About the Author

Alexander Marriott was born 6 February 1984 in Winfield, Illinois, outside of Chicago. He grew up in the Chicago suburbs, Jeddah, Saudi Arabia and Las Vegas, NV. He developed an intense interest in history while living abroad and made a career of it, going to graduate school and graduating with a PhD in American history from Clark University in 2013. He has taught American, British, European and Texas history at Wiley College and Alvin Community College since 2013. He continues to travel widely, read broadly and write whenever he has the time and opportunity.

THE SCHOOL OF HOMER

Alexander V. Marriott

THE SCHOOL OF HOMER

Vanguard Press

VANGUARD PAPERBACK

A CIP catalogue record for this title is
available from the British Library.

ISBN 978-1-80016-420-8

Vanguard Press is an imprint of
Pegasus Elliot Mackenzie Publishers Ltd.
www.pegasuspublishers.com

First Published in 2023

Vanguard Press
Sheraton House Castle Park
Cambridge England

Printed & Bound in Great Britain

Dedication

For my family and my friends, I cannot thank you enough.

Ουδέν κακόν αμιγές καλού

Contents

Lefkas
Ithaca
Kefalonia
Zakynthos

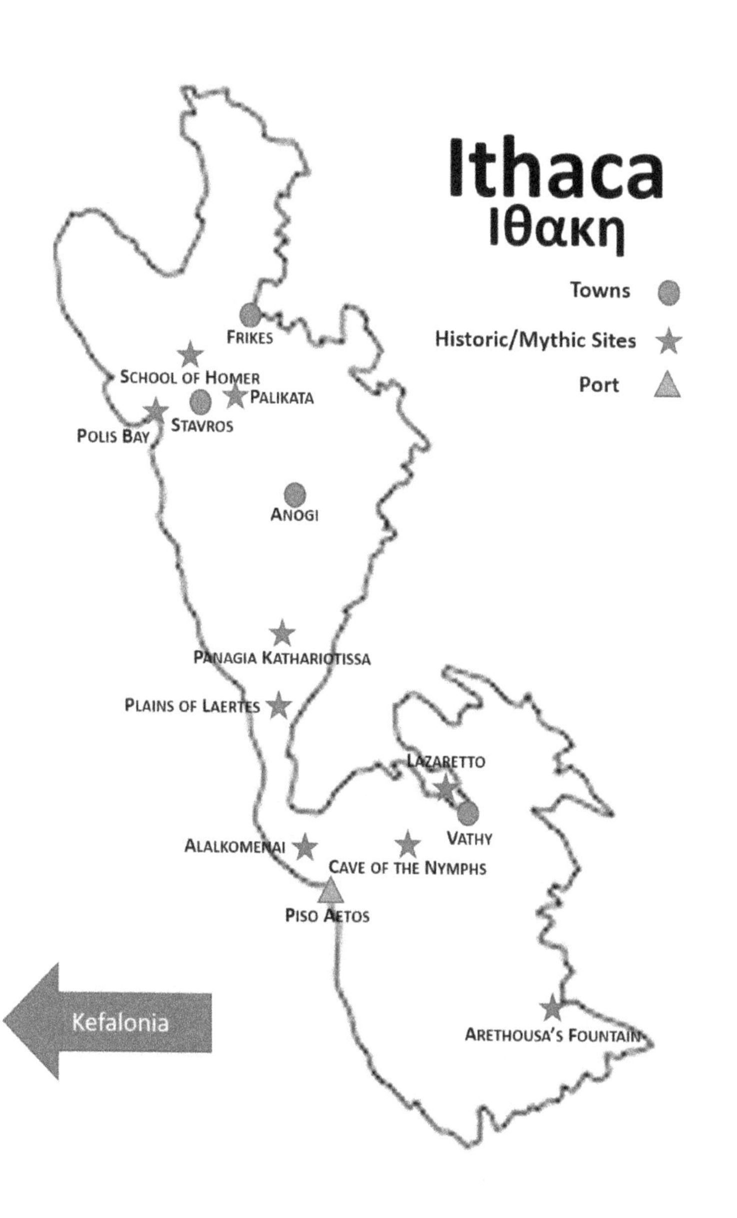
Ithaca
Ιθακη
Towns
Historic/Mythic Sites
Port
Frikes
School of Homer
Palikata
Stavros
Polis Bay
Anogi
Panagia Kathariotissa
Plains of Laertes
Lazaretto
Vathy
Alalkomenai
Cave of the Nymphs
Piso Aetos
Kefalonia
Arethousa's Fountain

PROLOGUE
ANCIENT ITHACA, CIRCA 1165 BCE

The eagle soared over the sea slowly. It had come down from its mountain on the isthmus. Eukalos watched the bird float on the wind as he sat in the sun, overlooking the city's harbour.[1] The sea appeared blue close to shore. On the horizon, it looked much darker, almost like the wines from the mainland. The land of his birth was over there, somewhere. The smoke from the offerings wafted over him as he stared. The burning fat of the goats smelled rather acrid, while the scented perfumes could not block it out. They just mixed into an unearthly joint vapor that blinded while it scorched the lungs and throat. Fit for the Gods, but not for mortals. Eukalos could not enjoy his perch any longer and had to move. He watched the eagle a moment, and then he jumped up, straightened his wool tunic, picked up the heavy sack that sat beside him and began the descent from the bluff.

When he reached the beach, he watched the priests and sailors continue their offerings in the bronze tripods on the platform in the narrow harbour's rocky side. He

---

[1] Pronounced "*Ef-ka-los*"

looked up to the bluffs directly over the platform where he had been sitting moments before. He tried to spot the eagle again, but the harbinger of mighty Zeus, an intrepid bird, had flown off somewhere. Maybe it had been a god and was now walking through the town. The thought made Eukalos smile. He had no doubts such things happened on this island, and often. Since his arrival — shipwrecked and orphaned on the coast — his adoptive family and neighbours had told him all about the island and its protective and jealous gods, especially Athena and Poseidon. As he pondered where the eagle had gone, he prayed that it had not flown towards the sea where the sun disappeared. That would be a troublesome sign.

He looked back at the supplicants on the platform. They mumbled mostly, but the basic invocation was for the missing king, Odysseus, to watch over these visitors to the shrine who made the appropriate offerings. They poured wine into the harbour and raised their arms to the sky, chanting. King Telemachos resisted this development as it conceded the death of his father, but he had relented when it was clear that the travelling mariners were not going to be deterred. Now, he taxed them when they came to worship his lost father who once ruled the island long before Eukalos was born. King Telemachos was older now than Odysseus had been when he left Ithaca for a second time, unable to stop wandering. The old dowager Queen Penelope still lived. She was a local shrine as well for those who were important enough to see her. Eukalos had never seen the wife of old King Odysseus and he worked at the palace — his hut was on the same hill. But he worked in the fields of the palace — only the queen's ladies, Telemachos and his family, and certain important visitors and priests were allowed up the stairs to see Penelope and her enormous olive tree bed, built by the lost king.

"Eukalos!" The familiar voice came from behind him.

As Eukalos turned, he saw his great friend, his older brother really, Okuwanos, striding towards him. It was Okuwanos' father, Mentor, who adopted Eukalos when he was found on the shore and brought to the city. Okuwanos was already mostly grown but had always treated Eukalos like his flesh and blood. He was a burly man with black hair everywhere in massive tufts. He was about ten years older than Eukalos, who had just grown his first beard — in patches. While Eukalos was still rather scrawny, resembling too closely the boy he so recently was, Okuwanos was all sinew and muscle.

"Eukalos," he said, closing in on his friend and brother, "where have you been? I have been looking for you! It is ready! Do you have the rest of the payment?"

"Yes, right here." He held the bag up to Okuwanos, who grabbed it and weighed it in his arms.

"Ah, it feels right! Come! Idomeneia is waiting for you. Athena herself will not be able to save you if we keep her waiting much longer!"

At that, they both laughed and jogged from the harbour, along the path north of the city, past the great fountain, slowly ascending the plateau towards the palace of Telemachos.

When they arrived at the palace, they stopped to catch their breaths. The walls around the palace were low and functional for keeping in animals rather than keeping people out. The palace itself had two floors, built into the hillside with stone blocks making the base of the first floor while the remainder of the structure was made from fashioned logs and slated wood. The roof was open over the great hall, while the rest was thatched together with mud, clay and straw. After they admired the view, with the sun riding through the sky behind the palace, they veered left to the workshop and cottage of Okuwanos and Idomeneia, the king's artificers. They kept busy making pottery, repairing metalwork, producing new pieces to order for the royal household and fulfilling side orders for friends and customers like Eukalos when they could. They lived comfortably together with their four children — when those hardy little ones were not roaming the island, sleeping under the stars, like most of the island's boys and girls. The skilled husband and wife were always busy. Okuwanos did the metal work and repair. He also crafted most of the pottery from wet clay to sun-dried intermediate finish. Idomeneia finished all the pottery. She painted and coloured all of it with elaborate designs, patterns and representations. She also served as the consultant and model for Okuwanos' bronze and gold jewellery creations. They shared their work and lives together, as most of Ithaca's men and women did. The island was simple, all the visitors said, but everyone seemed content. Being content is what brought Eukalos to the cottage of the king's artificers this day.

"Eukalos!" Idomeneia called out when the men sauntered in, giving her mountainous man a kiss. She then turned her attention back on their friend and relation, "Well, have you the payment?"

"I do, good woman!" Okuwanos dumped the contents of the sack on the floor and Idomeneia crawled about to examine the collection of cheeses, figs, and pears that had scattered about. She occasionally sniffed the specimens or took small bites. Then she looked back at Eukalos and smiled. While they were family, business was business.

"You did well, Eukalos! Very well!" The married masters of the cottage gathered the bounty together and put it all into a pit in the corner furthest from the hearth.

Then Idomeneia went outside. "She needs to get your piece from the kiln. It is quite something, Eukalos — possibly our best work. We were able to get Agelawos, he lived as a scribe in Pylos, to help us with the symbols you will see. He was a bit confused by the work, but I think it turned out well!"

Idomeneia came back in.

"You be the judge, Eukalos," she said, hiding a large item under a white fleece. She rested the object on the floor and beckoned the men to sit near her. They did as commanded. Idomeneia then removed the fleece dramatically, revealing a large bowl with two handles on either side of it. It was perfectly crafted by Okuwanos, and even more breathtakingly decorated by Idomeneia. The main motif was the representation of a humble Ithacan man — Eukalos — and a humble Ithacan woman — Amphidora — joining together. Amphidora was the woman Eukalos intended to join himself with and to live with as Okuwanos and Idomeneia lived together. Around the top of the bowl, as Eukalos examined it wide-eyed, were strange symbols that had been etched into the clay before firing. While they watched him, Okuwanos and Idomeneia glanced at each other, quite pleased with themselves.

"What are these?" Eukalos asked of his friends, as they monitored his reactions.

"The scribe," Okuwanos answered, "I asked him to include the names of the island's great kings and the queen — so it reads in order: Laertes, Odysseus, Penelope and Telemachos. Do you like it? We have never had sounds on anything we have ever made, even for King Telemachos." They both proudly smiled as they awaited the judgement of Eukalos.

Before he could answer, a shadow fell across the threshold. Eukalos looked but could not instantly identify the figure standing in the doorway.

"Okuwanos! Idomeneia! Eukalos!" the figure bellowed familiarly as he stepped into the cottage. His greyed beard and hair, still spliced with streaks of jet, along with his lovely tunic of the finest flax identified him as none other than Telemachos, King of Ithaca. They all bowed to their king.

"Please, get up!" Telemachos continued his bellowing. "I just need to borrow Okuwanos, I will let him come back to you in a moment." Okuwanos followed his king outside.

"So, what do you think?" Idomeneia inquired of Eukalos as soon as Telemachos and her husband exited.

"It is so much more wonderful than I ever dared imagine," Eukalos declared, "I must procure you a kid!"

"Oh, that's really not necessary, Eukalos," Idomeneia said, "you paid all that we agreed upon. We love you like a brother, a son even! We were happy to do this for you. And we cannot wait until you bring Amphidora here to the palace of the king as your wife!" At that, she embraced Eukalos and kissed his cheek.

Walking in at that moment, Okuwanos boomed, "Ah, what's this! I leave my wife alone with a rogue and suddenly I'm forgotten!"

Idomeneia smiled. "Oh, if I were going to trade up, it would be for King Telemachos!" They all laughed.

"This bowl is fantastic, Okuwanos," Eukalos declared to his friend, "I will bring you a kid!"

"And we shall feast on it together and offer the rest to Athena!" Okuwanos embraced his brother and friend. He pushed back. "When will you give it to her?"

"Now!" Eukalos smiled. "No more waiting, that is all I have been doing and I am tired of it! Amphidora knows how I love her like Odysseus loved Penelope. This bowl is the perfect offering for her. She is no slave, and King Telemachos has consented to letting Amphidora join the ladies of the queens as soon as she is my wife. I am leaving today, this moment!"

"Eukalos! You are such a hot-blooded man!" Idomeneia mockingly admonished her young friend. "But go and tell this woman of your passions and feelings before you forget!"

As Eukalos made his way to the door, Idomeneia called out, "Eukalos! Wait!" He stopped to look at her as she came to him and wrapped the bowl in the white fleece that concealed it earlier. She then placed the bowl in his sack and placed the sack around his neck and shoulder. "Do not break this bowl! This is a symbol of your love for her, and our love for you! If you break it before you give it to her, Eukalos, may Zeus on high Olympus strike you to dust with his thunderbolt!" She then kissed his cheek again, turned him around and pushed him out the door.

After watching the young man walk purposefully towards the city, Idomeneia turned to her husband and asked, "Were we so taken with each other and ourselves when we roamed the island at his age?"

Okuwanos strode to his wife, engulfing her in his arms. "Who said anything about 'were'?"

***

The walk to Amphidora's home, where she lived and worked as a servant to the wife of Telemachos' headman Ekhemedes, was a pleasant one. The fountain above the town of Ithaca had its usual line of supplicants. The offerings had been growing more and more desperate lately as less and less water was forthcoming. The assembly grounds were empty now. He remembered the most recent gathering, several moons ago, where the elders had discussed a trip to the oracle across the sea to ask the god about the water which the people needed, but which the trees, crops and livestock desperately required as well. The assembly had sent a delegation away with precious offerings.

They had not heard back yet. People were fairly lean-looking; times had been hard. Fortunately, Poseidon seemed less angry lately. Eukalos remembered the rumblings of his childhood; they had been frequent and damaging to the buildings in the city — some had even attributed Poseidon's anger to the saving of Eukalos, proposing to return the boy to the sea in order to please the god. Eukalos remembered this without bitterness as he walked along the side of Mt Neriton, whose heights were covered with trees. He could see them swaying in the winds as he looked up, nearly tripping and falling over.

"You must be careful!" Eukalos said to himself, touching the covered object in his sack to make sure it was still in one piece.

There was a small ship in the channel to his right, the sail full of wind. Okuwanos and the elders talked often about how the channel was once full of vessels going with the winds or stopping in the harbour to wait for the winds, trading and bringing news. Now, a ship a day was considered busy. Days without visitors were becoming more and more common. The elders said Odysseus had left again because he was cursed, that Poseidon would never leave the island alone so long as he was there. The shaking did eventually stop after he left. But now, these other problems were adding up. Hopefully, the oracle would explain how to get out of all this. What was taking so long?

Helios was approaching his final climb through the sky when Eukalos finally arrived at the farm and orchards of Ekhemedes. He looked down at the small, but bountiful, collection of pear, fig and olive trees. Goats bleated on the hillside near him. There appeared to be a sail far off to the left.

Two ships in a day? Eukalos thought to himself, *Gods be praised!* Eukalos took a sip from the sheep's bladder that hung from his shoulder. There was not much water left. Hopefully, he could have some from the cisterns of Ekhemedes. He was normally quite generous, but the sun blazed mercilessly. No one took it as inhospitable meanness to be denied water any more.

He descended into the orchards, looking for Amphidora as he strolled. Then he saw her, carrying a basket of pears to the storehouse. He stood to admire her, the woman he loved and that would be his wife. Her hips were wide, and she was a bit shorter than he was, especially lately. Eukalos had been getting taller. Okuwanos no longer seemed like quite the giant any more, though he was still quite massive. Amphidora's hair was long and black. She had a silver clasp, a gift from Ekhemedes and his wife, that held it together in the back to avoid having it blow about in the wind and get in her face. Her tunic ran down to the middle of her thighs covering her breasts, which were still small. She walked, as did Eukalos, barefoot. Sandals were for the likes of Telemachos, Penelope and Ekhemedes. When she re-emerged from the storehouse with an empty basket, Amphidora looked up to the sun and shielded her eyes. Then she looked straight at Eukalos. She obviously did not see him immediately blinded with the sun. After a few moments, she recognised him and blushed. She walked calmly over to him. She was covered in a sheen of sweat as she had been working hard all morning. She could not have looked better, Eukalos thought to himself.

"Eukalos? You have come all the way from the palace? Are you all right?" she asked her questions with concern and sweetness.

"Quite all right, my love!" Eukalos said, feeling the blood in his body move faster and faster.

Blushing again, Amphidora looked down. "Why have you come, Eukalos?"

"I have a gift, my love, for you!" He reached into his sack and brought forth the bulky white fleece.

"You have brought me a fleece? For a day like this? You said you loved me, Eukalos!" she even chided him sweetly.

He unwrapped the fleece and let it fall to the ground, revealing the elaborately decorated bowl. He presented it to her. "I had this made for you, my love! It will be our first bowl in our home as man and woman together!"

Bowls, cups, kraters and amphoras were highly prized everywhere on the island. Everyone kept them in their families as long as they possibly could. The breaking of a piece of pottery was a great tragedy, felt by every member of a household. Amphidora's family did not have more than a couple of pieces that were usable.

"You had this made? For *me*?" She took the bowl, a krater really, from his hands and marvelled at its decorations and craftsmanship.[2] She blushed as she recognised the representations of herself and Eukalos. She stared at the etchings before looking into his eyes and asking, "What are these, my Eukalos?"

"A surprise, even to me! Okuwanos and his wonderful wife, Idomeneia, made and decorated this. Without telling me, they had the old scribe Agelawos write down sounds along the top. Those are the names of the kings and the old queen. I do not remember which is which. But this is the only such bowl in all Ithaca! Do you like it, my love?" Eukalos asked with the greatest excitement.

"Do I like it? Eukalos, I would marry you with your empty bladder, your discarded fleece and your hollow sack" — she laughed as she pointed at his meagre belongings — "but this" — she grabbed the krater in both hands again, much to the relief of Eukalos — "this is of the gods, Eukalos! I do not know what to say at such a thing as this."

"That is enough for me!" He gently kissed Amphidora's lips, carefully avoiding crushing the pottery in between them.

---

[2] The handles and upward narrowing distinguish the krater from the simpler bowl.

"Eukalos!" The booming salutation came from the door of the cottage of Ekhemedes, from Ekhemedes himself.

Eukalos waved to Ekhemedes, who marched to the young lovers.

"You have finally come to pillage my orchards and take Amphidora to the north as booty, have you?" Ekhemedes was an intimidating and imposing man, but now he was all smiles.

"Yes, sir!" Eukalos stated with the confidence of love.

"Gods be praised!" Ekhemedes embraced them both as Eukalos and Amphidora desperately shielded the krater from being smashed by the force of his crushing arms. "This calls for a little wine, and sadly, even less water. Philona!" he called to his wife inside the cottage. "Bring some wine!"

Philona, in a long dress that reached to her shins, her feet clad in leather sandals, emerged after several moments with a jug of dark wine, mixed with far less water than everyone liked. It could not be helped.

"Amphidora!" Philona hugged her servant after she handed the jug to Ekhemedes. Amphidora showed her the krater. The third most elite woman in Ithaca — after Penelope and the wife of Telemachos, Nausicaa — was greatly impressed by the bowl. "Fit for a queen of Ithaca!" she declared.

Ekhemedes handed the wine jug to Eukalos. "On this day, young man, you drink first. Drink long!" He smashed Eukalos on the back so hard that he nearly dropped the jug. Ekhemedes roared with laughter and delight.

Eukalos put the clay jug to his lips and tipped it upwards until the wine reached his lips. It was so sweet and strong, he only had two gulps before bringing it down. Amphidora smiled and giggled as the wine dripped down his meagrely bearded chin. He handed the jug back to Ekhemedes, who refused it, pointing to Amphidora. Eukalos gave the jug to his love, who grabbed it with eagerness and put it to her lips. She drank quite a bit more than Eukalos had managed. She *was* thirsty!

When she brought the jug down and offered it to Ekhemedes, her mouth was as purple as the wine that dripped from her chin to her tunic. Before the imposing monolith of a man took his own drink, he commanded, "Kiss your wife, boy!" Then he took a mighty serving from his wine jug.

Eukalos did as he was told, embracing Amphidora to himself and enjoying her wine covered lips and tongue, forgetting that there was an audience. When he came up for air, Ekhemedes and Philona were staring at them, smiling. Philona's chin dripped of wine now too. The young lovers had kissed so long that they missed the great lady drinking to their love, health and long lives. They all laughed.

"You will stay tonight and eat with us! You can steal your wife from my service in the morning,"

Ekhemedes commanded. There was no way to refuse. Fortunately, there was also no reason.

"You are too kind, sir," Eukalos said, appropriately.

"We insist," Philona said, and she took the jug back to the cottage after handing the krater back to Amphidora.

After she had turned, shouts and acclamations were heard from the servants and slaves further in the orchard. One, then another, and another came running from the fruit trees. Some made their way to the mountain of eagles, others towards the slopes of Mt. Neriton. Eventually, one of them came to Ekhemedes and fell before him.

"What is the meaning of this!" the giant barked.

"Ships, master, ships!"

Ekhemedes, Eukalos and Amphidora made their way through the trees to the terraced ledge that would allow them a view of the sea over the terrace below. When they arrived, the sea below was full of sails, at least as many ships as pears on a healthy tree at high season. They were headed into the Bay of Phorcys. From this distance, the men aboard the vessels were distinctly visible. Odd-looking men, some with colour on their faces. The glint of their bronze spears and swords reflected the sun's light.

Turning to them quickly, Ekhemedes blared so loudly that Amphidora dropped the bowl on the terrace wall. It broke. None of them noticed. "Get to Athena's sanctuary on Neriton! Now!"

Eukalos looked to Amphidora, his eyes serene. "Go! Run to the sanctuary, I will be right behind you, my wife!" He kissed her again, still enjoying the wine in and around her mouth. He turned her to Neriton and pushed her, screaming, "Run!"

She ran across the rocks like a panicked deer, following the others up the slopes towards the sanctuary. She never looked back.

Eukalos turned to Ekhemedes, "Give me a weapon, sir!"

Ekhemedes laughed. "Ah, a man!" He slapped Eukalos on the shoulder and led him back to his cottage. Ekhemedes had his own armour, which he quickly put on. He gave his shield to the otherwise vulnerable young man. He picked up his bronze sword and leather scabbard, putting them over his neck and left shoulder. He hefted the two bronze spears that lay resting against the wall and handed one to Eukalos, before commanding, "Go outside, Eukalos."

The young man moved himself out the door with the heavy shield and spear, trying to get used to the weight and appearing a bit ridiculous.

Ekhemedes looked into Philona's eyes. She stared right back into his. Neither of them betrayed any hint of tears. "You need to head north, my wife. Get to the city and raise the alarm. Warn the king. If they are not under attack, have them send help. If they cannot, seek refuge in the palace and pray to the gods!" He kissed her gently on the forehead and then her mouth. "Go, now!"

She picked up her dress and tied it around her waist so that her bare legs might move more quickly. She ran from the house and turned left towards Neriton. She hugged the path on the coast of the channel and did not stop moving back along the route that brought Eukalos only a short time before. Ekhemedes came out with his spear glinting in the sun and his already imposing bulk even more threatening than usual.

He tapped Eukalos' spear with his own. "Do you know how to use that yet?"

"I think so," Eukalos said shakily.

Ekhemedes laughed thunderously. When he had finished, he said seriously, "Just stay by my side and try to make sure no one gets behind us — understand?"

"Yes, sir!"

"Well, my young friend, shall we?" He nodded towards the mountain of the eagles, where the pass into the lower island lay.

Without answering, Eukalos began marching. Ekhemedes followed him, laughing.

CHAPTER ONE
POSEIDON YAWNS

The amphora crashed to the floor.[3] The pieces scattered across the wood and the sound echoed through the room. Virgil Colvin was awake.

As he adjusted to his sudden consciousness, he noticed that the room was swaying. The fact that the invariably stationary room was moving struck him initially as unremarkable. After another moment or two, he realised it was unusual. He realised it was downright terrifying in the darkness to be swaying and rolling, as if at sea during a night squall.

Did I have that much ouzo? he thought to himself. He could not remember exactly how much ouzo he had consumed, or the precise details of his arrival in his unseaworthy bed. After another moment, he realised it was an earthquake — his first one! They did not have earthquakes in Chicago. In fact, the idea of an earthquake in Chicago — the city of concrete and steel

[3] An amphora is a clay vessel for the storage and transportation of goods — usually liquids; they typically are tall and vary in terms of width. Virgil Colvin's amphora was simply a miniature version of the larger trading amphora of the ancient Mediterranean.

skyscrapers — struck Virgil as more preposterously frightening than the unnatural undulations of the dark reality all around him.

Almost as quickly as his incredulity washed over him, the shaking stopped. It was replaced by an eerie stillness. It was not just the quiet — a whole universe suddenly silent — but everything seemed frozen. He gazed around the room, still bleary-eyed with sleep and last night's drinking. His head pounded dully, indicating mild dehydration and the fact that he had not slept long enough. Still, it was far easier to bear than the post ouzo headaches had been in his first weeks on the island. Instead of the overwhelming sensation of miners sapping the interior of his cranium, this was just a repetitive dull thudding. As his vision adjusted to the twilight, he noticed the disarray caused by the quake. Not only had the amphora smashed into bits, casting debris everywhere, but the pictures on the wall had fallen or become crooked. The picture of Janet, his wife, had managed to survive only slightly askew. Her strawberry blonde hair peaked out of her bucket hat, her tanned legs looked young and firm and she was still smiling at him as she was that day twenty-five years earlier in the bleachers at Wrigley. The Cardinals won, but it was a glorious day, and she rarely looked lovelier or happier. He got up and straightened it.

"Good morning, baby. You would have hated that!" She had been dead for almost a year, but he hadn't stopped talking to her yet.

He looked at his phone, under the sheets on the bed; it was a quarter past five in the morning — still an hour to sunrise. There was no hope of getting back to sleep. *Time to clean up a little,* he thought, *and then see what the rest of the villa looks like.* Inside first, outside once the sun made its appearance. Virgil knew that earthquakes were common in the Mediterranean, a surprisingly active tectonic and volcanic region geologically (and occasionally politically), but he had only been living on the island for a little more than five months. For some reason, Virgil Colvin never really believed the earth shaker would ever actually appear. Like most people who lived through their first earthquake, he was experiencing the narcissism of "I can't believe this is happening to me!" syndrome — as if the universe ever singles anyone out in such a manner.

He looked back at Janet; he was back in Chicago. He had buried her and was going to the 19th precinct in Chicago's North side, when he suddenly realised he no longer wanted to be in the city he loved. He no longer wanted to be working homicides. Not any more. Not without Janet and the life they had built together. When he thought about what he would do, or where he would go, he kept coming back to Greece. They had honeymooned there almost thirty years earlier and loved it. They both always wanted to go back, maybe buy a house and live out their retirements while the city's pension system still existed. These were their daydreams when they lolled in bed on weekend mornings, or their drunken fantasies when they had too much after long shifts — he at the precinct house, her at the hospital. They had never gotten around to seriously fleshing the dream out. They travelled to other places — Scotland, Florence, Normandy and Israel — when they weren't exploring the states. They saved as much money as they could and Virgil would occasionally read a book about the island and then try to get Janet to read it. There was a nice pile of them on her side of the bed when she had to go to the hospital as a patient three months before she died.

Chicago had become an oppressively haunted house for Virgil. He saw her everywhere. He smelled her everywhere. He felt her in the darkness of their vacant home. It was comforting in some ways, but the Janet of those days, weeks and months was the Janet at the end. Her vigour, her youth, her vitality, her 'herness' had all drained away inexorably before his eyes. Yes, she fulfilled all the clichés of heroically holding up against the onslaught of mutated cells destroying her body; against the barrage of poisonous treatments that helped sap her remaining strength; and adamantly opposed to the obvious temptation to give up and call it quits. It made no difference. She still died in the end. Everybody dies in the end. The ultimate cliché; true, but ultimately useless. The experience had drawn them closer and deepened their love. But when it was over, Virgil Colvin realised he had been thoroughly devastated and traumatised in slow motion. Nothing in the city gave him any solace. The Italian beef sandwiches they had enjoyed together now tasted bland, the skyscrapers seemed small and incapable of exalting his imagination as they had when he looked upon them with Janet at his side, the shore of Lake Michigan — where they had spent many days chatting and contemplating the cold vastness together — was stuck in the perpetual grey of utter meaninglessness. Even his favourite spot in the city, Wrigley Field, simply made him hollow and almost inconsolable. In short, everything about the city ruined him anew, and it didn't improve as the days passed.

Work didn't help. If anything, being immersed in the city's overabundance of death and petty motives which often lay at the heart of cases where husbands murdered wives, wives murdered husbands, gangbangers murdered each other or random passers-by caught in the crossfire, merely made Virgil bitterly angry at every stranger he encountered. He suddenly imagined all of them plotting to kill their loved ones — the very people they were fortunate enough to still have in their lives. It made pursuing leads tough. Hell, it made going outside a challenge. Friends and family could not break the sad curse that had overtaken Virgil's life. He knew it couldn't go on. The only thing that inspired him, gave him any happiness at all as he went through the drab motions of 'life' as a widower, the only thing that could make him smile was returning to this magic island of their past together. It became his *idée fixe* and nothing could deter him from abandoning the place where Janet had died for the place where she had so gloriously lived.

In a blink, he was back in Ithaca. He smiled at Janet. Her row of pearly white teeth, blue eyes and rosy cheeks smiled back at him from the past. He meandered his way to the kitchen to get a broom to sweep up the busted amphora. It was just a cheap miniature replica he had purchased as a culturally appropriate decoration from one of the tourist shops by the water. It was the sort of useless knickknack that Janet would have hated. As he stepped past the threshold of the bedroom, his foot hit upon an odd sensation that obstructed his contact with the floor. He looked down to see the familiar cylindrical blue cloth cap with the iconic red 'C' outlined in white.

"My amphora and my hat? You'll have to do better than that, Poseidon!" he called to the darkness, laughing to himself.

He picked up the hat and planted it lazily on his head. Given the time difference and the distance that prevented him from ever seeing them play live, Virgil was uncertain as to why he insisted on introducing every Ithacan he met to his beloved Cubs. But be that as it may, he persisted. He didn't have to leave *everything* behind, did he? Suddenly, he caught sight of his reflection in the window. He was stark naked — with a Cubs cap on his head.

"Jesus, I really did have too much ouzo," he muttered.

He looked over his body in the imperfect reflection in the transparent window glass. He had lost the weight that Italian beef sandwiches, deep-dish pizzas, Old Style beer and sitting in a precinct chair too many days had built up on his generally fit frame over three decades. Actually, he was thinner than he had ever been — and not in a good way. The ouzo diet was not amenable to putting on weight, apparently. His clothes still fit, for the most part, but they felt loose and verged on unacceptably baggy in his own estimation. His beard growth was getting beyond the shadow phase. Shaving had been a firm part of his routine every day in Chicago before Janet got sick. Wake up, shave, coffee, paper, shower, kiss Janet if she was home, out the door. You could set your clock by it. Now it was simply when he remembered or cared enough to expend the effort. He looked away.

After putting on some of his loose clothes, adjusting all the pictures and cleaning up the amphora shards, Virgil Colvin yawned. It was a satisfied yawn. Sure, the morning had begun with a somewhat alarming geological phenomenon that he playfully ascribed to Poseidon, the forgotten God of the seas and shaker of the earth, but ultimately it was like most mornings in his new home — pure relaxation. He looked over at the bookcase that took up his entire living room wall. It was full of histories and biographies, some books on crime, dozens of novels, some of the Greek and Roman writers of antiquity and an impressive collection of archaeological and other volumes related to Ithaca and the surrounding islands. He had determined to give up television when he left Chicago. So far, he wasn't missing it. Well, he missed the Cubs. But he had Ithaca's sometimes intermittent and weak Internet to keep him connected. Or, as he sometimes thought, distracted.

His eyes wandered over the book titles. *What will I start reading today?* he thought. He had paid a fortune to ship his small library across the world. Everyone thought he was nuts. The benefit of being a widower is that no one had the guts to say that to his face. He was a good enough detective to see it in their eyes when he told them where he was going and what he was doing. The books were a necessary part of his life — they gave him legitimate mental stimulation. They were probably the healthiest part of his life at the moment. He also did not read a word of Greek and spoke almost less. In more than five months, and during his obsessive planning phase in Chicago before, he hadn't bothered to learn the language. More than that, he hadn't even thought about bothering to learn the language. As such, he was still largely cut off from the true life of the island — its literature, its songs and its people. Like forgetting to shave, not bothering to eat well enough and his repetitive routine of ouzo — occasionally wine — this bizarre mental lapse went largely unnoticed. By Virgil, that is.

Suddenly, he was sitting across from his chief of detectives at Ditka's Chicago on Chestnut Street. They were enjoying the Tomahawk cut ribeye, an absurdly large and expensive steak that matched the ego of the restaurant's namesake. It wasn't even on the menu. You had to know it existed and ask the waiter specifically if they would make it for you. It was an indulgent treat they enjoyed twice a year — along with a decent pinot and a couple of Ditka's Signature Churchill maduros. Of course, you couldn't enjoy the cigars *in* Ditka's any more — heaven forbid you smoke the man's stogies in his own place surrounded by hard-drinking, steak-eating, cigar-smoking Americans! Virgil wasn't going to miss that supercilious aspect of the city he had loved all his life.

Though fleeing one of Janet's ghosts to commune with another one was Virgil's prime motivation for emigrating, the demise of the city's freedoms over the three decades he lived and worked there certainly did not encourage him to rethink the decision. Petty, small rules for everything enacted by petty, small people. In contrast, Ithaca's residents lived an almost laissez-faire existence by default. The population was so dispersed and scattered about the rocky mass that the anonymity of life in a truly large city was entirely impossible. Everyone knew and basically trusted everyone else, except for the tourists — but you needed them. There were so few authority figures on the island that you could go weeks without seeing one unless you went out of your way to check in on them, to make sure they were still there. Chicago seemed to exist in an alternate bizarro universe by comparison. Virgil did not miss it.

"Colvin," his chief asked in between bites forty and forty-one of his quarter section of prime beef, "why in God's name are you going to the middle of nowhere again? I mean, *really*? Why? Why would you leave this place? Leave *this*?" He implored incredulously, pointing at the beef with his 'Ditka Hatchet', an enormous razor-sharp dagger he used on the mammoth Tomahawk. It wasn't actually a hatchet, but Colvin and the chief endlessly thought it should be, given the mound of meat it was called upon to eviscerate.

"Look, Dick, I told you and everyone else a thousand times, I'm tired. I'm tired of this city and its bullshit. I'm tired of working murders. I'm tired of walking around this town, which used to make me smile, and only seeing people and places that remind me of Janet. I need to get the hell out of here." The raw emotional passion that infused his entire body as he finished had Virgil shaking from deep within, like an enormous vibration.

"Hold on, Colvin!" Dick Borneman interjected. "Won't you be reminded of Janet all over that damn island you're going to?" He had a puzzled smile on his face — happy that he caught his best detective in a logical paradox, but also genuinely confused. Borneman respected his detective and felt a fatherly and friendly regard for him. He wasn't simply worried about losing his best man, he was genuinely worried about Colvin's obvious distraction, if not decline, since Janet's illness and death.

"Yeah, Dick, I can see how you might think so." Virgil paused to chew and gather his thoughts. "When Janet and I were honeymooning in Ithaca before I joined your band of merry men, we had the best times of our lives. We were happy, in love and without a care in the world. Beyond that, the place has a magical charm — it exists away from all this chaos, murder and absurdity. What am I staying for? A few more years to get shot? A few more years to not enjoy my pension before this whole Ponzi scheme collapses?" he said waiving his hatchet around theatrically. "Sorry, Dick, but there is nothing holding me here any more. I need to get away and my mind keeps returning there." He chewed for a moment, redoubling his mental efforts. After swallowing, he continued, "This city is circling the drain, Dick, and everyone knows it. City Hall climbs further and further up its own ass. The businesses either leave or donate more money to the same old assholes to avoid having to leave before they finally leave anyway. No matter how many cases we clear, the prosecutors cut deals to let some of the monsters we lock up right back out again — and some of them are fucking nuts, Dick! They are prosecutors that don't want to prosecute anyone! What's the point? I can't even collect the psychic satisfaction of knowing I helped make the city safer. At the end of the day, that was the best part of this job. It's all gone now. Should I just stay here to shuffle paper and inflate my pension some more? Everything here is dead or dying. I don't want that for me. No, thanks!"

"Well, Colvin, I still think you're full of shit. When you're back here in a year, don't expect to get a good precinct. You'll probably end up in some hellhole in area two." This last part was not a threat in Borneman's estimation, merely a statement of fact about how HQ would almost certainly respond if Colvin returned in a year. Borneman didn't even think ending up in the South Side was that bad — lots of action! Hell, it wasn't some shit island with no people and nothing going on in the middle of fucking nowhere. He left that unsaid. He liked Virgil too much. "You still owe me a round of golf before you leave!"

Colvin blinked. The rays of Aurora were peeking through the window. He was ready to go outside and inspect the exterior for damage. As he exited his villa, his eyes adjusted to the darkness whose utter blackness had been violated by the opening of dawn. He chuckled, remembering that he still owed Dick a round of golf — he left before having to tell his chief that he didn't really like the game. At all.

He marvelled at the harbour below. It was almost too dark to see it from the promontory view from his villa's entrance, but trade-off of light from moon to sun had started shifting decisively to the latter and every second brought the water into clearer relief against the land. It was lovely to see it every morning, to enjoy some espresso, and do some reading in the crisp air. He never felt more certain of his decision to move to the capital of Ithaca than the morning. Vathy, Virgil's new home, was destroyed by an earthquake in 1953. That visit from Poseidon was far larger than the one which startled Colvin awake and ruined his 'precious' amphora. The islanders rebuilt their capital in the same strict Venetian style that characterised it for centuries. It was a style that created a picaresque mosaic around the horseshoe harbour of oranges, pinks, blues and greens. The city of Venice controlled the island off and on during the fourteen, fifteen and sixteen centuries as part of a large empire built on trade and naval domination against the nearby Ottoman Turks. Greece was caught in the middle in those days, perennially jostled and buffeted by the power and ambition of greater and more effective neighbours who saw the country as just so much real estate; rocky and rather unappealing real estate at that. Be that as it may, the period imparted to the capital a lovely and charming colour palette that Virgil always found beautiful, but most especially at sunrise and sunset.

While Vathy's harbour was connected to the larger Ionian Sea, and while Vathy was Ithaca's capital, Ithaca itself, of course, was supposed to be the kingdom of Odysseus, the wily and crafty hero of Homer's great eponymous epic. It was a small island on the west coast of Greece accessible by ferry and helicopter. It had no airport. Getting everything to Vathy — the books, the car and clothes and accoutrements of a home — had been a tremendous pain in the ass, costing Virgil a king's ransom. The honeymoon had been easier, but Janet had been so appalled by the bus ride through the winding mountain roads of the neighbouring island of Kefalonia to get to the ferry landing closest to Ithaca that she demanded they ferry back to the mainland directly rather than reverse the trip in order to fly out. She had nearly vomited in her hat, which she had used to avoid seeing the narrow roads, the oncoming traffic and the occasional precipice off to the side. Kefalonia not only had the functional commercial airport with its one runway, it was also much larger than Ithaca. Some even thought that Kefalonia was actually *the* Ithaca that Homer wrote about. The so-called 'Ithaca problem' dated back to antiquity, but emerged during the late Enlightenment when artists, intellectuals and the wealthy began to take grand tours of classical sites and ruins around Italy and Greece. Using Homer's poems as their guides, travellers could not square the island called Ithaca on their maps with some of the epic descriptions. Nor could they find adequate ruins for Odysseus' palace anywhere, nor of immortal Troy in Ottoman Anatolia. Until Heinrich Schliemann, the businessman turned amateur archaeologist, stunned the world in the 1870s with the announcement that he had found Troy, most had simply come to believe Homer made it all up. The problem of squaring the geography and the cartography of modern Ithaca with Homer's Ithaca had never vanished. Schliemann did not solve it, nor did those who came after him. There were many who tried. While every decade or so saw a new book describing a theory for a different island, or exploring why Ithaca was *the* Ithaca, the 'Ithaca question' remained without a definitive answer to the small community of those who even knew there was a question at all. For Virgil Colvin, it didn't make any difference at all. Ithaca? Not Ithaca? This island would still be the repository of his memories regardless.

His water cisterns seemed undamaged. "Thank god!" he muttered; those were expensive and laborious to replace, a sad fact he knew from moving in when he discovered that one of them was rotted to hell. Like a timber infested with worms and termites, except the clay version. They were a damn fortune given that they were essentially just giant clay jugs. The tiles on his roof were a different story. He saw a few piles of terra cotta rubble that once sat in semi-orderly rows atop his villa. *Probably twenty tiles in all*, he thought. Increasing daylight might reveal a few more. As he continued to make his way around the walls, he heard what sounded like a car driving up the road towards him. The straining sounds of a sad, small, outdated engine propelling a European car from one of those European countries no one outside of Europe even knows makes cars reached his ears. Finland, for instance. Or Hungary. Of course, it could just be an old piece of shit from anywhere.

Virgil stopped his inspection and made his way back to the side of the villa where his metallic grey Mercedes G-Class was parked. He still wasn't sure he liked it, it looked like the sort of thing some German asshole would drive around Bavaria. Or one of the plutocrats that ran Chicago. *No*, he thought, *those bastards always went with black paint*. In any event, when he bought a villa in Greece, shipped his things a third of the way across the globe and retired on more than $77,000 a year — *Jesus Christ!* he thought every time he pondered the pension system of the police department, the city, and the state he had worked and lived in for nearly 30 years — he decided to spoil himself with a sturdy vehicle for the pitted and serpentine roads, and paths passing for roads, of the island. He squinted as the headlights of the smaller car temporarily blinded him, but as the car parked next to his behemoth, he knew immediately who his visitor was. Virgil was both intrigued and annoyed. He was having a hard time picking which one should predominate. In the nearly six months he had been living here, he never had a guest this early in the morning. Unless he was still drinking from the night before, he reminded himself.

"Mister Colvin!" Costas shouted as he ambled from the driver's side of his 'cruiser'.

Ithaca police vehicles barely warranted that estimable title. *They barely warrant the title of car,* Virgil thought as Costas made his way towards him. But now that he saw Costas, he was intrigued — the man was impossible to find annoying.

"How many times, Costas, must I tell you — call me Virgil! We're friends now, aren't we?"

"Of course, of course. But until you can talk with me for a whole month only in Greek, you're going to be 'Mr Colvin', Mr Colvin." The smile on Costas' face was both incredibly charming and hellishly obnoxious. He was an interesting-looking man. He was younger than Virgil, who turned fifty-one after moving to Ithaca. About forty-five years old, Costas was shorter than Virgil, about five feet, eight inches tall. Virgil was six feet and a tad over an inch. While Virgil's hair was either gone or greyed, Costas still sported an impressive black mane of seemingly unyielding thickness, characteristic of some Greek men (in common, ironically enough, with many Persian men). His blue-grey eyes were arresting and full of life and good humour. His moustache reminded Virgil of Coach Ditka's except almost jet black. His legs were a bit shorter than they ought to be, leaving his torso correspondingly larger and more imposing than it should have been. He was irresistibly personable, but there was always an air of command and authority lurking beneath the inviting and amiable surface. He was the sort of guy that Virgil would have enjoyed working with in Chicago. Entertaining, competent and he could talk and smooth his way out of anything. A master of what they called 'community policing' back in the States.

"Coming to make sure Poseidon and our little ouzo party haven't ended my retirement prematurely?"

"I wish it was so pleasant a voyage, Mr Colvin." Costas' face became glum as he spoke. His English was competent and usually quite good. Sometimes, it veered into awkward, often for no obvious reason. In nearly six months of near daily conversation with the man, there seemed to be no pattern to his mistakes or errors. Drunk as he may very well have still been, however, Virgil could tell something was wrong. Costas was never in anything other than grand spirits. Who wouldn't be on this magical island where nothing dangerous or criminal ever really happened?

"Costas, what's wrong? You look like a pigeon just shat on your dog! Is there anything I can do?"

"Well, Mr Colvin," Costas stopped, "shat on my dog? Are pigeons doing that to your pets often?" he asked, looking genuinely concerned and curious.

"*Ha!*" Virgil laughed. "No, of course not, I was referring to a wiener, a sausage; you'd be pretty glum if a pigeon shat on one you were about to eat, wouldn't you?"

"And this happens in Chicago?"

"Forget it, Costas, what's up?"

"Well, Mr Colvin" — Costas returned to his original mission, still a little confused — "I don't know how to say this to you, and I don't want to impose upon you, Mr Colvin, but we have had some trouble in town and I wanted to know if you might lend me a hand?" He paused, smiled and then concluded, "A pigeon has shitted on our dog?"

Virgil was amused, but also mildly alarmed at this plea for help. It was a sudden dose of unwanted reality on their relationship and his life on the island. Since meeting Costas Pantakalas at the main ferry port of Ithaca almost six months earlier, the Chief had quickly impressed himself upon the veteran homicide detective as a talker and a charmer. Costas knew everything and everyone on the island. He handled petty theft, minor battery and traffic violation and altercation with aplomb, cheer and all the vigour his constitution, temperament and stature allowed.

To Costas, Virgil was an exotic. A big-city American homicide detective! Virgil Colvin was the stuff of legend and myth — every bit as unlikely as the heroes of Homer, so far as Chief Pantakalas was concerned. While Virgil wanted to know the lay of the land and the rumours and myths of the island, he now called home, Costas wanted to be regaled with tales of real crime and real detective work in the faraway land he only knew about from television and the movies. Their friendship was built around these mutually beneficial insights. And ouzo. Lots and lots of ouzo. Virgil remembered liking it during his honeymoon but had never really had any since. He was making up for lost times — and then some.

"Costas, what is it? Of course, I'll help you. If I can," he added.

"Oh, thank you, thank you, Mr Colvin!" Costas embraced his tired and startled friend.

"Jesus Christ, Costas" — moving out of Costas' sudden hug — "will you tell me what the fuck is going on, already?"

"Yes, Mr Colvin, I am sorry. You see, we have had a killing."

"A killing? You mean someone died from the earthquake? Was it more serious in town? It didn't seem too big up here, but it was my first quake, so I don't really know."

"No, Mr Colvin, I apologise for my English" — Virgil felt bad for making his friend feel awkward — "I meant, we have had a murder. In Vathy. Will you come to assist me? Now? Please?"

Shit. Virgil had not missed his old job at all during the five months he spent settling into life in Ithaca with his walks, his books, the fresh Ionian seafood and his ouzo. And yet, here it was. Murder had followed him like the Furies of Greek myth that hounded heinous criminals until they went mad. OK, so it wasn't quite *that* bad, but this was the last thing Virgil wanted or expected or needed. But he had to say something to his poor friend. Costas had never handled a murder. They had talked about it at length. Apparently, nothing very exciting in terms of crime ever really happened on the island. *Costas was out of his league*. *Unless*, Virgil thought, *it was a crime of passion and the murderer had passed out nearby, covered in the victim's blood.* He did not say this to his friend. "Costas, of course, let's go."

"Mr Colvin!" Costas grabbed Virgil with another hug, and then ran for his car. "Please, get in, I drive! I will tell you what I know as we head for the plaza!"

"OK, let me get my phone from the villa," Virgil said resignedly on his way to the door.

"Oh, Mr Colvin, you haven't noticed? The phones, the Internet, they are all dead. Your friend, Poseidon, decided to give you the real island experience!" The Chief was downright gleeful.

Virgil stared at Costas' white-and-blue Kia Sportage. The standard vehicle of the Hellenic Police, islands like Ithaca received the hand-me-downs of the major cities. Costas Pantakalas was still using the 2001 model that had first seen service in Thessaloniki, before being sent to Crete. When the Cretans sent it to Kefalonia, they probably half-hoped the transport tanker would sink so they could pocket the insurance money. Costas received it in 2019 after the Kefalonians decided it was ready to die in Ithaca. It was small, it had an obsolete and used-up engine and Virgil dreaded stuffing himself into it, having to listen to its death throes up close. Every time he did so, he seriously pondered what turn or hill would be its last, and possibly his? As Virgil climbed into the passenger side of the car, he couldn't help but wonder how long this unsought 'adventure' might last and how far he might have to go to be left in peace?

CHAPTER TWO
AT THE FEET OF ODYSSEUS

Dawn was in full command of the sky when they arrived. The body didn't look dead. *They sometimes don't*, Virgil remembered. But as they drew closer, it was clear that the man *was* dead. His pallor was off. There was a little blood pooled under his head. There is something utterly unnatural about a perfectly still body that always eerily communicates death. It all came rushing back as Virgil circled the scene, taking it all in. The sun illuminated the impressionistic statue of Odysseus, wandering king of Ithaca, presiding over the usual plaza of Vathy, and this morning, the unusual corpse deposited at the base.

Whoever did this, had an odd sensibility. Not only was the act of dumping a body in the middle of the largest city's public square fairly brazen and/or utterly foolish, but planting the victim at the base of the island's most notable statue of its most famous supposed resident was, thought Virgil, either a circumstantial oddity or a peculiar message of some sort.

"And you say you don't know this man?"

"No, Mr Colvin," Costas answered, watching Virgil intently. "Like I said in the car, he is a British tourist. He's been here at least two weeks, but I haven't been able to corner him into a conversation — very unusual!"

No shit, Virgil thought. Costas was a good friend by now, but there was no doubt that the man was a little pushy ('involved' if one wanted to be diplomatic), never stopped talking and could put away inhuman amounts of ouzo. For a moment, Virgil wondered if Costas was the ouzo version of Pan or Dionysius, but then he remembered there was a case and got back to looking at the lifeless body before him. Costas was hospitable to a fault. For a tourist to be on the island for two weeks and not be cornered and charmed by Costas was highly unusual and unlikely — unless the person were deliberately avoiding the chief. Who would do that? Who *could* do that? Why? *How?*

Virgil needed a coffee or espresso, but remembered that Costas looked up to him. The big city homicide detective from America! He needed to be focused and present. But he could still taste the distinctive anise of last night's ouzo. Virgil had to help with the case and look like he knew what he was doing. *He couldn't be whining about the lack of caffeine! How the hell was Costas wide awake? He drank so much more ouzo last night! Damned if he's not made of ouzo!*

"OK, so a British tourist is dead in your capital city's main square. Someone placed him here at this statue…" At this moment, Costas cut him off.

"How do you know someone put him here? Why is he not killed here?"

Before Virgil mockingly dismissed this question, he remembered that Costas had never dealt with a murder before. They had traded 'war stories' for months, and as best Virgil could tell, the greatest caper that Costas Pantakalas ever confronted in Ithaca was the mysterious case of the man who loved his goats. There was a fellow in the hills south of town, a neighbour of Costas' whom many suspected of having carnal relations with his goats. Such things happened among pastoralists from time to time, but the island was quite pious, and the community was in an uproar. Naturally, they came to their chief for relief. The great complication of the case, as Virgil recalled, was that the man's goat cheese was renowned not only in Ithaca, but also Kefalonia, Lefkas and Zakynthos — all the nearby Ionian islands. Costas had spent weeks ingratiating himself with the farmer, whom he knew as a neighbour, but not terribly well beyond that. They talked about goats. Costas would pet the goats. Costas would pet the goats some more, while talking about how lovely goats were — trying to goad the man into revealing his dark secret. When that hadn't panned out, Costas had taken to showing up at all hours of the day and night, hoping to discover some manner of routine or pattern to the alleged aberrant behaviour. After several months of this, the man grew suspicious that his neighbours were plotting against him and stopped making and selling goat cheese altogether. Costas was then visited by the man's accusers, as well as notables from other parts of Ithaca and the other Ionian islands, to correct the wrong that had been perpetrated against this man. And so, Costas had assured the allegedly amorous goatherder and cheesemaker that he was under no suspicion and that everyone loved his cheese. After several weeks of such cajoling, along with a lot of ouzo, normalcy returned. Whether the man loved his goats too much was never proven one way or the other, but everyone seemed to realise that they didn't care about that more than the cheese, so they stopped thinking about it. *That* was the biggest case to fall upon Costas Pantakalas until this morning at the feet of Odysseus.

"Well, Costas, we have a couple of things that suggest that that's very unlikely," Virgil said in his authoritative detective voice that he so often used with the rookies. He didn't miss breaking those kids in. "First, we should assume the cause of death was this nasty head wound here at the back of the skull, which seems to have been crushed — I would guess with repeated blunt trauma. I don't see any splatter around here, Costas, do you?" Costas immediately began scanning the areas around the statue before affirming that there did not seem to be blood scattered around the base. "When did you say you discovered the body?"

"Right after the earthquake, Mr Colvin. I drove into the plaza to see if anyone needed help and to survey the town and then I see him here like this! I recognised him, I told my lieutenant Kyriakos to keep an eye on things and then I come for you. Now we are here!"

Virgil looked at the dough-faced young Gen Z lieutenant, who had silently observed the chief and the American at a wary distance. His hair was combed straight back and as black as his chief's. He had an inordinate number of moles on his face for such a young man — Virgil had counted at various points over the last six months, it was somewhere between six and eight, maybe nine. He was a little taller than his chief, but he was in fairly flabby shape. He sweated profusely most of the time. Even though it was barely past dawn, he had already markedly sweated through his uniform shirt. He talked very seldomly, and then in the very unconfident tones of people his age due to the combination of technology-induced social awkwardness and only being comfortable speaking authoritatively to people their own age.

Kyriakos was a good egg, in Virgil's estimation. *He probably would have been a shitty cop in Chicago*, he thought, *but he could certainly handle the beat in Ithaca*. The 'beat' in Ithaca mostly consisted of doing 'gopher' work at the behest of Costas most of the day, and providing designated driver services for his chief, and his American friend, Mr Colvin, at night. In fact, Kyriakos had driven Virgil to the base of the hill ascending to his villa only a few hours earlier. Virgil could still sort of remember the jumble of images of his stumbling trek up the now well-trod path from the base of the hill to his villa. Kyriakos performed this service dozens and dozens of times over the past half year. Kyriakos looked back at Virgil, his face betraying only a faint hint of scepticism.

"Good, well that was about an hour ago," Virgil said. "You will notice that the stones at the statue here are pretty cool and the temperature here is… what? About seventy-five degrees, or so?"

Costas looked amused. "Still no Celsius? You need to abandon this Fahrenheit! This is Greece, we have advanced to metric! But yes, it is about 22 or 23 degrees now," he said, smiling broadly. Always able to be amused — that was Costas Pantakalas.

"So if it is about 25 degrees cooler than the body while alive and healthy" — again, Costas looked amused — "and the stones here are themselves very cool to the touch, how is the body still rather warm? If it had been out here in the dark of night for three or more hours in this cool air and on these cold stones, we should expect the body to be a bit colder at this point. You see what I mean?" Costas nodded slowly; Kyriakos followed suit. "But he's stiff as a board, Costas. He's been dead at least a few hours, I'd wager. This suggests he was moved here from some other place and kept warm. Not the crime of passion, you see?" Again, the Greeks nodded slowly. "You need to get pictures,

Costas — we need to assume whoever did this possibly chose this location for a reason. There may be clues, either way."

Costas immediately relayed orders to Kyriakos, who fumblingly got to the business of taking pictures with his otherwise useless iPhone.

Once Kyriakos, working under the direction of Virgil's right index finger as he followed the young man around the scene and the body, saved a sufficient number of pictures, from a sufficient number of angles, Virgil began to deal with the corpse. Costas Pantakalas produced medical latex gloves from his pocket.

"From the hospital?" Colvin asked, putting the thin latex on gingerly. He was used to the sturdier stuff of crime scene investigation gloves back in the States. These were the dainty things of Janet's business.

"Yes, Mr Colvin, why?"

"It's nothing," Virgil lied. He began to feel the dead man's limbs, abdomen and then finally the neck and head. Deliberately and slowly, making sure he didn't miss anything. As he began to feel around the head, his fingers touched a sickening patch of soft and giving area on the normally firm posterior of the skull. It felt like a thawed steak. The fact that the rest of the body was leaden and hard as stone made the feeling all the more disconcerting.

"Yes, the head is definitely caved in at the back of the skull," Virgil said while verifying the most likely spot of the fatal injury, "it doesn't seem like the wound really broke the skin, though, which is interesting." Virgil grimaced slightly at the fingers of the glove, there wasn't much blood. *You don't really get used to it,* he thought, *unless you're one of those fucking medical examiners. Weirdos.*

Virgil suddenly was back in the stairwell of his first precinct house as a homicide detective in the Chicago PD, walking down to the medical examiner's office and the morgue to talk about her findings on one of his first cases. One of the city's developers had been shot in the face by his wife's lover. Fourteen times. *The fucker reloaded!* Probably wouldn't be much the ME could add to the basic facts that Virgil noted at the crime scene. As he came into the office, he quickly saw that it was empty. So, he casually walked into the morgue and then stopped. Kim Sadlowski was standing in front of him, her eyes closed. There was a slow Chopin piano piece playing from some unseen speaker. The developer's cold, dead hand was held firmly to Sadlowski's face, caressing her. She seemed quite transfixed. Virgil backed away, slowly. Kim never knew he was there, and they worked together cordially until his transfer to the North-side four years later.

Janet believed his account instantly and told him of her own peculiar interactions with pathologists in Med School and her subsequent career. Just as suddenly as he was reliving Kim Sadlowski's étude with a corpse, Virgil was back in Ithaca. He hadn't told Costas this story yet — he had never told anyone except Janet. It was too weird. Costas, no idea of the bizarre scenes running through the American's head, feasted on everything Virgil was doing and saying with eyes and ears, like he never saw or heard anything quite so interesting.

Virgil moved deftly around the victim. After assuring himself that the hangover was not making him miss something, he reached into the pants pockets of the dead man and extracted their illuminating contents. "Let's see here," Virgil continued to narrate for Costas, Kyriakos and whichever of the gods or goddesses cared to watch and listen, "we have what appears to be a hotel key" — *Jesus, when is the last time I saw one of these?* Virgil thought to himself as he hefted the dull, heavy iron key — "Hotel Familia, Room 4," he read the engraving on the side, "Well, I guess we know where we are going next, Costas." He shot the Chief a wry smile — the chief blushed.

The Hotel Familia was a well-known destination in the city, with a fine bar and restaurant, plenty of rich and elite tourists in the high season and a proprietress that the local men vied for in a shamelessly open and sadly ineffectual way. Costas Pantakalas, for all his native charm and obvious devotion to the woman, was like so many Achaean heroes staring pathetically at the walls of Ilion. It was the only great mystery of the island that had presented itself to Virgil Colvin since he arrived. How could this most charming and magnetic of men be so lonely a bachelor? All he had been able to gather from the locals was that Costas had been married once, long ago, but that the union had dissolved in some great controversy less than a week after the wedding. The wife was gone. The island had been scandalised and Costas refused to discuss the topic with anyone. He had not even come close to remarrying since. Virgil had yet to find the right moment, or the intimate familiarity, to broach the difficult discussion with his new best friend

"International driver's license!" Virgil exclaimed, pulling the last article from the dead man's pockets. "Now we will know this fellow's name!" He flipped the document open and then slowly read aloud, "Reginald Wellesley? My god, could his name have been any more insufferably British? I hope he at least didn't go by Reginald, what an awful name!"

"What is wrong with this name?" Costas asked, showing that the American's humour had still not fully calibrated to his new setting and audience. "Isn't your name unusual?"

Virgil suppressed his desire to defend his name — his great grandfather's name. He remembered the story his parents had told him about great granddad Virgil's reaction to the news of the honour bestowed upon him: "I hate that name!" Virgil Colvin the younger, however, was quite fond of it. There were very few other Virgils running about. He liked it that way.

"Oh, nothing, Costas, I am merely trying to make light of this situation. You know us Americans, still have a chip on our shoulders with the Brits! Before we head to the hotel, is there anything else we can glean here..." as he spoke, he looked around the plaza for faces or clues. His eye caught a lovely glint. "Costas, these cameras around the plaza, please tell me they work, they are pointed right over here!" he exclaimed as he waved his right hand lazily at the three cameras seemingly covering the plaza.

Before Costas answered, Virgil knew what was coming. A look of shame swept over the usually joyous face of his friend. "Mr Colvin, I am sad to bear the bad news, but the cameras are simply a fright and trick. They do not record." His shame was deep, and his eyes sought a path to Tartarus in the ground around him.

Virgil suppressed a desire to laugh. *Got to stay professional! Poor Costas is counting on me to play the role of heroic big city homicide detective! Don't laugh at his island, damn it!* These and similar commands impeded the impulse, though only just.

"OK, well don't worry, Costas, we solved plenty of murders before cameras were posted everywhere." His friend immediately looked up, happy that the island's rustic provinciality did not condemn him in the eyes of the big-city detective. "We will just have to see what your girlfriend at the Hotel Familia has to say about poor Reggie here." Virgil was beginning to fully awaken and could not help poking fun at the well-known pursuit by the island's eligible class of single men of the alluring, independent and available hotelier who ran the island's most cosy and comfortable *x-en-o-do-he-o*.[4] The modern Greek word hotel evoked the ancient Greek concept of *ex-en-ee-a* — the obligations that hosts and guests owed to each other and the ever-

---

[4] In Greek, ξενοδοχείο.

watchful Zeus, whose charge it was to punish transgressions of this incredibly important value of the Greeks.[5] For Ithacans, *xenia* was as critical to their conception of just behaviour as it had been to their wandering hero, Odysseus, who condemned the Cyclopes to blindness for his failure to observe its laws. The Cyclopes had, of course, murdered and feasted on Odysseus' men, seeking shelter and hospitality. As Virgil glanced up at the hero's statue, he thanked his good fortune that the islanders were a bit more welcoming and tolerant of him.

"Mr Colvin, please! You know this is not true!" As Costas began his standard denials that protested the truth more than too much, the familiar refrain was interrupted by the approach of an equally familiar face.

The Mayor of Vathy was a bloated-looking man, as joyless and grave as Costas was lively and ebullient. Panagis Metaxas hoped, like nearly all mayors of Vathy, to simply wait for retirement and the end of the daily grind of having to walk around the town and make small talk with everyone. While there was a regional governor for the Ioanian Islands as a group, he was based in Kefalonia and made the rounds to the smaller island every four or five months. Vathy's mayor, therefore, took responsibility for the island's other towns and villages. *It really was too much!* Panagis always thought to himself around noon of the four days of the week that

[5] Ξένια — xenia

he worked. And then this accursed day had befallen him! First the earthquake to startle him to blighted consciousness. Then the word of murder in the plaza — a murder! In Vathy! In Thiakí! And now this awful news to relay to the chief, and that odd American who had moved to the island. *A drunk, dark and gaunt-looking fellow,* Panagis often thought. *Why did Costas bother? And now he, Panagis Metaxas, Mayor of Vathy, had to interact with this man pleasantly to avoid offending him, and Costas Pantakalas by association. The job did not pay enough or add enough prestige to a reputation to warrant any of this labour. Heracles committed great and unspeakable crimes before being so burdened!* These self-pitying and dyspeptic laments usually awaited his quitting time ouzo — at 15:00 on the minute. But this day truly was cursed!

"Panagis!" exclaimed Costas. "How are you, my friend?"

"Costas," replied the mayor, "how much misery can one day bring to us? Sadly, I have more awful news."

"Worse than this?" Costas pointed to the body of Reginald Wellesley.

"With all respect to the dead, yes." He touched the orthodox cross pinned to his jacket below the Greek flag pin as he said this. "I have just come back from the harbour at Aetos. It is gone. Claimed by St. Nicholas.[6]

[6] St. Nicholas usurped Poseidon's command of the seas in the early Christian era.

Fallen into the ocean. The earthquake was apparently far more severe on that side of the island! Frikes is not really a replacement and who knows what has happened up there anyway!"

Virgil marvelled how the port of Frikes, which was less than twenty kilometres away and on the same island, sounded like it was in another universe when uttered by this frightened man. Panagis' face was ashen and his panic poorly hidden. His eyes looked to Costas for reassurance.

This was remarkable news. Piso Aetos was the main (dis)embarkation point for the large ferries that brought people to the island from Kefalonia and mainland Greece. For the port to collapse into the sea meant that no sizable ferries would be able to bring people to or from the island for the foreseeable future. Everyone was effectively stranded. More precisely, the tourists who'd flown into Kefalonia and then ferried over, or ferried directly from the mainland, were stranded. The tourists who sailed to Ithaca, and the fishermen, were as free as the eagles for whom the fallen port was named. It was the high season. The island and its few thousand denizens relied on a few months of tourists to get them through the rest of the year. It was not too much to say that Vathy's residents would consider this a disaster nearly as devastating as the calamity of 1953. But that was only because they had forgotten what their parents and grandparents had told them of that catastrophe.

"On the plus side, gentlemen," said Virgil, breaking the stunned silence, "whoever killed this man probably cannot leave the island for the moment."

"Any idea when the port can be repaired?" Costas asked the mayor.

"None. With the phones and Internet down," the mayor sadly droned, "there is no telling when the rest of Greece will remember us. Especially given the crisis with the Turks before this happened!"

Virgil and Costas moaned their assent to these general truisms. There was always some crisis with the Turks — this one related to how the Greeks were supposedly mistreating Muslim refugees in Lesbos. The real issue was a battle over the mineral and energy extraction rights for the seafloor of the Aegean off Turkey's coast. But it was always something. There were few topics, Virgil had quickly learned, capable of animating everyone on the island as quickly and as passionately.

"Panagis, we need to take our investigation to Katerina's place." Costas said this knowing full well that the mayor was on the same errand as he was with the hotel's owner. Metaxas, immediately blushing at the news, did not take Costas' cheeky farewell in good spirits. "Good luck re-establishing communications with our eastern friends, Panagis!"

Muttering his goodbye, Metaxas continued on his usual rounds to see just about everyone in Vathy — wondering how Sisyphus himself could claim to have a worse fate. He was quickly onto thinking about how to circle back to the Hotel Familia without being too obvious about it. The detectives watched his slowly shuffling amble take him away and then got back to work.

"Kyriakos! Get this body to the hospital at once, make sure they keep it cold!" Costas glanced at Virgil for approval of this order. Getting it, he continued, "Once you are done, try to catch up with us at the Hotel Familia, room 4!" With that, the young lieutenant ran off towards the hospital south of the plaza. Costas was dumbfounded.

"KYRIAKOS!"

The young man stopped dead in his tracks and slowly looked back at his chief. Virgil sensed that the lieutenant had never before heard this bellowing tone. He wasn't sure that *he* had heard it before either. It was alarming, to put it mildly.

"What in God's name are you doing?" Costas was decreasing the volume rapidly, but the iron in his voice was unmistakable. "You cannot abandon this body! Your radio still works, call the hospital to come and collect Mr Wellesley! Do not be like that ass Midas — not today!"

The younger man simply moved quietly and quickly back to the body while reaching for his radio to call for the hospital.

Virgil recalled the story of Midas — not the familiar one of the foolish king, whose golden gift soon proved a horrifying curse, but the prosaic story of the Ithacan provincial, Midas Velopoulos. As best Virgil could tell, Midas Velopoulos existed in a remote antiquity of Costas' management of the Vathy police. Like Kyriakos, Velopoulos was a similarly bright-eyed lieutenant aiming to please his chief. As Costas told the tale, Midas Velopoulos had been foisted upon him by one of Panagis' predecessors. Everything the man touched turned to dross. He couldn't file paperwork properly or remember orders and commands from ten minutes earlier. And he couldn't be fired! It had gotten so bad that eventually Costas had to write down elaborate instructions for Midas that took him on long pointless errands all day. After a month of this, Midas finally started to become suspicious that these 'missions' were not as essential as Costas was pretending. When he confronted Costas, the chief told the pitiable man that he wasn't cut out for the job and should try to find something he liked and could take pride in doing. Costas then gave him his instructions for the day. Midas took them, left and was never seen again on the island. No one knew what became of Midas Velopoulos, but he remained *the* standard of foolish obliviousness and inept incompetence ever since. Kyriakos never knew this Midas, but it still stung when his chief compared him to the long-lost boob.

As they walked towards the Hotel Familia, Costas continued to observe and take in all that Virgil Colvin did and said like his life depended on it. His career certainly might depend on it. He occasionally asked clarifying questions that showed he was both paying attention and processing. Colvin continued to silently debate in his head whether Costas would get chewed up in one week working Chicago homicide, or own the town. As he went back and forth, he suddenly remembered that he, Virgil Colvin, was the masticated one.

CHAPTER THREE
HOTEL FAMILIA

The Hotel Familia was a seven-room boutique establishment to the west of the square where Reginald Wellesley's body was discovered. A converted olive mill, the hotel was a quaint yet luxurious establishment that charged some of the highest rates on the island — and got them. It was roughly four blocks to the hotel — small and truncated Ithacan blocks at that. These weren't the enormous city blocks of American grid city plans, like Chicago, where a five-minute walk would maybe get you past two of them. They were the curious and irregular blocks of very old towns and cities, built centuries before cars and Enlightenment-inspired straight lines. It was less than five minutes' walk from Reginald Wellesley's body at the feet of Odysseus. It was still a little early, though, and Virgil could smell the espresso brewing in the cafés surrounding the plaza.

"Costas," he asked, "do you mind if we get some coffee before visiting the hotel?"

"Of course, Mr Colvin! Of course!" replied his ever-conscientious host.

"Great!" Virgil said with relief. He needed to eradicate the taste of last night's ouzo. "Sesto's?" he suggested.

"Yes! They have the best *fi-ni-ki* in Vathy!" Costas eagerly led the way.

It was the resumption of a months' old campaign to get Virgil to eat the confections and odd delights of the Greek café. The coffee, espresso and cappuccinos were all fantastic. Baklava, once in a while, was a decadent delight. But the cookies coated in powdered sugar, the indulgent overuse of honey in and on nearly all the treats and snacks and the fried phyllo stuffed with cheeses, spinach and who-knows-what never looked all that appealing to Virgil Colvin. Janet's years of training and cutting sweets out of his diet had become part of his creed and constitution. Ithacan cuisine for lunch and dinner was the freshest of Mediterranean and Greek seafood, caught that day and served with fresh oil and herbs — but the breakfast and snack trade was a glutton's paradise. Costas insisted, every time they got coffee, that Virgil eat some best version of something terribly bad for you "in the city" or "on the island" or "all of Greece". It was one of the few aspects of his friend that grated on his nerves.

They arrived at Sesto's café in about a minute of brisk walking as it was just off the southern end of the plaza. The young girl working the register and the coffee making apparatus was a bit plump and homely looking. Her smile didn't help. Costas insisted on ordering a cappuccino for his friend, a straight Greek coffee for himself, and some unappetizing-looking phyllo dough concoction from the display case. Virgil glanced at the floor behind the counter, the pile of broken ceramic mug, cup and saucer sherds was substantial. The earthquake may have wiped out the entire supply. Poseidon wasn't environmentally conscientious, it seemed. When the drinks and the hot triangle of dough arrived, Virgil quickly took up his paper cup and pushed the mystery object towards Costas.

"Please, Mr Colvin!" Costas urged the paper plate back towards Virgil. "I did not order you sweets, but the tiropita; it is delightful and will help you wake up!"

"Cheese pie? Nothing could sound worse at the moment, Costas. I thank you, but no." He drank his cappuccino as emphatically as he could for finality.

"You don't eat, Mr Colvin!" He padded Virgil's abdomen, pushing past the loose-fitting shirt. "Please, for your friend, eat! If not you, then me, yes? Eat!"

Virgil guiltily took a small bite of the buttered dough full of melted cheese and eggs. It wasn't the worst thing he'd ever put in his mouth, he told himself. But he still wasn't hungry.

"Good, thanks, Costas," he said, replacing the tiropita on the plate and resuming his cappuccino. Costas could tell he wasn't going to eat the rest. He had a look of fatherly concern and disappointment on his face. He proceeded to drink his Greek coffee in silence.

They both finished, said goodbye to the ugly girl and left Sesto's for the short trek to the hotel.

The two-storey building was made of large stones fashioned into irregular oblongs, much like bricks, but enormous — five or six times the standard size. The stones were a yellowish beige, while the terra cotta roof, ubiquitous on the island, capped the charming temple to *xenia*. As they arrived, a tad past eight, the friends forgot the awkwardness at the café and got to discussing how to handle the next steps of their incipient investigation.

"So, Costas, you should probably be in charge of smoothing over a search of Reggie's room with Katerina," Virgil suggested.

"You just enjoy watching me talk to her! You can talk to her, I will be there to suggest it is, as you're fond of saying, 'OK'." Costas deflected.

"Costas, don't be silly, you're the police here, not me. She is far more likely to listen to you and take you seriously. Besides, you're better than all the other louts who waste her time. Don't blow an opportunity like this. You're going to look very authoritative demanding access to Reggie's room for a murder investigation. Women love a man who confidently wields authority — even if they aren't interested in that authority ever being applied to them." Virgil was mostly serious, but he couldn't help being somewhat flippant with Costas on the topic of Katerina Stasinopoulos. *Besides, Janet always loved it when he was playing 'Mr Cop' — stood to reason Katerina would be similar, right?*

As they entered the hotel's small lobby, they saw shattered glass strewn about the floor and an awful lot of water. The floor had a lovely, though entirely superfluous, glass-covered illuminated seawater floor panel. The earthquake had made quick work of this charming touch of the décor. Katerina was sweeping up glass.

She was probably a shade past forty years old. Virgil wasn't quite sure. Her skin was beautifully olive tinged and largely unblemished by sun, age or wrinkle. Her hair was long, black and curly. You could tell it must look marvellous when down, but she almost always wore it up — as she was now — bound in some intricate way while concealed beneath a traditional Greek wrap for the purpose. Hers was white and blue. Her black locks peeked out in luxurious tufts around her brow, while also emerging at the top of the conically shaped and wrapped hair mountain atop her head. The effect was very becoming, if Periclean. As they entered, she had her back to the door, affording the detectives a moment to admire her figure. She wore a long blue skirt, with a white loose-fitting blouse. She had the solidly built frame of a woman who worked for a living, yet she still curved and jutted in all the areas that most men on the island seemed to find nearly hypnotic. Now she was a silent siren. As she moved to and fro, back and forth, sweeping, neither man could bring himself to interrupt her. All at once, she stopped what she was doing, and slowly turned to see the Chief of Police, who she knew all too well, and the strange American whom she had only seen once or twice — usually with Costas. Her eyes were deep as Homer's wine-dark sea and her nose was of the round Greek variety without being so big as to detract from the loveliness of her face. She smiled often, and when she did, you wanted her to issue a command. Why? So that you could pay back the debt to her and the universe for the privilege of *that* smile.

"Gentlemen — were you just going to let me ignore you? What sort of host would that make me? And what sort of guests would that make you?" She was smiling, and yet she knew what they had been up to and the smile somehow managed to reproach them.

Remarkable woman! Virgil Colvin thought to himself. He liked her all the more and would have spoken to apologise, but now it was his turn to study, observe and soak in everything his friend did, and said.

"Katerina," said Costas, vaguely less self-assured than usual — Virgil could only tell because of the hours they had spent drinking together over the last several months — "we need help. One of your guests, Reginald Wellesley. Please, Katerina," he said with renewed and intense confidence, "he is dead. Killed. We must see his room, #4, immediately."

"Costas!" Katerina had a look of alarm in her eyes, though her face remained calm, almost with the hint of a concerned and empathetic smile. It was almost as if she had trained the muscles in her face to smile subtly and in perfect accord with all potential circumstances. "Yes, of course, you know where the room is, do you need a key?"

"No, Katerina, we have his key." He produced it, adding alarm to her already shocked eyes. "Could you please tell us about this Wellesley? When did he get here? What was he doing here? Had you seen him before? Did you speak with him at all?"

Katerina's eyes regained their normal brightness and her smile now became that mild upturn of helpfulness. Virgil was impressed with the torrent of pertinent questions Costas unleashed upon her after gaining her acquiescence to visit the room.

"Eeee, I'm surprised at you, Costas! A person on this island escaped your attention and charm!" Katerina obviously delighted in teasing her most charming suitor.

"It seems that way, Katerina. Please, my questions?" He said this with a tone of tenderness Virgil hadn't heard before. Costas continued, "Also, can we please have a list of guests?"

"Of course, Costas," she replied, as she led them to the check-in desk, just behind the smashed floor décor. "Well, I believe this was his first time with me — I did not recognise him or his name. I do not believe this was his first time on the island. He knew about Circe already! What else did you want to know? I'm sorry, I was just a little shocked at this news, on top of this sudden escape of *ee as-kee too A-o-loo*."[7]

"Yes, certainly, Katerina" — the same tenderness, Virgil smirked ever so slightly. "When did he get here?"

---

[7] In Greek, Οι ασκοί του Αίολου — a reference to the winds of Aeolus, imprisoned in a large leather sack to allow Odysseus to get home in the Odyssey. Sadly, Odysseus stayed awake day and night after leaving the island of the wind god and collapsed from exhaustion just before reaching home. His men, convinced that the sack held treasure that their king was hiding from them, a gift from a god no less, opened the sack within sight of Ithaca and unleashed the torrents of the winds, blowing the ship away from the island and preventing all of them from ever getting home, except Odysseus. His journey continued for nearly another ten years, while everyone else perished along the way. This Greek expression aims to recreate that sense of disaster and misfortune.

She handed a printout of the guests to Costas, who took it without looking.

"Oh, almost two weeks ago, I think? Today is Thursday. He arrived two Fridays ago."

Shit, thought Virgil, *he really had given Costas the slip!*

"And what was he doing here? Did you talk to him about that? Did he mention anything?"

Before she could answer, François Deflers entered the Hotel. "*Messieurs! Bonjour!* What excitement we have had, *non*?"

Costas, suddenly quite red, looked down at the list. He then angrily folded it and stuffed it into his shirt pocket.

Virgil could detect a look of annoyance in Costas' glance his way before embracing the Frenchman and his affectionate greeting. Virgil just stuck out a stiff American hand with a formal "Good morning, Mr Deflers."

As Costas and François discussed the morning's events — the earthquake — Virgil looked the other foreigner over. He was tall, tanned and affable-looking — in his mid or late 30s. He had a little grey in his hair, which was otherwise wavy, black and full. The effect was to give him the gravitas of older age without actually making him any less vibrant-looking. He was always immaculately dressed, like a Frenchman on the Riviera — relaxed, yet pure class. It was actually a great look for Ithaca. He had vibrant blue eyes, a great smile and seemed in excellent shape. Maybe a runner? Virgil suddenly felt like a bit of a slob, simply wearing jeans, loafers, a polo and his Cubs hat. *Oh well, ugly Americans!* He sensed the Frenchman thought worse of him than that.

Virgil knew the rest of François' story through Costas. He was the construction liaison, agent and representative of a large consortium of international investors planning to build a major five-star resort on the island's isthmus, called 'Project Odysseus'. The island was quite divided over the development. Some believed it would provide a far steadier stream of tourists — and money. Others believed it would destroy the isolated and unique feel of the place. Having just escaped there himself, Virgil tended to side with the latter group, but what could he do? If murder was going to follow him to this place, what chance did he have in stopping everything and everyone else?

Deflers *always* stayed at the Hotel Familia when he was on the island. Costas, and most everyone else, suspected the reason why. Virgil wondered how François and his consortium were going to react to news of the port at Aetos collapsing into the sea. And a murder! Would this make Ithaca even more appealing to tourists tired of the Aegean islands? Or would it simply highlight what a remote pain in the ass Ithaca was in the first place? Anyway, he wasn't about to let François know there had been a murder at all — that was Costas' prerogative. Though if Costas had asked his advice on the matter, he would have suggested telling no one else unless absolutely necessary.

"François, we have had some unpleasantness; one of the guests here was murdered," Costas said, making his first big mistake innocently. Virgil winced noticeably enough for Katerina to see it and she began to look quite quizzically at her ugly American guest.

"*Non*! Who?" François appeared genuinely surprised. Of course, if he was the murderer, it would hardly be the moment to *not* act surprised.

"Your neighbour from across the sea, Mr Wellesley." Again, Virgil winced. Again, Katerina noticed.

"*Mon dieu*!" were the words François exclaimed, but there was something in his expression, Virgil thought, that betrayed a happy, almost joyous, reaction to the news. He wondered if Costas noticed it. "I cannot believe it! When? How?"

At this point, Katerina intervened, "Costas, I will show you to the room with your friend here" — motioning towards Virgil — "and answer your questions."

Costas, taking the hint, finished his conversation with François abruptly. "I am sorry, Mr Deflers, I cannot divulge that information, we are still investigating. Should I have any questions for you, as a guest here, I will be able to find you, no?"

"But of course, *mon capitaine*! I will either be here, in the plaza for espresso or lunch, or out at the project."

With that, François Deflers took his leave of the policeman and the retired detective. As he walked by Katerina, he whispered inaudibly in her ear while pressing himself rather closely to her. She playfully pushed him away. He strolled to his room, laughing.

"Katerina, you can do better than that man who will ruin the island!" Costas let his jealousy get the better of him with this premature reproach. Again, Virgil winced ever so slightly.

"Costas! Who do you think you are?" Katerina dressed him down instantly. "If I were you, I would stick to this case, and follow the counsel of your friend here before you do something foolish." She continued her walk ahead of the two men — which normally would have been a moment for silent reverence. Instead, Costas gave a rare glare Virgil's way as they walked up the stairs. Virgil did his best pantomime of the guy who can't shrug emphatically enough.

Katerina interrupted this interlude with her final answers to the questions Costas had now forgotten. "He and I did speak, a couple of times. I was not able to figure out exactly what he was doing here. He talked with me, as I told you, about Circe and whether she was still on the island and still running her taverna.[8] He also wanted to know about the fishermen, about Nikos and about François. The fishermen, he was curious if they were always the same people or if new people ever came

---

[8] Like many words in modern Greek, ταβέρνα does not need an explanation for the English speakers of the world.

into Vathy. With both Nikos and François, he just wanted to know what they were doing on the island and if either of them had made any 'waves' or 'noise' lately. These are the words he used."

Virgil waited for a moment. "And who is Nikos?"

"Ah, my friend," Costas answered, "he is a man I hope we do not have to talk with today. He runs a political party here on the island. Frankly, I don't know why, or anyone who is supporting him."

"What political party?"

"The KKE," said Katerina, "the Greek Communist Party."

"Ah, yes," Virgil realised, "I have seen their HQ over by your place, Costas — quite the sight! Kappa Kappa Epsilon. Sounds like a frat!"

Costas and Katerina exchanged a puzzled look.

They arrived at the door to room #4. Costas apologised to Katerina and thanked her for answering his questions and helping them up to this point, but told her she could not disturb the room. She might as well get back to what she had been doing before all the interruptions. Virgil expected disappointment or annoyance. Instead, she beamed a lovely smile, as genuine as it was attractive, and wished them luck. She made her way, perfectly poised, back down the hall to her business. *What a remarkable woman!*

He had not thought of women too much since Janet's death. He wasn't really thinking of Katerina now, she was already being pursued by a half dozen men (or more) on the island, including his poor friend. But he did feel that stirring of longing for the sort of sensible, feisty and determined woman that Janet was before the cancer took her from him. He saw Costas staring at him again with that endearingly annoying fatherly concern.

"Shall we?" Virgil asked.

***

Room #4 was fairly cosy, about twelve by fifteen feet. The entryway was narrow before opening on the room. The queen-size bed (the king-size beds Americans were accustomed to once they reached gainfully employed adulthood were almost unknown on the island) was to the left. Immediately in front of them was a narrow couch and the sun-drenched windows that looked towards the sea to the east. The wispy coverings fluttered slightly in response to the opening of the door. The bed was immaculately made. Either Reginald Wellesley was a fastidious obsessive compulsive, or he hadn't slept there since the last maid service of the room. There was a small suitcase on the couch and an attaché case on the floor next to it. A small desk ran parallel to the bed against the opposite wall — there were books and papers piled upon it as well as a bottle with some amber-coloured liquid. The bathroom was next to the desk, on the right. It had been finished with impeccable taste. Its floor was a very dark grey, almost black, stone tile while the finishings from the tub and sink to the shower were all marble and polished chrome. It looked almost unused as Virgil poked his head in.

"Mr Colvin," Costas finally broke the silence, "I must apologise for what happened downstairs. I am professional…"

Virgil cut him off, "Costas, please, we don't need to go over it. This is your first murder case, people make mistakes."

Costas looked confused. "What do you mean?"

"You told François about the murder and told him who the victim was," Virgil said absentmindedly while examining the room.

"No, I was talking about Katerina" — Costas seemed genuinely confused — "why should I not tell François — we don't think he did it? Do we?"

"That's the point, Costas, we have no idea. Someone killed Reggie…"

Costas was the one to interrupt now, "Reggie?"

Virgil laughed, "Yeah, Reginald is so stiff and unlike a name, I gave him a nickname to make him more personable and alive; it helps sometimes in an investigation." Costas still looked confused, but Virgil continued where he left off. "That someone then moved Reggie's body from someplace else to the statue. We don't know what Reggie was doing on the island and we don't know who he was dealing with, talking to or pissing off. It doesn't look like he slept here last night, but we can't tell for sure." Costas immediately examined the bed and Virgil could see the self-reproaching look on his face for not having noticed sooner. "I could have sworn François looked somehow pleased by the news when you told him. That could just be the bizarre way everyone idiosyncratically responds when they hear that someone is dead. But maybe not. The news of the murder and the victim's identity needs to be something you keep in your pocket and only reveal when you absolutely must. Or, when it is to your advantage to reveal it."

"Ah, I see. Well, now I am sorry for this, too!"

"Forget it, Costas. But remember, until we can start figuring out what Reggie was doing, we cannot start eliminating suspects. This room is full of potential clues, Costas! Are you ready to search it?"

Costas clapped his hands in excitement. "We are going to 'toss' the room, now?"

"Something like that — though probably a bit less drama." Virgil laughed as he walked to the couch. "We will start with the suitcase — do we have more gloves, Costas?"

The chief of Ithaca's police pulled two pairs of the hospital gloves from his pocket, handing a set to Colvin who put them on quickly and efficiently — it was a skill he developed more than two decades ago. It was a skill no one besides detectives, nurses and doctors would even know was a skill until you put on so many pairs of gloves that you almost felt exposed without them. He unzipped the suitcase.

"Several changes of clothing," Virgil said aloud as he carefully removed each piece of clothing from the case, all very nice and all perfectly folded. "I'm starting to notice a pattern with Reggie, the man seemed to like things very neat."

"Is this a clue?" asked Costas.

"Maybe it is, but it may just be helping us get to know Reggie a little better. I always found that understanding the victim helped in understanding what brought them to their deaths. Almost no one is ever murdered purely out of the blue through totally random chance. A series of decisions and actions, a large context, almost always brings about a person's murder and since we don't have the murderer to talk to about that yet, we have to settle for trying to 'talk' to Reggie." Costas nodded and watched.

"Well, the bag seems perfectly normal, just clothes. He's been here almost two weeks, and I see, at most, five- or six-days' worth of clothes? And that is counting what he was wearing. He must have done laundry twice. Let's take a look at this attaché case, shall we?" Virgil repacked the suitcase carefully, and then closed it. He then picked up the attaché case and placed it on the couch next to the suitcase. It was made of leather, aged and used, very soft. It smelled marvellous as only fine aged leather can. Perhaps Italian? It had a securing clasp over the top which Virgil loosed and moved out of the way, spreading the case open.

"Well, what do we have here, Costas," he said as he pulled out a small crimson book and handed it to the chief.

It was a British passport. But it was different than the ones Costas had seen in the past — the crimson colour was unusual. It said at the bottom: 'DIPLOMATIC PASSPORT'.

"What!" Costas exclaimed. "He was a diplomat! What was he doing here? Why didn't he come to me? Or Panagis?"

"Yes, that is curious, isn't it?" Virgil pulled out two collections of paper that were each bound with combed coils and covered in hard crimson plastic. He handed one to Costas and opened the other, the cover page said simply: 'PROJECT ODYSSEUS'. What followed seemed to be a government report about the entire resort project, the individual investors, with high glossy photos of all of them, including François (they caught him in an unflattering pose while talking on the phone), along with detailed maps of the area on the isthmus where the project was planned. "He seems to have been looking into your pal François' business."

Costas was too busy staring at the report he'd been handed to notice the reference to his frustratingly suave rival. His face was draining of blood.

"What is it, Costas?"

The chief shook his head and handed the report to Virgil. The first page was a bit more verbose than the other report: "AN ANALYSIS OF ROUTES OF

ILLICIT ARMS SHIPMENTS FOR SUBVERSIVE GROUPS IN TURKEY." What followed was a lengthy analysis of eastern-European arms shipment routes through the Black Sea in the east towards Northern Turkey and through the Ionian Sea in the West around Greece towards the island of Rhodes and from there to Izmir, Turkey — with the same penchant for high glossy pictures and maps of the previous report. One of the maps caught Virgil's attention. It was a close up of Ithaca and Kefalonia with arrows pointing to several different locations in Ithaca. He looked at the text on the other side of the report, opposite the map: "Ithaca's low population, remote location and relatively light tourist season, in addition to its many coves, bays and obscured landings present an ideal waystation for weapons shipments making their way to those preparing for the overthrow of President Gündüz."

Virgil looked to Costas as he handed the report with the passage and map back to him, "Costas, what does this mean to you?"

After quickly looking over the map and the written description opposite of it, Costas looked back to his friend, "He thought that guns were being run through Thiakí on their way to Turkey! Ridiculous!"

"Well, he *is* dead, Costas — murdered — so let's not cut off our inquiry quite yet. The places on the map, you know them?"

"Yes, of course, you know them too, one is to Aetos, one to Frikes, one to *Agros Laertou* and one to the cove at the base of Arethusa's."

"Yeah, I thought so — looks like this is going to be a *long* day! Back to this Turkey business — did I miss something? Is there unrest there?"

"Not in the sense of revolution, not yet anyway," said Costas, "but who knows? The earthquake has cut us off from the world!"

"Is it impossible to believe any Greeks might want to help disgruntled elements in Turkey?"

Costas stopped his impulse to lustily defend his countrymen and to condemn all things related to the Turks. He needed time to think and weigh what he was about to say. "Well, some Greeks, as you know, are still very bitter at Turkey. Gündüz has expanded Turkey's military presence in the eastern Mediterranean and the chaotic power vacuum of Syria and Iraq while silencing his critics, mostly communists and western-oriented liberals. Some Greek liberals, communists, maybe others, might be willing to do more than protest the Turkish embassy and consulates. Perhaps, as you say." He voiced this conclusion with great reluctance that made it all the weightier and more persuasive. He added, realising what he had just said, "But very few and certainly no one from Thiakí!"

"OK, OK, I get it, but let's just, obviously, keep these clues to ourselves, right? Reggie is making the context of his death more and more interesting — which of course means more and more difficult to untangle." Virgil removed the last item from the attaché case, a heavy item wrapped in cloth. He knew what it was instantly. The weight, the feel, the way it had been wrapped and tucked away in the case. He did not unwrap the obviously substantial item, instead staring at it before handing it gingerly to Costas.

Costas took it, immediately knowing what it was as well, quickly letting the cloth wrapping drop to the floor. The Sig Sauer P226 rested in his hand unnaturally — the Ithacan police force was unarmed. "Well, Mr Colvin, this is not standard for diplomats, no?"

The odd double negative, so common in modern Greek, momentarily confused Virgil before he responded in kind, "Not that I am aware of, no. A diplomat who does not introduce himself to anyone or announce his presence? A diplomat who somehow got a gun past all the customs and people who check for that sort of thing? A diplomat who carries a gun!" Costas frowned, seeming to take the failure of his law-enforcing Greek comrades upon himself. "It seems fairly safe to speculate that our friend Reggie was working for Her Majesty's Secret Service," Virgil concluded seriously. "Someone killed a British spy on your island, Costas!" He couldn't contain his excitement, knowing that this case would be a career-defining moment for his friend. Come to think of it, it was now a substantial case for him, too.

Costas just looked worried. "What now?"

"Well, there is nothing else here aside from the desk, so I guess that is our next stop before we move on. I'd hold onto that gun if I were you, Costas."

"Certainly, but only until I can scare Kyriakos by giving it to him to put in my office!" And the gleeful smile was back.

They moved to the desk, which had several items upon it clearly not part of Katerina's typical *xenia*. There were four books, a bottle of whiskey and a small envelope with Greek letters on it. Virgil handed the envelope to Costas while taking a look at the bottle and the books. The bottle was familiar and surprising to see — but he supposed no more surprising than working a homicide in the place he had fled to in order to never work homicides again. Redbreast Irish Whiskey had a lovely and slightly sweet taste to it, a bit unusual in whiskeys. It had always been Dick Borneman's favourite spirit — which made his yearly Christmas gift exceedingly easy. Borneman received more than a dozen or so bottles from his squad every Christmas, and he always ran dry by June. The bottle was about a quarter full. It wasn't unusual to see an Irish whiskey in Greece, but this wasn't a ubiquitous label, even in Athens. *Peculiar that the spy had discovered some out here. Maybe he brought it with him?* Looking to the books, Virgil was surprised to see that he owned three of the four. He was also a little ashamed that the spy's copies were so much heavier with annotation and battered by use than his own. The book that he did not own was in Greek so he handed it to Costas, who was still pouring over the letter that had been inside the envelope.

"Anything good?" asked Virgil.

"Did you see a glass in the bathroom?"

The chief's eyes were still reading the letter, he seemed to be going over it repeatedly.

"Wow, that juicy, eh?"

Costas went into the bathroom with the letter and the Greek book and turned on the faucet. *Oh well*, thought Virgil, *the magnitude is finally catching up to him!* He examined the remaining volumes. Two were nearly identical little green books that Virgil recognised instantly when he first walked into the room. Up close he saw that they were Murray's translation of Homer's *Odyssey*. That had been one of his guesses as to their identity, but he only knew for sure that they were two of the Greek volumes of Loeb's Classical Library.

He had several dozen such volumes back at the villa — a few had fallen from the shelves during the earthquake earlier that morning. Almost every page had some sort of a notation, on both sides of the text (Loeb editions of Greek and Roman texts displayed the original classical Greek or Latin on the left, and the English translation on the right). *A spy and a classicist?* Virgil remembered that some elite British schools still fostered learning in classical languages, but he still felt inept in comparison to this dead man's obvious intellect. The last book was familiar to everyone on the island. It was the principal document in the 'Ithaca isn't the real Ithaca' argument and therefore was widely considered fit only for the flame by most Ithacans. Or, fit only for a Kefalonian. Virgil kept his own copy somewhat hidden in his villa to avoid offending visiting neighbours.

Suddenly, it was his first morning in the villa again after moving to the island permanently. Marina, his seventy-year-old neighbour, came by to welcome him — bearing a basket of olives, figs and the cheese of the yet unheard-of man who loved his goats. They chatted haltingly; her English was ephemeral, and his Greek was nearly non-existent. He invited her in and offered her espresso and she began admiring his collection of books, commenting in extended Greek monologues as she came to the works of Homer and Aristophanes. Virgil smiled and nodded, handling some of the figs to have something to do. Then she saw *the book*. Her countenance darkened and the friendly welcome ended abruptly. She had picked up the volume and shook it at Virgil while speaking in such a rapid string of staccato exclamations that would have eluded him even if he knew some modicum of the language. She then tossed the book to the ground, repossessed the basket of gifts and left peremptorily. It took Costas a week of conveying Virgil's apologies until Marina returned to apologise and welcome him, again, to the island. She brought two baskets, but Virgil could tell she was looking around for *the book*. Now, here it was, in the dead man's hotel room.

Sir Nigel Blasingame's *Getting Odysseus Home: Finding the Real Ithaca* was an impressive-looking book. Its dimensions were both wider and taller than standard hard-cover works from academic presses — Oxford University Press lent its imprimatur to the work, even though Blasingame was an amateur historian. It was over five hundred pages long and had well over seventy-five full colour pictures, maps and satellite images. It was a tremendous investment and an equally tremendous flop — even for academic presses, who were in the flop business. The book never made it to paperback and the only people who seemed to know it existed were academic classicists, the residents of Kefalonia who insisted that the 'real' Ithaca was part of their island, as Blasingame contended, and the residents of Thiakí who, of course, insisted the Kefalonians and Blasingame were craven lunatics. Just like the copies of Homer's epic poem, nearly every page was heavily annotated and flagged.

Virgil was impressed, again, and a little confused. The room seemed to belong to two different men. On the door side of the bed, the spy had his government reports and a loaded pistol, but here on the bathroom side of the bed, a classicist seemed to be interested in an esoteric and ultimately pointless debate shrouded in myth. *What was Reginald Wellesley doing here? Were the two sides of the room equally important to figuring out the context of his murder? Why was the gun still in the bag? Didn't spies carry those around? And what about the bed?*

Suddenly, the water in the bathroom turned off and Costas came back with the book, the letter and a single empty glass in one hand, and a towel with which he was drying his face in the other. He handed the letter and glass to Virgil.

"Oh, Mr Colvin," he said from behind the towel, "this is quite a terrible case. You did *this* every day?" He tossed the towel into the bathroom sink and looked at his American friend with a mixture of envy and disgust. He saw Blasingame's book on the desk and did his best phantom spit sound and motion of contempt. Most of the Ithacans Virgil had seen in the book's presence made the same gesture and sound. It would be funny, and he had laughed when he first witnessed it, if his Ithacan friends weren't so deadly serious about it.

"Well, sort of," Virgil said, ignoring the prideful digression of his friend, "but honestly, Costas, this case is pretty bizarre. The room is not really helping me make sense of who Reggie was or what the hell he was doing here. What was in this letter and what was the book?"

"Pour us some of the whiskey first, Mr Colvin. I am sorry for the one glass, the other seems to have fallen, probably during the earthquake, but I don't think we can't share, no?"

"Of course, Costas." Virgil poured a stiff double and took a quick swig before passing it to Costas, who drained what remained with alarming insouciance. He passed the glass back, indicating a refill was in order. Virgil poured, then ransomed, "The book, Costas, what the hell is it?"

"It is about Hellas! Greece. Today. I have not read this one. He seems to have been interested in the portions dealing with the history of KKE and also with the Turk — he makes lots and lots of little notes. I do not recognise the writing so I do not know what he says. Now, Mr Colvin, hand over the prisoner!" Virgil took another swig before letting Costas repeat his feat of unaffected absorption. It was good stuff, but was Costas even enjoying it? Virgil had this thought often when drinking with the chief.

"OK, that seems to track with the reports in the case. What about this letter? It is literally 'all Greek to me!" Virgil quoted Shakespeare with a smile.

"Oh ha! How many times will you quote that line? Shakespeare — you English speakers and your Shakespeare! He is nothing with Aeschylus and Sophocles! And when are you going to finally master my language — you should not have had trouble with this!" This was not the first time Virgil had heard this speech. Like a good epic poet, Costas had a stock of memorable lines always at the ready.

"OK, Costas, I promise when this case is over, you and I will speak only your language."

"*Or-a-ah!*[9] Now that I have raised a sufficient ransom from *you*, I will tell you about the letter. It is quite the clue, Mr Colvin! But it is a terrible clue. This spy was a busy man — *very, very busy*."

"Out with it, Costas, for God's sake!"

"Yes, yes, I read you the letter," and Costas proceeded to translate the letter for his friend:

Dearest Apollo,

We must meet each other again as soon as possible — in our usual place. I long for your touch and your presence within me. Deep within me. I do not sleep, I cannot eat, I must see you. Do not make me wait, oh sweetest of men! Every moment with this swine is a degrading hell. I will be where we always meet all morning. Till then, I am yours in mind and yours in body.

Lovingly,

Calliope

When he had finished, Costas looked at his friend. "You see what I mean, Mr Colvin? A busy, *busy* man!"

"No kidding, but who the hell is Calliope?"

Costas' left eyebrow went up in surprise. "You don't know? I thought you had mastered our old stories, Mr Colvin!"

[9] In Greek, ωραία — great, beautiful.

"No, not that, I know the story of Apollo and Calliope, Orpheus and all that. I meant do you have any idea who this letter is actually from?"

"Oh, of course, Mr Colvin, yes, I do. I have lived on this island all my life and I know everyone here, and I have seen many of them write things down. Sometimes, I have seen things they have written many, many times." Costas stopped there. He seemed unready or unwilling to continue, content to wait.

"Damn you, Costas! Spit it out, will ya?"

"I have no doubt at all that this letter was written by Zoe Kordatos."

Virgil was shocked there wasn't a more pronounced look of triumph in the chief's eyes and face.

"What gave it away?" He looked over the letter again in some amazement at this legitimately impressive piece of observation, good fortune and some damned amazing amateur hand-writing analysis.

"Her manner of writing her *thel-ta* is unmistakable — I have never seen another like it, not in Thiakí."[10] Now Costas was beaming a little, still looking less proud than the moment truly allowed him to be.

"Finally, something in this case is starting to unfold and come together without additional shit!"

"I am afraid not, Mr Colvin."

"What? Why? What's the matter?"

---

[10] The Greek letter Δ/δ (δελτα) is pronounced *thelta*.

"Sadly, this woman is married, Mr Colvin. And she is married to Mr Kordatos."

"And? So? Who is Mr Kordatos?" Virgil asked, drawing a blank.

"*Nikos* Kordatos," Costas said with marked disappointment.

Virgil wracked his memory. He was still groggy, even with the cappuccino and all the excitement. "Nikos? What, the guy we were just talking about with Katerina? The Greek communist leader on the island? Reggie was schtupping *his* wife?"

"Mr Colvin, while I do not know this word, I assume I know it — and yes, it seems that this man who was murdered was some sort of British agent, sent here for some reason related to the Turks, and that he was having an affair with the wife of a person he may have been sent here to watch, work with or even to make killed. And *I* missed all of it! It was right under my moustache the whole time!"

Quick to reassure his shaken friend, Virgil convincingly said, "You may make a solid murder detective yet, Costas. These things happen sometimes and there isn't anything you can do about it. This handwriting thing is a real breakthrough — could solve the whole case!" His friend beamed at the compliment. Turning back to the clue, Virgil asked, "I don't suppose you have any beat on this location she alludes to in the letter?"

"Oh, Mr Colvin, no. But I know where we go next!"

CHAPTER FOUR
KKE

Costas asked Katerina to lock room #4 and allow no one but himself to re-enter it until further notice. He then asked her about the comings and goings, times specifically, of Reginald Wellesley. She recalled all the details she could as Panagis Metaxas entered the lobby. The mayor and the police chief exchanged wary glances with one another. Katerina finished her recollections, largely recapitulating what she told them earlier, and the detectives took their leave. The mayor was telling Katerina of the disaster at Piso Aetos as they exited the hotel.

"Unbelievable!" muttered Costas.

"Now, now, my friend, all's fair…" retorted Virgil.

"Yes, yes!" exploded Costas, reclaiming the clear lead in the early morning walk back towards the plaza where Reginald Wellesley was discovered. "We need to drop off this evidence" — waving the reports, the passport, the letter, and the gun, now rewrapped in cloth — " and then, we look up Nikos!"

As they walked back through the plaza, the sun now clearly illuminating the pure blue water of the Ionian

Sea in the horseshoe harbour of Vathy, people were slowly beginning to emerge in the light of Helios. The island filled with tourists about four weeks earlier. The current batch would only just start to realise that they were temporarily trapped on the island until the ferry service was restored in some fashion. Virgil looked towards the statue of Odysseus as they re-entered the plaza — Kyriakos was standing guard. Reginald Wellesley was gone. Virgil noticed that Costas kept his eyes always before him, not glancing at Kyriakos. They were both content to march, rather than talk.

The plaza was quite lovely in the morning and the crisp breeze — crisp somehow even though it was already in the upper 70s — from the sea reminded Virgil of his first encounter with this place nearly thirty years before. Suddenly, there they were; two young, tanned Americans pointing like tourists at everything as they walked through the plaza. The centre contained a large bust of Homer, the immortal bard whose wily hero continued to inspire the trickle of tourists away from the general torrent bound for the more popular Aegean islands. Odysseus had called both Virgil and Janet to the island — that they both wanted to honeymoon there had been one of those beautiful mutual coincidences of wants that embellishes the joy of love. Just as then, the horseshoe bay contained a mixture of local fishing boats and the small or midsize sailing yachts of the wealthier Ithacans and those who still visited the island in the classical fashion. The plaza was bordered by a mixture of hotels, souvenir shops, tavernas, restaurants and the Vathy post office. All of them were beginning to open. Virgil never saw the town during this part of the day, almost every morning he needed these precious hours to recover. He could hear lamentation and the noise of broken glass being swept across tile and concrete floors floating through the air as they cut through the plaza diagonally to the south. The cabbies leaned against their eclectic assortment of cars with their coffees at the northwest corner — all of them here for the tourist season. Most were Athenians. They smoked, told tales and gesticulated with each other in grand exaggerations while waiting on the sleepy tourists to emerge from their hotels for transport to the other towns and the historical sites. Most were north of Mount Aetos and the isthmus of the island.

Island cab fare ran anywhere from five to ten times higher than fares in the metropolis. The cabbies who could get themselves to the islands made a substantial portion of their entire income for the year, just like the Ithacan hoteliers and restauranteurs, in just a four-month window. Depending on weather, political turmoil, global pandemics, terrorism and economic collapse, that window shrank considerably, or disappeared entirely.

When the island's population was four times larger a century ago, it was a far different place. Virtually no tourists came then, except rich phil-Hellenes like Heinrich Schliemann — the man who most famously trumpeted the reality of Troy at Hisarlik, Turkey, in the 1870s. The entire economy was built on currants, olives and figs. Goats, sheep and a few pigs groused the island in those days like they owned the place. Not many remained. Most of modern Ithaca's 3,200 or so residents were either tied to tourism and the services that went with it or lived part-time on the island before working elsewhere seasonally. The 1953 earthquake depopulated Ithaca just as it had Kefalonia. The depopulation likely would have occurred anyway due to long-term economic trends that depopulated all of rural Greece — feeding the tremendous growth of Athens and the unmanageable sprawl around it. But the earthquake (really earthquakes, as there were 'smaller' tremors before the big one struck on 12 August) hastened that process by decades. Virgil thought about the seismic faults of the region when he planned the move from Chicago. He was trading a very sleepy fault zone (there had been an enormous earthquake in the Mississippi

River valley in 1812 that was so catastrophic that it was felt on the east coast and temporarily made the mighty river flow north) for one of the most predictable and violent tectonic areas on the planet. Major earthquakes — beyond 6 or 7 on the old Richter scale — could be expected every fifty years on average. The African plate was subducting beneath the European plate only a few dozen miles off to the west-southwest. He had hoped he would have a little more time to prepare for the earthquakes. *Thank God, he had insurance!*

As they walked south on Enmeou Street towards both the hospital and the police station of Vathy, Virgil could tell what his friend and fellow policeman was thinking. He recognised the pensive silence. When they reached headquarters, they quickly made their way to Costas' office where the chief deposited the key evidence of the case — so far. He unceremoniously dumped it all into a deep and unlockable desk drawer. Virgil did his best to avoid laughing.

"I know, my friend," Costas apologised, at long last breaking his silence, "that this is not ideal, but it is the best we can do under the circumstances."

"I understand," Virgil lied. "Off to find Nikos Kordatos?"

Costas nodded.

As they turned to leave, Virgil noticed that the police headquarters only had two other people working in it besides Costas. He realised he had only been here once or twice — and only Kyriakos had been on duty, hadn't he? The memories were a little fuzzy. The entire building was non-descript. White plaster walls, pictures of the Greek president, prime minister and Mayor Metaxas. There was a Greek flag, filing cabinets and a few desks with a few obsolete computers. The desks had pictures of smiling families and other idiosyncratic kitsch. He suddenly thought about the fact that he and Janet had not had children. Both had decided early that they didn't want children. Both had decided late — too late — that they had made a mistake. Tens of thousands of dollars, two attempts with IVF and a miscarriage later left them exhausted and spent. *God, of all the shitty memories!* Virgil shook his head to get back to the present. These faces and people, did he know them? He walked by without stopping to chat, or really notice them at all. Now he noticed bits of glass and other broken fragments and pieces of decorative objects no longer extant in the trash bin outside Costas' office. The earthquake. More evidence of destruction. Within Vathy, it seemed to be limited to breaking pottery, glass and other fragile items that weren't tied or bolted down. The combination of last night's ouzo, the sickening shaking of the solid earth, the morning with too little coffee and the surreal quality of working this murder case was contributing to his trouble focusing. The memories of not being a dad weren't helping. *Not good for a detective,* Virgil thought to himself.

Suddenly, he was back in the 19th precinct at his own desk with his own idiosyncratic kitsch. There was the magnifying glass — a clichéd tool of the trade, but actually useful more times than he could count or remember. There was the dual standing picture frame displaying Janet and himself at their wedding, and opposite that their honeymoon on this island. Sunset, Polis Bay, outside Stavros. The noise was constant and loud. The other detectives chatting about their cases — picking each other's brains about clues, *modi operandi*, usual suspects and all the rest. For a moment, he missed the smell of the city drifting in through the open windows. The noises of the street and the L train. The murmur of Cubs fans walking to and from Wrigley, mere blocks North, in summertime. The excitement of the work. Then, he was back. Ithaca. So small. So different. So unusual. *Same goddamn murder*. He suddenly realised that he had seen these Ithacan police officers the first time Costas brought him here months earlier. Uncharacteristically, Costas had not done the introductions with the rest of his force — and Virgil had not forced the issue. *Why had he only been back once or twice? Had he been purposely avoiding it? Had Costas been avoiding bringing him here? Was he embarrassed?* Virgil put the thoughts away as Costas introduced everyone.

"Ah, Mr Colvin, let me introduce you to the rest of my force, except for the other shift, they sleep!" Costas led Virgil to the young man, who was inputting data into the nearest computer. Interrupting the twenty-something's work, Costas excitedly said, "Mr Colvin, this is my junior officer, Alexis Konstantinos."

"Pleasure to meet you, Alexis." Virgil almost yawned, suddenly realising how tired he still was. "I am sorry, I'm very tired, suddenly."

Before Alexis could respond verbally, Costas quickly dragged his friend to the nearby young woman standing by the station's phone at the large greeting desk oriented towards the front entrance, "And this, Mr Colvin, is Officer Konstantinos' wife, Ariadne."

Virgil noticed that this mythically named policewoman was very pregnant as he extended his hand, "Pleasure to meet you! Did you save Alexis from a Minotaur?"

"He only wishes he save me from such a creature!" Ariadne returned, smiling from ear to ear.

Costas interrupted the repartee, "Did we get the report of the baby — do you have an Alexander or an Alexandra?"

Blushing, Ariadne replied, "It will be a boy."

"And have you chosen a name?" Costas couldn't help himself now, obviously quite excited at the news.

"Telemachos," Alexis suddenly interjected, "appropriate, yes?" His question seemed directed at Virgil.

"Oh yes, indeed, quite so — and congratulations!"

"They are my kin, you know," Costas added.

"Really?" Virgil wasn't actually very surprised — it did not take anything approaching six months on the island to show him on numerous occasions how interrelated the native inhabitants oftentimes were. This must have been the fifteenth or twentieth of Costas' relations he had been introduced to or heard mention of. Given his current condition, it was quite possible that Costas had mentioned them before. *Had he? Hell.*

"Are you helping Costas with the murder?" Ariadne asked with obvious interest, though she had an eye on Costas to gauge his reaction to the question.

"I don't know if I would say I was helping. Consulting, really, is all. Costas has the case well in hand," Virgil lied, again.

"Enough, enough!" Costas interrupted. "You two parents get back to work, and I will owe you both something good for baby Telemachos Konstantinos — who will one day be a great policeman like his mama and papa!"

As they took their leave of the proud parents-to-be, Costas explained the Byzantine paths of relations that made him kin to not only the two people they left behind, but also Kyriakos who was presumably still doubling as Talos next to the statue of the island's most famous part-time inhabitant.[11] No doubt making sure no one got too close to any potential evidence. Virgil's mind was boggled. While a family of cops wasn't that

---

[11] Talos was an enormous, and animated, bronze machine that stalked around Crete, protecting the island from attack. This is, until he was 'killed' by the cunning and magic of Jason and Medea.

unusual in Chicago, Virgil had never seen an entire interrelated department.

"So you're actually related to your entire staff?" Virgil asked, still somewhat flabbergasted that this admission had been delayed this long given that they had spent three or four nights a week — hell, at least five — drinking and talking together for the previous half year. And during the sleepiest of months without tourists and a sizeable portion of Ithaca's 'permanent' population!

"Yes, so it seems, Mr Colvin!" He said this as if he really had not pondered the idea before.

At this point, they were just outside the station on Enmeou Street. Before turning left for the short walk to the KKE office of Ithaca, Costas quickly briefed Virgil about what was coming.

"Look, Mr Colvin, Nikos does not really speak English, so I will have to translate between all of us. He really speaks no English at all, it is not like the act of a French politician."

Virgil smirked at the dig about French linguistic duplicity — he suspected the chief's real target was François Deflers rather than Jacques Chirac or François Hollande.

"That's fine," said Virgil, "I trust your translation skills. I don't think we will have much trouble with him."

"This is no accident — he hates the British and your countrymen. He is going to be unpleasant, Mr Colvin. I will leave his bile out of translation, but you will see in his eyes and face. I really don't know who on the island is giving him hope of political success!" At the first intersection with a named street, Telemachou Street almost unbelievably, stood the remarkably unimpressive headquarters of the island's votaries of Karl Marx. They hadn't seen it while walking to the police station, despite walking right by it. It was that non-descript.

The Κομμουνιστικό Κόμμα Ελλάδας, known to outsiders as the Communist Party of Greece, had a long and checkered history in both the land of the Hellenes and the world.[12] After the Second World War, the party attempted to parley the success of having led significant portions of the Greek resistance to Italian and German fascism into political dominance. Sadly for the Greek communists, most of the Greek resistance who fought under their leadership never actually became communists. And they showed them no particular love or sympathy when the anti-communist leadership in Athens, with British and American support, crushed the armed forces of the 'People's Democratic Army of Greece'. Victory in the Greek Civil War by the anti-communists contributed to the KKE's prohibition between 1947 – 1974.

After the legal proscription ended, the KKE never achieved much beyond 10% in any Greek election —

---

[12] Com-moo-neece-ti-ko Com-ma El-lath-as.

even when it seemed like the market economy was in tatters and Greece was nearly bankrupt. It was excluded from all coalition governments outside of a couple of bizarre caretaker situations in the late 1980s — when they teamed up with the Greek conservatives! In fact, the KKE's fortunes, like the communist parties in nearly every European nation, had been bleak since 1991, when their mortally ill patron collapsed into oblivion.

Ithaca's KKE headquarters was a drab two-storey affair with a front façade maybe fifteen feet wide. The bricks of that façade were a cheap-looking off-white, while the doors looked beaten, old and ill-maintained — about what you might expect from a group of people who believed no one properly owned anything for themselves. The hammer and sickle were still a bit disconcerting to Virgil. There were plenty of effete intellectual communists in Chicago who lived in high-rise apartments and drank champagne with the mayor, or the Obamas when they were in town. The poorer neighbourhoods had their Marxist street organisers and their socialist priests and ministers.

It was not the idea that communists existed that was off-putting to Virgil Colvin — it was that a party that openly identified with some of the greatest mass-murdering regimes in history could still be found with an iconic symbol every bit as genocidal and deadly as that used by Germany's national socialists. The swastika was infamous and unusable forever, but here were a dingy hammer and sickle, drenched in blood but seemingly guiltless. No matter how many times he mulled it over, it would never make sense. In any event, this was not a threatening bastion from which to pursue Marx's dream of a global worker revolution. The symbol of a power that once threatened the world with mutually assured destruction, now leading the vanguard from this pitiful hovel! It was a pathetic and laughable remnant of ideas and impulses that Virgil wouldn't even allow to grace history's dustbin.

When Costas knocked on the ramshackle front door, they only had to wait about five seconds before a bespectacled man in his mid or late fifties — at least — appeared. He opened it quickly and pushed his way outside the door, closing it behind him. *He obviously did not want them to see the interior of his bastion of revolutionary plotting*, Virgil mused. His look of contempt for Costas was remarkable to Virgil. It had seemed to him impossible that anyone — aside from the other men pursuing Katerina — would not instantly like or love Costas. As he marvelled at this, he was similarly struck by the look of disgust that the man shot in his direction. While Virgil listened to Costas and what must have been Nikos Kordatos converse in Greek, he looked the man over closely. His glasses hung onto the very end of his very long, yet very bulbous Greek nose. The eyes were a very deep brown, almost black, the equally deep bags that hung below them were pale and a sick-looking yellowish grey. Atop his head, he sported the classical colouring of the skunk, jet black with a line of white and grey, but slightly over half was also missing in action. What was left was greasy and 'combed' by hand, going by appearances. He was a bit beyond 5 feet, 6 inches in height and seemed entirely without any sort of muscular or physical presence at all. He also seemed a bit stooped — even hunched — over. *No wonder the robust and younger Reginald Wellesley was cuckholding this sad specimen*, Virgil thought.

"So Nikos, as expected, has not given you a warm welcome to the island, Mr Colvin," Costas said, taking a break from chatting with Nikos to translate what had happened so far. Nikos watched them both warily as the translation continued, "I have of course asked him where he was last night and this morning and he, of course, has told me I have no right to ask him these questions. He and I have been debating these legal questions back and forth. He seems to want to drag this out or force me to take him for an official interrogation, I think."

"Well, that seems like a delay from getting to Mrs Kordatos — ask him where she is, Costas," Virgil was beginning to find Nikos as distasteful as Nikos regarded both of them.

"Ah, of course!" Costas resumed his conversation with Nikos. After what seemed to be the question about Zoe, Nikos went into a long and somewhat animated speech. The glasses came off and the hands flew in every direction. Small groups of spectators began to mill about within earshot to the left and their right as Nikos carried on. Costas seemed both mildly amused and remarkably patient under this verbal assault. It almost seemed like Nikos had this speech chambered for just this sort of occasion. Virgil tried to follow the words himself, but the only word that really stuck out to him was "*Amerikanikokratía*" and mostly because Nikos looked at and pointed at him when he sneered it.[13] After nearly five interminable minutes, Costas turned to his friend, "Well, as you might imagine, he has not answered the question."

"*Ha!*" Virgil was not surprised. "What the hell was he just gassing on about?"

---

[13] The word is used to convey a critique of Greece's position in the early days of the Cold War — where the United States supposedly became Greece's imperial guardian, dictating internal politics in exchange for protection.

"Oh, the same list of complaints he always parades about — that you and the other Americans stride the world and buffet Greece about as if you own everything. That American-backed Greeks betrayed his great-grandpapa in the civil war and exiled him to a prison on some island in the sea of Aegeus, where he died. His grandpapa and papa were arrested during the dictatorship and mistreated. Nixon gave the colonels cover and approval. On and on he goes. Still blaming the CIA for the downfall of Papandreou — whom he also did not like — Wall Street for the economic collapse and so on and on. No answer to the question we care about." At this point, Costas was clearly out of ideas.

"Tell him that Zoe is in danger and that we need to find her immediately, that if he doesn't tell us, you will have the dangerous American criminal policeman do the questioning and I don't know Greek. Tell him all that. Now." Costas was a bit taken aback by these commands.

"But Mr Colvin, I can't let you…" Costas was about to explain how he couldn't allow Virgil to threaten Kordatos, but at this point, Virgil grabbed the threadbare lapel of Kordatos' cheap suit jacket and got within a centimetre of his gargantuan nose and said in flat, cold, emotionless but unmistakeable English:

"Where is Mrs Kordatos?" Costas translated, but Nikos, who now looked quite terrified having the much larger and athletic man looming over him — his own imagination and propaganda creating no end of horrible scenarios if he did not do as this savage American wanted — hardly needed the prompting from Costas.

"*Sta kanónia! Sta kanónia!*"[14]

Virgil let go and motioned to Costas to walk away with him. As Costas was opening his mouth to translate, Virgil waved him off. "Even I know that one, Costas. Let's go!"

As the two policemen quickly marched off toward Drakoulis Street, the little crowds whispered, giggled and guffawed. Kordatos straightened his jacket and replaced the glasses on his nose. He then emphatically spat on the ground where Virgil and Costas had been standing, shouting "*Amerikanikokratía!*" after them.

---

[14] Στα κανόνια! Στα κανόνια! — At the cannons! At the cannons!

CHAPTER FIVE
VENETIAN CANNONS

"You're telling me that guy isn't even forty years old?" Virgil exclaimed; his incredulity couldn't be any greater. He always prided himself on his ability to read character and age from faces and deportment. Almost thirty years of being a cop honed the skill. He was rarely so off. *Jesus. Nikos Kordatos looked like shit.* Again, no wonder Mrs Kordatos was stepping out. *But was he letting prejudice against Nikos Kordatos cloud his judgement?* Nikos had a *compelling* motive to kill Reggie. That he was a cuckolded runt with lousy ideas didn't mean he couldn't murder a man. He remembered some of the unlikely murderers he had made cases against in Chicago; an old lady who murdered her adult daughter for drugs, a diminutive librarian who terrorised the city's commodities traders for thirteen months as she serialised her tapestry of murder through eleven instalments, and a thirteen-year-old boy who murdered a five-year-old girl in his neighbourhood because he was curious to know what another person's blood felt like on his hands. He had no real reason to discount

Nikos Kordatos, he kept reminding himself as they walked.

"Well, he will be this year. Very stressful to run the party, it seems?" Costas laughed.

"I'm glad I at least rightly predicted that he would fold like the cheap suit he was wearing. I think we would have wasted time at the station interrogating him, Costas, if we hadn't pushed things a little. I'm sorry if I stepped on your toes."

"*A-khil-ee-os pt-er-na*!" Costas laughed.[15]

"Pardon?"

"Oh, Mr Colvin, you found his weak point — just like Homer's Paris!" Costas continued to enjoy his laugh as they walked.

"Oh," he said, chuckling, "good thing his weak point is so common to men of his ilk — cowardice. Had it been his heel, we could have been stuck there all day!"

"Mr Colvin," Costas said quietly as his laughter faded and they continued their walk through the plaza towards the east side of the harbour, "I cannot play the evil cop as you call it, no one could believe it — not even that rotten fig, Nikos. But is certainly fun to watch you do so. Only in films have I seen this. I will let you know if you do wrong."

"Again, I'm sorry, Costas."

"Not another word, Mr Colvin!"

---

[15] Αχίλλειος πτέρνα — Achilles' heel, the weak point.

After they exited the plaza, hugging the water along George Drakoulis Street — the main thoroughfare of the city — they walked several more blocks in silence. The Drakoulis family were long-time Ithacans, and constructed one of the buildings that was not completely wiped out in the '53 earthquake. The Megaro Drakouli.[16] Virgil and Costas passed it by as those familiar with the island did — quickly and without examination. It was an impressively large mansion, especially for Ithaca. Neo-classical in parts, but not overly so. It resembled a box in many respects, with some columns attached. Somewhat incongruously, the same family was in the vanguard of Greek's socialist movement, sending one of the favourite sons to the Greek parliament. Drakoulis Street ended and the policemen veered left to continue following the harbour towards Loutsa Beach — with its painfully large pebbles and rocks substituting for the sand that Americans typically associate with their beaches. It was nearing ten a.m. and the sun shone prettily upon the water of the harbour. The greenery of the island was pronounced, but it was not from lush grass or all that many trees. Rather, Ithaca was covered with brush and anaemic Greek shrubs spread out from one another far enough to reveal the rocky ground beneath even at a distance. Among the Greek islands, it was considered quite lush, mostly because many Aegean islands were

---

[16] Literally, the 'Dracula Mansion'.

arid, dry and bereft of colourful vegetation. Even on this supposedly verdant island, cactuses were common.

Behind them, to their left, they could distantly spot Virgil's villa in the hills south of town, across the harbour. They also passed by Lazaretto Island as they worked their way around the east-side of Vathy. The small bit of land inhabited the middle of the harbour and was home to the Orthodox chapel Metamorfosi Sotiros.[17] In prior ages and epochs, the island served as a leper's prison and a quarantine waystation for traders during the days when the plague still stalked through Europe.

The promontory to the right of the road just before the beach emerged into view indicated the path towards the "Ενετικά Κανόνια." The unpaved path to the

---

[17] The Transformed Savior.

cannons the Venetians installed in the 18 century to guard the harbour from an Ottoman threat that never came was easy to follow. It only became mildly steep in the last several steps before coming level with the abandoned artillery. The Venetians secured Ithaca for the final time in the wake of the Treaty of Passarowitz in 1718. The final eighty years of Venetian government of the island had finally, and unironically, been serene. It came to a sudden and alarming end in 1797 when the island became the political plaything of Napoleon Bonaparte after he extinguished the thousand-year Republic. Ithaca was joined to its neighbours after Waterloo under British protection as the United States of the Ionian Islands, where it remained until 1864, when Britain turned the islands over to independent Greece.

As Virgil and Costas emerged onto level ground with these relics of a dead republic's defence against a ghostly empire, they saw a tall, slender woman looking out on Skartsoubonísi Island. She clearly spotted them as they started on the path towards the cannons and made no effort to announce herself— *Or escape,* Virgil thought. She was nearly six feet tall. She was fetchingly lithe and her hair had a rusty hue. She wore jeans, white tennis shoes and a red short-sleeved blouse. Her arms were toned and tanned. She appeared to be in her early thirties or so. Virgil based this hunch almost entirely on the fact that she wasn't wearing a bra. It was a crude methodology, but it seldom failed him over the years.

He remembered how shocked Janet was when he first described his theory of estimating a woman's age by the perkiness of her breasts when she wasn't wearing a bra. Soon she was whispering her own guesses in his ear on shopping trips, walking in Grant Park or along the Lake Shore, vacations to the Dells or cruises on the Lake, and ball games at Wrigley. Her skill quickly exceeded his. She was still doing it in the hospital when the opportunity presented itself, up until the final week or so.

"Costas!" Zoe ran over to the policeman and gave him a kiss and a hug.

How the hell is this woman married to that hunched and rotten specimen back in town? Virgil wondered this as loudly as his mind would tolerate without forcing the words out of his mouth.

"Zoe, how are you, my lovely friend?" Costas, all smiles and charm.

"Oh, you know, just coming up here to think and enjoy the morning." Zoe's eyes searched Costas' face quickly, before looking Virgil over. "And who is this friend of yours, Costas?" Her English was crisp and precise, with a very lovely accent. *Yet another contrast with the ogre waiting for her at home!*

"Oh, Zoe Kordatos, my manners! This is Virgil Colvin!" The two shook hands and exchanged hellos. "He is living on the island now — from America — almost half a year. A policeman, like Costas!"

Zoe looked Virgil over more carefully than before. She smiled very slightly.

"Apollo isn't coming," Virgil said suddenly.

Zoe's face darkened just as suddenly. Virgil studied it carefully. She seemed surprised and a bit alarmed.

Costas gently interceded, "My dear, we need to talk with you about the letter you wrote to Mr Wellesley about meeting you here."

Zoe paused, for only a brief moment, barely noticeable, "What do you mean, Costas?"

"Zoe, please, no one else writes your *thelta.* I recognised it at once. Either we can discuss this here, or we can head into town and talk it over at my office." Costas did not have a threatening tone — he made the threat sound amiable. *Remarkable,* Virgil thought to himself.

"No! No. Not there," Zoe said quickly and definitely. She did not look worried, exactly, but she was clearly determined to hold this conversation here at the cannons rather than be walked through a fully awake Vathy.

"Good. So, Mr Wellesley confirmed he was going to meet you here?" Costas had produced a small notepad from a pocket and a pen from his sleeve.

"No, I left the letter under his door at Katerina's. He always came to me. Where is he? What has happened to him?" There was a mild alarm creeping into her voice. *Very natural,* Virgil thought.

"Momentarily, my dear." Virgil was proud, Costas wasn't showing cards unnecessarily. "How long have you and Mr Wellesley been, ehhhhh, meeting?" Costas blushed slightly.

"We have been seeing each other since he arrived in Vathy. Marcus needed some directions and asked me to show him the town. We spent the whole day together and then the whole night." Zoe did not seem embarrassed in the least.

Virgil was impressed and mildly amused, thinking back on her pill of a husband. But how had this beautiful woman, this strong-willed woman, this Calliope, how had *she* married that cretin in the first place? *Also, why did Reggie tell her his name was Marcus? He did not seem to be laying that low on the island. Though he had somehow avoided Costas. Still. Marcus?*

“And your whereabouts last night and this morning?” Costas was looking straight at her as he penned notes of her answers perfectly within the lines of his notebook. The name Marcus didn’t seem to faze him.

“Last night, I was home. Nikos was there when I went to sleep. I woke up with the earthquake. I spent the morning cleaning the mess.”

“Was Nikos there when you woke up?” Costas asked nonchalantly.

“No, you know he is in his office before the sun is up. All the important things he is doing. I heard him rummaging around down there.” She said this curiously devoid of tone — the delivery was totally flat. It was off-putting for reasons Virgil couldn’t quite identify. He suddenly realised that Nikos and Zoe lived above the decaying party headquarters. Again, no wonder she jumped at the opportunity presented by Reggie.

“When did you leave the house? Did you go anywhere before you came here?” Costas was scribbling.

“No, I walked here at around nine after showering. I have been waiting since then. Then you two arrived. That is my morning. What has happened?” Zoe was clearly losing patience, as her voice was starting to inflect with a modicum of emotion.

“Soon. Please tell me what you know about Marcus’ work and why he was here in Vathy — did you two discuss those things at all?” Costas’ natural charm and gentle demeanour put her back at her ease for the moment. Virgil appreciated the seamless transition to "Marcus."

"We did, not often after the first day, though. He was here to investigate the antiquities market of the islands — he said he came from Zante and was headed to Kefalonia and Lefkas next before returning to London. He told me he helped museums and collectors around the world add to their exhibits and collections. He was quite interested in figuring out whom to talk to about archaeological digs and finds on the island. He didn't want to deal with the archaeological museums here and in Stavros. I took him to Circe, of course. After the first day and night we met, he was gone most days and we only conferred in the mornings to discuss our next… meetings." Zoe explained this all naturally enough. Virgil did not sense any obvious untruths in her narration or delivery.

"Your letter, Zoe, was quite advanced. Were you planning to leave with this man? Was there any chance that Nikos knew about what was happening?"

"*Ha!*" Zoe laughed heartily at this last question. "Costas, do you really think there is any chance that Nikos notices anything that doesn't involve the party?"

Costas laughed. "I do not suppose not."

"Leave with Marcus? He never suggested it, and neither did I. When Marcus is gone, I resume my happy life with Nikos." She was back to total flatness.

"Do you have any questions, Mr Colvin?" Costas surrendered the floor to his silent 'consultant'.

"Yes, Mrs Kordatos. How did you and Mr Kordatos come to be married?"

"We are in love." Again, he detected no lie.

"And Apollo and Calliope?" Virgil matched her flat tone.

"That was Marcus' idea, he is quite taken with the nonsense of these islands and the mythos of this country." Virgil detected disapproval.

"I meant the affair?" Virgil asked again.

"What about it?" Her lips curled slightly in an amused semi-smile. It was both a becoming and annoying look for her thin lips. Virgil felt some understanding for Reginald Wellesley's error in sleeping with her. *But was it an error?*

"You are in love with your husband, but you are carrying on a passionate affair with a relative stranger who just arrived? You said some nasty things about Mr Kordatos in that letter. You don't see the tension there?"

"No." She was perfectly serious. "I manage my affairs as I see fit, as do you, from what I have heard." She stared icily at Virgil.

"Now, now, this is not necessary," Costas interjected.

"No worries, Costas," then turning to Zoe, "that's fair enough, Mrs Kordatos. Just one more thing — the Circe connection, you said you took him to her?"

"Yes."

"How did that work out?"

"He says that she is exactly what he is looking for. He mentioned several times that they are doing business of some sort or another. I am not terribly interested." Her tone ironically picked up as she described her indifference. She seemed *quite* interested. *Jealousy? Or something else?* Virgil continued.

"Did Marcus mention anyone else on the island, or ask you about anyone else? Did you see him with anyone else at any point?"

"He did not mention anyone else — he asked me about Nikos until I asked him to stop. I only ever saw him talking to Katerina, like all of you," she said this while looking directly at Costas, who abruptly stopped writing.

"What did he want to know about Nikos?" Virgil asked, trying to get back to business for his embarrassed friend.

"He asked a lot of questions about where is Nikos, what is Nikos doing, how confident I was about when Nikos leaves and returns, things like this. I told him that we had better things to do than talk about Nikos. This usually ends the questions." Back to flat.

"Forgive me, why is it impossible for the man who loves you, and whom you love, to figure out that you are seeing another man? To become jealous?" Virgil asked this as delicately, but firmly, as he could.

"Because Nikos only thinks about the party. We are in love, but I am his second love. The party comes first," she concluded, quickly adding, "for Nikos."

"And he cannot detect when you are coming and going at unusual times? Or when you are lying to him?"

"He has no real conception of unusual times for me. I never lie to Nikos," she ended with total sincerity and seriousness.

"And, finally, Mrs Kordatos, what do you do?"

She smiled broadly. "I work for Nikos, in the office. I'm his chief clerk."

"*Chief* clerk? Are there others?" Virgil saw that his questions annoyed her.

"No," she replied blandly, suppressing her perturbance.

"Thank you, Mrs Kordatos. I am sorry we had to interrupt your morning." He turned to Costas. "I'm done, Chief."

Costas scribbled a few more notes, it seemed as if he had filled up six or seven pages in his little book. He then looked to Zoe Kordatos. "My dear, you have been of much help to us! Please do not tell anyone of this conversation just yet. Even Nikos, if you can avoid it."

"And Marcus?"

"I am sorry, my dear," Costas did not seem entirely remorseful, "but I cannot share any details yet. However, Mr Colvin was correct, there is no reason for you to wait for Marcus any longer, he cannot join you."

“Costas! You deceived me!” Zoe seemed hurt and angry, more the latter.

“I am sorry, my dear, sometimes the job requires these temporary suspensions of ethics. You will know everything soon enough, Vathy has no real secrets, does it?”

She laughed. “I am off to Loutsa for a swim, then. Give me a call when you will tell me what is happening, Costas.” He nodded, and with that she headed down from the cannons, in the direction of the road. Loutsa Beach would be to the right, Vathy was to the left.

When she was out of earshot, Virgil spoke, “Interesting woman, Costas.”

“Yes.” Then he paused for almost a minute of silence. A pleasant breeze blew as the sun began to blaze more severely overhead. “Have you solved this case yet, Mr Colvin.”

“Shit, was I supposed to solve it before noon? You should have said something!”

“I am serious.” There was a look of worry on the chief’s face.

“Costas” — Virgil patted the chief on the back, getting his legs moving again as Virgil moved towards the road, and back to Vathy — “no, I have not solved the case yet. We still haven’t figured out what the hell Reggie was doing here — aside from Zoe Kordatos. Ironically, at least we know who has the balls in the Kordatos family. But we will kick some more information loose eventually.”

“Are you sure?” Costas asked for reassurance.

“No, Costas, I’m not. Every case is different and some of them get away from you. Fortunately for us, and unfortunately for the murderer, you and I literally have nothing else to do now. The real question is whether you are ready for Circe’s?”

“Mr Colvin! When I am not ready for a break?”

“No break, Costas. This is a professional visit.”

“Ah, yes, of course, but I think we should take a break soon and discuss case, yes?”

“On that, Costas, we are in agreement. Not until after we talk with Circe, though. Fortunately, it is not a long walk!” Nothing in Vathy was a long walk.

They marched back towards Drakoulis Street and the town. The blue Ionian reflected the glorious golden orb onto their faces as they marched to the place where they had imbibed away much of the previous night.

CHAPTER SIX
CIRCE'S WELL

Vathy was too small and compact to really have a locals-only area, or a hidden hideout — tourists in the high season went everywhere with ease, clumsy innocence and curiosity. However, Circe's Well taverna was as close to a locals-only haunt as one could find. Fishermen, merchants, the mayor, the police and island denizens like Virgil Colvin all came to know and love Circe's Well. The food was solid, fresh and hearty. The drinks were plentiful and varied — for Greece generally, let alone a small Ionian island. The prices were exceptionally reasonable, especially for regulars. The lighting was bad, except during the day, when the sun did all the work. The smell of the place was generally of fish and the sea — the day's catch was displayed on ice just inside the door by the late afternoon. In the morning, the display cooler was exceptionally lonely, bereft even of ice. The Greek 'evil eye' was tiled in mosaic on the wall behind the bar. The three shades of blue and the black centre had a mesmerising effect if you stared at it too long. It was supposed to ward off bad spirits and ghosts. The taverna's bar formed an unbalanced L with the long vertical running parallel to the entrance, and the small perpendicular end running away. A throughway covered in curtains ran into the kitchen and Circe's office space. Despite what must have translated into lost business, the back area of kitchen, officers and living quarters consumed nearly half the downstairs space. There was a second floor as well that could only be accessed from the hidden half of the ground floor. The rest of the taverna's décor was made up of antiquities that were the hobby of the proprietor. These included vases and amphoras, small statues and figures (some quite lewd to many tourists not used to seeing erect phalluses so casually depicted and displayed), daggers and a splendid bronze *xiphos* — the short swords of the Greek hoplites. Engravings and prints of famous Homeric scenes decorated other patches of blank space on the walls. Here was the death of Patroclus. Over there was the massacre of the suitors. There was Achilles chasing Hector around the walls of Troy. And on that wall was the meeting of Odysseus and Nausicaa. There were tables scattered around the floor of the taverna, numbering between six and twelve depending on people combining the tables and chairs together for larger parties. The tablecloths were a dark blue that looked clean from afar. Aside from the conversation of the customers almost constantly present and the subdued intermittent chattering of the wait staff, the lapping of the waves against the brick harbour wall was always nearby to break any temporary silences. Occasionally, local performers would play traditional Greek music at Circe's Well when she felt inclined to invite them. No other forms of entertainment beyond conversing were tolerated. Given that Greeks liked nothing better than speaking their language, except perhaps hearing their language spoken, this rule was very widely approved and appreciated.

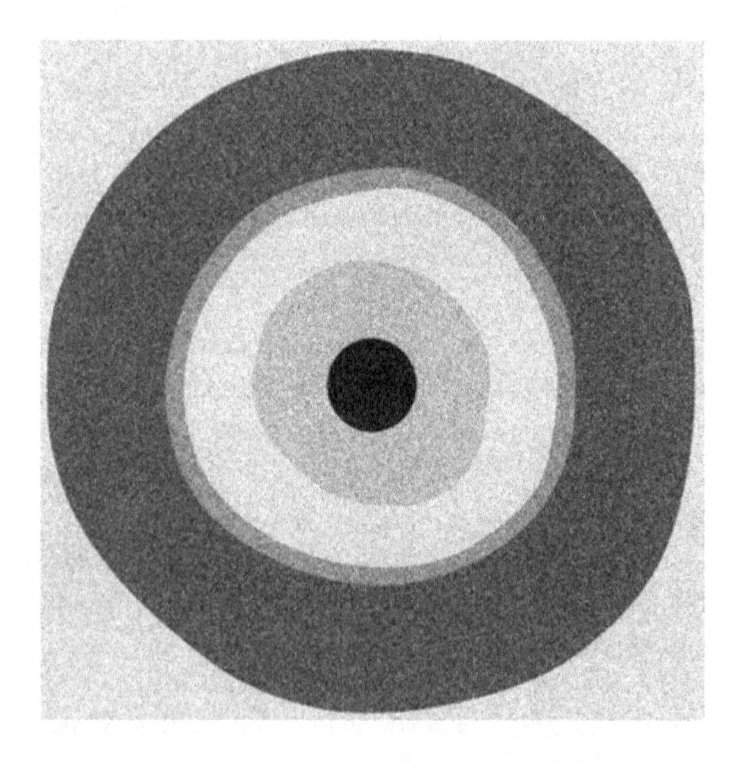

But this was not an establishment built upon Greek *demokratía.* The ruling *tyranna* was herself the largest part of the draw of the place. Circe, just Circe, did not appear to be much older than thirty or thirty-five years old. And yet, as long as anyone could remember — Ithacans were fairly bad with tracking the passage of time — she owned and operated this taverna. She did not seem to be present when Costas and Virgil arrived. They were both disappointed, but they decided to wait for her to appear. Aside from having questions about Reginald Wellesley to pose to her, she was a charming woman to talk with. Her conversation was lively, intelligent and captivating. She was well-versed in history, art, literature, politics, current events, fishing, alcohol, antiquities and archaeology. And she could drink every man on the island into oblivion while remaining seemingly immune to the effects of the effort. The fact that she shared the name of the witch who turned sailors into swine and who hosted Odysseus for a famous extramarital interlude of his decade-long journey home from Troy merely added to the allure of it all. Costas and Virgil almost always ended their nights together here with a bottle of ouzo, or two, before stumbling off to their homes, or Kyriakos' waiting car.

They immediately sat at the bar and asked Yiannis where his boss was. He suggested, without disclosing where she was, that she would be back within fifteen or twenty minutes. Virgil finally ordered another espresso; Costas ordered a mythos, a Greek beer. Virgil raised his eyebrows at this request.

"What? It is for thirst and calories! It isn't ouzo, you know?" Costas was only half-defending himself.

"Just don't forget the whiskey from earlier," Virgil reminded.

"Oh, that wore off the moment I drank it. I might hide it, Mr Colvin, but this case is running on my nerves" — he drank some of his beer after this clumsy description of his feelings — "and I am having trouble avoiding the thought that we cannot solve this without outside help."

"That may be the case, Costas" — Virgil hammered his espresso, ordering a cappuccino chaser, noticing another bottle of Redbreast Irish Whiskey behind the bar as he did so — "but who knows how long that might take? The murderer might slip away by then."

The detectives enjoyed their drinks in silence. Virgil turned to survey the other customers. All of them were, by now, familiar to him. Loyal locals from the town and some of the fishermen. All except one. He appeared to be a fisherman, sitting in the far corner of the taverna, his back exactly against the meeting place of the two walls and his eye able to survey the entire place. His *eye*. It was hard not to stare at the fisherman once you first saw him. He wore a fisherman's cap emblematic of the Aegean and Ionian docks the world over. His orange hair peaked out around the brim of the cap all around his head. His beard, which was quite a bit darker than the flames that jutted from around the cap, was long but uniformly maintained at about an inch and a half around his face and over his upper lip. He was casually reading a Greek newspaper, but not so much that he couldn't keep his eye upon the taverna. The eye that remained, his left eye, darted around the paper, but Virgil could tell the man was keeping part of his vision on Costas and himself. His right eye was gone. The skin of the eye lid had grown over the vacant cavity and an ominous scar ran down the right side of his face from the lower brow to the cheek and into the beard, directly through the area that once contained the eye. There was no attempt to cover any of this, it merely sat as quiet and ominous testimony to some past trauma or accident. His black jacket indicated that he was recently at sea and the rest of his outfit and his shoes were in line with the accoutrement of the fishermen who visited the town, and Circe's Well, regularly.

Virgil elbowed Costas gently and motioned towards the door. When Costas turned to examine it, Virgil did not even need to whisper about the fisherman in the opposite corner. Costas immediately began the very examination Virgil had just concluded.

"Do you know him, Costas? I have never seen him — I certainly would have remembered," Virgil whispered as naturally as he could without looking at the fisherman.

"No, Mr Colvin. But I will! *X-en-os!*[18] I am tired of all these strangers floating around my island! As soon as we are done with Circe, we talk to this man. Strangers, like this spy, are all suspicious, right?"

---

[18] Ξένος — stranger/foreigner

Costas was trying to whisper but was still too loud. *Maybe the fisherman did not speak English?* Virgil hoped.

"Maybe, Costas, but we haven't really had cause to rule out much of anyone yet. I agree though, a brand-new person might not be a coincidence."

As they faced the entrance, a familiar figure entered in swift, purposeful strides. She was short with beautiful olive skin and black curls draped around her ears and neck, bouncing with her steps. She was wearing a short yellow sun dress with leather sandals accentuating her very toned and lovely legs. She saw the gumshoes and smiled wonderfully — *She always did,* Virgil thought with a vague sense of discomfort as he realised he was staring a bit too closely. Eurydice Pantakalas was in her mid-forties, had a basket full of cheese slung on her left arm and was one of Costas' first cousins. She plopped the basket on the bar, which Yiannis began to empty of its contents, and then she turned to her cousin and his American friend.

"Well, what a delightful surprise! My boys! Already at Circe's? Early, no?" She was perfectly friendly and radiant in every way from her recent exertions.

Costas came around to hug and kiss his petite and very well-formed cousin, before clearing out of Virgil's line of sight in the most unartful and obvious way. *Why must he always do this?* Eurydice and Virgil simultaneously wondered.

"We are working!" Costas said defensively, once he was out of the way. "Mr Colvin is helping!"

"Mr Colvin! My god," she chided, her voice very accented, with a sweet and gentle timber, "do you still not call him Virgil? Why?"

"Because I don't speak in Greek with him yet," Virgil interjected, "this is his way of incentivising me." He regretted the words as soon as they left his mouth.

"Ah, yes!" Costas exclaimed. "And you know who teaches Greek, Mr Colvin? My cousin, Eurydice! You can take lessons, it is perfect!"

"Of course, I would be happy to teach you my language, Virgil. I am sure you have already picked up quite a bit hanging around this character" — poking her cousin's chest — "so much!"

"Maybe," Virgil said as enthusiastically as he could. This attempted setup, this offer, this conversation had happened at least twice before. *Did Costas think he didn't remember?* Yiannis slid some money across the bar to Eurydice which she quickly folded and put into the small leather pouch draped across her body, resting under her right arm. She then looked sincerely and caringly at Virgil, smiling.

"Well, Virgil, maybe when your case is over, Costas will give you my phone number and we can talk about lessons?"

She was alarmingly forward, Virgil thought. He was quite uncomfortable now. *It must be showing,* he thought.

"Ummm, OK. Thank you, Eurydice," as he eked out the best smile he could.

She smiled back. Then she hugged and kissed her cousin, grabbed her empty basket, turned and resumed her determined stroll out the door. Virgil caught himself staring again. Then he realised Costas was staring at him. *Oh, God!* he thought.

"Ah, Mr Colvin, I think she likes you! And you need to learn Greek! Why not, no?"

Virgil didn't want to respond crossly to his friend. He knew that Costas was only trying to be a good friend. Eurydice was a lovely woman, certainly. Very lovely. But he hadn't been with anyone at all for well over a year — not Janet in the final months, the illness was too severe. He was obviously devastated and traumatised by her death — he quit his job and left his home and country behind to chase the phantoms of better memories. How could he explain this to Costas? How could he tell Costas that his cousin made him feel awkward and guilty and uncomfortable? There was plenty of time to learn Greek. He was getting by without it. He was bosom buddies with the police chief, after all.

"Maybe," was all he could muster. He could tell Costas was concerned. But what could he do?

He turned back to the evil eye behind the bar as two obvious tourists walked in. They were young, maybe in their mid or late twenties. The coconut fedora the man was wearing wasn't entirely out of place on the islands, but only the tourists seemed to wear them anymore. The woman had a bizarre orange complexion indicating a severe vitamin imbalance or, as Virgil thought more likely, an unhealthy penchant for artificial tanning creams and products. Her straw hat seemed like a cheap afterthought bought before the plane took off for a vacation. They conferred with each other and then took up seats on the small elbow of the bar, separated by a chair on the perpendicular from Virgil Colvin and Costas Pantakalas. They both seemed fairly happy and fit — his clothes appeared somewhat ill-fitting, loose and uncomfortable. The man stared at Virgil's hat before reaching out his hand, "Hey there! I assume you're an American? Cubs fan?"

Despite pandemic predictions that handshakes were to be discarded and done away with, Virgil Colvin took the hand and shook it firmly. "Absolutely, guilty on both counts. This is my friend and the chief of Ithaca's police, Costas," as he made the introduction of the chief, the couple introduced themselves as Blake and Ellen Sheridan, from Houston, Texas.

"When did you two arrive in Ithaca?" Virgil asked once the preliminary introductions were made.

"We got in yesterday afternoon," Blake said, "Ellen is exhausted from the harrowing bus ride across Kefalonia to Sami. Once we got into town, she collapsed into bed." He looked at her for affirmation, but she was preoccupied with her disconnected cell phone. She seemed to be using the selfie feature on her phone's camera as her husband continued, "But the earthquake certainly woke her up — I slept through it!" They all laughed at that, Ellen Sheridan belatedly as she had not heard what was said. "We're in Greece for our honeymoon," Blake said, "and here on Ithaca for the next three days."

What was wrong with this woman, Virgil wondered loudly to himself? *Who came on their honeymoon and buried themselves in a fucking phone? Who came to this place — this magical island, this local gem and instead of soaking it all in, wasted time on a screen? Didn't she know where she was? Didn't she know what was possible for lovers on this island?* She didn't even seem to know that her uncouth behaviour might set tongues wagging and eyes rolling, or seem to care. This late millennial and Generation Z obliviousness was not something he had missed since leaving America behind. One of the wonderful things about Ithaca, he now realised as he watched this orange avatar of intellectual surrender scrolling along with a single finger, was that he hadn't seen *this* in months. Suddenly being reintroduced to this aspect of modernity made him queasy and enraged. He tried to make sure his reaction was not apparent, but he wasn't sure he cared if it was.

Suddenly, the rage melted away and Virgil was back on Ithaca nearly thirty years earlier, climbing to the summit of Mount Aetos, Janet in front of him. Her tanned legs were young and long, the muscles defined and flexing with each stride as she ascended the slippery narrow steps like a panther. Virgil was huffing and slightly nervous about losing his footing and plummeting to an embarrassing death on the rocks and cliffs descending into the channel separating Ithaca and Kefalonia. As they neared the summit, they silently explored ruins of walls that were thought to be the remains of Odysseus' palace by the earliest amateur archaeologists who visited Ithaca. Heinrich Schliemann most famously in 1868 when the German literally brought a worker to the summit and began clumsily digging around, breaking artefacts as much as unearthing them. Then they admired the breath-taking views of the island's two halves that the peak above the isthmus afforded all those brave enough to make the climb. The sea was a deep and frightening blue; the island appeared rocky, hilly, rugged and green in both directions. They had both seen nothing like it before. They embraced and kissed, long, deep and hard. There was nothing else in the world that mattered to either of them. The magic of the place and the reality of their love combined in a passionate and unforgettable moment. It was forever seared in his memory. Virgil had thought of it often in the years afterwards whenever they quarrelled. Somehow, he had not thought of that moment since Janet died. But now, here it was again, visceral and all-consuming.

He snapped out of it, to realise that Costas had stepped in with his congratulations and had ordered a round of ouzo for the four of them to celebrate properly. The clear distillation of anise was poured into tall and narrow glasses by Yiannis, who then added two ice cubes (really oblongs) to each of them. The misty cloudiness resulting from the addition of water to ouzo commenced slowly at first but soon turned all the glasses a milky and impenetrable white within a couple minutes. When satisfied with the result, Costas raised his glass to the couple, paused as if summoning from a recess of his mind the proper recollection, and said, "May the gods give you all that you want in your hearts; may they grant you a husband — or a wife — and a house and sweet harmony. For nothing is more enduring, nor better, than when a man and his wife have a household with harmony in mind. It causes much grief to their enemies and pleasure to well-wishers, and they will feel it the most!" At that, he drank most of the ouzo in his glass in one go; Virgil tried to follow suit and nearly succeeded, Blake drank about half and Ellen had a sip before passing the glass quietly to her husband. They would have noticed her turning slightly green had the unnatural orange not masked the effect.

"What was that?" Blake asked. "It sounds very familiar."

"It was what the most famous Ithacan of all told the beautiful maiden Nausicaa," Costas beamed. "I do not remember too many passages by heart, but I have always found that one especially perfect for these moments, no?"

"Absolutely!" Blake raised his glass again, and successfully completed the second half.

They chatted for another ten or so minutes about the earthquake, their lodgings and places to see on the island. They recapped their stay in Athens, the loss of their luggage, Ellen's bag being delivered before the flight to Ithaca and Blake's poor fitting clothing to replace his missing wardrobe. When it became clear that Ellen was bored with the setting, she quickly bounded out of her chair and crushed the conversation in mid-exchange. As quickly as they entered the bar, they were off and out.

Virgil turned to Costas. "Well, she's pleasant!"

Costas shook his head. "Are many Americans orange, now?"

Before Virgil could finish laughing and get around to some manner of witty reply, the proprietor of the taverna suddenly appeared in the doorway. Circe commanded attention wherever she went. She wore a dark blue jacket over a traditional linen shirt. Her shoes and pantaloons were those of traditional Greek men from a century earlier. She did not wear her black frizzy hair up in any of the customary Greek fashions, instead letting the humidity and weather decide its general posture and direction. While it was clear that she washed and brushed it, and cut it from time to time, evidence of much other interference in the natural ways of things was minimal. Her English was decent, and her accent was heavy. She was strikingly beautiful, with an athletic yet feminine build accentuated by her curious mélange of clothing. The fates favoured her five-foot, three-inch frame with appropriate and generous endowments. Her eyes flared a greenish colour when struck by the light at the right angle, but most often appeared almost grey. She had an angular face with an aquiline nose and a melting smile. While Katerina's coterie of champions was a well-known bit of island gossip, there was absolutely nothing known of Circe's love life. There wasn't even a drunken braggart known to be lying about winning her favours. As she made her way into her place, she caroused briefly with her regulars. She eyed the man in the corner, whose own eye studiously avoided her. Then she made her way behind the bar, facing Virgil and Costas with a broad smile.

"Gentlemen, gentlemen! What a morning we have had! The island, it shakes; the taverna, it survives; the Aetos, it collapses; and we are all cut off from everyone! How are you?"

Costas took the lead here. "Circe, you left out one bit of business this morning, I am sure you are aware."

She continued smiling, but now rather mischievously. It was enchanting, "Ah, that!" Then she spoke more quietly, her vision in some way vaguely oriented towards the back corner and the mysterious fisherman. "Yes, I know about it a little bit. Quite sad, really, he was an interesting fellow."

"And now you know what we are doing here," Costas tried his best to whisper. "What were your dealings with this man? What did you know about him?"

"He called himself Marcus," Circe began, "but the name did not fit. I think he was lying. Clearly British, not the slum British like David Beckham, but someone of some substance. He came here talking about the antiquities of the island and the various places associated with the Bronze Age and Odysseus. He wasn't lying about that, but he wasn't telling me everything either. He was curious about my collection and where I procured or found things. He also wanted to go over a map of the island with me and to get some ideas about where he might go to explore and do a little, um, digging." She said this last bit cautiously, to see how Costas would react.

"You are going to need to be as specific about the locations and his interests and questions as you possibly can," Virgil interjected.

"Yes, of course, anything for the police! Let me get a map." She swiftly vanished behind the curtains. After about five minutes, she re-emerged with a folding map of the island, walking and examining very slowly. When she returned to where Costas and Virgil were sitting, she cleared the bar of their drinks, turned the map so that they would be able to read it right side up, and then paused. "Costas, have you heard anything from Hellas?"

"Not yet, Circe, why?" The policeman looked as deeply into her eyes as he could. He knew her about as well as anyone did. She rarely became so serious and humourless in tone.

"I have a radio upstairs; it is what delayed me. The news had a bit on the earthquake — apparently of moderate size, they seem to think a bigger one or more may be in the near future for us. But they were also talking about Gündüz." Her reference to the Turkish autocrat perked up both Virgil and Costas.

"Oh, what about *him*?" Costas inquired.

"A coup," she said.

"Successful? Is he dead?" Virgil asked.

"That wasn't known, just reports of gun-fighting on the streets of Constantinople and Smyrna and a few other cities. Liberals and communists and the like." Her use of the old, pre-Ottoman, names for Istanbul and Izmir was without affect or pause.

"And? And?" Costas was impatient, something aside from this coup was bothering her.

"They said that Gündüz's government lodged an official complaint in Athens and in the United Nations alleging Greek support of the coup and threatening military retaliation." She still seemed to be holding something back.

"Ah, that's no good! Onur Gündüz is an inveterate, shameless liar!" Costas delivered in epic understatement. "Anything else?"

"Is this not enough?" Circe asked.

"OK, well if this is it, we will put it to the side for now. Tell us about this map and Marcus and what he was interested in." Costas redirected the conversation back to what would otherwise have been the greatest excitement of his life and that of the island.

"Yes, well, um." Circe regained her focus slowly at first, but then quickly told the detectives about the mutual interests she shared with the late 'Marcus'. "He was very curious about Eumaios — the well of Arethusa in particular and *Pera Pigathi*, I told him the point of interest was really the excavations above the well at the top of the cliffs, but he was not to be persuaded. I never found out why. He also wanted to know about the nymph cave above *Dexia*. I told him it was a pretty view, but had been explored by the previous diggers pretty thoroughly. I am sure he visited, because he confirmed a few days ago the absence of anything truly interesting. He asked about the summit of Mount Aetos and the digs that occurred there and what had been found. He seemed to know a lot about those excavations already. North of Aetos, he asked about the Homer School. I told him what I thought would be more interesting places, but he insisted on that location. He never would say why. I think he was here to find antiquities, but I could never pin him down. He also was only interested in those to be unearthed — I could not interest him in buying any of mine."

Costas laughed heartily.

Circe was not amused. "Costas, you *are* a boy!"

He finished chortling. "Oh, Circe, forgive me. But I'm amazed this man could resist your various charms, especially since you have his favourite drink here." He pointed to the bottle of Redbreast. Virgil was glad to see that Costas had spotted it, too.

"Yes, he actually brought that to me, in partial payment for my advice about where he was going."

"Oh, what was the rest of the payment?" Costas was a bit more serious now.

"I don't believe I need to answer that," she said defiantly.

"Circe, this is true, but not answering my questions now will just lead to me asking them again later down the street and searching your rooms." Again, Costas made the threat sound pleasant.

"He paid cash, and he promised me another *xiphos* or amphora upon the completion of his work here."

"What else, Circe? What else did you two discuss or deal for?" Costas pressed her.

"Nothing, I swear it!" She placed her hand across her mouth once she had sworn it. Then she removed it. "But he did ask about something else, not related to our mutual interests. He asked about other places to go — places tourists do not explore. Of course, I don't know much more than anyone else, and I told him what I know," she lied. Circe was more knowledgeable about the antiquities of the island than anyone in western Greece. "This Marcus was an interesting man, Costas," she continued. "He spoke *El-ee-nee-ka* well, and the ancient tongue better than me. I do not like admitting that, but we held nearly our entire dialogue in the old language."[19]

"Nothing else, Circe?" Costas' tone was hard.

"Nothing, that is it!" she insisted in a raspy whisper.

Costas looked to Virgil. Virgil looked to Circe. "And the man in the corner with one eye, who is he?"

Circe, not once glancing to the man in the corner who had just stood up and was walking purposefully, but without haste, to the door, quietly said, "I have not seen him before today. He was here before I left the taverna — he is why I left. Despite his clothing, I do not believe that he fishes for a living. My friends among the cabbies and at the harbour do not know him either. His boat is tied up out there. They think he arrived this morning or last night. They did not quite seem certain. It looks like any of the other fishing boats, but I think it is cover for something. Don't ask me why, I just sense these things about people." Costas and Virgil knew it was more than just feelings and sensations. Circe's dealings had their own aura of illegality at times. Her obsession with antiquities could easily lead her into the limited underworld of the islands.

While she had been talking, the cycloptic fisherman exited the taverna. Not wanting to lose him, Costas quickly asked the final and necessary question, "Circe, where were you last night and this morning before sunrise?"

---

[19] Ελληνικά — Greek

She smiled. “I was here in my taverna, where I always am. The cook left around one after cleaning up. Then I was alone with myself until the earthquake. I cleaned up most of the morning and then opened. You can talk to the cook for part of this, but in your detective adventures, you would call this a flawed alibi?”

“Maybe,” said Costas, “but we will not bother you any longer!”

Virgil was tugging at Costas’ elbow as he made his goodbyes to Circe, and they emerged into the full blazing day. Adjusting to the full sunlight again took several moments. The blue sea of the harbour invited them forward, but as they looked in all directions, they could not see the fisherman anywhere. They quickly marched toward Drakoulis Street, and fleetly covered real estate back towards the plaza. The man vanished. Vathy did have many other streets and haunts, but if he were heading back to a docked vessel, they should have caught up to him. Once they reached the Megaro Drakouli, they slowed down and halted. They then looked at each other. The temptation was either to laugh or upbraid the other for this foul-up. In the end, the mutual and antagonistic impulses cancelled out and they quietly looked at each other, before turning to the serene waters of the harbour.

CHAPTER SEVEN
VATHY PLAZA

Eventually, they began slowly walking towards Vathy's plaza again without discussing the fact that they lost the incredibly noticeable one-eyed stranger. Two trained and veteran policemen! Given the slip by a one-eyed Greek fisherman ambling through an incredibly small town. *Thank God Dick Borneman couldn't see this*, Virgil thought. As they walked, they began a peripatetic review of the case and what they knew so far about the murder and the various suspects. Costas retrieved his notepad from his shirt pocket and scribbled as they ambled along.

"Reginald Wellesley is a British agent," Costas was saying, "here for a variety of reasons, right?"

"Yes, at least four that we have discovered so far, Costas."

"Four?" Costas seemed put out by this number. "The Turks, Project Odysseus, what else?"

"Zoe Kordatos, for one. We cannot lose sight of that among his espionage activities. She's a little too much the beanpole for you, I think, but I can see why

Reggie found himself making that mistake. Over and over again." Virgil laughed.

"Who says I don't find Zoe attractive?" Costas asked unpersuasively. "She's a lovely woman! Mr Wellesley was a lucky unlucky man!"

"I find it hard to believe Nikos would so carelessly let a western imperialist like Reggie have his way with Zoe. His belief in collective ownership couldn't go that far—"

Costas laughed "Can we really believe Nikos Kordatos killed Mr Wellesley?"

"Kidding aside," Virgil said, "we shouldn't dismiss people with compelling motives and no alibis. There is no better motive for a murder than a jealous rage. Kind of like when a certain Gallic interloper ends up dead."

"No! I do not kill the guests of this island, my home! Though I would like to kill Mr Wellesley for ruining this day — but someone already does it and ruined it. So, I guess I may suspend my ethos for that person!"

"Do you think it might have been Zoe?" Virgil asked seriously as they arrived at the edge of the plaza and stopped to finish their review.

"Ah, the fatal woman! Like your Sharon Stone in *Basic Instinct*!" Costas was quite excited again to be working 'the big case', no matter his crocodile tear protestations.

"I was more thinking Barbra Stanwick in *Double Indemnity*, but yeah, you get the idea. What do you think?"

"Sweet little Zoe Kordatos? But why?"

"Well, I don't know," conceded Virgil, "but you don't really think she's all that sweet, do you?"

"Why?"

"She married that cretin, Nikos, for some reason, Costas — there is darkness there somewhere…"

"Certainly not on the exterior!" Costas resumed the campaign to convince Virgil that he wasn't romantically so predictable.

"It's OK, Costas, I know your type. Curvy, sensible hotel owners whose sense of courtesy, welcome and *xenia* surpasses even your own. The island is crawling with those!"

They both laughed.

"Where were we? Oh yeah" — Virgil resumed the scent quickly — "Reggie's reasons for being here. Sampling the island's 'hospitality' aside, the antiquities — his interest seems genuine as best I can tell, though maybe also connected to his work? Or was he just trying to get close to Circe? Reggie was a busy man, it's a wonder he found any time to sleep!" Virgil laughed.

"Deflers?" Costas resumed.

"Yes, François has potential motives related to whatever Reggie was doing regarding Project Odysseus. Anyone else somehow related to this Turkish coup may have had motives as well. Almost everyone seems to have had opportunity to murder Reggie. We don't know where he was murdered yet. The fact that his body was moved tends to cut against the various women in the case, but it is not impossible that Zoe or Circe hefted or dragged Reggie to and from a car. Circe is certainly more up to the task than Nikos Kordatos!"

Costas laughed deeply. He may have been feeling the effects of the whiskey and the ouzo — it was only just now eleven a.m.

Kyriakos came running across the Plaza. When he arrived, it took him a moment to catch his breath — it really wasn't that far from his post at the statue. His white shirt was blotted with translucent patches where the young man had sweated through.

"*Ar-khe-gos*!" breathing, gasping, yet more loud breathing. "Alexis took my place at Odysseus, can I go lunch?"[20]

Costas had stopped laughing. "Kyriakos!" he said with the full tone of despotic authority. "You did not receive any orders to be relieved from your post! And why you not come to the hotel, like I ask?"

"*Ar-khe-gos*, I did not want to leave the scene, or let anyone disturb evidence," Kyriakos pled.

Costas calmed down before continuing, "Before you can go to lunch, I need you to look into something. It is important and I expect good work from you, Kyriakos. Not like that fool, Midas!"

---

[20] Αρχηγός — chief

The young policemen, was clearly disappointed at the delay of lunch, but recovered sufficiently to put on a brave pose he imagined appropriate for a murder investigation. "*Ar-khe-gos*, yes?"

"There is a fisherman here," Costas explained, "he only has one eye. He arrived last night or this morning. I do not know his name. He has a long beard, red hair and has an Athena on his head. Find out all you can about this man. His name. His lodgings. His boat. His friends on the island. What he catches. Where he is from. Everything."

Kyriakos could not hide his dismay. "Anything else?"

"No, get going!" Costas sent him off running. He then turned to Virgil. "Mr Colvin, this young policeman is lazy! I hope to break him of this, or he will never be good at this job. And then I will have to tell his mother that I cannot use him and then there will be drama the likes of which Euripides and Sophocles could never have contemplated!"

"Well, I hope he's up to the task you just gave him, it might be important," Virgil said pensively as they continued their way into the plaza. Most of the cabbies were gone at the other end, now. "Costas, what do you say to visiting the locations that Circe discussed with Reggie? The fountain, the cave, Mount Aetos and the School of Homer?"

Costas stopped walking and looked at his friend, amused and aghast. "Mr Colvin, why? Why would we be doing this?"

"We could keep treading over the same group of suspects over and over, we can keep combing over the statue and Reggie's room until we go blind, but Reggie must have gone to these places for reasons related to one or more of the reasons he was here. Plus, it's a beautiful day, isn't it?" Virgil asked.

Costas looked into the sky. "*Nai*, Mr Colvin, but shouldn't we talk with *Monsieur* Deflers soon?"[21]

"Indeed, we will, Costas, but we know of two reasons that François is not going to be running away all that quickly. He, like you, loves…" he was saying this with fiendish delight, waiting to see how his friend would rise to the bait, when they were interrupted again.

"Costas!" boomed the unexpected Panagis Metaxas, projecting something approximating authority for once.

"*Yia su*, Panagis!"[22] Costas was all charm, sensing his superior's mood.

"Costas! It is all over the island! What are you doing? Please tell me you are close to being done?" The mayor's voice was approaching a slightly higher, almost comical pitch, even though he appeared frightfully agitated.

---

[21] Ναι — Yes
[22] Γειά σου — Hello

Costas answered quickly in Greek and the two of them then carried on an almost incomprehensible conversation that was clearly more reprimand than back and forth. Virgil couldn't be certain, but Panagis' body language, gestures and looks at various points in the tirade seemed to be meant for himself. *What did I do?* Virgil thought. Once the mayor seemed done with the dressing down, the English returned.

"Enough of this! I don't want to hear any more about this *ko-pros tou av-ghee-ou*! I want a report in Frikes, tonight!" Panagis said and stormed off. He didn't bother to say hello or goodbye to Virgil.[23]

"What the hell crawled up his ass and died?" Virgil asked once Metaxas was out of range.

"*Po po*! What were you saying before about getting out of here for a bit?" Costas was clearly a bit rattled.[24]

"Costas, what did he just say? Was it about me?" Virgil couldn't help inquiring.

Before Costas could recover his usual good humour and respond, he caught sight of something in the plaza that made him pause. He made his phantom spitting motion, and Virgil followed his eyeline across the plaza past the bustoe of Homer to the figure of the very tall man with grey hair in a tweed jacket. The man was looking into the harbour with his arms folded. He was

---

[23] Κόπρος του αυγείου — Impossible to fix, chaotic situation. Americans might prefer the more prosaic translation: shitshow.

[24] Πω πω! — Oh my!

quite tall, at least 6 feet, 4 inches. The overdressed hulking outsider turned and walked in their direction, as his hands moved to his pockets and his head stared at the ground ahead of him, seemingly lost in thought. Costas began walking in an intercept trajectory. Virgil thought he could hear the chief muttering something as they neared the stranger. It was clear as they got closer that not only was the man very tall, he was also very broad and well-built, muscular in spite of what appeared to be his years — maybe sixty or sixty-five? As they got within ten or so yards, Costas shouted out to the man, "Sir Nigel! I cannot believe that *Thiakí* has the pleasure of your presence!"

Sir Nigel Blasingame looked up, stopping his contemplative walk. He removed his spectacles, which were incredibly thin, almost invisible from any distance. His grey and white moustache resembled something that would have been common in the days of Theodore Roosevelt and Rudyard Kipling. Two blue eyes were a tad too close together and his large Roman nose easily consumed nearly half the real estate on his face. The man's cheeks were flushed; a bit hollow otherwise. As soon as he realised where the salutation came from, his eyes gleamed happiness and recognition.

Blasingame smiled. "Costas! You old goat! What a pleasure to see you!" His British accent was about as refined as Virgil had ever heard — exactly the sort of crisp Henry Higgins elocution Americans had come to expect from the British aristocracy. His voice was deep and authoritative, adding to the impressive effect of his upper class bearing and fidelity to the mother tongue.

"How long have you been here? You don't come to see your old friend?" Costas feigned insult and hurt.

"Well, I was going to call on you before I left, I have only been here a couple of days. Looks like a couple days more with the earthquakes. Hello, sir" — Sir Nigel reached out to Virgil — "I am Sir Nigel Blasingame, how do you do?"

Virgil shook the vice grip offered to him. "Virgil Colvin, pleasure to meet you, Sir. I have read your book, it was quite interesting."

"Sir Nigel, it is a terrible day, but I am always happy to see old friends. Speaking of that book of yours, what brings you to *Doulichion*?" Costas was never good at hiding his simmering distaste for Sir Nigel Blasingame's theory that ancient Ithaca was actually the western Paliki peninsula of neighbouring Kefalonia. Modern Ithaca was, Sir Nigel argued, actually the island of Doulichion mentioned in Homer's poem as the home of fifty-two of Penelope's suitors. *If only he knew of the similar army of men constantly hovering about Katerina Stasinopoulos*, Virgil thought, *it would surely convince him there was something in 'Doulichion's' water!* Blasingame's book, of course, merely increased the long-standing rivalry between Ithaca and Kefalonia. The denizens inhabiting them competed for the annual bounty of tourists and their money. The tourists came for Ithaca — not Doulichion. More importantly, however, was the pride of being the true homeland of legendary Odysseus. Every resident of Ithaca, particularly natives like Costas Pantakalas, viewed Homer's wandering hero as something of a patron saint and founding father. They all imagined some sort of serpentine descent from the hero, just as Odysseus had claimed his own descent from Zeus. Sir Nigel Blasingame's theory threatened to burst that bubble and everything built upon it, both real and imagined.

"*Ha!* You know me, Costas, curiosity never rests in the quest to figure out where Odysseus walked, where Eumaios herded the swine, where Penelope slept at night, and where Telemachos addressed the assembly. Mr Colvin, what did you think of my theory? Are you here visiting as well? American — Chicago?"

"Yes, the hat is always giving me away, right?" Virgil laughed. "I've actually moved here permanently, Sir, um, Blasingame." Virgil did not know the preferred way of addressing a knight of the realm.

"Please, just call me Nigel," Blasingame sincerely requested.

"OK, Nigel, I was a homicide detective in Chicago. I retired. My wife and I honeymooned here almost thirty years ago and I couldn't think of a better way to enjoy my retirement."

"Retired already! You're so young! And where is Mrs Colvin now?" Sir Nigel asked innocently.

"She passed away last year. Cancer." Virgil said, concisely.

"Oh, please accept my apologies, Mr Colvin. I am so sorry; I did not mean to be insensitive."

"Please, call me Virgil. It is no problem at all, Nigel, there is no way you could have known. And thank you."

"Sir Nigel," Costas interjected, "what do you say to spending the day with us as we visit some of the sights — Arethusa's, Marmarospillia, Alalkomenai, and Agios Athanasios? Perhaps we stumble upon the tomb of Odysseus? And then you pay for dinner and pay your apology to Thiakí!" Costas was only half-joking.

"You chaps just doing some sight-seeing? Has the earthquake eliminated crime? Poseidon is *generous*, is he?" Blasingame bemusedly inquired.

"Actually, we are investigating a big case, Sir Nigel" — Costas beamed — "and you may be able to help us!"

Blasingame looked intrigued. "Well, if you think I can help, then of course, my friend! Do I have time to change into some more appropriate clothing — I assume we are driving?"

"Yes, of course!" Costas said. "Mr Colvin will need shorts as well. Me also!" He looked down at his uniform slacks, then at Virgil. "Of course we are driving — well, Mr Colvin is driving. His brand-new Mercedes is better than my old war horse. Let's meet here as close to noon as we can, yes?"

They all agreed to do so, and split up in haste, heading in three separate directions: Costas back to the police station, Sir Nigel back towards the cabbies and presumably towards his hotel or rental and Virgil Colvin continuing along the harbour and into the western hills overlooking Vathy harbour where he had left his villa nearly six hours earlier.

CHAPTER EIGHT
THE SWINEHERD'S FOUNTAIN

Colvin arrived on foot at his villa twenty minutes after leaving the plaza. He had a good sweat going as it was almost entirely uphill. He peeled off his jeans, tossed them onto the bed and quickly put on some decent Polo hiking shorts. He looked at his hiking sandals. Before he reached for them, he suddenly remembered the hike to Arethusa's Fountain. The walled cistern on the side of a sheer cliff was the supposed location on the island where the swineherd of Odysseus, Eumaios, drove his lost master's fattening pigs for a reliable drink. He did so often to prepare new batches for the ever-rapacious suitors laying siege to Odysseus' harried wife, Queen Penelope.

Virgil hadn't done the hike in nearly thirty years, but he remembered a couple of things distinctly. One of them was the bugs. Spiders, specifically. The idea of them crawling on his feet or between his toes made him squirm uncomfortably. The web-spinning spiders on Ithaca were heinously massive things. He shivered slightly at the thought. He put on hiking socks and his L.L. Bean boots instead. Better for the toes and ankles on the rocks, he rationalised — masculinity safely intact. He kept the Polo shirt and Cubs hat. It had all taken little more than a minute.

He looked at the picture of Janet again. She looked so happy. So tan (naturally so, he reminded himself, not the weird unnatural orange of Ellen Sheridan). So young. So *not* dead. He suddenly realised that he had not revisited these places since he moved to the island — the magical and mythical places of Odysseus. His honeymoon was joyous and inspiring. They knew their love, like that of Odysseus and Penelope, would stand against all the obstacles, the way all newlywed couples do. They had a good run before the cancer came, the biggest obstacle of all. They almost beat it. Their own heroic epic. But the cancer was like a tide that receded before, like all tides, it came back. Poseidon's revenge for their hubris, Virgil thought morosely while staring at his dead wife.

Now he was returning to the great landmarks of their honeymoon. *Had he been avoiding these spots subconsciously? Was he afraid of seeing them without Janet? Would they not match the memories? Could they? Was the whole point of being in Ithaca to keep her alive?* He realised he was wasting time. *Enough!* He thought. All these questions would be here when he came home. He found his keys on the desk and began to walk for the door. Then he noticed the crack in the corner where the walls met the ceiling in the kitchen.

"Fuck!" he said aloud. "Well, that will wait, too," he said to the emptiness. He rushed out into the blazing sunlight of the Ithacan summer and jumped into the brand-new G-Class. The engine kicked into life immediately and he shifted into reverse to back his way down to the mountain road that led back into Vathy. He had less than 5,000 kilometres on the car. It was still a baby. It was also a manual transmission, which he had not driven in twenty-five years since he and Janet upgraded to his and hers BMWs as a Christmas gift to each other — and to celebrate the end of her surgical residency. On his salary, it was more a hers and hers gift to them both, but Janet always let him pretend it was still Dutch.

The first few days of driving, first across Greece and then the always ascending and descending roads of Ithaca, had been a little rough and occasionally embarrassing. But he was an old pro again. No more screeching and humiliating stalls. It made the driving a little more fun and involved, just as he had remembered it.

Virgil made his way back to the plaza of the capital in less than five minutes. He made excellent time. It did not seem like Sir Nigel and Costas had been waiting too long when he pulled up just beyond the statue of Odysseus.

"Hop in!" he yelled through the open windows, in front of the humorous-looking pair. The contrast between the tall, enormous Brit, now in shorts and rubber-soled boat-style hiking shoes along with a light-blue Polo-style shirt, and the smaller moustachioed Greek in uniform shorts, his white short-sleeved uniform shirt and black boots was a visual juxtaposition. While Blasingame had put on a foldable twill bush hat, Pantakalas merely let his thick black mane protect his head from the sun's rays. The height difference made them look like an old vaudeville comedy team. *Nigel and Costas,* Virgil thought to himself wryly as the two men opened the doors on the passenger side.

Sir Nigel Blasingame, who looked awkward in shorts — like he should never wear them and never did — climbed into the passenger seat. Despite the sheer size of the man, he did not look large in the Mercedes. Costas slipped into the back seat quickly, he had a bag of something — almost certainly food, Virgil thought. He slid the machine into gear as they quickly got out of town on Enmeou Street, sloping uphill past the police station, the hospital and into the southern mountains of the island. The distance they would cover was nearly five kilometres, and it could be covered in about ten minutes during normal times, but with the earthquake, Virgil drove slowly out of the town.

The road led to three mythological locations — the fountain Eumaios used to water the swine of Odysseus (Arethusa's Fountain), the sties and home of Eumaios and his herd of royal pigs (Marathia), and the craggy rock of ravens' nests that told 19 century Philhellenes they had found the right place (the rock of Korax).

As they drove slowly up the steeply inclined road, wide enough for one car and a little extra, Costas reached to the radio and turned the dial until a constant Greek chatter came clearly through. Both Colvin and Blasingame looked at each other with the common shame of those abroad who don't know the local language.

"My apologies, Costas, my ancient Greek is better than rusty, but my modern Greek is for reading only!" Sir Nigel explained.

"Yes, uhhh, me too!" Virgil chimed in.

"Both of you! One lives here and one is around all the time, like he lives here!" After the outburst, Costas began to summarise the radio voice as they made their way towards the home of some of the island's most lasting legends. "It is talking about Gündüz and the coup taking place. Fighting… there is fighting… in Izmir, Istanbul and Ankara… Gündüz has issued a statement… the coup is a plot of Americans, Kurds, Greeks and traitors… Communists, secularists and liberals… retribution if evidence is found linking coup to state actors… report of Turkish naval vessels roaming through Aegean… warnings from United States, Britain and Greece… NATO and United Nations envoys headed to the region… and then it starts over," Costas, once he finished offering this essentialised translation, moved the dial again to another incomprehensible fast-paced garble.

Again, he provided translation, "Earthquake centred off the coast of Kefalonia, to the west, fifteen to twenty kilometres… 5.3 magnitude… scientists expect more shaking in the next few days… could be like 1953, much bigger shaking… could be just the reverse… reports of the destruction of Piso Aetos and property damage throughout the islands… major damage in Argostoli… tidal waves… injuries on all the islands… one death in Thiakí." Here, Costas' voice modulated slightly. While Virgil noticed it, he doubted that Sir Nigel did. "Now it repeats again…" Costas reached up and rotated the dial again. He settled upon an indecipherable dialogue that was melodramatic even by Greek standards — the conversation was broken up with short bursts of *kementzes* and *kanonaki* music.[25]

"Ah! This is my favourite! *O-he, ba-ba*!" Costas said during one of the stringed interludes. "It is the story of a father who is assailed by everyone — his wife, his children, his boss, his dog, his mistress — the universe is always against him!"[26]

"And why do you like to listen?" Sir Nigel asked as the dialogue resumed.

"Well, here we have the father — Paul — arguing with his wife," Costas listened for a few moments

---

[25] These are both stringed, lyre-style instruments — their contributions to Greek music reflect the influence of larger Mediterranean, Turkish and Arabic music cultures on modern Greece.

[26] Οχι, μπαμπά! — No, Daddy!

before continuing, "they are back and forth about their oldest daughter, Christina. How will she marry without money? Who will have her?" Another voice joined the radio drama. "Now the daughter is here," Costas continued, "she doesn't want to marry… she wants to move to Athens… she wants to live alone…" The actor playing Paul's voice emanated from the G-6 speakers in a highly agitated and almost comic tone at this point. "Now Paul is saying he needs to go to the taverna before he goes insane… his wife is yelling at them both… *fantastic*!"

"Costas," Virgil interrupted, "can we turn the radio off?"

"You don't like the drama, Mr Colvin?" Costas asked as he turned the radio off.

"It's not that," Virgil lied, "I have a headache."

"Do you believe," Blasingame said gently as he tilted his head back towards Costas, "that your government offered or supplied weapons to this coup? Seems pretty reckless, does it not, my friend?"

"It would be crazy!" Costas replied with scepticism. "Also," he added wryly, "we do not have the euros!" Everyone chuckled at Grecian financial mismanagement.

"What about your government?" Costas inquired of Sir Nigel.

"Oh, I don't think so, quite the opposite actually. The connections between the Gündüz regime and the British government are deep. My government will actually be working with Gündüz to find out who is behind the coup, believe it or not." Sir Nigel did sound genuinely disappointed. "If that Fethulla Gülen chap were in the UK and not the US, for instance, my government would sail him to Istanbul in chains — I'm not joking! Personally," he said reflectively, "I wouldn't mind seeing the Royal Navy in the Aegean to send Gündüz a message. But I imagine they will just be there to do his dirty work for him."

"And the radio report about the UN, US and UK warnings?" Virgil asked.

"Well, the United Kingdom does have a longstanding commitment to the territorial integrity and independence of Greece, after all," Sir Nigel explained. "Suffice it to say, detectives, it is complicated!"

"And we thank you!" Costas added.

"And the death?" Sir Nigel asked. "I didn't hear about that in town."

"Well, we don't want to alarm everyone," Costas said, but did not seem inclined to keep talking. Following his friend's lead, Virgil stayed quiet and focused on the road. To the right were occasional turnoffs for houses and villas — at other times, it was just walls or sheer hillside. The walls looked like they were composed of stones belonging to a much older era. Ithacans had long pilfered their own stone ruins to repurpose the building material. Archaeologists fretted about it, but who could blame them? To the left was the rolling plateau towards Vathy harbour or the sea to the east. It was constantly covered with olive trees, fig trees and wine vines. The houses were a little smaller, befitting the farmers of the island who worked hard and lived comfortably, but who never became truly wealthy from their efforts. The sea beyond the sloping hills shone brightly as the midday sun had an unobstructed path to Poseidon's realm. Virgil remembered why he moved here as he stole glances at the view.

They made their way very slowly around a bend to the right. You never knew when some careless driver might swing around. They now saw many small boulders littering the road. Small, yes, but still, *boulders*. Virgil stopped the car when they arrived at the barrier and all three men whose midday had passed by jumped out to clear the way. A shepherd, his goats behind him, and another man were just off the road to the left. *They must be in their forties or fifties*, Virgil thought, *hard to tell*. They looked good, though a bit weathered from their years in the Ionian sun. Costas smiled and shouted out to them both. They smiled back and came up to the paved path. *Of course, he knew them*, Virgil marvelled.

The five men imperfectly saluted one another, and without any clear understanding between them all, began to toss the boulders off the road. The heaviest required four of them to heave out of the way, but none was larger than that. They were quite sweaty when it was finished. Costas spoke with the two Ithacans in Greek for a moment and then shook hands — which the locals insisted be extended to Colvin and Blasingame. The historian, the chief, and the ex-detective then climbed back into the Mercedes and proceeded on their way to the starting point for their walk. Virgil cranked the AC to its highest setting.

"What did you chaps say back there?" Blasingame asked.

"Spyridon and Giorgios just wanted to invite me to their homes to eat figs and cheese and drink *retsina*. They tell me that I have been a bad friend and have not visited in a long while. They say that now that they moved boulders that I am no longer able to deny my responsibilities. Those men — and their long-suffering wives — are what makes Thiakí 'magic', as Mr Colvin is always saying, not these out-of-the-way tourist spots! Giorgios! Spyridon! They are right, I will need to visit them. But — I will take Mr Colvin with me! He *loves* the *restina*!" Costas chuckled.[27]

"Hey!" Virgil responded. "I think you and the rest of the Ithacans are the real magic of this place, but that doesn't mean I can't dream about the mythical past too, Costas. But why focus on those old shepherds when I have Circe, Zoe Kordatos and Katerina running about?

---

[27] Retsina is a Greek wine deliberately mixed with pine resin. The taste was acquired by Greek wine connoisseurs in ancient times when wine amphorae were sealed with the resin, which naturally leaked into the wine, giving it a unique aromatic quality and palate.

That is magic, eh, Costas?" *Also, I'd rather drink goat piss than retsina,* Virgil thought to himself.

"And Eurydice!" Costas re-joined, looking squarely into Virgil's eyes in the rear-view mirror.

"Yes," Sir Nigel added, "Doulichion is a charming place in its own right!" The historian seemed to take genuine childish delight in his fun with Costas.

The actual location of the island of Doulichion, one of the four closely associated Ionian islands that Homer describes as participating in the Trojan War, sending fifty-two of the hundred and eight suitors that came to win Penelope's hand, had bedevilled all writers on Homeric geography since Strabo. Strabo, a first century AD Greek geographer, synthesised reports on the physical and place-name geography around the known Roman world and beyond in seventeen surviving books.

In Blasingame's theory, modern Ithaca was ancient Doulichion. But nearly every modern writer on the problem had a different candidate for the 'lost' island. Some put it to the north, some to the east, and others maintained that it was most, part, or all of neighbouring Kefalonia. Still others insisted that Homer simply was writing pure fictions, or that his geography was so bad that heads or tails could never be made of his descriptions. The most famous of the latter was the ancient pre-Strabo geographer and mathematician Eratosthenes of the third century BC, who said, *"You will find the scene of the wanderings of Odysseus when you find the cobbler who sewed up the bag of the winds."*[28]

Costas stopped chuckling when he heard Sir Nigel's flippant remark. Fortunately, they had made it to the turn off for Arethusa's Fountain. Virgil pulled off the road to the right and turn off the car, saying "Well, boys, here we are!"

Everyone made their way to the path on the left side of the road overlooking the sea at elevation now. The path began its immediate descent before veering off sharply to the right around the hillside. It was beautifully paved with stones, offering the illusion of a descent and easy walk to the fountain. Virgil remembered this, too. He and Janet scoffed at the hike at first, like all the unwitting adventurers before them. He knew better now. It was going to take nearly an hour each way. After the first fifteen hundred feet or so, the nice and easy path would end. As it was, the stones often got slippery in the summer from the brief and fierce rains as well as the near constant humidity. The stones were replaced with a well-trodden dirt path that would eventually devolve into a hillside of large stones that obviously served as the bed of a torrential stream whenever it rained heavily.

As they moved around the hillside — occasionally guided by comically small yellow arrows with no

---

[28] Quoted by Strabo's *Geographica*, see J V Luce, *Celebrating Homer's Landscapes: Troy and Ithaca Revisited* (New Haven: Yale University Press, 1998), 7.

indication of distance or progress — it morphed into a narrow dirt path again before a steep descent to the landing that offered two choices: to the left, another narrow and hillside descent to the *Pera Pigathi* (the beach 'beyond the well'); and to the right, to Arethusa's Fountain, a walled-in collection point for the water that fell from the sheer cliffs above, but which was up one more precarious and short hike across a narrow gorge in the hillside. Almost the entire way, especially in spring and summer, they would be assaulted by flying insects that seemed to be waiting for hapless tourists to make the walk to the fountain. Above, large spiders would seemingly float in the ether, never actually intending to descend from their invisible environs, but menacing all the same. *One gust of wind*, you would think, *and that damned giant would fall on my head!* And then, as you struggled to kill it, over the side of the steep mountain you would go. Another dead tourist on the walk to Arethusa, they would say in the tavernas that night. Of course, that never happened. But you would think you were going to be the first in some horrific and embarrassing mistake almost a dozen or so times as you made the hike back and forth. This verdant and alive world clearly belonged to the vegetation, the flying insects and the arachnids, while the goats, sheep and tourists were mere passers-by. Interlopers to be pestered and tormented. Still, it was very beautiful when you weren't fighting off the elements.

"When is the last time you made this walk, Costas?" Virgil asked, knowing that the answer was going to be humorous. One of the things he remembered well from thirty years earlier was the awe in which the locals held Janet and himself when they heard about their successful hike to the fountain — and back! Most of the locals never made the trek at all, they had admitted in semi-embarrassment.

"I was a child," Costas said, himself somewhat embarrassed by the admission. "My father insisted I do it. Was his first time, too! His Swede friend, Henrik, was visiting. He insisted on seeing things."

"Well, gentlemen, shall we?" Sir Nigel said, seizing a youthful lead, heading down the path, taking the bend to the right in confident downward strides. Costas and Virgil assented and followed along. "Such an improbably baffling candidate to be Eumaios' fountain for hundreds of swine!" Blasingame yelled as he bounded easily along the well-paved path that lured in the saps who did this every year.

They all appreciated the scenery to the left — the broad sea that separates Ithaca from mainland Greece — for several minutes, in quiet.

When they arrived at the end of the stone path, Virgil ventured a question to break the silence, "Sir Nigel, at the end of your book, you talked about the need for geologists and archaeologists, and such, to help validate your theory that Ithaca is actually the western penin — ah!" He smacked the right side of his face awkwardly as some large flying thing swiped by with a glancing blow. "Sorry, peninsula, of Kefalonia. How has that gone since you published the book?"

"Oh, Lord!" Sir Nigel exclaimed, waving his bush hat at a flurry of winged tormentors and making his way cautiously down the constant declination. "I am sure you might expect the difficulty to be in the deep-sea geology to prove that Paliki was once a separate island, or boring holes hundreds of meters into the side of Mt Imerovigli, but the actual difficulty has been with the damned archaeologists! You Americans imagine they are all adventurers, ready to move at a moment's notice. Nothing could be disappointingly further from the truth!"

"Yes," Costas interjected, his shirt already showing wide blotches of sweat stains at the chest, the stomach and under his arms, "because they only have to look at a map to know where the real Thiakí is!"

"Oh, Costas!" Sir Nigel laughed. "If only it were a matter of cartography!"

"Does the name hurt your case with the archaeologists?" Virgil asked seriously.

"I wish it were only a matter of *that!*" Sir Nigel exclaimed as he nearly lost his footing heading into the first stones that made their way steeply downhill and to the left. "Actually" — once he regained his balance — "it is the fact that I so heavily relied on Homer to support every aspect of my theory. That has made the archaeologists extremely reluctant to undertake major digs at the sites I proposed at Paliki. Unless, of course, I produced some other sort of evidence from the historical record of the classical, Hellenistic or Roman periods. They think they have already pursued all the probable dig sites in Paliki."

"Really?" Virgil asked, stopping in the stones for a moment to remember how he and Janet had egged each other on at this point of the hike, asking each other if they wanted to turn back at various points and refusing indignantly at the suggestion that they would be the one to turn back. They shamed each other to get through it. When it was all over, they felt like they achieved something remarkable. He snapped out of the reverie, asking Sir Nigel, "Archaeologists don't like Homer as evidence?"

"As a matter of fact," Sir Nigel said calmly — Virgil was impressed that he didn't seem winded at all for a man his age as they crept slowly down the smooth and slippery rocks winding their way through the hillside — "no."

Costas, on the other hand, was breathing fairly loudly — *He must be regretting that drinking from earlier,* Virgil thought.

Sir Nigel continued, "They most certainly do not. I could not have picked a worse source as far as most of them are concerned."

"I'm surprised!" Virgil sympathised.

"You cannot believe how surprised and disappointed I have been. They all think Homer himself was a myth, and that whoever wrote the *Odyssey* obviously never got within hundred kilometres of these islands. I swear, the evidence on Paliki will convince even the most hardened sceptic that that cannot possibly be true!

"I have spent almost fifteen years trying to convince British and Greek archaeologists to invest the time and money to investigate sites that I have already done the preliminary work on! I proved the concept and the plausibility in a lavish and major work, published by one of the premier academic publishers in the world. And to know it does not even have anything to do with an alternate theory! The bastards simply do not care!

"Basically, it boils down to whether or not you can finance the operation and secure institutional backing from a major academic archaeological program and the government in Athens." Sir Nigel's blue shirt began to show signs of sweat. "Cambridge and Oxford have been supportive in ways that do not include archaeological funding, the British School at Athens will not devote resources, the Greek government does not want to get involved in the inevitable dust-up among the islands themselves and the University of Cincinnati has put Paliki on the 'short-list' of 'alternate' sites every year since I published. Not once in fifteen years, have they excavated at Paliki!"

"No money?" Costas' question was more an accusation.

"*Ha!*" Sir Nigel replied. "These digs in remote places like Thiakí and Paliki cost a small fortune, Costas. There are no Heinrich Schliemann's or Lord Rennell of Rodd running around anymore to finance these operations."

"I thought you were a knight and a business magnate!" Costas accused again, treading onto uncomfortable ground. Virgil was both happy and sad to be between the two men.

"Well, my friend," Sir Nigel said as disarmingly as possible — *a natural diplomat* Virgil thought, impressed — "as successful as we modern knights are, modern archaeological digs in far-off places cost quite a bit more money than even we possess. This is not like the days of Schliemann, where you could just show up with a spade and a couple of day laborers and start stabbing at the earth, destroying the last resting places of Odysseus and Penelope and such."

"He found their last resting places?" Virgil asked, surprised that he did not remember that.

"Oh, god, no!" Sir Nigel laughed. "Schliemann was a pompous Prussian popinjay who claimed that the ashes he found in some pots up on Aetos must be Odysseus and Penelope. He had no proof or reason to conclude such, and none has been produced ever since. It was his first dig and the magic of these islands got the best of him."

"And so you are not any closer to proving your theory!" Costas exclaimed, as they turned the corner on the watered stones to the right, working slightly uphill for a moment before reaching dirt and the downhill slope again.

"Not at all, my friend," Sir Nigel said pleasantly, still leading the way with vigour. "The geologists have added to the theory quite a lot. They have bored holes both in the sea and on the isthmus between Paliki and Samé — by which I mean the rest of Kefalonia, of course — for a fraction of the expense the archaeologists demand to do preliminary work!"

"And, what have the geologists suggested?" asked Virgil, with genuine curiosity.

"Everything the geologists have brought up suggest that the theory is sound!" exclaimed Sir Nigel. "Everything is consistent with my theory of rockfall from Imerovigli into Strabo's channel that now makes up part of the isthmus between ancient Samé and Ithaca today! And still, the damned archaeologists will not dig!"

"*HA!*" The beginning of Costas' laughter pierced the thickness of the cliffside humidity and trailed off into the distance of sea and legend, followed swiftly by his continued chuckling and giggling.

"Oh, Costas!" Sir Nigel said as they began their way down the final narrow path towards the fork. "You cannot possibly believe this impossible path was taken by Eumaios to slack the thirst of hundreds, or even dozens, of swine three thousand years ago?"

Costas might have laughed anew if he had not nearly lost his footing on the steep declension to the final fork. Instead, he merely exclaimed incoherently as if both laughing and screaming simultaneously. The effect the noise produced was merely to reinforce the historian's point. Virgil smacked the back of his neck for the fortieth or forty-first time, he had lost count — missing for the fortieth or forty-first time. Given the size of the things flying around, though, he was not quite sure that he actually wanted to be successful.

"And have you found an appropriate alternative in Paliki?" Virgil asked.

"Well, like the multiple candidates for Nestor's Pylos, there are numerous springs of Arethusa in Greece" — laughed Sir Nigel — "but, of course, I have found an appropriate candidate for the fountain near my proposed candidate for the Eumaios sties on Paliki. It even has the good fortune of being directly on a local fault line, and thus is a likely source of perpetual water — at least in the timeframe we are talking about. It also has the decency to be accessible to pigs and men and not at the end of a god-forsaken path such as this!"

"You know, I read your book," Costas reinserted himself, stating a fact rather than posing a question.

"Yes, I always assumed you did, old friend!" Sir Nigel said playfully. "Especially since I went to the trouble to publish it in Greek. Oxford was certainly not easy to persuade on that score — they made me pay for the translation! I was trying to make an impression with the Greek archaeologists — all the good it did me!"

"And," Costas said in between carefully deliberated steps on the final decline before the fork, "I thought you imagined yourself a bit closer to the world declaring you correct. But you seem not to be, fifteen years later! You never even happened upon any pots until the very last moment, and then only because an archaeologist showed up! Notice how he never came back?"

"Well, Costas, you are not wrong, but you might have thought that the archaeologists would respond to the knowledge that there were sherds on Mt Kastelli in Paliki, but you would then be mistaken! And as you point out, this is even after it was a fellow archaeologist who suggested the more likely site for the palace than where I originally thought it was." Blasingame was nearly at the fork.

"And you think this is entirely to be attributed to archaeological scepticism of Homer?" Virgil asked, slowing down for the final steps.

"Yes, I do," Sir Nigel said definitively as he took his last steps before level ground.

Costas made sounds that were unintelligible. Sir Nigel Blasingame and Virgil Colvin might have followed up had they not reached level ground to stretch and catch their breaths. Then they looked around. To the right was the relatively short climb to Arethusa's Fountain, fed by the adjoining cliffs. To the left was the steep path through brush and trees bearing down sharply towards the beach, which was in full view more than three hundred feet below them. Beyond that was the island of Lygia, a small crag that broke through the sea on the way to Greece and nearly made a breakwater for the small cove below. More interesting than the scene itself was the fishing boat that was anchored in the cove. This was not a spot for the fishermen of the islands but rather the sailing and larger yachts and tourists who owned, hired and rented them. The fishing vessel appeared entirely out of place with the small tourist speed boats and yachts also laying at anchor nearby.

When Costas arrived, he immediately looked to the left. His eyes fixed on the fishing boat. Virgil pointed slightly down and to the left of the fishing boat. Following his index finger, Costas immediately saw the faraway figure of the one-eyed fisherman from Circe's Well. There was no mistaking his getup. Even the gap where the missing eye should have been was identifiable from this distance. It was also readily apparent that the one-eyed mariner was looking up at the cliffs directly at them. As soon as he had ten seconds or so of realising who some of them were, he ordered the man next to him to get the dinghy on the beach behind them ready to go. The other man quickly obeyed, and both were away in what seemed like twenty or thirty seconds.

In a minute or so after that, they were aboard the fishing boat. There was someone else on the vessel that the one-eyed captain was clearly talking to, but they could not see the figure from the cliffs; perhaps a minute or so later, the fishing boat began its way out of the cove beyond Arethusa, making its way to the right, away from Lygia to Cape St John on the south-eastern extremity of Ithaca.

"Did you catch the name of that vessel, Costas?" Virgil asked.

"I am sad to say, I did not, Mr Colvin — my eyes must be getting old and useless!" Costas lamented.

"Yeah, me neither, it looked like maybe, *Po-*, or *Pe-*

something? God, I used to be able to read license plates speeding away at 50 yards or more — I might be losing my gift, Costas." Now it was Virgil offering up the ritual lamentations of the aged.

"Well, I am sure we will see that man again, Mr Colvin. I can still use your help, even now that I know your infirmity!" Costas laughed.

"Now what?" said Virgil to Costas, not as amused at the joke as his friend was.

Sir Nigel Blasingame had already made his way to the right up to the walled-in boundary of Thiakí's claim to the fountain of Arethusa. He was engrossed and oblivious to the question posed.

Costas looked at Virgil and then at Blasingame before whispering, "Why did Reginald Wellesley come here?"

Virgil looked around, there was nothing in plain view that suggested any particular reason a spy should come to this spot. There also did not seem to be anything out of place at the fountain or the cliff landing leading up to it.

Looking back to Costas, Virgil said, "Maybe he came here to see what we just saw? If there was some sort of arms shipment making its way through these islands — through Ithaca — then maybe non-descript fishing boats are just the right sort of smuggling vessels? Maybe this area is some sort of waypoint? It *was* marked in the report we saw at the hotel, remember?"

Looking up the incline back to the road, Costas told them both, "We go back to the car. Now!" And with that, he instantly took the point. Virgil noticed, as he followed, that Costas' shirt had turned entirely the see-through to which damp white cotton shirts were prone. Before he could laugh, he noticed that his own Polo shirt had transformed into a darker shade as well. Looking back at Sir Nigel Blasingame, Virgil Colvin was amazed that there were still clear distinctions in his shirt between sweated-through and dry. Remembering that the amateur historian's age was at least a decade beyond his own, Colvin could not help but feel genuine admiration for the shape the man kept himself in.

The three men made their way back to the car quietly, and at an accelerated pace. Still, it took nearly three quarters of an hour and all three men looked like they had wallowed in a Roman bath when it was over. The return trek was almost entirely uphill, so the effort they expended was substantially greater than during their rickety descent. The flying pests also had missed the memo to leave them alone. Oddly, and appropriately, they all felt fantastic as they reached the road again. They took a triumphant look at one another and grinned.

Costas ran across the road to the car and opened the driver's side back door. He rummaged for a moment while Virgil and Nigel enjoyed the breeze and the view of the sea. When he came running back, his hands were full. Two figs, a napkin, and a small bottle of Souroti — Greece's answer to San Pellegrino — for each man. Figs, Virgil had discovered since moving to Ithaca, were ubiquitous. It was not a fruit many Americans had experience with — but they were easy to eat and sweetly fibrous. They appeared oddly obscene on the inside, Virgil always thought as he tore into them. Maybe that's why Americans never bonded with the fig? Costas ate his figs whole, skin and all; Virgil and Nigel peeled the skins off theirs as they devoured the midday replenishment. They grunted their satisfaction as they made quick work of the small green fruit.

Taking a long drink of his sparkling mineral water and wiping his hands, Virgil resumed, "Well, Costas, what would we do without you!" He belched loudly, and the men chuckled. "Where next?"

"The Cave of the Nymphs, my friend," said Costas Pantakalas, before adding, "sadly empty now!"

They took one last look at the view from the head of the path Eumaios once followed to fatten his pigs and then walked to the G-6. Before getting into the vehicle, Costas radioed Kyriakos, saying something that neither Virgil nor Sir Nigel understood. *How did I not notice his radio?* Virgil thought, *I must really be losing it*. After they were all aboard, Virgil ignited the engine and began to reorient the vehicle to the downward path upon the road. As they made their way downhill, all three of them suddenly realised how damp and nasty they all felt. Virgil Colvin turned off the air conditioner.

CHAPTER NINE
THE CAVE OF THE NYMPHS

The Cave of the Nymphs was the place where Odysseus stored, or rather where Athena stored for him, the treasures given to him by the Phaeacians when they learned of his identity in Book XIII of Homer's *Odyssey*. The poet's description is wonderfully evocative and curiously precise.

"There is in the land of Ithaca a certain harbour of Phorcys, the old man of the sea, and at its mouth two projecting headlands, sheer to seaward, but sloping down on the side towards the harbour. These keep back the great waves raised by heavy winds outside, but inside the benched ships lie unmoored when they have reached the point of anchorage. At the head of the harbour is a long-leafed olive tree, and near it is a pleasant, shadowy cave sacred to the nymphs that are called Naiads. In it are mixing bowls and jars of stone, and there too the bees store honey. And in the cave are long looms of stone, at which the nymphs weave purple webs, a wonder to behold, and in it are also ever-flowing springs. Two doors there are to the cave, one toward the North Wind, by which men go down, but that toward the South Wind is sacred, and men do not enter by it; it is the way of the immortals." *Odyssey*, XIII, 96 – 112[29]

Just as with Eumaios' haunts, every ancient Ithaca theory hypothesised some version of this 'Cave of the Nymphs' and this 'Bay of Phorcys'. For those who favoured the modern island of Ithaca, the Bay of Phorcys is typically located to the west of Vathy at Dexia Bay while the only plausible nearby cave candidate is Marmarospilia Cave. The problem with Marmarospilia is that it is two and half kilometres away from the bay, up a winding mountain road at an altitude of nearly six hundred and fifty feet. Sir William Gell, who visited Ithaca in the early 1800s, found evidence both real and circumstantial attesting to a large and substantial cave at Dexia beach that had collapsed in on itself a decade or two before his visit. The islanders told Gell, and he still saw evidence of it, that they took the stones of the collapsed cave for construction in Vathy. That process eventually cleared away all the evidence of whatever it was that had collapsed. But as with so much else in the past on these islands, the cave was now long gone and forgotten, leaving only Marmarospilia to entice tourists and dreamers that would follow in the footsteps of legends. It was to this interesting, but rather unlikely, sanctuary for Odysseus to hoard his Phaeacian

[29] Homer, *Odyssey, Books 13 – 24*, translated by A T Murray, revised by George E Dimock, Loeb Classical Library 105, 2nd ed. (Cambridge: Harvard University Press, 1995), 9 – 11.

treasures that the detectives and the historian now made their way.

While there was an old shepherd's path through the hills from the site of the Raven's Rock and the sties of Eumaios directly to the area just above Marmarospilia Cave, the drive was faster (though far more indirect) as they went back into Vathy before making their way around the west side of the harbour. Just before driving past Dexia Bay, Virgil swung the G-6 to the left and up the flank of Mt Merovigli. Again, they had to get out and remove rocks and boulders from the road. The normally 20-minute drive took the better part of an hour — it was now around four in the afternoon when they arrived.

During the drive, they had come down from the euphoric high of the walk to and from Arethusa's Fountain and lazily discussed the problems posed by Marmarospilia, while Costas kept asking after the alternative proposed by Sir Nigel Blasingame. This was a sore spot for Sir Nigel because, as he described in his *Getting Odysseus Home*, he had had to abandon his original candidate for the Cave of the Nymphs on the north coast of the Paliki peninsula once he had determined it would have largely been submerged when Odysseus woke up on the nearby beach three millennia earlier. His alternative location for the cave did not resemble a cave at all, but rather an overgrown series of rocks obscured by vegetation and olive trees. He speculated that archaeological probing of a supposed void in the area would reveal the lost Cave of the Nymphs. Of course, such excavations had not yet been seriously contemplated, let alone executed, by anyone with the requisite skills in the fifteen years since the book was published. Costas knew all about it and wasn't anxious to let Sir Nigel forget it. When Virgil parked, they all rather sorely exited the vehicle and ambled their first few steps with some audible griping.

"So here we are — Marmarospilia Cave, the Cave of the Nymphs!" Sir Nigel laughed as they looked at the entrance for mortals awaiting them. Virgil could not help but empathise with both men. Blasingame, the amateur historian, whose own theory was notably weak on the cave's location, was looking to spread the misery to Costas. And the native Ithacan, wishing to press his advantage after the long trek to the unlikely source of water for the swine of Eumaios and now trying to remind the Englishman that Paliki had no cave at all.

They walked single-file into the cave, which descended a bit before landing on a level expanse. His first experience with this cave thirty years earlier with Janet had been a quick one between sightseeing stops that were much prettier, though he did remember fondly the quiet coolness of the cave and the kisses they stole within it. Despite that nice association, spelunking never emerged as a subsequent 'bucket list' item for Virgil Colvin. His return certainly did not make him regret it — and remembering Janet suddenly made him melancholy.

Watching Sir Nigel cram himself into the cave's opening was fairly amusing for Virgil and Costas. The large Briton was barely able to decrease his stature and profile to get to the projecting ledge of the cave, before stairs to the lower floor allowed him to regain his normal shape. The cave's dimensions certainly would have accommodated the Phaeacian treasure, and a small opening in the 'roof' could have allowed the crafty gods and goddesses entrance and egress. The large stalactites projecting from the ceiling were supposed to be the stone looms of the nymphs to make their purple manufactures, but business had seemingly dried up long ago. No honey could be found in the cave any more, nor was there any obvious source of water. The 'looms' though, suggested that that was not always the case.

"Why would Mr Wellesley come here?" Costas whispered to Virgil as lowly as he could.

"No clue," Virgil muttered while looking up and down over different sections of the cave's walls.

As the three men ambled around in the semi-darkness, a voice at the cave entrance called down quite loudly, "*Ar-khe-gos*?"

Costas immediately replied, "Kyriakos! I am coming!" He bounded quickly up the steps, Virgil following. Sir Nigel was touching the cave wall furthest from the steps, seemingly content to remain in the darkness.

At the opening of the cave, Kyriakos stood mostly outside and backed away when he saw Costas and Virgil walking out. “What have you found?” Costas inquired quickly.

“No one knows who this one-eye is. He showed up sometime in the last few days. He looks like a fisherman. He has a fishing boat. I wrote down name, here.” He handed a small piece of paper to Costas who read it quickly, laughed, and handed it to Virgil. It read, simply:

Πολύφημος[30]

---

[30] Polyphemus

Virgil looked at Costas, who misinterpreted his expression. "Mr Colvin, please! You have been here almost half a year; you must be able to read this!"

"Of course," Virgil retorted, "but is this serious? He named his ship after the Cyclopes that Odysseus blinded? At least we know this man has a sense of humour."

"Kyriakos" — Costas returned to his subaltern — "please, what else?"

"Well, he does not seem to venture out to the normal places to fish. He always heads away from the other trawlers. None of the seaside restaurants in Vathy have done any business with him yet; in fact, not one even knew he was a fisherman. I have not talked to everyone in Frikes or Kioni yet, but it sounds the same so far. He has not even started preliminaries with anyone. Asked no one about prices, demand, anything like that; he looks the part, *Ar-khe-gos*, but that seems to be it." Kyriakos seemed finished.

"This is *all* you have found? We saw him in the cove beneath Arethusa and Korax, he left when he saw us. He had a mate and there was a third person on his vessel. Do you have any information about these associates?" Costas was unrelenting with his subordinate, putting him through his paces — if he had answers, his chief would be pleased; if he did not, he would learn a valuable lesson about thoroughness and initiative. Virgil was enjoying his role as spectator on the side-lines.

"Well, no... no one suggested any associates or employees. There is a lot of gossip, but I could not substantiate any of it. Idle town rumours." Kyriakos was pleading more than stating.

"*I* will decide what is idle, and what is not," Costas said firmly. "What did you hear?" At this point, Sir Nigel emerged, squeezing his artificially shrunken body out of the cave's entrance, taking up a spot next to Virgil to watch the proceedings.

"Just rumours really. Some are speculating that he is here to move antiquities for Circe. He does seem to be at her taverna quite often. Some speculate that he's her lover, just visiting. Some think he has something to do with the earthquake, the murder..." — he stopped himself, suddenly aware of Sir Nigel's presence — "to do with all the happenings in town lately. There is talk about the coup as well. Crazy things."

"Hmmm, well, that is pretty good work, Kyriakos, you do good! But I need you to go back and continue with questions. Radio in the name of the ship and a description of this man to the mainland and see if they can tell you about it. Then I want you to find Nikos Kordatos, take Alexis with you, and ask Nikos about this fisherman and the coup, see what his reactions are, his face, his eyes — even more than what he says. Then have Alexis watch Circe — she lied to us earlier. There must be a reason," he trailed off, before regaining focus. "Then you come and find me in Frikes, I will be having dinner there with Mr Colvin, on the water."

"Yes, *Ar-khe-gos*, right away!" He moved quickly off and then stopped as if he had hit an invisible wall, turned around and came up to Sir Nigel Blasingame. "Are you the British historian? Nigel?"

"Indeed, I am, how do you do, sir?" Sir Nigel extended a hand.

"I was given this" — he handed a piece of paper to Sir Nigel rather than his hand — "by Katerina at the Hotel Familia, she wanted me to tell you that your room has been extended a day and that your new checkout is fine. I must tell you though, that the ferry service is still uncertain."

"Oh, quite right, thank you, sir." Sir Nigel pocketed the paper without examining it. With that, Kyriakos turned again and ran to his car to carry out his next mission.

"How's the Hotel Familia, Sir Nigel? It always seems to be where all the interesting visitors on this island stay," Virgil Colvin asked as they watched Kyriakos drive off. He noticed Costas, behind Nigel, remove the list of guests Katerina had given him that morning from his back pocket. He obviously had not gotten back to examining it. He scanned it for and moment before quietly crumpling it in disgust.

"Oh, you have not stayed? It is lovely! Katerina might just be the most magical thing about this island, eh, Costas?" Sir Nigel had a fiendish delight in his eyes as he turned to his friend. "I am, of course, married, but if I were a single man again, I might consider this island as ancient Ithaca if *she* asked me to do so."

"You old devil!" Costas blasted, seemingly in jest, but Virgil noticed a firmness and sublimated rage beneath the façade. He wondered if Sir Nigel noticed it? He did not seem to take the exclamation as anything but the appropriate response to his ribbing.

"Have you run into your countryman staying there? Reginald, I think his name is, right, Costas?" Virgil asked, looking at Costas with a quick wink once he caught the other man's eye.

"Reginald?" Sir Nigel asked ponderously. "Yes, I think he and I shared a drink a few nights ago at Katerina's bar. He is a quiet fellow, seemed more interested in drinking and listening than talking — kept looking at his watch, as I recall. That is the only interaction I have had with him."

"Really?" Virgil was surprised. "He did not want to speak to you about your theory?"

"Really, Detective Colvin, you flatter me. While I would certainly like to believe that everyone knows of my work, I have to try to temper my ego!"

"So, while he was quietly keeping the time, what else were you doing?" Virgil continued.

"I was talking to that chap Deflers. He was telling me about the golf course they are planning to build next to their resort. Fascinating stuff — ironically, it is likely going to result in a major archaeological dig before they can begin building anything. Got me to thinking about how to move my own archaeology problem. It seems that only the prospect of building things on top of potential finds gets the archaeologists and the Athenians moving these days. Probably because they make the builders pay the expenses. If I can get someone to propose a development on the northern end of Paliki, I will get my vindication. However, then I will be dealing with the problem all of you are dealing with."

"Which is?" Virgil asked.

"Well, the destruction of the very sites I want excavated and preserved — the creation of a global heritage site for all future generations to come and be on the same ground where Athena imposed peace, at long last, on a warring world. I daresay that this island is going to be overrun with the world's least engaged and ignorant snobs whose only concerns are euros, dollars and yuan rather than sherds, grave sites and Cyclopean walls. Rather sad, when you think about it."

"On this, we are agreed, Sir Nigel," Costas said, looking up at the sky, and then his watch. "Mr Colvin, the day does not stop. Alalkomenai?"

"Certainly! After you, gentlemen!"

As the two other men moved towards the doors on the passenger side of the vehicle, Virgil Colvin gazed out on Dexia Bay below. It was a beautiful and clear view — the small dinghies and sailing boats were quite easy to see in detail along with their passengers. Mt Neriton was off to the left in the distance. The Gulf of Molos was in between. *Another clear view of the sea.*

Did it mean anything? Was this view what Reggie had come here to have a look at, rather than the cave? He realised that Sir Nigel and Costas were now looking back at him, waiting. They all got into the G-6 and began their way down the mountain towards the sea, leaving the cave for the winds and the gods.

CHAPTER TEN
ALALKOMENAI

When Heinrich Schliemann, the man who established the archaeological reality of historical Troy rhapsodised by Homer in *The Iliad*, spent a week in Ithaca in 1868, he had yet to conduct any archaeological digs. In fact, Schliemann was not an archaeologist. He spent his young adulthood and mature years as a clerk in trading houses and then as an independent merchant. His comparative advantage in the competitive markets of Europe was a high facility with languages. Through dedication and a work ethic that made his early archaeological digs look all the more haphazard, and inept, Schliemann mastered new languages in a little more than two months at a time, becoming literate as well as fluent in speech. French, Russian, English, Dutch, Italian and Polish; the man was prolific! It was to become a defining characteristic. Such a skill made him the nexus between markets and between merchant communities. From his perch in St Petersburg, Schliemann built a fortune during the Crimean War that allowed him to spend the rest of his days investing, travelling the world and conducting archaeological digs of increasing sophistication. And eventually, of increasing competence. He added Spanish, Italian, Greek (ancient and modern), Turkish and Arabic to his repertoire in 'retirement'. That second-act was also noteworthy for a nasty divorce, remarriage to a Greek woman, having two children (Agamemnon and Andromache), building himself a marble mansion in downtown Athens and elaborate burial in the city after an ear infection spread to his brain and killed him in Naples in 1890.

The 'dig' in Ithaca in 1868 seems to have come about through a combination of motive and opportunity. The 'opportunity' was the general laissez-faire environment of the nineteenth century — no one systematically monitored any of the supposed historic sites throughout Ithaca (or the rest of Greece and much of the rest of the world for that matter). Permits were theoretically required everywhere but were practically ignored or sought retroactively in nearly all the earliest cases. Certainly, this was so in Schliemann's early career. In fact, his notoriety for spiriting finds away from illicit and authorised digs alike almost certainly led to a clampdown in the enforcement of laws and regulations related to archaeological excavations. The 'motive' is more complex. Schliemann would subsequently suggest that he burned with the desire to uncover Troy and the classical past since he was a small child, having been told of the Trojan War and the destruction of the great city of King Priam by his father.

However, this was almost certainly a romantic fantasy that Schliemann invented or heavily embellished *post facto*. More probably, Schliemann's turn to archaeology developed from a general interest that became much more specific during the early phase of his retirement from active business affairs in the 1860s.

In any event, the magic of Ithaca caught the German amateur's imagination during his July stop. After concluding this all-important first tour with a visit to the Troad and the site at Hisarlik that would make him internationally famous, Schliemann subsequently published to the world his first amateur and clumsy findings. He provided elaborate descriptions of reading Homer's *Odyssey* to the Ithacan locals and of taking a man to the mountain above the harbour of Piso Aetos to investigate the visible stone walls on the saddle and the summit. It would be misleading to even categorise the spade work of Schliemann and his workers on Aetos as an archaeological dig. At best, Schliemann inexpertly aped the techniques he had witnessed earlier in his trip in Italy while applying a limited theoretical knowledge of archaeology gleaned from lectures he had attended in Paris. With a few tools and several workmen over the course of two days, Schliemann claimed to have found pots with human ashes in them (of Odysseus and Penelope, no less), figurines, some bronze artefacts, and some bones. He left convinced that Odysseus called the summit of Aetos home — as was the prevailing opinion at the time.

Subsequent archaeological research following Schliemann's publication, including by Schliemann himself a decade later, cast so much doubt on the Aetos theory that the consensus now places the city and palace in the vicinity of Polis Bay, much further north of the isthmus of Ithaca. The dwellings and religious/ceremonial ruins atop Aetos are still a common stop for the more adventurous tourists who visit the island every summer. Despite the steep and sometimes slippery climb, and the hidden goats guarding the trail, ready to alarm climbers with their sudden appearance, the view alone was worth it. The entire island could be surveyed on a clear day along with the strait in between Ithaca and Kefalonia, and the neighbouring island itself for many miles. One could also see Zakynthos to the south, and Lefkas to the north. It certainly evoked a certain Bronze Age chieftain surveying his world before and after his fateful voyage to sack Priam's city at the entrance of the Hellespont.

The fifteen-minute drive from Marmarospilia was not extended by rubble clearing this time — the road to Alalkomenai was the same road to the Piso Aetos port, which was investigated and cleared by others earlier that morning. When the three men got out of the G-6 to begin the initial hike, it was about a quarter past five. The initial ascent was not terribly difficult — in fact, the easy gradient lured sceptical tourists to proceed before things got hard. It seemed a common theme in the Ithacan tourist sites. The steep goat trails that presented an unremitting series of switchbacks up the mountain were carefully hidden at the base of the climb. Once they arrived at the saddle, the stone walls, or bases of walls, unfolded in rows up the mountain.

"Alalkomenai," Virgil asked aloud, "why is this place called that?"

"A good question, Detective," replied Sir Nigel Blasingame as he looked around at the walls, still walking towards what could only be described as the remnants of a walkway to the summit. "It goes back to Strabo's *Geographica*. His report was a compilation of earlier geographical writings — he was never here himself. When he wrote about that tiny island in the strait, which we shall see momentarily if it is clear enough, he reported that there was a town on it, Alalkomenai. He then said it was located on the isthmus itself, or something to that effect. Well, there is no isthmus on that tiny little spec of land, let alone any cities. So, as might be expected, all subsequent hunts for the actual locations have sought to place an 'Alalkomenai' upon the relevant nearby isthmuses. This is modern Ithaca's version, especially now that no one seriously believes this was Odysseus' palace."

"Looks good to me!" Costas harrumphed as they made their way up the 'path' that led to the summit of Aetos.

The precarious hike up the mountain to the final archaeological site upon the summit was both exhilarating and a bit scary. The climb was far steeper than anything they did on the trek to or from Arethusa's Fountain and it required attention and relative silence. It was as Virgil remembered it; except this time, he wasn't trying to impress Janet by keeping up with her strong confident strides — she nearly leapt up the side of Aetos as he remembered it. He also remembered that he was totally outclassed. Virgil Colvin smiled.

After several minutes of concentrated effort, they arrived at the somewhat levelled apex of the mountain. The walls below were impressive and the obvious ruins of the carefully paved ascent were intriguing, but it was the view that was spectacular, as it had been when he last saw it. The lone columnal remnant hinted at some lost temple or shrine, maybe to Poseidon? The sun's rays, coming from the west at an angle were not as illuminating as they were at midday. The hazy horizons did not allow them to see the two far-off islands to the north and south, but they could certainly see the rest of Ithaca, as well as the small island of Deskalio in the strait, nearer to Kefalonia.

"You see that runt of an island?" Sir Nigel pointed, "Asteris, my foot! Certainly not, and without Asteris, the island in the strait where the suitors waited to kill Telemachos, there is no Ithaca!" He breathed heavily as he relived his own deductive triumph, his eyes appearing nearly aflame as they caught the angled rays of the sun.

Virgil and Costas wandered around the summit, examining the ground and getting further away from Sir Nigel.

"Gods save us, why did I invite this man?" Costas whispered.

"*Ha!*" Virgil laughed as unobtrusively as he could. "Let him relive his life's work. Anything up here look off to you? Out of place? Askew? Different?"

"Sadly, Mr Colvin, it has been many years since I have visited this place, what about you — please tell me you have visited since your residence!" Costas looked positively giddy as he awaited an affirmative response.

"I'm sorry, my friend, I have not revisited any of these locations since my honeymoon." Virgil felt guilty both for disappointing his friend, and for what the admission represented in terms of dealing with Janet's death.

"Well, it is fine, Mr Colvin." Costas' tone took on a fatherly character, full of concern. "I think that if Mr Wellesley found or did anything up here, it might be obvious. Do you think it is possible he used this vantage point for the same purpose we think at Arethusa?"

"Ah, you mean to survey the boats and ships? Very possible. A good pair of binoculars would certainly make it easy to track boats on a clear day, so long as they were in the strait or the eastern coast. There were no binoculars in his room, though."

"Yes, you are correct. I do not understand this man! He comes to the island, he has a mission, but he brings the books of a scholar or hobbyist? He talks to the antiquities dealer, but not this historian. He carries on a brazen affair with the wife of a man he is here to investigate. I just do not understand this fellow!" A mild disgust was beginning to creep into Costas' voice.

"Yeah," Virgil said quietly, checking to see that Sir Nigel was still out of earshot, "Reggie was a puzzle. We should assume, however, that there was some method to what seems like madness — even if it only made sense to him. Marmarospilia had a great view of Dexia Bay, just as the Arethusa vantage point had a great view of the cove on the landward side of Lygia, and this place has an even broader view. That may be the connection since he did not tell Circe about visiting Korax, Marathia, Pelikata or even Polis. The School of Homer, as I recall, has a spectacular view of Aphales Bay, doesn't it?"

"Yes! It does!" Costas brightened up.

"Well, we have about two and half hours of daylight left, what do you say to us getting over there?"

"Well, my friends, where are we off to next?" suddenly, Sir Nigel interrupted from quite close by, it was unclear how long he had been there.

"We are heading towards Agios Athanasios, you still want to join us?" Costas politely, but rather coldly, inquired.

"Of course!" Sir Nigel couldn't have looked happier. "Though I hope you do not expect to find Odysseus *there*!" He removed his bush hat and wiped down his head with a handkerchief that he then folded meticulously and replaced in the right pocket of his shorts.

Before Costas could respond, Virgil intervened, "Costas, we are so close to the port, do you mind if we examine it? Quickly?"

"It will be so sad! But yes. You are the driver, after all."

After taking one more, long look at the panoramic and luxuriant scene of blue and green, they hiked back down to the car and began the slow, and quite short, drive to the south to see whatever remained of the main ferry entrepot of Ithaca.

CHAPTER ELEVEN
PISO AETOS

The drive was only a few minutes, but it was down a serpentine path that wound back and forth until the final descent to the port itself. Then a right turn brought one to the ticket office, a small parking lot, a small open-air café of sorts, and the 'avenue' to and from the docked ferries so that cars could drive on and off orderly and quickly. As they came around the bend before the final descent, Virgil stopped the car and turned the engine off. They all just stared in amazement at what used to be the principal port of entry to the island. The abutment of land where the large ferries from Sami in Kefalonia slowed down before lowering their ramps to disembark cars and passengers before reversing the process for those leaving Ithaca was, simply, gone. Not just the slip, but the entire facility.

Indeed, the side of the mountain to the left of the road had clearly fallen away during the earthquake. Some of that rockfall cluttered and totally blocked the road below where Virgil had stopped. Some of it covered the former spot of the parking lot and the ticket station, both of which were no longer visible at all. The collapse of this much earth must have created a tremendous wave on the other side of the strait. Simply put, the scene was a testament to the colossal destructive power of earthquakes — even relatively small ones.

The three men got out of the car to venture down as far as they dared. They surveyed the scene with the sea breeze on their cheeks and the intermediary medium of windshield removed. As they silently examined and inched, they heard another engine approaching from above. As Sir Nigel and Costas looked back towards the bend, Virgil Colvin continued to stare at the former port itself.

It was nearly six months earlier and he had just driven the G-6 off the ferry, finally 'home'. He parked in the lot and then got out to enjoy the smells and the feel of terra firma. He also wanted to get an Epsa *por-to-ka-lath-a* — the Greek answer to Orangina. Janet had always loved them and insisted on getting them whenever possible in the States. He didn't really enjoy orange pop (he was still a Midwesterner), but he associated the drink with Europe — with Janet — and it seemed appropriate as an arrival ritual. If Janet had been there, she would have insisted, so it seemed even more appropriate. He was debating to himself whether the gods and goddesses would be offended more by his *pouring* or *not pouring* out some of the drink for them, when he suddenly heard a man yelling in Greek.

When he turned to the voice, Virgil saw what appeared to be a Greek policeman, with a full head of black hair, an iconic moustache and an imposing torso despite his somewhat diminutive stature. He had a teenage boy in arm and was chastising him while pointing at Virgil Colvin. He was dragging the kid towards the confused novo-Ithacan. Virgil swallowed a swig of *por-to-ka-lath-a*, grimaced and then said, as well as he could, and more as a question than a salutation, "*Yia su*?"

"*Yia su*! Ah, tourist!" the policeman said and then shook and yelled some more at the kid, who was maybe fourteen or fifteen years old. "Sir, your wallet?" The policeman, indeed, had Virgil Colvin's wallet in his free and outstretched hand.

Blushing in shame, Virgil felt the right side of his ass, where the wallet lived. It was gone. He took the wallet and examined its contents. Everything was still there. "Thank you, sir, I can't believe *I* let this happen!"

"Oh, no, sir, please! This thief is a regular and is always doing such things as this thing. He belongs on Kefalonia!" He shook the thief and yelled some more. Then he made a pantomimed spitting motion in the direction of the larger neighbouring island. "I apologise that this is how you are greeted on *my* island! Please, let me know where you are staying, I will give you a ride!"

"Oh, no, thank you, Officer…?"

"Costas Pantakalas!" he beamed while still holding the kid in a vice. "I am the Chief of the Thiakí police. And I am at your disposal until we make your arrival right!"

"Chief Pantakalas…" Virgil began.

"Oh, please, please, my friend, call me Costas — I insist!"

"OK, Costas," Virgil said awkwardly, "my name is Virgil Colvin. Believe it or not, I was a policeman myself for the last thirty years! In Chicago. Either this young pickpocket is very good, or I have lost a step *very* quickly. I just retired. And believe it or not, I am now your neighbour! I live in Vathy — I bought a villa there about a month ago."

"Ah, Mr Colvin, this is wonderful news! You have car?"

"Yes, and please call me Virgil, we're colleagues after all, right?" he pointed at the parked Mercedes.

"Excellent car! Follow me, Mr Colvin, let me load this" — shaking the thief — "into my car and then you follow me to your villa! What is the address?"

Before answering, Virgil poured the *por-to-ka-lath-a* into the sea. "For you, baby," he whispered. Then, he turned to Costas, "Why not lunch? *O Batis*? It's on me!"

"Mr Colvin! Are you certain you just moved here? I meet you there — thirty minutes!" the Chief turned with the thief and marched to his comically unimpressive car.

Suddenly, Virgil was back on the road that once led to the very port where he first met Costas Pantakalas nearly half a year ago. He looked back up towards the bend. The other car had arrived. It was a black Citroën

Elysée. It looked new, clean and fully loaded. François Deflers was making his way to the three men. He looked as suave as ever. He looked angry.

"Ah, *Monsieur* Deflers!" Costas greeted him.

"*Merde! Merde! Merde*!" François retorted. He *was* angry.

"*Monsieur* Deflers, please, what is the matter?" Costas asked as disarmingly as he could.

"You! *This*!" pointing to the destroyed port. "The dead body in the plaza. There are rumours all over town about some one-eyed vagrant and this coup in Turkey against that *connard* Gündüz. In one day, the investment my company has made in this island has been entirely jeopardised! I can't even get a hold of *you*! Just your junior underlings. What *are* you doing about it?" Even the act of venting did not seem to take the edge off the anger as he pointed his right index finger alarmingly close to Costas' face.

Without looking annoyed or angry, Costas calmly replied, "Please, *Monsieur* Deflers, you know I did not cause this" — pointing over his shoulder to the destroyed port — "and while I cannot give you the particulars, we are working on the other issues. My associate and I" — this time pointing to Virgil, François did not take his venomous stare off Costas — "are pursuing it now."

"Really!" he sputtered, clearly exasperated. "*Merde*!" he shouted it almost to himself as to any of three men there with him. "It looks like you are sightseeing! My company will send in detectives to assist you. I can fly them in by helicopter — TONIGHT!"

"Yes?" asked Costas, with a heavy dose of humour in his voice. "Yes, send in detectives as the island recovers from an earthquake and everyone is worried more and larger quakes will come. We certainly need detectives; not doctors, not nurses, not first aid. This will look good, right?"

"Well, what do you expect me to do, wait for you two to figure it out? Are you even close?"

"Where were *you* last night and early this morning, *Monsieur* Deflers?" Virgil suddenly interjected.

"You must be joking?" Deflers finally took his eyes off of Costas.

"Not at all."

François looked back to Costas, this time incredulously.

"Well?" Costas asked.

"You cannot possibly think I killed this man? Why would I? Murder on this island, especially of a foreign tourist, is the last thing I need!"

"I still haven't heard an answer, *Monsieur* Deflers," Virgil responded.

"Fucking Americans, you are not even police here! *I* don't have to answer to those who wash up in a sea of ouzo every morning!"

Virgil was stunned by the bluntness of the attack. He couldn't even be angry; he was simply taken aback by the ruthless cut to the quick.

"*Monsieur* Deflers, please answer the question — this time, it is from me." Costas no longer sounded all that pleasant.

"Oh, you! I will report this to Athens as soon as the communications are back up!" François was back to pointing now.

"This is fine, but answer the question. Or I will have to take you in for interrogation. I would like to avoid that as much as you, no?" Costas said all of this in his inimitable charming manner again, smiling disarmingly.

"I was working at Project Odysseus last night, trying to turn this place into somewhere people actually want to come to and to make all of you rich! What do I get in return? A flatfooted Greek policeman and his American dog accusing *me* of murder? Unbelievable!"

"And early this morning?" the American dog asked.

"I was asleep at the hotel." Then he looked with a fiendish glimmer at Costas. "Ask Katerina, if you want verification, she was there."

"Very good" — Virgil quickly precluded any reaction from Costas — "you are free to leave, *Monsieur* Deflers. We will be in touch. Needless to say, don't leave the island."

"Fuck you! *Merde*!"

As he stamped off to his waiting car, Virgil suggested non-verbally to Sir Nigel to get back into the G-6. The large Briton nodded and headed for the passenger side door. François fired up the Elysée and backed up so that he could, quite dramatically, speed up the heavily inclined road. The rubber peeled loudly as he did just that. *What an asshole,* Virgil thought to himself.

"You OK?" Virgil asked his friend.

"You know the answer to this."

"Yeah, I do. You *going to be* OK?"

"Yes, give me a minute, my friend." Costas turned to the sea and took several deep breaths, admiring the sun as it continued its inexorable descent. There was no more hospitable, welcoming and patient man in Virgil's lifetime of acquaintance. But Virgil had noticed during their brief friendship that some took advantage of what they assumed was a weakness or a vulnerability. He knew that Costas was aware, and that it irked him greatly when it happened. But he never stopped being who he was. Virgil quietly admired his friend as he stared into the strait.

After a couple of minutes, Virgil gently asked, "What do you make of his attitude and alibi?"

Taking a few more breaths, his eyes closed, Costas turned from the sea. "He is right about the murder clearly not being good for business; especially *his* business."

"Yes, that certainly doesn't mean he wouldn't have done it in the heat of the moment, but it doesn't make him a likely candidate for premeditation," Virgil concluded.

"Heat of the moment? Why?"

"Well, Katerina perhaps," Virgil said gingerly. "Reggie worked quickly with Zoe, he may have had a large appetite and maybe that got him into trouble? But also, it could have had something to do with Reggie's file on Project Odysseus. Maybe Reggie confronted François with bad news, or a damning *J'accuse*, and our French friend lost it? It certainly helps to explain the attempt to get the body somewhere else — out of the hotel. The Odysseus statue is not far from the hotel and François would certainly be capable of the move, right?"

"Yes… Look, my friend, I am not sure I can make fair decisions regarding *that* man and this case. I am going to need your help with *that* one."

"Of course, you know you can count on me! Shall we get to the School of Homer before we lose the sun?" Virgil tried to pick his friend up with a diversion and some enthusiasm.

"First, take me to *Kathariotissa*, it will only take a moment." Costas sounded odd, almost forlorn. It was not a tone Virgil had ever heard from his constitutionally joyous and ebullient friend. He was worried. He was not sure how best to deal with this new tone and posture.

"Costas, we are running out of daylight, are you sure?" Virgil asked weakly.

"*Nai, nai, nai*."

CHAPTER TWELVE
PANAGIA KATHARIOTISSA

They made their way north through the isthmus in silence. The scenery was spectacular as the sea on both sides sparkled and radiated the reflected illumination of the sun. They approached the fork that led to Stavros on the left and Anogi on the right. Stavros was the island's second biggest 'town' at roughly a seventh the size of Vathy. Mountainous Anogi had been the capital of the island during the years of Turkish coastal raids. Before the fork, they passed *Chani*, shuttered and slated for destruction. It had been a lovely restaurant just south of the flat plain in the isthmus, nearer the Gulf of Molos than the strait separating the island from Kefalonia. Plain was a generous term. It was as flat a stretch of ground as could exist in a perpetual rocky mass like Ithaca. The land was now owned by Project Odysseus and destined to be part of the resort complex overlooking the Gulf. The ambitious projectors planned to somehow blast an adjoining nine-hole golf course into the hills beneath the road leading to Anogi. It was rumoured Tiger Woods was going to lend his name and prestige to the design. The plain was a beautiful spot that the locals called *Agros Laertou* — the Field of Laertes. Was *this* actually the spot where Laertes, the father of Odysseus, lived out his retirement, tending his figs, pears and vines? Could *this* be the location where Odysseus came the day after killing off the suitors, their servants and his own collaborating servant girls, to mount a defence against their angry relatives? Did old Laertes kill the father of the suitor Antinous when he brought a mob of enraged citizens to have vengeance on their past, present and future kings *here*? Most drove by the rocky 'plain' not pondering any of this. It was a beautiful spot on the spine of the isthmus. It didn't need to be more than that for them. But it did not strain the imagination much to picture Athena delivering the traumatised and legendary veterans of the Trojan War to a denouement at such a place as the *Agros Laertou*. Now it was surrounded by construction fences, guarding the trailer HQ of 'Project Odysseus'.

At the fork, Virgil went right, up into the slopes of the highest peak on the island, Mt Neriton, spoken of often in Homer's *Odyssey* as the island's defining feature — and certainly the landmark most essential in Odysseus' description of the island when he revealed his identity to the Phaeacians:

"First now will I tell you my name, that you all also may know of it, and that I hereafter escaping the pitiless day of doom may be your host, far off though my home is. I am Odysseus, son of Laertes, known to all men for my stratagems, and my fame reaches the heavens. I

dwell in clear-seen Ithaca; on it is a mountain, Neriton, covered with waving forests, conspicuous from afar; and round it lie many islands close by one another, Dulichium, and Same and wooded Zacynthus. Ithaca itself lies low in the sea, farthest of all toward the dark, but the others lie apart toward the dawn and the sun — a rugged island, but a good nurse of young men; and for myself no other thing can I see sweeter than one's good land." Odyssey, IX, 16 – 28[31]

Since the days of Odysseus, Mt Neriton continued to be the spiritual heart of the island. It served as the protective bastion of the islanders whenever bands of unwanted 'guests' invaded. During the centuries of Turkish invasions of the Greek mainland, coastal raiders made their livings in the eastern Mediterranean, including the Ionian Sea. Ithaca's few lowlands became hazardous and untenable. To Neriton the islanders escaped. Some of the island's most important churches and shrines were still found on Neriton's slopes, in and around scenic and mountainous Anogi.

Moni Panagia Kathariotissa, a monastery, housed what was perhaps the most holy shrine to the Virgin Mary in the islands. Built at the end of the 17 century, local legend had it as being built upon the ruins of one of the ancient shrines or temples of one of the Greek

[31] Homer, *Odyssey, Books 1 – 12*, translated by A T Murray, revised by George E Dimock, Loeb Classical Library 104, 2nd ed. (Cambridge: Harvard University Press, 1995), 317 – 319.

goddesses. Since it was Ithaca, the name of Athena was not far from these rumours. The shrine housed wall frescoes, a beautiful reredos and a supposedly miraculous icon of the Virgin that attracted the pious locals and wandering pilgrims. A religious festival, or a *paneyeri*, is the highlight of the shrine's religious calendar, held every 8 September.

Virgil Colvin, an indifferent atheist made more indifferent by decades of working homicides in Chicago, was still getting used to the very serious nature of Orthodox worship in the islands. While the tourists and Philhellenes came for Odysseus, the locals stayed and lived for *Khristos* and the *Panagia*. Fortunately, they blended their piety with *very* healthy doses of feasting, music, dancing, laughter, wine and ouzo. Even an atheist, indifferent or otherwise, could get behind that.

The twenty-minute drive from the ruined port to the holy shrine passed in pensive slowness. When Virgil parked the car outside the monastery, Costas handed them the bag from the back seat.

"I will be back soon! Here is some bread, some goat cheese — the finest in all Thiakí, and a bottle of Rosé and cups. Please, my friends, my apologies. Enjoy!" With that, he jumped out quickly without saying anything else and made his way into the courtyard before arriving at the front door where he knocked and waited. After a few moments, the door opened, and he disappeared inside.

"Shall we enjoy the view, detective?" Sir Nigel inquired, grabbing a hold of the bag and examining the contents.

"Absolutely!"

They both exited the car and avoided the monastery entrance that had swallowed up Costas. Instead, they ambled to the left towards the belfry and its magnificent overlooking view of Vathy and Dexia harbours. The belfry was narrow, about forty-five feet tall, and topped with a stone Orthodox crucifix. While the top of the belfry was not the Grecian sky-blue dome so familiar to tourists who roam the islands of the Aegean, the door to the belfry was framed in the iconic colour, beautifully complementing the sea behind it. Around the right of the belfry, a low stone wall prevented the casual sightseers from falling to a rocky doom while they distractedly tried to catch their breaths.

Sir Nigel distributed the vittles — both men put their cups on the stone wall while nibbling on the fresh Ithacan bread and goat cheese. Virgil didn't bother to tell Sir Nigel about the provenance of the cheese, or the rumours about the maker's proclivities. He just let the salty and fresh cheese melt on his tongue while sipping his wine and admiring this new view of his recently adopted town. The second thoughts on *that* case were wise and just, Virgil decided. The cheese was fantastic!

The amber rays of the steadily setting sun still cleared the summit of Mt Aetos and the hills around the harbours, but only just. The sailing vessels were still out on the calm and dark blue waters of the Gulf of Molos, each cutting their way towards Vathy harbour or still meandering around the coast. They were white specs upon a blue floor that surrounded the greenest of the Greek isles. The boats would discharge their sailors into the tavernas of town in another hour or two. Poseidon, or no Poseidon, nervously forgetful merriment would be the order of the evening in Vathy.

Virgil breathed it all in. He and Janet had not come here. They had been so glued to the ruins and the myths of the island that they had missed these Orthodox spots of majesty and serenity. Majesty and serenity. There was no other way to describe it. The monks attributed this view to heaven, Virgil to the grand and terrible beauty of an unfathomably large universe, but the reverence they all felt for the unparalleled scene was the same. The breeze added to the calming sensation he felt as he thought about Janet. It smelled of the sea. If you liked that sort of thing, there were few better spots on the globe. Time seemed suspended. Janet was gone, but here, now, he was alone with his own spirit. He was happy for the first time in many months.

"What brought you here, Detective?" Sir Nigel's sudden interruption was an infuriatingly swift punch to the gut from reality. He had entirely forgotten the historian was standing several feet away.

"My wife," Virgil responded robotically, returning his gaze to the transcendent view.

Sir Nigel waited several moments before speaking, "Did you two come here often?"

"Here, never." A tear rolled down his cheek. "Ithaca? Just once. Our honeymoon. Almost thirty years ago, now."

"Ah! I know the feeling." If Sir Nigel noticed the tear, he moved over it seamlessly. "When I first came to Greece with my wife and children, I knew I would keep coming back. When I got onto this hunt for Ithaca, it got to be so taxing on my wife and family that she made me buy a villa over in ancient Ithaca — Paliki, of course. So, we spend half the year back home and the other half popping around these islands."

"Is that why you're here now?" Virgil asked mechanically, still trying to hold onto the reverie.

"Well, umm, not quite," Sir Nigel said haltingly, "I mean to say, we spend the summers back in England, and come to the islands in the off-season — much easier to work without the tourists around. I am here, in the islands, now, to meet with some people regarding tests for the theory."

Virgil continued staring at the harbours. He was wishing that Sir Nigel would get lost or be quiet. He glanced at his watch — Costas was already at the shrine almost ten minutes. "Shouldn't you be in Kefalonia? Or are you testing Doulichion, now?" Virgil asked, slipping back into the present.

"Not exactly, no. This *is* ancient Doulichion, Detective. I know that cannot be comforting to you, but there can be no question on that point," Sir Nigel said with an obnoxious note of stridency.

Colvin suddenly realised that Blasingame was in his element. This mountain bluff was now a monastery. Before that, an ancient temple probably. Priests and priestesses, holy men and supplicating pilgrims — this was *their* hill. Blasingame's conviction was always tangled up with unprovable and non-falsifiable assumptions and presuppositions. It wasn't his fault in some respects. When dealing with events in the Mycenaean, it was still largely pre-historic. Homer and the archaeologists allowed us to get glimpses of that world, but it was shrouded in mists and voids that were as lost in Homer's time as they still were and would always be. Blasingame's certainty was not alarming to Virgil because it was certain, but because it was not moored any longer to evidence or an honest appraisal of the lack of evidence. A lack of evidence that ought to prevent a rational man from being totally certain on answers to this particular set of questions and mysteries. Blasingame had unwittingly constructed his own faith around this theory of his, every bit as unmovable as that of the keepers of the shrine of the *Panagia*, or the long-vanished guardians of whatever goddess was worshipped here three thousand years earlier.

"It has been a while since I read your book, Nigel, but I always thought calling this place Doulichion was the weakest part of the whole thing." Virgil did not really want to get into this argument — what was the point? But he couldn't help himself. The man ruined his happy moment. He *had* to pay.

"Oh?" Sir Nigel was curious — maybe annoyed, Virgil thought. "Please, if you will, share with me your reasons for being sceptical?" He ate some of the goat cheese after he posed the question.

"Well" — Virgil warmed to his vengeful task — "one thing this rock always seemed to have going for it, it seems to me, is the utter impossibility of it supporting large farms of wheat and grain. This place sending more than fifty suitors for Penelope! While Kefalonia and Zakynthos were not able to send half so many?" He could see, from the blood in Sir Nigel's face and the look in his eye that the battle was joined. *Good!* He stopped arguing with religious people for these very reasons: it was just about scoring points and ultimately went nowhere. But his transcendent blissful moment had been stolen. Now he wanted to crush this well-meaning, but myopic, pedant. Virgil was in it now; there was no withdrawing.

"Oh, don't underestimate this rock, Detective. The plain behind Vathy harbour is certainly fertile and verdant as we saw earlier. To the north of this very spot where we stand now, there is some very lovely farming land. Kefalonia, for all its mass, is intersected by enormous mountains almost everywhere you look. The disparity of arable land is not as much as you might think. Besides, as I argued, when we properly identify ancient Ithaca, we must figure out where Doulichion is

— the alternative theory places it on a small island over by mainland Greece, wholly inadequate for the purpose, not matching Homer at all. On the whole, when you compare the dozens of geographical clues in Homer as to the identity of these islands to the geographical and geological realities, Doulichion is really all that makes sense for this place." Sir Nigel beamed at the conclusion of this little speech — there it was, the 'reasoning' of the fanatic. It *was* because it *had* to be. He was *quite* annoying. Virgil did not say *that* out loud.

"I don't know, I don't see it — there is no way this island was ever that much more verdant and fertile than the others. And that brings back the archaeology." Virgil was surprised by how much he cared about the outcome of this conversation. He drank a little of the Rosé before continuing on, "This island is the most tramped around of the lot. You would think if it were Doulichion that all those diggings would have turned up evidence of it by now. At Pelikata, Marathia, Tris Langadas near Polis Bay and the diggings in and around Stavros, or on Aetos? I mean, for your own Ithaca candidate, the Paliki peninsula, there haven't been any finds there of relevant pottery or other artifacts for your case, right? At least Ithaca, here, has some of those all-important sherds, and those thirteen bronze tripods at the Polis cave, right? There was some lingering and long-lasting cult and shrine activity on this island associated pretty clearly with Odysseus from my recollection, right?"

“Not exactly, Detective. Since the 1930s, when Sylvia Benton found those tripod fragments at Loizos,” Sir Nigel lectured, “the meagre archaeological finds on this island have diminished in significance in terms of shedding light on the Mycenaean period of settlement. The fact that there may have been cult worship of Odysseus at Aetos or Polis Bay, or even a ceremonial set of games called the Odysseion hosted here, merely suggests how early the islands became jumbled and confused in local geography. Even the subsequent digs here have merely emphasised the lack of a city at Polis and the lack of a palace at Pelikata. Without the cartographical prejudice, this island would be in the same boat as Paliki in more minds than mine. This is the case I keep making to the archaeologists; ‘You have already dug up Thiakí, why not take a stab at Paliki?’” Blasingame was quite animated now, imagining his archaeology antagonists were there before him.

“What about Linear B?” Virgil asked.

Sir Arthur Evans’ (the most important archaeologist not named Howard Carter in the first half of the 20 century) discovery of clay tablets at the ruins of the palace in Knossos, Crete, sparked a half-century attempt at deciphering a forgotten and lost language. The written script, in a familiar linear format, was dubbed ‘Linear B’ because a different linear script, ‘Linear A’, was discovered in prior diggings. Both were first discovered in Crete and were assumed to be some lost Minoan script, for a lost Minoan language.

Philologists, classicists, archaeologists and ancient historians spent fifty years arguing and postulating about what the odd images meant. Imagine the surprise of trained academics everywhere when an amateur, in this case the genius architect Michael Ventris, claimed to have solved the secret of the mystery language in 1952.

The greater surprise was that Linear B was an early shorthand language for early ancient Greek, not a lost Minoan language at all. While it may seem obvious now that tablets of writing discovered in lands speaking Greek for as long as history has been recorded should be an early form of Greek, all the weight of educated opinion for that half century — and all the assumptions of Ventris himself until the moment of epiphany at the end — were that the mysterious language had to be Minoan. The ideograms and syllabic symbols of Linear B did not resemble the Greek alphabet in any way at all. This, combined with the fact that the language was presumed to be of a culture and people far different than those who eventually became the 'Greeks', made solving the riddle a matter of imagination and risk taking. No wonder it took a non-academic!

Sir Nigel started for a moment, then coughed before saying with a smile, "Detective! You're more of a classicist than you let on! What about it?" Sir Nigel seemed pleased to see that Virgil knew something more about the questions that dominated his life for nearly two decades.

"I read some of John Chadwick's stuff in between cases years ago," Virgil relayed, and then resumed his questioning. "But Nigel, what I am trying to ask is, at places like Crete, Nestor's Pylos and Agamemnon's Mycenae, tablets with Linear B have been proof positive of Mycenaean era settlement, right?"

"Indeed, sir!"

"Have any pottery sherds ever been found with Linear B?"

"A few, Detective, but only very few. Most often, the script is only found on clay tablets used to record administrative and bureaucratic minutiae at large palace archives," Sir Nigel said, sadly.

"But if Linear B were to be found, here in Ithaca for instance, wouldn't that be conclusive evidence that this island *was* Odysseus' island?" Virgil was legitimately curious now.

"Hmmm" — Sir Nigel pondered for a moment, scanning the horizon as he did so — "well, I suppose it would depend on what the sherd or tablet said exactly. But it would certainly lend much credibility to the existence of Mycenaean settlement and the likely existence of a palace and scribes."

"And, so far," Virgil continued, "no Linear B has ever been found in these islands, right?"

"That's right, Detective, only the familiar Greek alphabet, borrowed and adapted from the Phoenicians long after the fall of the Bronze Age Mycenaeans. Long after Odysseus was already the subject of the bards."

"But again, more sherds, bronze, references to Odysseus, etc., have been found here than your candidate, right? Has anything at all been found at Paliki?"

"But Detective, please" — Sir Nigel had turned quite crimson, and his sudden fit of stammering created an odd effect that was curiously hilarious and slightly ominous as he concluded semi-coherently — "you cannot, really, hold the absence of sherd evidence, at all, at Paliki, to be… evidence… for… Ithaca. Again, the archaeologists…"

"Oh, don't worry, Sir Nigel" — Virgil regained the diplomatic posture in the interruption, satisfied that he had exacted some cosmic justice — "it doesn't really matter to me — I love this place, be it Ithaca *or* Doulichion. Should you ever be able to prove that your peninsula was the island of Ithaca, I will be the first to drink to your success." When the words left his mouth, Virgil was quite startled to realise he was lying. He *did* want Nigel to be wrong. It *did* matter to him.

At that moment, they were interrupted by a joyous sounding Costas. "Friends! The light, it is fading, yes? Shall we get ourselves to the last stop, before we cannot see?" He noticed that some of the Rosé was left in the bottle. He poured it into Virgil's empty cup and drained it like it was water.

"Yes, let's get on with it." Virgil quickly latched onto the escape from his interlude with the aristocrat historian.

They all walked to the car. While Virgil and Costas chatted about the lovely weather on the bluff, Sir Nigel Blasingame moped along in silence.

CHAPTER THIRTEEN
THE SCHOOL OF HOMER

Agios Athanasios — the 'School of Homer' — was one of the true oddities of Ithaca's archaeological tourist stops. The stone structures on the elevated plateau were alternately billed as Mycenaean; or, part of a burgeoning Dark Age settlement; or, it was simply a Hellenistic and Roman era shrine that was subsequently used in early Christian worship on the island. To that modern oracle, Google Earth, there was no uncertainty, it *was* 'King Odysseus Palace'. The 'School of Homer' honorific seemed drawn from rumour and lore as a possible spot for the actual Homer to have come to regale auditors with his sublime craft. The name was bestowed relatively recently, the story goes, by a crafty 19 century landowning Ithacan who knew how to draw the rich foreign tourists and archaeologists to his land. Different waves of archaeologists had dismissed and hailed the site in turn. It was currently enjoying one of its periodic upswings of popularity and presumed importance amongst those intrepid diggers of the stratified earth.

Virgil made his way back to the fork — heading to Stavros through Anogi, they all agreed, was unwise due to likely road obstructions. Ironically, even with the backtracking, the greater quality of the roads on the west side of the fork made the driving time, about thirty minutes, equivalent to the eastern route that only looked faster on the maps. Costas turned on the radio again, providing his translation of the updates on the situation in the islands and in Turkey.

"More fighting… Gündüz is still in control… the coup seems to be succeeding in Izmir… it is over in Ankara… more warnings to Turkey… more warnings from Turkey… American 7th fleet heading to Aegean… fighting in Turkish Kurdistan… sounds like big mess." He turned the radio dial to the other station for internal Greek news. "American navy sending vessels to Ionia and Adriatic… hundreds injured in Kefalonia… ferries being organised for Thiakí, Kefalonia and Zante… now repeats." He turned the dial until the *kementzes* and *kanonaki* music interrupted the silence — *O-he ba-ba*'s dramatic dialogue was back. Costas resumed his role as play-by-play commentator. "Paul is having dinner with his mistress and his boss… she pretends to be the wife."

"Why doesn't he just bring his wife to the dinner?" Nigel inquired disinterestedly.

"Paul is convinced that the mistress can flirt with his boss better than his wife… *po-po*! She is flirting too well! Paul is getting jealous… he just tells the boss that he met his 'wife' when she worked with a traveling carnival… *ha!* She tells the boss that Paul could not be pulled away from the bearded woman!" Costas turned off the radio while laughing uproariously. Nigel and Virgil kept their peace, while exchanging confused glances.

They chatted about the coup and the archaeology of the northern part of the island during the remainder of the drive. Ever since Heinrich Schliemann's second visit to Ithaca in 1878, after he had learned to be much more professional in his diggings and assumptions about what he found, the archaeologists had shifted their attentions almost exclusively to all points north of Mt Aetos. Schliemann's last and most talented professional archaeological collaborator, Wilhelm Dörpfeld, came back to Ithaca in the early 20 century after achieving his own immortality at the Hisarlik site of ancient Troy. While digging in the northern half of modern Ithaca, and not finding the same sort of dramatic evidence that all the late 19 century archaeologists came to expect, he had the sudden epiphany that ancient Ithaca was really the 'island' of Lefkas. The problem was that Lefkas' status as an island was in historical and geographical dispute. The 'island' seemed to almost always be a peninsula, attached to mainland Greece by a truly narrow isthmus that even ancient engineers ambitiously conquered with a canal. However, the canal did not stop the silt from refilling and defiling the passage. During the epochs since that engineering triumph was first attempted, Lefkas had reverted to peninsula before being reborn as an island yet again. Dörpfeld's *Alt-Ithaca* theory had launched the 'Ithaca question' among professional and amateur archaeologists that had persisted for nearly a century. Sir Nigel Blasingame's Paliki theory was actually the *second* Paliki as Ithaca theory in the debate. Two Dutch scholars named Goekoop, grandfather and grandson — the grandfather had worked in Ithaca with Dörpfeld — posited that ancient Ithaca was actually part of the larger neighbouring island of Kefalonia. The elder Goekoop believed the southwest quadrant suited Homer perfectly, while the grandson made convincing arguments for the north-eastern peninsula, *Erissos.* Going by Blasingame, the Goekoops, and Dörpfeld, ancient Ithaca was everywhere, *except* modern Ithaca.

The British, aside from Blasingame, largely remained convinced that modern and ancient Ithaca were one and the same through the British School of Archaeology in Athens. In the 1930s, due to the Philhellenic interest, spiritual and material, of James Rennell Rodd (raised to Baron Rennell of Rodd in 1933), British archaeologists came to the island to prove that Ithaca really *was* Ithaca. W A Heurtley and Sylvia Benton found much to support their cause over several seasons of digging and exploring before the war interrupted their aspirations — including fragments of twelve bronze tripods in the Loizos 'cave' in Polis Bay. A thirteenth had been recovered, before vanishing, by the very Loizos who owned the 'cave' that now carried his name. Subsequent work on the 'cave' had determined that it was an open platform carved into the side of the bay by man, nature, or both, rather than a collapsed cave. They did not discover the 'Cyclopean' walls — made of stones so large that only the mythical Cyclopes could have moved them into place — that made the finds at Mycenae, Tiryns and Pylos such legends among archaeologists. However, they had unearthed hundreds of pottery sherds and bronze fragments that largely ended the professional question that Dörpfeld had opened. Goekoop the Younger and Sir Nigel Blasingame were swimming against a rather satisfied and complacent tide of professional archaeological opinion.

After they had driven through charming little Stavros, they turned left onto a dirt road that was nonetheless levelled and well-travelled. A couple of minutes along with several twists and turns and they came to a stop in a slight widening of the dirt path. They exited the G-6, slowly and sorely from the day's long exertions, and made their way to the ruins. Even though the School of Homer was a constant archaeological site, it was usually open to anyone who happened by if the archaeologists were gone for the season. Between digging seasons, they protected their active trenches with wooden frames attached to crinkled aluminium coverings. While intrepid 19 century glory hunters like Schliemann never would have been put-off by such flimsy obstacles, they seemed to do the trick for 20 and 21 century tourists.

The walls at the base of the site certainly appeared 'Cyclopean' enough and the ruins on the overlooking saddle that were a stand-alone shrine or temple were built with very large stones as well. While the site had once been relegated to the 'uninteresting' Hellenistic and Roman periods of the island's history, much evidence had been uncovered during successive digs in the 1930s and the 1980s onwards, establishing that the site's importance to the island's habitation stretching back to the Late Bronze Age Mycenaeans and even into the neo-lithic period. As the three men made their way up into the site, they thanked the gods that the climb was hardly worthy of the name after their earlier treks. Costas and Virgil stayed near the upper ruins to confer and view Aphales Bay, hoping to see the *Πολύφημος* again. Sir Nigel Blasingame drifted to the back of the site where the temporarily abandoned trenches lay protected by their shelters.

"Well," Virgil whispered, looking at his watch, "we have less than an hour to sunset, Costas, but I don't see the boat, do you?" The Italian cypress evergreen trees standing sporadically between the ruins and Aphales Bay blocked a direct line of sight and required Virgil and Costas to try to contort and position themselves to see around them as they scanned for the one-eyed man's elusive vessel.

"*O-he*, Mr Colvin, no sign of it. Could our friend, Mr Wellesley, have come here for some other purpose?"

"It's possible, have any ideas?"

"Maybe I am tired, Mr Colvin, my mind is empty." Costas did, in fact, look tired for the first time since Virgil met him.

"Well, Circe is rather notorious in the antiquities trade, right? Maybe he came here to do something for her in order to get information?" Costas shrugged dejectedly. "But I think our best bet is that he came here to observe the bay while serving his own curiosity in the history of the island. It is a rather lovely spot."

Virgil was watching Janet on the walls with Aphales Bay in the background, flexing and posing like the heroic ghosts that tourists came here to hunt. He took her picture and winked at her. Then she looked towards the bay and was perfectly still with her arms spread out, collecting and enjoying the mid-afternoon sun. The other tourist who had been milling about when they arrived had moved on, so Virgil could enjoy the view — his wife's tanned and fit body as well as the gorgeous bay that complemented her loveliness and the curves of her figure. In a few moments, he would propose they make love there amid the ruins and be laughingly rebuffed. Then they would kiss on the wall for what seemed like an hour. The kisses were soft, slow and infused with their own mythic meaning. When they finished, they walked up the adjoining stone path to the other mountain hideaway of the island, Exogi, before retracing their steps and descending to the Bay of Frikes for dinner. It was Virgil's favourite day of the honeymoon.

"Oh, gentlemen," Sir Nigel suddenly interrupted, again, "please come here." He was still standing near the archaeologists' trenches. He sounded a bit forced. A bit peculiar, like he was being held at gunpoint.

As they approached, they could see Sir Nigel, pale as a bleached sheet, pointing at one of the trench coverings. It was clearly quite damaged, as if it had been deliberately pried open with a crowbar or some other manner of leverage tool.

"Could it have been the, ummm," Sir Nigel stammered, "the… earthquake?"

"I do not think so, my friend." Costas sighed. He then trudged up to the opening and reached underneath the covering to see if it would move. He lifted easily and the cover moved as if it weighed nothing at all. The gaping hole was more than large enough without moving the cover for an average-sized man to slip into the trench. Someone had clearly gone into the trench. Recently.

"Costas," Sir Nigel said, with grave panic in his voice. "Do you and the island's police patrol these archaeological sites to make sure no one disturbs these ongoing digs?"

"Yes, my friend, we do," Costas said gravely, "but it is not a thing we do all days. Generally, though, we try to focus more on the living than the dead."

"How often do tourists try to get into these things, Costas?" Virgil asked.

"Mr Colvin, until this moment, this today, I have never known this to happen."

"Well, another crime for you, then?" Sir Nigel said without humour, still clearly worried.

"Nigel," Virgil turned to the historian, "give us your expert opinion here; why would a person — say not the typical tourist — pry into one of these trenches?"

The colour slowly filled back into his face as he considered his response, clearly deliberating quickly, "Well, I suppose a dealer or smuggler of antiquities might want to gain entry. You can still make quite a bit of money in the illegal market for sherds, coins, bronzes and things of that sort. Beyond that, I cannot imagine why anyone would do this."

"Not even for glory?" Virgil asked seriously. His tone was accusatory — it was meant to be. Apparently, not enough cosmic justice had been exacted.

"My God, man!" Sir Nigel stared at him with some amount of alarm and venom, Virgil could not tell which predominated, but he knew his insinuation had clearly bothered the historian. "No one is playing Schliemann these days, least of all me!"

Costas, somewhat lost and looking at Virgil, interjected, "Pardon, Mr Colvin, but do we think Sir Nigel broke into this trench?"

"Now look here, Pantakalas!" Sir Nigel turned his glare on the Greek.

"Calm down, Nigel," Virgil intoned, "if the tourists have never done this, all the possibilities need to be considered. I did not mean to accuse you," he lied, "but I cannot so easily discount the possible explanations."

"Well, I am very decidedly tired of *this*." Sir Nigel indignantly regained some of his composure. "I have spent my day with you men, rendering service and aid for your murder case, and I do not propose to remain here to be accused of petty criminal activity. May we please return to Vathy now?"

"Who said anything about murder?" Virgil asked pointedly.

"That frog-faced windbag at the harbour did! And so did that lieutenant at the cave! You are not trying to suggest I had anything to do with it, are you? I am just a historian for God's sakes!" Sir Nigel's anger was subsiding, slowly, into annoyed bemusement.

"Of course not, Sir Nigel! My friend, Mr Colvin, was just curious — yes, Mr Colvin?" Costas clearly wanted this altercation over with.

"Obviously, Costas, yes" — turning to Blasingame — "Look, Nigel, my apologies if I have offered you some offense here. It has been a long day. I'm sorry, sir." Virgil did feel bad — his emotions from earlier had clearly gotten the better of him.

Sir Nigel brightened at the apology, and the end of the interrogatories, "Do not trouble yourself, Detective. Let us forget it. Vathy?"

Virgil removed the G-6 keys from his pocket and handed them to Sir Nigel. "Please, take my car back to your hotel and leave it there, I will collect it later. Just leave the keys with Katerina."

"You're not going home? It is almost sunset, Detective," the Briton's voice seemed laced with genuine concern.

"Yes, my friend," Costas stepped in, "but we have dinner plans in Frikes this evening. We will walk down. My lieutenant, Kyriakos, will fetch us later. Please give my regards to Katerina, please?"

Sir Nigel smiled. "Of course, Costas. You gentlemen take care of yourselves!"

They all shook hands and then Sir Nigel stalked off towards the dirt path and the parked Mercedes.

The detectives walked back to the walls and scanned Aphales Bay again — still no sign of the *Πολύφημος*. It was nearly eight o'clock, sunset less than half an hour away.

"Mr Colvin, let us get to Frikes, no? I am quite hungry and even thirstier!"

"*Ha!* Costas, I could set a watch by your thirst. But yes, I am hungry too. Let's make a deal; no talking the case until we have some food and drink before us?"

"It is deal!" Costas stuck out his hand.

Virgil shook it firmly.

CHAPTER FOURTEEN
FRIKES

As they made the meandering descent to Frikes Bay, they discussed the weather, the Turkish coup, earthquakes, food and women. The path went first though fields and farm land, trees lined the left and fields opened on the right. Eventually, the stoned terrace steps leading up to the School of Homer and Exogi beyond, re-joined the roads dipping down to the bay. The rest of the walk was through the narrow town that lined the roads to the water. It was quaint and easy walking, but the trees and fields were prettier. Even the cactuses were charming. After thirty-five minutes or so of steady downhill walking, they arrived at the horseshoe waterfront of Frikes, enveloped in the darkness that was almost done dismissing light from the sky. The lights of the restaurants and tavernas were all on. The noise of conversations, laughter and stories told again and again greeted the detectives who had once again sweated through their shirts. The euphoria of the exertion was back and their minds, rested with irrelevant conversation, added to the effect. The bay was full of small and medium-sized sail boats owned by locals, rented by tourists staying in one of the nearby hotels or were the lodging of that special species of Mediterranean tourists who floated around for the season, spending every night in a new lovely port, eating the best food and enjoying the best scenery on earth.

"Costas!" the voice of Panagis Metaxas boomed from the left as they arrived at the sea. The stalky mayor marched upon their flank, glowering in the darkness. "Please tell me you bear news of success!"

"Panagis!" Costas pretended to be happy as well as he could. *After such a long day, he was losing his touch*, Virgil thought. "Not yet, sadly. But I think Mr Colvin and I are getting close. Right, Mr Colvin?"

"Oh, yes… very close, Costas, very, very close!" Virgil lied for his friend while not particularly trying to hide his disdain for the obnoxious mayor.

Metaxas glanced at Virgil Colvin with impatient contempt, before turning his ire back on Costas. "Unacceptable, Costas, unacceptable!"

"Truly, Panagis, there is not much to help it, the case is… complicated," Costas apologised.

"I'm sure! Dead body in the open, no family, no friends, not from here. No one can leave the island and you have unlimited time to question everyone you want. Sounds simple to me, Costas!"

Pantakalas stared silently until the mayor changed the subject.

"What is this I hear about you two harassing François Deflers?" he glared at Virgil as he asked.

"*Ha!*" Costas dropped his charming patience. "We could hardly harass that interloping frog! He came to us in the middle of investigation and yelled and behaved poorly! We did not seek him out! Do not speak to me of this man!" Panagis and Costas carried on in Greek for several more minutes until the mayor threw up his hands and stalked off up the road out of town that the detectives so recently used to make their entrance.

After several moments of silence, watching the stumpy man struggle up the hill out of town, into the darkness, Virgil turned to his put-upon friend. "*Ageri*?" he asked.

"*Nai!*" Costas enthused.

Ageri — in Greek, Αγέρι — was part of the ring of tavernas and restaurants that rounded the mouth of the bay. Once upon a time, Frikes had been part of the northern defensive line of the Venetians. A couple of the stone towers the Venetians used to fire upon raiders and observe the sea still overlooked the bay, providing phantom protection against the incoming ghosts. When the raids ended, during the final Venetian occupation of Ithaca, the islanders who sought refuge in Anogi and Exogi came down from their hills to places like Stavros, Kioni and Frikes. The latter two were now charming stops, especially for seafaring tourists, to enjoy the island with the locals and each other while avoiding 'crowded' Vathy. Many of them never even bothered to venture to places like Marmarospilia, Alalkomenai or the School of Homer. Virgil and Costas dined in Frikes every other week, almost always at *Ageri*, the best restaurant in the town and one of the most noteworthy in Ithaca.

"You going to order?" Virgil asked sheepishly once they were shown to their usual table, right on the water.

"Mr Colvin! You mean you cannot order a meal still? Why are you so afraid of the Ελληνικά? You know my language is lovely! Why do you resist her charms?"

"Because yours is so lovely! Why would I want you to listen to my stuttering butchery of such a pleasant tune?" Virgil smiled, knowing that flattery always did the trick.

"Well, if you insist, but we are going to change this, and soon!"

"Ouzo?" Virgil asked, hopefully, swatting at one of the lumbering wasps they descended upon all the diners at every outdoor table on the island.

"*O-he*!" Costas said firmly. Virgil knew the tone. There would be no changing his mind.

Costas called the waitress over and immediately fell into chatting with her familiarly. Virgil leaned back in his chair to admire Costas in his element. Interpersonal relations were always where Costas excelled. He was a master craftsman when it came to lively, engaging and charming repartee — with women and men, but women especially. On a small island like Ithaca, that was still devout in its Orthodox observance and riddled with gossipers and rumourmongers, one could hardly afford to be a womanising rogue before creating an untenable situation in more ways than one. In many ways, everyone felt that Costas was their friend and a surrogate father of sorts. And in many ways, he was.

Once the conversation ran its natural course, Costas proceeded to order a bottle of wine — always wine at *Ageri*, never ouzo — a local red from Kefalonia. His antagonism to the neighbouring island did not deter Costas Pantakalas from admiring its wine, its food or its women. He then placed an order for tzatziki and bruschetta with fresh anchovies. Finally, he asked for the traditional repellent of wasps for the table, a contained of smoking coffee grounds. The waitress walked away to get their first round going, eventually she might also remember their futile war against the persistent, fat, and slothful winged antagonists.

"Well, Mr Colvin, first pick your entrée and then we talk murder!" Costas smiled slightly.

"Linguine with fresh shrimp, and let's wait for the wine before we get to the murder, OK?"

"Excellent choice, Mr Colvin! Also, excellent idea; wine will get me talking freely! *En-tax-ee!*"[32]

"If only you needed the assist, Costas!" Virgil rolled his eyes and they both laughed.

The waitress arrived with the wine, a bottle of sparkling water, two water tumblers and two wine glasses. Despite only having two hands, she also had the smoking coffee grounds. Somehow, it did not look awkward. She gave each man a healthy pour — she knew them and their habits quite well at this point. She would bring the second bottle, a Rosé, without prompting. Costas placed the order for food, choosing the fresh baby octopus for himself. She went away again, promising appetizers shortly. The wasps were, at best, mildly deterred.

"Well, now we have wine, Mr Colvin. But before murder, one more vice!" Costas smiled as he reached

---

[32] Εντάξει! — OK!

into his pocket to remove a very sturdy cigar holder that had been keeping two prime Cubanos fresh and moist during their day's adventures. He removed them, grabbed the cutter from the other pocket, quickly clipped the ends and handed one to Virgil.

"*Par-a-ka-lo*, Costas![33] I had no idea you thought so far ahead!" It was more flattery — Costas *always* took care of these sorts of things. "What happened to those nasty Nicaraguan things you're always peddling?"

"Please, Mr Colvin! This is a murder investigation — only the best!" Costas lit his cigar with a zippo lighter with a very worn Greek flag etched into it. He slowly rotated the end of the Cubano in the dancing flame, evenly lighting the finest cigar on the planet. He then closed the lighter, puffed flamboyantly several times and handed the incendiary to his friend. Virgil quickly lit his cigar and put the lighter on the table, taking two very long puffs off the Cubano and luxuriating in the very quick sensation the tobacco brought to his famished and mildly dehydrated body. They enjoyed the silence and moon's reflection on the water for a few moments. He thought about how impossible this scene would be back in Chicago. He thought about his wife — the physician; the surgeon — making him rinse his mouth out with Listerine after

---

[33] Παρακαλώ — Thank you

cigars at Ditka's with Dick Borneman. He was content and easy — remembering.

"Well, Mr Colvin, we have food, we have drink, we have cigar — now… murder?"

"Indeed." He grabbed some of the hard, thinly sliced bread and slathered some tzatziki on it, chomping down upon it ravenously. After it was on its way to his stomach, he asked Costas, who was masticating bread and anchovies, "Who did it?"

Costas nearly spat his food out, managing to just save himself, and his friend, the embarrassment of such a faux pas. Once he recovered and ingested the appetizer, he cleared his mouth and said, "Mr Colvin! Please, how can I know that after the very odd day we have just had?"

"Well, I thought maybe you had a guess, or had solved it, you never know," Virgil said, grinning. "But let's do it the systematic way. Who are the most likely suspects?"

Costas put some bread and tzatziki into his mouth, leaned back, chewing slowly, and thought. When he swallowed, he took a deep drink from his glass and then took a long pull from his cigar. He sat silently for a few moments before speaking. "Well, I think the top of the list has to be our one-eyed captain. Both of these men, Mr Wellesley and the Cyclopes, are strangers to this place. They were here for same reason. They got in the way of the one and the other. Mr Wellesley lost. We find the Cyclopes; we solve the case." At that, he drank some more wine and then incongruously put more anchovies in his mouth.

"What about Nikos Kordatos, or Zoe for that matter?" Virgil asked in between gulps of wine.

Now Costas replied quickly, passing the cigar between his lips now and then. "Nikos is a weakling. He talks, talks, talks. He does not do. Zoe is much more the murderer of those two. But! She was loving Mr Wellesley. And how would she move his body? *O-he*, no, I think Nikos and Zoe are no good for murder."

"And Circe?" Virgil now tried one of the anchovy bruschetta morsels before Costas consumed all of them.

"*She* could definitely kill a man, but I cannot think of a reason for why she murders Mr Wellesley. Do you?"

The anchovies were fresh and briny. The yogurt of the tzatziki was local from Stavros, rich and creamy. *Perfect, as always,* Virgil thought. He finished chewing and then pulled on the cigar, rotating it slowly while doing so to keep the ash even. He stared at the red glow of the Cubano for a moment. "Well, Costas" — he blew the smoke while talking — "part of Reggie's mission here had to do with the running of arms to the Turkish opposition. You heard Sir Nigel; the British government is in bed with Gündüz. If Reggie got in the way of the gun runners, whoever they happen to be" — he pulled on the rotating cigar again, exhaling lazily — "and it must have been part of his mission to do so, they would all have a rationale to kill him. If they worked as a group, moving his body would certainly be no trouble."

"A group! Oh no, I had not even thought about that!"

"It is all right, Costas, I am just thinking out loud." He took a healthy swig of the Kefalonian red. It was a little sweeter than he liked for a dinner wine, but it had a punch that felt good after the long day. "This Cyclopes fellow cannot be working alone, we saw him with two others earlier and he was hanging around Circe's for some reason, watching us and everyone else. If he already had all the weapons he was moving, there would be no reason to stop here, and even less reason to lurk and linger around. He is followed by rumour and gossip wherever he goes. People are talking. He must know this. He must be waiting to contact someone, or a group of people. Reggie may not have discovered who all the players were and been taken unawares. He was a spy, but he seemed a bit cavalier — sleeping with Zoe Kordatos — and a bit of a multi-tasker, preoccupied with the mythos of this place on top of his mission."

"What you say makes sense, Mr Colvin, but I do not know how we prove it."

"Yeah, that is certainly tricky, but there is also the matter of another suspect."

"Yes… *him!*" Costas violently pulled on his cigar, emitting an enormous cloud of smoke which he then followed up by draining his glass before refilling it.

"François Deflers presented an alibi, but there is no particular reason to believe it is airtight even if it happens to be true in the main," Virgil spoke gently on that point, drank some more wine, and then continued, "François still had the opportunity to murder Reggie, the proximity and strength to move the body and the motive of preventing Reggie from digging too deeply into whatever it was he and his associates are up to here — aside from a golf course. Given that we don't know what that was precisely means you will have to look through that report we found more thoroughly — enjoy the homework tonight!" He ate the final bruschetta, washing it down with some of the sparkling water.

"So, we have Deflers, we have Cyclopes, we have Circe, we have Nikos Kordatos, we have Zoe Kordatos… am I forgetting someone?" Costas leaned back to enjoy his wine.

"*Ha!*" Virgil said, taking his cigar out of his mouth to flick away the ash into the black water. "Not enough for you, Costas? Should we add Sir Nigel Blasingame just to make it an even number?" He laughed and smoked his cigar in between chortles.

Costas did not laugh. He looked troubled, even mildly annoyed. "You are not serious, are you, Mr Colvin?"

"Well, not really, no. But Sir Nigel is an odd fellow. Probably just because he's an academic who has been living with a myopic obsession for nearly twenty years without vindication — or even really any attention at all. He reacted… how should I put it? Somewhat bizarrely? When I posed some problems in his theory while you were worshipping — and then again in the ruins when he saw the trench had been disturbed. But he is more likely to murder one of the local archaeologists, I think," he finished, chuckling.

"Well, Mr Colvin, you *did* accuse him."

At this point, the conversation paused as the waitress arrived with the food and the carafe of Rosé. The cool night air, the cascading solar reflection off of the moon's dead surface and the sounds of others enjoying themselves made it all seem like it wasn't real. This feeling of falseness had struck Virgil Colvin frequently since he moved to Ithaca. It wasn't an unpleasant feeling. He liked being in this unreal world, but it was still a little off-putting when it suddenly hit him in these moments. He recovered quickly and dived into the linguine and shrimp, while avoiding watching Costas devour the baby octopi on his plate. No matter how often he tried to eat this local delicacy, or saw others eat it, Virgil could not overcome his aversion to the image, sensation and thought of eating that particular cephalopod.

The linguine was perfectly al dente, coated in a butter sauce and fresh herbs. The shrimp were fresh, like everything else on the island; plump and succulent. It was a sturdy repast, the healthy Mediterranean fare that Virgil had so gladly become accustomed to since the move. Occasionally, he missed the Italian beef sandwiches, Chicago-style hotdogs, steaks and deep-dish pizzas of Chicago, but not as often as he thought he would. After eating about a quarter of his portion, and drinking the rest of his wine, Virgil finally replied, "Well, only because I thought he left out a motive that he himself would be tempted by under the right circumstances. His response confirmed it. You only have to read his book — he admits often his willingness to go trampling all over what he insists are the most important archaeological sites on the planet. He should have laughed at my accusation. Instead, he became extremely upset. He knows, as much as he would pretend to be separated from Schliemann, that he is just as motivated by the glory that drove that Prussian dandy. And unlike Blasingame, Blasingame knows that Schliemann *actually* attained the glory, the respect, the fame and all the rest."

"But still," Costas said while chewing through the last of his octopus, "we are not adding him to list, no?"

Refilling his glass with the Rosé, Virgil laughed. "Not yet, no." He suddenly noticed the wasps were gone. Not just mildly deterred, but entirely absent. *A miracle?*

Greek Rosé functioned almost like water on the islands. It was cheap, ubiquitous and was the perfect palate-cleanser. Of course, unlike Greek sparkling water, the Rosé packed a minor alcoholic punch.

As he picked up the glass, his seat began to shimmy and shake while a low rumble permeated the air, drowning out the other noises that died off almost as soon as the shaking commenced. Sudden splashes about a hundred yards from where they were sitting indicated that rocks were cascading down the hills into the bay. From the sounds, some were obviously quite large and possibly from the Venetian towers though it was impossible to tell in the darkness. Screams from some of the moored boats dangerously close to these splashes added to the acoustic terror of the tremor. After what seemed like five minutes, but was only about 30 seconds, the shaking gradually stopped, and the rumbling noise abated. Virgil looked over at Costas, who had calmly smoked his cigar through the entire earthquake while holding his wine out away from his body, managing to spill none of it. The bottle of Kefalonian wine was not as lucky, having slid off the table onto the rocks. Fortunately, it did not break and was already nearly empty.

"Well, Mr Colvin" — Costas exhaled smoke as he spoke — "you are getting the full welcome from Poseidon."

"Indeed, I am — he can stop *now*," Virgil said in all seriousness.

"Mr Colvin, you chose this place known for Poseidon's favour. This is a part of our lives. For all the lovely wonder of my island, it shakes. It shakes almost every year. Sometimes, it shakes very badly."

"I'm sure I will get used to it — it's only my second earthquake, Costas." Virgil downed his glass in one gulp and placed it next to the rest of his linguine — his appetite was gone. He put the cigar back in his mouth and stood up to stretch and to survey the cliffs to the right. As he looked around, he saw a woman approaching them. He quickly turned to Costas and got his attention focused on the figure making her way to their table.

"Ah, Mr Colvin, this could be the ghost in the machine coming to save us!" he whispered.

Virgil smiled at his friend. Then he looked back at Zoe Kordatos, who was dressed in black slacks and shoes, with a Grecian blue blouse accentuating that she still wasn't wearing a bra and that there was a slight chill in the air. When she arrived and said hello, Virgil offered her his chair while he grabbed one of the vacant seats at a nearby vacant table. She did not seem to mind his bourgeois sense of decorum and manners.

"To what do we owe this pleasure, Mrs Kordatos?" Virgil asked, putting the cigar in his mouth to chew for a bit.

"It is Nikos, I am worried about him," she said with only a very vague hint of worry in her voice.

"Why?" asked Costas.

"He is not telling me where he is going when he leaves any more, and he is out at strange hours for long amounts of time."

"Wait, *you* are worried about *him* being dishonest?" Virgil was a little too incredulous, but he couldn't help himself. A lazy wasp meandered by his face, heralding their return.

"Please, Mrs Kordatos," Costas interrupted, "what else?"

"He is having odd people over." As she spoke, she stared a dagger slowly into Virgil Colvin.

"Like who?" Costas followed up.

"Circe, for one. We never consort with rapacious capitalists like her, but, suddenly, she is coming over frequently."

"Whoa," Virgil stopped short. "Is Nikos stepping out with Circe?" He was obviously a little buzzed but did not care as he refilled his Rosé. When he went to pour for Costas, the chief covered his glass.

Zoe glared fire in Virgil's direction. "No. They just talk. And some fisherman. He is missing an eye. He comes over, too."

"What is his name?" Costas asked immediately.

"I do not know. Nikos never uses it. He just calls him 'the fisherman'. He is a strange man."

"What else, Zoe?" Costas pressed forward familiarly.

"He is just talking very bigly, very importantly, saying that events are happening soon that will change everything for everyone. I am frightened, Costas!" There were tears flowing down her cheeks by the end. Costas seemed to buy it. Virgil thought it was an act — poorly performed.

Costas immediately came alongside to offer her a hug, which she accepted. They spoke softly in Greek while they embraced. Virgil blew smoke rings while trying to be unobtrusive, though he hoped that he was failing. After several moments, they disengaged and said their farewells. Zoe Kordatos walked back into the night. Virgil smoked his cigar, now quite close to its end, and admired the moon's illumination on Zoe Kordatos' backside. He found the woman repellent, but there was no denying her some *very* alluring qualities.

"Well, Costas, is the case solved now?" Virgil blew a few more slow smoke rings. The waitress, knowing their habits, brought them separate checks, which they signed.

"Sadly, no. I do not think so, Mr Colvin."

"Oh? Why not?"

"Because, like you, Mr Colvin, I do not believe much of what Zoe Kordatos says."

"Sure, you have eyes, ears, a brain and the rest, but why does she come to squeal on her old man? What good does it do for him or her to have us look more closely at the four of them? Pure balls coming in here like that, though, I will give her that. And how did she know where to find us?" Virgil picked up the wine bottle and dumped the remainder of the cigar inside it. "Whatever their game is, Nikos couldn't have pulled that off in a million years!"

"I must admit, it all puzzles me." Costas dumped his cigar into the bottle as well.

"Well, my thought is that she needs us focused on all of them for some reason, or rather, focused on all of them except her. But it's too late and I'm exhausted" — he yawned at the end of this — "where the hell is your man Kyriakos?"

They waited for another fifteen minutes before Kyriakos came running up, offering profuse apologies to Chief Pantakalas — none to Virgil Colvin. Then he offered the interesting and potentially consequential news that ferry service to Frikes, which could not accommodate the larger ferries that went to Piso Aetos, would resume at some point tomorrow from the mainland to evacuate tourists and Ithacans seeking to avoid the islands until the shaking subsided. Obviously, this could allow potential suspects to escape the island as well. But then came the more immediate bad news, "*Ar-khe-gos*, the quake, *mik-ros*, just now, it caused a landslide at the isthmus. There is no way the road will be cleared until morning. We are trapped here."[34]

"Oh, Kyriakos! We are never trapped in Thiakí! Wait here a moment."

Costas walked towards the pier that ran along the right side of the bay, while Kyriakos sat in his boss' vacated chair. Virgil looked the young man over. Despite being at least thirty years younger than the Chicago PD veteran, it was the boyish Greek gendarme who appeared exhausted.

---

[34] Μικπός — small, little

"Long day?" Virgil asked, remembering his own weariness.

"The longest," he said mechanically.

"Cases, big cases, have the curious effect of slowing time down until it is almost interminable. Every moment seems so consequential, so meaningful, so critical to solving it that they all linger for ages. It is taxing."

"Do you get used to it?" Kyriakos asked.

"Yes, and no," Virgil said unhelpfully. "You get better at managing the sensation and filling the interminable moments with meaningful work on the case. But no, the slowness never changes. Unless you stop doing your job, or stop caring," he added darkly.

"Is that what happened to you?" Kyriakos' damned European bluntness would have been offensive were he not such a green, innocent provincial.

"Sort of, yes." Virgil looked away, at the sea.

From the pier, standing beside a fifteen-foot motorboat whose skipper was untying the mooring ropes and making his vessel ready for the sea, Costas shouted, "Come, Kyriakos, Mr Colvin, we leave for Vathy!"

***

They all boarded the boat and sat down in the aft benches while the motor purred into life and quickly moved the vessel through the Bay of Frikes. Once they had cleared the headlands, the skipper spun the wheel to the right and the they began their southern trip into the Gulf of Molos. They were not going terribly fast, maybe seven or eight knots, but they would be in Vathy Harbour in less than an hour. The water was choppy, and the temperature plummeted at least ten degrees once they left the bay of Frikes. Virgil did not enjoy the sensation.

"Kyriakos," Costas intoned over the sound of the motor, "what happened when you questioned Nikos?"

Kyriakos looked a little nervous as he shouted his answer, "We never find him, *Ar-khe-gos*!"

"What?" Costas yelled. "Why not? Where did he go?"

"We never found out, *Ar-khe-gos*. But he is gone… no one seems to know where!"

"*Po-Po*!" Costas was quiet for a moment, before yelling at Kyriakos again, "When we get to Vathy, please go to Alexis' house and let him know that you and he are going to need to work with Demetrios and Alexandros tomorrow to keep an eye on Nikos and Zoe Kordatos, Circe and the Cyclopes fisherman. If *you* can find *him*!"

"Demetrios and Alexandros! Aren't they working all night?" Kyriakos asked with alarm.

"Not for long, I dismiss them as soon as I get to the station. I will stay at the station tonight. I have work to do," Costas authoritatively roared over the motor. "You understand what I ask you to do?"

"*Nai, Ar-khe-gos!*"

"One more thing, Kyriakos," Virgil said loudly as he fought back oncoming nausea, "you cannot let them leave the island once the ferry service resumes! And don't let them board the *Πολύφημος* either!"

"*Nai*, do not let them out of your sight — try not to be too obvious, yes?" Costas added loudly.

"*Nai, Ar-khe-gos!*"

"Costas," Virgil yelled, breathing as he tried to keep his composure, "Zoe Kordatos… why was she… what do you…" Virgil plunged his head suddenly over the aft-starboard side of the boat and returned his dinner to the sea.

"Mr Colvin, why not wait until solid land, no?" Costas shouted while patting Virgil on the back.

They waited until they arrived and disembarked to resume their conversation. They were in Vathy Plaza again, where Virgil Colvin, Costas Pantakalas and Sir Nigel Blasingame had set off for their exploration of Reginald Wellesley's visitations nearly half a day ago. It seemed both longer ago, and like they were just there. The moon illuminated everything brightly, both from its direct reflection of the sun and from the albedo of reflected moon rays off the surface of the harbour itself. The air was cool and clear and slightly salty.

"I will see you tomorrow, Kyriakos," Costas told his subaltern. "Now go, quickly, to Alexis!"

Kyriakos nodded and ran off, leaving Costas and Virgil alone in the plaza. There were a few locals and tourists out for strolls and smokes. The detectives began to make their way in the direction of the Hotel Familia again.

"Mr Colvin," Costas said after a minute, "we should meet in the Plaza tomorrow morning. At 7. Yes?"

"That sounds good, Costas. What are you planning to do this evening?" The taste and smell of vomit permeated his entire head. While unpleasant, it was not totally unfamiliar of late.

"Read through those reports we find in Mr Wellesley's room," he said pensively. He then noticed where they were headed, and stopped walking. "Mr Colvin, who do you think broke into the trench at *Agios Athanasios*?"

"That is a good question, Costas! We had not really circled back to it yet before Poseidon interrupted us. I was thinking Reggie."

"Mr Wellesley! Why?" Costas looked confused.

"Well, who else? You yourself said no random tourist had ever done such a thing, so that seems unlikely. Circe has a motive, but she's never operated that way before, why is she suddenly starting now? Blasingame might have a motive, but again, he's around these islands all the time, and he now begins to pilfer archaeological trenches? No, neither of them seems very likely. Only the Cyclopes and Reggie were outside variables lately who might do something very unusual, and only Reggie was up there so far as we know — and had some potential motives to do it. Yeah, I think Reggie is the best bet — the issue then is, why? And of course, what — if anything — did he find and remove from the trench? And where did it, whatever it was, if it was, go?" He smiled mischievously at his tired friend. *May as well spread the discomfort around*, he thought.

"Mr Colvin, this is too many questions! I am tired. I am going to go to my office and send my men home to sleep. Then I sleep in my office. Enjoy your bed! Good night, my friend!" He waved and turned around, marching briskly back to the plaza.

Virgil Colvin laughed. He walked to the hotel and entered the front door — noticing that the floor fish tank was now covered with wooden boards. Katerina was behind her bar, looking lovely as ever. When she saw him walking towards her, she hailed him with a greeting and one of her million-dollar smiles. She slid the keys down to him when he got to the bar. "A drink, Mr Colvin?"

"Oh, sure, just a beer please, something Greek." He sat down on a stool, suddenly quite tired.

She placed a Mythos bottle on a napkin in front of him. "On me, Mr Colvin!"

"Oh, no, Katerina! You suffered damage — please, let me pay." He fumbled for his wallet.

"*O-he!* I will not accept your money… *tonight*!" She smiled again, and Virgil stopped resisting.

"Well, thank you, Katerina. I appreciate it. How was your day?" Virgil took a swig of the Mythos. It tasted like a standard American pilsner. *Nice to have the vomit subside a little,* Virgil thought.

"Long and strange!" she said with a smile. "I had to clean up the mess, console guests, extend reservations, refund money and keep people from the room. I was very busy!"

"Someone tried to see the room? Who?" Virgil asked with pure innocence and curiosity covering the serious urgency with which he awaited the answer.

"Oh, it was nothing, François is just paranoid. He said he found out that the British man was trying to stop his project and that he wanted to know why. He tried to charm his way in there, but he is not so charming as he believes!"

"Did he come back yet? We saw him earlier over at Piso Aetos — he seemed a little upset."

"Oh? *O-he*, he has not returned. I was expecting him earlier, but he keeps his own hours most of the time, Mr Colvin."

"I have two questions for you, Katerina, and then I must leave for my villa and my bed. Is that OK?"

"Of course, please, I want to help you and Costas!"

"Good; the first is whether you ever saw the murdered man, Reginald Wellesley, chatting with the other British guest you have here, the tall man, sixties, Sir Nigel Blasingame?"

She thought about it for a moment and then slowly shook her head. "*O-he,* Mr Colvin, only in passing, here at the bar."

"They never chatted at length or about history or the island or archaeology — anything like that?" Virgil persisted.

"*O-he*, I don't think so — at least, I never saw or noticed. So sorry, Mr Colvin." She smiled slightly guiltily.

"Good, thank you, and please forgive this question, but I have to ask it." He took a long drink and then cleared his throat quietly. "Were you staying with François last night? If yes, could you please tell me the times he was with you?" Virgil winced slightly at having potentially caused grave offence.

Katerina smiled lovingly, though she did not blush with any sort of embarrassment, "You do not need to worry about offending me, Mr Colvin. We are both old enough and wise enough not to be offended and embarrassed by things such as this, right?" Virgil nodded, relieved. "Yes, François and I spent part of the evening together, he arrived about eleven last night, and he went back to his room around three this morning. Do you have any other questions, Mr Colvin?"

"Katerina, you are a wonderful tribute to *xenia*, please have a wonderful night!"

"*Kal-ee-nicht-a*, Mr Colvin! It was a pleasure to see you again!" She gave him one more smile for the road. Virgil finished his beer and waved goodbye as he turned to the door.[35]

---

[35] Καληνύχτα — good night

When he arrived at his car, he paused to enjoy the silence of the Ithacan twilight. He took his G-6 back up to his villa. He did not notice any new or additional damage to the villa upon a cursory inspection. He stumbled into his room and crashed into his bed, falling asleep almost instantly, his mind at the mercy of Morpheus.[36]

[36] Morpheus was the minor Greek god of the world of dreams.

CHAPTER FIFTEEN
RETURN TO CIRCE'S WELL

His eyes opened before he realised where he was. Virgil's head did not hurt as much as it had the previous morning, but he had a headache. He woke up in a heap on his bed, still tired. He was reminded of Janet's admonitions about burning the candle at both ends on a case.

"You are going to shave years off your life, Virgil!" she would sternly frown. "Why don't you take better care of yourself on these cases? You know I want to enjoy many years in retirement with you, right?" she would ask, again, and again, and...

The memory made him smile before he remembered the sad irony that it was Janet who died too early, snatched from the happy retirement years they were both looking forward to spending together in places just like this.

Virgil sat up and looked at his watch. It was a quarter past six, and the morning sun blazed through the window. He put some espresso grounds and water into his stovetop maker and quickly whipped up some eggs while pulling a couple of figs from the refrigerator. It was a rather Spartan affair, but he perked up quickly while he waited for the espresso to finish percolating. He quickly showered — and here most of his countrymen would have balked at a long-term relocation to Ithaca. Quick showers were required to live on the island where fresh water was scarce practically the entire year, but especially during the tourist season. Most of the islanders went days, often many days, between full attempts at even a brief rinse. He put on khaki pants, tennis shoes, a Chicago Cubs t-shirt and his Cubs hat with sunglasses. He drank his espresso quickly. Before heading out, he looked at the crack in the corner again. He couldn't decide if it had gotten bigger or not since he first noticed it. He took a picture with his phone.

"Fuck!" he said while looking at the picture for a moment.

He took another look outside to see what sort of exterior damages the villa had sustained from the two quakes the previous day. Aside from the remnants of terra cotta roof tiles in heaps on the ground, he noticed to his dismay that the crack in the corner of the kitchen and the anterior perpendicular wall was also visible on the outside of the villa. "Fuck!" he said again to the universe. He decided to leave the villa to the gods — what else could he do?

He jumped into the car and made his way down into the capital below. When he arrived in the plaza, he could already see Costas gesticulating at the cabbies on the northwest corner. Virgil parked along the south side, on Papoulaki Street, and then strolled leisurely across the plaza to where Costas was holding forth and telling a grand tale of one sort or another. The air was still quite cool from the preceding evening, but there wasn't a cloud in the sky. It was going to be a *hot* day.

As he came closer to Costas and his auditors, he could hear the strident yet melodious cadence of Greek that poured forth from his animated friend in torrents. The assembly of cabbies listened intently, occasionally exchanging nudges and side jokes or simply laughing along with the story Costas was telling. They may have heard the chief tell the same tale a hundred times, but they were enthralled by it regardless. One did not need to understand a word of it to recognise their pleasure at being so entertained. Some of the cabbies' eyes drifted in Virgil's direction as he came close enough to be obviously trying to join them. Costas stopped to turn to his friend, smiling as he recognised Virgil's unshaved face.

"Ah! Mr Colvin! You are precisely on time! Very good! We have business. One moment, please." He turned back to his dawn constituents and quickly pattered off what seemed like several paragraphs that garnered both laughter and the disappointed sighs and grunts of those who wanted more. They all shook hands and then Costas came alongside Virgil Colvin, grabbing his elbow lightly, starting them towards the Megaro Drakouli. "So, I have news, Mr Colvin!"

"Yes? So do I. You want to go first?"

"No, you go, I am the actual policeman here." He winked.

"Very well. Katerina cannot account for François' whereabouts all evening and morning of the murder. He was free of her before eleven p.m. and after three a.m. Between three and five in the morning was more than enough time to murder Reggie and dump him at the statue before the earthquake brought you and others outside."

"That *is* interesting," Costas said in a controlled tone. "Have you discovered anything else, Mr Colvin?"

"Is it? François, if he is the murderer, certainly would have known that his alibi with Katerina was not going to be terribly useful. I actually think the information just as easily lessens the chance of his involvement as anything. Say what you want about the guy, but he's not a fool. If he killed Reggie, then he would know precisely when he needed to have an alibi — the fact that he offered an alibi that actually leaves him all the time he needed to kill Reggie and move his body either makes him incredibly and suddenly careless or disappointingly innocent," he concluded in solidarity with his friend.

"Mr Colvin, I notice that every time we discuss the case, you offer ideas or thoughts about the suspects only to reverse course and get back to where you started. It is, *sig-no-me*, my friend, annoying!" Costas suggested gently, but no less seriously.[37]

"Well, Costas, what the hell do you expect? This case is a fucking mess. Back in Chicago, we used to call cases like this a graduate of Chicago public schools."

"What does this mean, Mr Colvin?"

"It's not going anywhere anytime soon, and it's going to continue to be our problem indefinitely."

Costas still seemed confused, but Virgil moved on.

"It is possible that he is terribly careless, but from what I have observed of him, he is not. A hot-head and a passionate man in many ways? Yes. Careless and stupid? No."

"Well, it is still annoying!" Costas said definitively. For several paces, he was quiet and then he resurrected his question in his old friendly manner, "Did you discover anything else?"

"Yes, but I'm not done with François yet. Before he came to scream at us yesterday, he somehow discovered that Reggie was here to observe him or interfere with his business in some way — or so he told Katerina — and then she caught him trying to get into Reggie's room!"

"*Thav-ma*! Mr Colvin, the case — what more can we hope for?"[38]

"Well, it is incriminating, no question. The problem, of course, is that if François murdered Reggie,

---

[37] Συγγνώμη — pardon me/I'm sorry
[38] Θαύμα — wonderful, miraculous

he had plenty of time to go to the room and find the report or anything else he wanted. Why wait until so much later, when it might cause just this problem?"

"*Po-po*! Again, Mr Colvin!" Virgil laughed at the accusation, understanding his friend's frustrations. "Is this all you have found?" Costas asked when the laughter ended.

"It seems that, at least so far as Katerina knows, that Sir Nigel's interactions with Reggie were perfunctory at their deepest."

"You asked her about Blasingame? Why?" Costas was legitimately confused.

"Just checking on what he told us at the cave. He had the same opportunity as François. You want to be thorough in these things. Relax, Costas," — Virgil chuckled at the perplexed annoyance of his friend — "he seems not to have been lying, so that certainly cuts in his favour. But what the hell was Zoe Kordatos doing out at Frikes last night, talking to us? I still don't understand it, do you? What have you found out?"

"Zoe Kordatos is playing a game, Mr Colvin. I do not know what the game is, like you. As for the others," Costas said as they passed the Megaro Drakouli — they were now clearly headed towards Circe's Well — "the reports that we found in Mr Wellesley's room were *very* interesting, Mr Colvin. I think we have a gun smuggling syndicate in Thiakí!"

"And how many of our suspects are involved?" inquired Virgil, not particularly surprised by this news given that they essentially deduced this the day before. *Hadn't they?*

"All of them!" Costas said, stopping in his tracks and beaming with self-satisfied pride, knowing he had caught Virgil off-guard after lulling him with some non-news. At this point, Costas picked up his radio and called out to Kyriakos. They exchanged a few cryptic messages in Greek, and then Costas replaced the radio.

"All of them?" Virgil asked, curious as to what Costas was up to, but allowing his friend to reveal his purposes at his leisure. "What, even François? What possible reason could he have for being involved in running weapons out of eastern Europe to a Turkish coup?" Virgil was befuddled.

"Well, the short version of the story is that the investors for Project Odysseus include a lot of Eastern-European and Russian oligarchs — lots of money and lots of antagonism towards a regionally strong and aggressive Turkey. *Monsieur* Deflers manages not only good aspects of the business, he takes care of the black parts as well. Having Mr Wellesley around here, an allied agent of Gündüz, would give him quite a motive, no? What do you think, Mr Colvin?"

"That's some good work, Costas. Though it still jibes with the idea of François trying to search the room after someone else murdered Reggie. Why are we heading to Circe's Well?" Virgil did not like the sensation of being led through the case by his friend, whom he adored, but who never had worked a murder case until this moment. It was like Virgil had lost his moorings and was adrift. He wasn't quite queasy yet, but it wasn't a pleasant sensation by any means. He nauseously remembered the boat from the night before.

"Ah, Mr Colvin, on that you shall see when we arrive!"

He was so pleased with himself as he confidently strode along Drakoulis Street that he was mildly annoying, Virgil thought to himself. He hoped he wasn't as annoying when he knew something that Costas did not, but he quickly assumed that he was and smiled.

As they neared the front of Circe's Well, it suddenly became quite clear why Costas had led them here. In front of the taverna, the proprietress was engaged in a very animated conversation with a very well-dressed and well-formed man with luxuriant black hair, sprinkled with a little grey. He was just as animated in the discussion, or was it an argument? Circe saw the two detectives first and quickly succeeded in getting François Deflers to halt his end of their exchange, which he did mere moments before turning and being hailed by Costas Pantakalas.

"*Kal-ee-mair-a*, friends! What a great coincidence to find you both here! I had no idea you knew each other — is this not convenient, Mr Colvin?" He turned to Virgil and whispered, "You see?"[39]

---

[39] Καλημέρα — good morning

"Yes, quite," Virgil said subtly. "Good morning, Circe! François."

Both Circe and François seemed entirely on their heels with the appearance of the detectives. Aside from stammered good mornings and *kal-ee-mair-a*'s, neither of them ventured much more at first.

Then François hissed, "Well, Pantakalas, have you wrapped up this case?"

"*Monsieur* Deflers, I came here to talk to you about that! Circe as well!" Costas beamed and smiled broadly. His charm took on a malevolent cast.

François Deflers was clearly simmering with anger now. "You dare to talk to me in an accusatory tone? You ought to talk to your mayor, policeman."

"Oh, Panagis? He and I spoke this morning on the old phone line. About what would you like us to speak?" Costas inquired with an irritating faux innocence.

"*Merde*! I have had enough of this bullshit! If you want to talk to me, policeman, with or without your mutt, here" — pointing now at Virgil — "call my lawyer. I already gave you my whereabouts!"

"Yes," Virgil joined in, "sadly, that alibi leaves you free during the exact moment of the murder and the disposal of the body."

François looked suddenly a bit alarmed. "But you cannot possibly believe I killed this man — I barely even talked to him! Why would I kill a stranger? I don't hate the Brits that much or else I would have to kill that giant historian, too!"

"What did you do once you left Katerina's room?" Virgil asked.

"I went to my room, showered and slept until the earthquake woke me up!" François exclaimed with exasperation. He still couldn't stop himself from briefly managing a smirk at Costas.

"Can anyone vouch for that? Did you see anyone as you went from Katerina's room to your own? Did you hear anything?"

"*Merde*! Does the dog do all the work, policeman?" he asked Costas who simply shrugged with a smile. "No, no one was out in the hotel. I did not see or hear anyone and as far as I know, no one saw or heard me. Now, unless you have some manner of evidence connecting me to this man, I am going to the isthmus. Are you stopping me, or no?" he asked, looking at Costas again.

"You are free to go, *Monsieur* Deflers" — Costas bowed his head politely before adding — "*for now*."

"Just one more thing, François" — Virgil was pleased to be able to channel his inner Lieutenant Columbo — "Why did you try to gain entry into Reginald Wellesley's room yesterday?"

François froze. He was clearly trying to formulate a careful response. "I was told that this man was spying on me. I wanted to know why. You two had already been in the room, so I assumed it would be acceptable to have a look. I did not actually get into the room. So, no crime contemplated, attempted or committed." François had regained his suave confidence.

"And who informed you that this man was spying on you?" Virgil asked.

"I have friends in high places," he said with smug insouciance, "beyond that, again, my lawyer is *always* available for you. Now" — he sneered — "may I leave?"

"*For now*," Costas repeated.

"*Merde*!" the acerbic Gaul blasted. He marched angrily to his black Elysée, jumped in and sped off with the squealing rubber of suddenly engaged tires.

"God, that guy's an asshole," Virgil declared as they watched him disappear down Drakoulis Street.

Now they looked to the enigmatic taverna operator who had quietly receded into the background during the back and forth with François Deflers.

Costas fired the opening salvo, "Circe, my dear, how do you know this unpleasant man?"

"Costas! Everyone on this island knows François and what he is up to!" Circe replied defiantly — and correctly.

"Certainly, but we do not all argue with this man early in the morning, before business," Costas calmly parried.

"*Ha,* isn't that what you two were just doing with him?" Again, defiant; again, correct. "He and I have business, a disagreement about business, that is all. It has nothing to do with your investigation." Circe was not to be outflanked easily.

"Well, Circe, my dear, I will have to judge that. This man, *Monsieur* Deflers, is a suspect in a murder in this city. I must ask you again, what is your business with this man?" Costas asked quite firmly.

"He is digging up the isthmus, *Agros Laertou*, to build his hotel and golf greens — I wanted to have access to the spot before all the saintly archaeologists showed up. We were arguing about it" — she smiled beguilingly — "you cannot blame a girl for trying, can you, Costas? Detective?" She alternated her entrancing gaze between the two men.

The story did have the ring of truth to it. It might very well be just as she said it was. Without something more, it was hard not to accept her admission of foiled law-breaking (unauthorised antiquities acquisition, dealing, etc., had been a moderately serious crime in Greece since the late-19 century). Costas moved onto a different, though possibly related subject.

"What do you know about the illegal destruction of the trench protections at *Agios Athanasios*?"

Circe looked puzzled and alarmed. She thought for a moment before answering, "This is the first I have heard of it. What was taken?" she asked.

"We have no idea — we only just discovered the sabotage yesterday," Costas added. "But you know nothing? 'Marcus' did not mention this? He did not go there looking for some sort of object? *For you?*"

"He did not tell me anything about this, Costas, I swear it!"

Costas looked at Virgil, who shrugged.

"The one-eyed fisherman who was waiting in your taverna yesterday, the master of the *Πολύφημος*, you know him?" Costas continued the interrogation in his authoritative tone.

"Yes, I know him — *I* know all the mariners and *they* know me, Costas. And *you* know this!"

"Good! I do know this, and I am pleased you do not lie to us this time! Tell us what you know about him — what is his name? What does he fish? Why is he here? How long? Everything you know, please." Costas was not begging.

"Why do you not ask him yourself?" Circe smiled — she knew the answer already.

"Because the man is a ghost!" Costas exclaimed. "And why hunt a ghost when I have the witch?" Circe's smile disappeared at this reference to her namesake.

"Costas! That was beneath you!"

"Maybe it was, but please, answer the questions I ask."

"I will not," Circe replied defiantly.

Costas was caught off-guard by this reaction and stood there in quiet shock. Virgil picked up the fumble. "And why would you not answer such innocent questions from the constituted legal authority on this island?"

"Because I know this man has done nothing to your precious victim, Mr 'Marcus'," she said with biting gusto, "and I will tell you this. The man you seek, the master of the *Πολύφημος*, he is a true Greek patriot! He has devoted his life to *El-la-tha*, to the ancient fight against her enemies. He is a blessed man. I would be forever cursed if I were to betray such a blessed one. I will not, no matter what!" Circe's eyes blazed with passion and conviction. She had, somehow, become even more mysterious than before.[40]

"Circe!" Costas returned. "This man threatens to bring ruin on this island! Ruin on this country! We cannot have this activity here! You know this, no?"

"The mission of this man is sacred. The enemy of *Ελλάδα* will fall and all those who stood on the right side will share the blessing, Costas. You know *this*, no?"

Costas looked crestfallen, but responded after several moments. "Circe, you know I will have to stop this man. Please spare us the possibility of unpleasantness, of injury to someone, with your cooperation? Please?" He was genuinely concerned for Circe rather than anyone else, including himself.

"I cannot, Costas." She stood firm without apology. "And, please, leave this man alone. I would hate to see something happen to anyone in Thiakí. To *you*, especially!"

---

[40] Ελλάδα — Greece

Costas did not take the implicit threat well. "Circe! We have been friends, this is why I have been nice, but you are withholding information in the investigation of a murder. You need to know that you are placing yourself in jeopardy. I can arrest you as a material witness. You can be prosecuted. You can go to jail. You can lose this lovely and beloved taverna." He sounded quite melancholy at the last bit.

"So be it, Costas," she said flatly. If anything, she was even more redoubtable than before.

"Circe," Virgil interjected, "we obviously don't want anything bad to happen to anyone else, but we need to talk to this man. Might you not at least suggest where we might go to find him without yourself being the author of what happens when we leave you here?"

"Talk to Zoe Kordatos," she said without any softening.

"Zoe?" Virgil asked. "Not Nikos?"

Circe relaxed from her ramparts and let out a cathartic and echoing laugh that suggested Virgil had unintentionally told the world's greatest joke. She kept laughing, and laughing, and laughing. It must have lasted twenty seconds or more before it began to subside and she was able to compose herself well enough to speak. "You two are professional detectives?"

She burst into laughter again and turned towards her taverna, disappearing through the front door. They could still hear her cackling for a while after she was gone and they looked at each other while they listened, puzzled. More, they were both annoyed to not be in on the joke.

"What do you suppose that meant?" asked Virgil, after a minute or so.

"Why do we not go find out, Mr Colvin?"

CHAPTER SIXTEEN
RETURN TO KKE

The stroll back to the headquarters of the Greek Communist Party in Ithaca was brief. The cool air of the morning had not dissipated in the warmth of the sun's glare quite yet, but it was noticeably warmer than it had been when they walked out of the plaza only a half hour or so earlier. The building was as ramshackle as ever, still the most fitting monument Virgil could imagine for one of the least compelling and morally hollow political movements of the last century. As they neared the door, they could hear a low electronic hum emanating from the interior. They knocked on the door and announced themselves. The noise ceased. They knocked again. Nothing. Then the noise resumed. They stood listening for several moments until Virgil Colvin suddenly realised what they were listening to. He tried to open the door, but it was locked.

"Costas, can I break through this door? Do I have your permission? There is evidence being destroyed in there!"

"If it is as you say, Mr Colvin" — Costas backed away to give Virgil space — "but, I hope you are correct. I will be answering for it forever if you are mistaken. The paperwork!"

Virgil backed away from the door a few paces. He took a breath and then took a quick step to the door before hiking up his left leg, his foot landing squarely to the immediate right of the door's handle and locks. The rickety barrier immediately yielded, smashing away from the lock and crashing into the interior wall as it flew perpendicular to the door jamb. Costas immediately rushed into the KKE building, Virgil following. They saw the paper shredder on top of the desk at the back of the front room, papers were disappearing into its teeth as they entered.

A stunned Nikos Kordatos stood looking at his uninvited guests. In his hands were papers ready for the shredder, but his mouth stood open and he was frozen in place. Costas made his way to the shredder quickly, yanking the plug violently from the wall. He then slapped Nikos Koradatos across the face, hard. The frightened and already quite diminutive man somehow shrank further as he dropped the papers across the desk and floor while retreating into his chair behind him.

"Nikos!" Costas said in a low shout as the prelude to dressing the communist leader down in a flurry of incomprehensible and angry Greek paragraphs. Occasionally, the bespectacled little man nodded, or quietly muttered a *Nai*, or *O-he*. The 'conversation' lasted several minutes before Nikos Kordatos regained some of his composure and stood up, still behind the desk, and began making his own impassioned case. Again, for Virgil, the performance was in the non-verbals and the tone, rather than the meaning of the actual words both men used.

In some ways, he imagined that this conversation paralleled the famous encounter between Odysseus and the hideous Thersites at the Greek camp outside Troy in the second book of Homer's *Iliad.* Most modern scholars tended to view that encounter as emblematic of the undemocratic nature of Homer's heroes.

In this modern parallel, Costas was not going to resort to ruthlessly beating the powerless civilian for disobeying his authority — but he was going to assert that authority and apply acceptable force if necessary. Kordatos, like Thersites, sneered at the detectives and obviously was engaging in accusing invective while his arms, hands and fingers flailed this way and that. Sometimes, he looked squarely at Virgil before turning and pointing with rhythmic motions at Costas who now took his turn as listener — though he did not interrupt with answers. It also did not seem like he was invited to do so.

When Nikos seemed finished, Virgil asked Costas, "Was any of this anything I need to know right now?"

"Not really, Mr Colvin," Costas said, turning towards him, looking around at the drab office for the first time. There were flyers, posters, pamphlets and other literature collected in disorganised piles everywhere. There was a portrait of Karl Marx on the wall behind Kordatos, and another of the Greek communist leader of the resistance to fascist German and Italian occupation in the 1940s, Athanasios Klaras, on the perpendicular wall to the left of the front door. It did not appear the place had been thoroughly cleaned in many months, or possibly years. It smelled of dust, sweat and stale smoke.

"Well, have you asked him about the fisherman yet? Or where Zoe is?" Nikos glared at Virgil at the mention of his wife's name.

This started another round of cacophonous speech between Costas and Nikos as they went back and forth in a much steadier dialogue, speaking simultaneously as Greeks so often did, as different from their competing harangues as the two men were in the eyes of their neighbours. After several minutes of this, the conversation ended, and Costas removed handcuffs from his belt and walked over to Nikos announcing what must have been the Greek version of a Miranda warning. He placed the cuffs on Nikos' hands without putting his arms behind his back in the familiar American fashion and put him back into the chair with his hand firmly on Nikos' shoulder. The small leader of the KKE sat down, his face now a steady blank.

"Please, Mr Colvin, can you help me find a box of some sort to impound these papers and the shredded bits?" Costas inquired, looking around the dumpy interior for such a receptacle as he did so. They scoured the front room before finding two small boxes in the pantry holding a few old cans of vegetables and boxes of dehydrated noodles and rice. They dumped these contents onto the floor unceremoniously before sweeping the papers on the desk into the boxes. Virgil removed the top of shedder, shaking lose the few long strands of paper that had yet to fall away. As he turned the shredder's bin upside down into the other box, Costas was on the floor, collecting all the single pieces of paper that had fallen from the desk — his back was to the front door.

At that moment, a figure appeared in the doorway. Virgil looked to see who it was. His eyes took a moment to adjust as the sunlight outside the door created a disconcerting corona around the figure, making it appear as a formless shadow or silhouette rather than a defined person. Just as his eyes adjusted to compensate for the light, the figure bolted out of the door quickly. Virgil dropped the bucket on the floor as he sprinted into the street without bothering to say anything at all to Costas.

As he flew onto Telemachou Street, he quickly turned to the right, sprinting in the same direction as the Cyclopes fisherman. Fortunately, there was not a street or alley to have ducked into during the momentary delay when Virgil lost sight of the fleeing one-eyed mariner. The Cyclopes was trying to use the downhill to his advantage, avoiding the first turn to the left in order to turn right at the next opportunity, continuing the descent back into Vathy Plaza. Virgil surmised he was trying to get to his boat and thanked his lucky stars he had put on his tennis shoes that morning. He ran at top speed, gaining steadily on the sea legs of the Cyclopes. When the alleged fisherman got to the right turn towards the plaza, Virgil had caught up and was right on his heels.

In another two or three strides, Virgil braced himself for the open-street tackle he was about to make as the early morning walkers and businesspeople watched the two men race by. Lunging forward, Virgil grabbed a hold of the man's torso and pulled to the left as he let gravity assist his tackle. Buddy Ryan would not have been terribly impressed, but it got the job done. They crashed violently onto the paved road and rolled a couple of times, but Virgil did not loosen his grip on the man's body.

He noticed, while holding on through the scraping of the ground and the violent initial roll, that the man was seemingly made of steel. He hid a tremendously compact bulk beneath his jacket, and it was all muscle. Running him down was one thing, grappling with him would be quite another if he decided to fight it out. As it turned out, the Cyclopes took the worst of the crash to the street, which broke his fall with his face. He turned the scarred side of his head to the ground in the second before impact, wisely protecting his remaining eye from damage, but still seriously stunning him and scraping a swathe of skin from the side of his head.

Disoriented, face bleeding and stinging badly, the Cyclopes was not prepared to contest Virgil's quick moves once that came to a halt. This allowed Virgil to position himself on top of the downed mariner with one knee pressing on the centre of his upper back, the other one on his left arm, which was pinned close to his body. All the while he held the right arm of the Cyclopes firmly behind the man's back in such a way that he could snap the limb if he needed to.

He figured, however, that the Cyclopes would know the peril of losing any more access to limbs, and faculties once he realised the exact situation he was in. The only problem Virgil had now while he caught his breath and kept the man's arm taught was that he couldn't go anywhere. With no handcuffs, he couldn't afford the risk of getting up. He just had to remain there, awkwardly positioned over this potentially dangerous grappler of a man.

"Well, shit," Virgil muttered. He nodded to passersby and gawkers. More and more of the latter appeared with each moment. People were talking to each other. It was only a matter of time before they began to ask Virgil why he was holding a seemingly innocent man in such a way. *Where the hell was Costas?* he thought.

The man began to regain his bearings and Virgil could feel the strength begin to test the limits of his confines tentatively at first and then powerfully enough to cause Virgil some minor difficulty in maintaining his leverage advantage.

"Hey, cut that out!" he said in a scolding voice while he tweaked the man's arm a bit to communicate his meaning, in case he didn't understand his language or tone. Apparently, the pain this caused had the desired effect as the Cyclopes grunted and stopped moving.

"Do you need help, Mr Colvin?" Costas grinned as he walked leisurely towards them, another pair of cuffs dangling from his left hand.

"Hey, you left Kordatos alone?" Virgil tweaked the arm again for good measure, in case the man thought Virgil was distracted. The Cyclopes groaned a bit to register his complaint and the troubling sensation of knowing a person could break your arm without there being anything you could do about it.

"No, no, Kyriakos was not far behind you. He was following our friend here." Costas put the first cuff around the wrist of the arm Virgil was holding onto, and then Virgil got up, grabbing the other arm and pinning it behind the Cyclopes' back as Costas completed the vice. "When he saw you run out of the office, he looked inside and I told him to keep an eye on Nikos, before I come to find you. We seem to be catching all sorts of fishes today, Mr Colvin! Everyone is planning meetings, and no one invites us!"

"*Ha!*" Virgil and Costas heaved the Cyclopes to his feet. Costas quickly announced his legal rights before Virgil resumed, "It must be me, Costas, because you're the most charming man in Ithaca. Also, I'm a mess!" He looked down at the holes torn in the left leg of his khakis where he had gone down first. His elbows were scraped and scratched up, bleeding superficially. His left knee also throbbed a bit from the fall, causing a slight limp in his gait initially as they began walking back to the KKE with their new prisoner. When they arrived, Costas took charge of both arrested men while Virgil and Kyriakos finished filling the boxes with papers and shredded scraps. The five of them all marched up Enmeou Street to the station. While it was uphill, the distance was less than a hundred yards. When they arrived, Costas put Nikos in a detention room — he was already demanding his attorney (*How bourgeois of him,* thought Virgil) — and escorted the fisherman into his own office, planting him in the corner of the room opposite Costas' desk.

When he came outside the office, he looked at Virgil, Kyriakos and the curious eyes of Ariadne Konstantinos. "Please, Kyriakos, tell Alexis find Zoe Kordatos, immediately. Once you do that, then you and Alexandros go to the *Πολύφημος* and search it for weapons and other relevant evidence. Go, now!"

"*Nai, Ar-khe-gos*!" and off the young lieutenant went quickly, still excited by the major arrests and action of the morning.

"Ariadne, dear" — Costas turned to his very pregnant officer — "please get the coffee going, yes? Then, please begin these documents" — pointing at the boxes. "Start with the ones that are not shredded — we will deal with shredded ones later. Please take notes and organise them by sequence or category, whatever makes more sense. I will get you help soon!"

Then, turning to Virgil and with a creeping and broad smile spreading across his face, Costas asked the question he had been restraining himself from posing since they cuffed the Cyclopes, "Mr Colvin, are you ready to find out who this man is?"

CHAPTER SEVENTEEN
VATHY POLICE STATION

Good police work, of course, delayed the long-awaited conversation with the master of the *Πολύφημος*. As Virgil Colvin had related to Costas Pantakalas over many glasses of ouzo during the past six months, you should never rush into a major interrogation of a principal suspect until you knew as much as you could. Such a delay would make the questions better, more pointed and more relevant. Such a delay would allow the interrogator to know more about what answers were lies and deceptions, and which answers were truths or at the very least plausible. Finally, such a delay allowed the suspect to worry and panic — not knowing what was in store for them as the interminable minutes passed by with their excruciatingly slow regularity. So, instead of rushing into the interrogation blind, they left the one-eyed mariner locked in the chief's office while they drank coffee and offered aid to Ariadne as she sifted through the papers that had not been shredded by the island's vanguard of the people's revolution.

The documents seemed to be in some manner of coded shorthand. The numbers seemed clear enough, but they were associated with seemingly random letters. The contents of a typical piece of paper that had not met the teeth of the shredder appeared as follows:

Φ — 134

Π — 28

Θ — IIII II

Ψ — 6

There was no explanatory information about what the Greek letters referred to, or what the numbers themselves referenced — nor why some of them were designated in the Roman numbering system. The other papers appeared potentially relevant, between the Thiakí KKE and the main KKE HQ in Athens. There was no obvious smoking gun about weapons or Turkey or coups in the documents — if anything, the documents appeared to be excruciatingly boring and mundane. Perhaps there was a code? Maybe the numbered documents provided a key to interpreting these letters? Why they existed as letters rather than emails was curious. The KKE represented ideas and aspirations of the last century, but they had a website — certainly they could use email, right? In addition, they were not addressed to Nikos Kordatos specifically, but to 'Thiakí KKE'. Whether that was a mechanism to avoid individualism in a collectivist enterprise, or a deliberate swipe at Nikos as a leader worthy of being named, was unclear. All of these possibilities and questions, among others, they discussed while allowing the mysterious

Cyclopes and the insipid Kordatos to stew in their respective rooms.

After a few hours talking, working and drinking coffee, they had not gotten much information from these documents. Kyriakos returned to the station, hopefully with some more relevant and illuminating clue. Costas went to confer with him quietly near the entrance. He seemed somewhat annoyed and perplexed. He issued some commands and Kyriakos left. Costas came back to the desk where the American and the pregnant Ithacan were working.

"Zoe Kordatos is disappeared," he announced clumsily.

"What?" Virgil responded, sipping his coffee. "How?"

"Demetrios was following her this morning and lost her in the confusion of the fisherman's reappearance and arrest. They did not tell me earlier because they were hoping to find her and not have to tell me," Costas said, with obvious annoyance in his voice.

"But where could, or would, she go?" Virgil asked.

"They have no ideas, they still look," Costas said, dejectedly taking his seat at the desk.

"Well, I'm sure she'll turn up, Costas, don't worry!" Virgil reassured his friend who was obviously despondent about this reversal. Virgil knew, however, that Zoe Kordatos would only reappear when she chose to do so. Whatever game she was playing, she was currently winning.

"We did get good news, though" — Costas brightened — "we have the *Πολύφημος*!"

"That's fantastic, Costas! Was there anything on it? Or anyone?"

Costas looked to the entrance of the station, which opened seemingly with the power of his gaze, and in marched Kyriakos, Demetrios, Alexis and Alexandros, carrying a couple of large crates in two-man tandems. The crates were made of military-green-coloured wooden planks. They had no markings. Costas' men set the boxes down behind the front desk where Ariadne was stationed on normal days. Demetrios used the crowbar atop the crate that he and Alexis set down and pried open the lid. Once he and Alexis removed the lid, the contents were instantly recognisable as Model 1974 Kalashnikov automatic rifles, about a dozen from the looks of it. They looked greasy and new. The crate corners each had a tall ammunition box. Alexandros and Kyriakos removed the lid from their crate, revealing two RPG-7 launchers and ten single-stage grenade cartridges.

"This was *all*?" Costas said, surveying the firepower that just made him the most powerful warlord in Western Greece.

"*Nai, Ar-khe-gos*!" replied Kyriakos.

"Good, Kyriakos, you need to find Zoe Kordatos and bring her here quick! As quick as possible. Alexis, please assist your wife with the documents. Demetrios, please find Circe and bring her here as well.

Alexandros, find and follow François Deflers, do not arrest him. Stay in contact with radio, yes?"

All of his deputies acknowledged his orders and immediately followed Costas' directives. While Demetrios, Alexandros and Kyriakos all marched out quickly, Alexis strolled over to his wife. He looked over her shoulder as she took notes and worked. He leaned over and kissed her head and then her lips as she smiled up at him. Watching, Virgil Colvin thought of his own wife's death, at their home in Chicago's northside. He had held her hand and kissed her forehead as she died, tears rolling down his face in simultaneous grief and relief — and then guilt for the latter feeling. It had all been so peaceful and serene at the end; had anyone walked in, they would have thought he was only kissing her as she slept. Those last two weeks had been impossibly hard — he had help from Janet's sister and a home hospice nurse — but he hadn't thought about it since, until this moment. *Stupid memories!* He didn't even realise he was crying, there, in the Vathy Police Station.

"Mr Colvin, are you feeling all right?" Costas pulled him out of the melancholy reverie.

"Ummm, yes, fine" — Virgil was lying only to himself, there was no way Costas believed him — "shall we talk to Nikos?"

"*Nai*" — Costas let his friend pretend, and then pretended not to notice the quick wiping of his tears — "but I do not expect he speaks!"

They walked into the holding room where they had left Nikos Kordatos. He was standing in mid-pace, still with handcuffs on. He immediately laid into Costas in a storm of Greek invective that quickly filled up the rest of the station before Virgil could close the door. Costas offered to undo the restraints, which seemed to calm Nikos down a little. Once the cuffs were removed, he rubbed his wrists and obviously asked Costas for a cigarette because the chief produced a pack from his pants pocket and gave one to Nikos before passing him his Greek flag zippo. Once Nikos had a few drags from the cigarette, he sat down, and calmly said a few words to Costas. Costas then turned to Virgil Colvin.

"He wants to know where is Zoe."

"Don't tell him we don't know where she is; ask about the fisherman and the arsenal," Virgil suggested.

Costas, who now lit his own cigarette and left it in his mouth, turned back towards Nikos and leaned in to question him about the fisherman and the boat's cargo. From the body-language and repetitive use of '*O-he*', Virgil figured they were going to go nowhere fast with Nikos Kordatos. He opened the room's door and went back into the station to get some air. He didn't mind the smoking; he just hadn't really calmed down from his melancholy run down memory lane. He closed his eyes and breathed deeply, then again. At the end of a long second exhale, Costas' hand touched his left shoulder lightly. Virgil turned around and opened his eyes.

"How are you now, Mr Colvin?"

"Better, thank you, Costas."

"*Ve-vay-os*, my friend."[41]

"Did he say anything?"

"Only that he knows nothing. Doesn't know the fisherman. Doesn't know the boat. Doesn't know the guns. Only he knows he wants his lawyer, and his lawyer lives in Tripolis, works for the party. Won't say anything else until the lawyer arrives."

"Can we hold him?" Virgil asked, not really knowing if the laws of Greece paralleled those of England, or France, or the United States, or some completely different legal system.

"Oh, yes, at least for a few hours — longer if these two find something we can use!" Costas said this while walking to the desk where Ariadne was trying to work while Alexis lightly touched her resting left hand with his right hand's fingers, slowly moving back and forth. Costas smacked the back of his head and said something by way of mocking reprimand in Greek. Alexis picked up some papers and tried to at least appear busy. Ariadne giggled and smiled at her adoring husband.

"Shall we finally talk to that fellow in there?" Virgil asked, pointing at Costas' door.

"Well, we certainly have much evidence here" — he waved at the heavy weaponry — "*nai*, let us talk to the mystery mariner of Thiakí!" Costas led the way to the office and opened the door.

---

[41] Βεβαίως — certainly

As the detectives entered, they both separately noted the remarkable fact that the fisherman appeared not to have moved since they left him there hours earlier. The Cyclopes turned to the detectives, expressionless, as Costas took his own seat behind the desk while Virgil closed the door and remained slightly behind and to the left of the captive.

"*Pos se len-eh*?"[42] Costas asked, while examining irrelevant papers on his desk to look only mildly interested in the expected answer.

No answer from the Cyclopes.

"*Pos se len-eh*?" Costas asked his name again, this time staring into his eye directly.

The blood on his face had long ago coagulated, and he looked quite grizzly and threatening, but he said nothing. His face made no expressions at all. The eye simply stared back at Costas, blinking with clock-like regularity.

"*Ka-ta-la-vai-neis ang-li-ke*?" Costas asked, changing tacks. Still, nothing. Costas looked at Virgil, hoping for an idea.[43]

"Stand up!" Virgil said, coming over to the Cyclopes. The man did not move, so Virgil lifted him out of the chair and moved him to the desk, pinning his legs against it while he rifled through his jacket and pants pockets. They were all empty except for a couple of €1 coins. Virgil then frisked the man's body, legs,

---

[42] Πώς σε λένε — What's your name?

[43] Καταλαβαίνεις αγγλικά; — Do you understand English?

groin and midriff before putting him back into the chair. He noticed a large bulge on his chest during the frisk and reached for the neck of the Cyclopes. The captive moved his head away, grunting, making his first noise or self-generated movement of the entire interrogation. Virgil gripped the back of his head and pulled him back to the centre while fishing for the object down the man's shirt. He pulled it out over the incoherent grunting protest of the Cyclopes. It was a rather large golden Orthodox crucifix. The two crossing bars, the lower not perfectly perpendicular to the vertical bar, made it quite easy to identify with the Byzantine Church of the East. Virgil let the weighty icon fall heavily back to the man's chest. He then tossed the coins on Costas' desk and gave him the look of a man searching for a new idea.

The door opened suddenly. In walked Panagis Metaxas. "Panagis!" Costas popped up instantly, coming around the desk, shaking the outstretched hand of the mayor while trying to reverse his course, back into the main office; failing.

"Costas!" Metaxas appeared winded and annoyed, and he was sweating profusely. "What is happening? What are these things?" he said, pointing towards the arsenal in the other room.

"Well," Costas replied gently, "we have uncovered an illegal weapons trade on the island, I think it has to do with what is happening in Turkey."

"What?" Panagis exclaimed. "Who, Costas? Who is doing this? You must tell me!"

"Well, we think Nikos Kordatos, and we are sure about this man," he replied, pointing to the Cyclopes. "His fishing boat was loaded with the weapons."

At that, Panagis put himself on Costas' side of the desk, and looked squarely into the eye of the fisherman. He then boomed, "*Pos se len-eh*?"

The fisherman stared back. He said nothing.

They stared at each other for a minute or so, and then Panagis said, calmly, again, "*Pos se len-eh*?"

The Cyclopes shifted in his seat, his hands still behand his back, his throat dry and parched. After a few shifting moments, he spoke, saying slowly, one syllable at a time, and in husky English, "No-bo-dy." When he was done speaking, he smiled slightly but otherwise added nothing.

Panagis Metaxas looked to the detectives. Costas motioned with his head silently for them to move into the main room of the station. They all exited, leaving Nobody in Costas' office. Virgil shut the door, again.

"The man's sense of humour knows no bounds." Virgil laughed.

"Has he been like this since you arrested him?" Panagis asked Costas.

"No," Costas replied, "before you arrived, he said nothing at all."

"What do you know about him?" Metaxas asked.

"Almost nothing," Costas said. "We first saw him at Circe's taverna, then at *Pera Pigathi*. When we caught Nikos destroying this evidence" — pointing to the table where Ariadne continued to fend off her husband while working — "he arrived at the door and then fled down the street. Mr Colvin got him. He had a fishing boat, but now we have it."

"Where is it?" Metaxas asked.

Costas did not reply. There was a sudden realisation coming into his eyes, and Virgil knew what it was. When he sent all his deputies along, he forgot to send someone to guard the *Πολύφημος*. Virgil, his friend, had quickly become so engrossed in his own memories, he hadn't thought to give his friend this obvious advice. Guilt flooded over them both.

"Well, it is down in the harbour," Costas sheepishly replied.

"Who is guarding it?" Panagis inquired.

"Well…" Costas stammered, moving his left hand to the back of his neck, rubbing it.

"Costas!" Panagis thundered. "How could you make such a mistake!"

"I am sorry, Panagis, I simply overlooked it once we had the cargo up here. I will go and take possession of the boat now."

"Good, and call me when you know more! I don't like finding things out by rumour, Costas!"

"Yes, Panagis, I apologise," Costas said. "Where will you be?"

"I am going to Frikes to coordinate the relief ferry — call *Ageri* to get a hold of me. I mean it, Costas, call as soon as you have something!" Panagis then marched out of the station, offering a friendly smile and wave to Ariadne and Alexis. He ignored Virgil Colvin.

"I'm sorry, Costas," Virgil said, "I should have said something."

"No, Mr Colvin, please! This is my mistake. Shall we get over to the harbour?"

"Of course!"

"Alexis!" Costas barked. "Bring Nikos Kordatos a cup of coffee and a package of cigarettes. Tell him we are trying to get in touch with his lawyer and to be patient. Any other question, say you don't know! Then bring some water to that one-eyed man in my office. Offer to pour some in his mouth. Do not, under any circumstances, take off his handcuffs. Do not, under any circumstances, get very close to him while you pour water into his mouth. He is a dangerous and unpredictable man. Do not say anything else to him; do not answer any questions if he asks any — but take note of those questions! We will not be gone for very long. Hopefully Kyriakos will be here soon with Zoe Kordatos to keep you company. Or Demetrios with Circe. Or, both! Understand?"

Alexis assented his understanding, getting a cup of coffee ready before fetching cigarettes and matches from his desk. Virgil and Costas headed out, turning left towards the harbour.

***

"It's going to be all right, Costas," Virgil lied as they looked at the boats moored in Vathy Harbour. The *Πολύφημος* was not there. It was gone.

"Mr Colvin, this is kind of you, but very uncharacteristic. You do not coat with honey. This is not good. Not at all," Costas said dejectedly.

"Look, you have the skipper, you have the weapons, the boat is not as important any more" — Virgil tried to lie more convincingly — "and, in a stroke of luck, Metaxas is on his way to Frikes — who knows, maybe we will have the boat before he shows up again?"

Costas just gave Virgil a look.

"It has been a long morning, Costas. All your people are out doing their jobs. Fretting will not make the missing boat reappear. Cyclopes isn't chatting, and neither is Nikos. Let me buy you lunch. *O Batis* is right there," he said, pointing to their favourite harbour-side restaurant — 'The Sea Breeze' in Greek.

"Are you sure? We shouldn't go back to the station, Mr Colvin, and resume the interrogation?"

"Take it from me, Costas, sometimes the best insights on a case come when you force yourself to slow down and replenish. Come on." He started walking towards *O Batis* without waiting for Costas to consent. After a moment, Costas followed.

They sat down, ordered ouzo and fresh bonito, caught that morning, admired the harbour and the still cloudless sky from beneath the protection of *O Batis*' stand-alone canopy, guarding most of its outdoor tables.

Those tables provided the overwhelming majority of the seating as maybe four people could comfortably eat inside the restaurant. Virgil did not recall ever seeing anyone inside the place except the owners and employees.

The waiter brought them sparkling water and glasses of ouzo. He also set down a glass of ice with tongs, before leaving to collect the bonito. The detectives took their turn to add a few cubes of ice to the ouzo. Then they sat in silence as the ice and ouzo reacted with each other. Slowly at first, clouded wisps suspended within the glasses began to form at the edges of the ice blocks. As the reaction continued, the wisps began to spread from the blocks like the tentacles of ghostly octopi, taking up more and more of the glasses. After a minute, the glasses were entirely opaque. After another half minute, the glasses appeared to hold a very watery and viscous milk rather than the clear distillation of anise flavoured ethanol.

Both men swirled their glasses around a few times and then clinked them together before enjoying their first drinks of the day. The ouzo effect, the clouding of the spirit when water was added, did not really alter the taste of the drink. But given the theatrics of the spirit, enjoying the show certainly seemed the right thing to do before imbibing. The obscuring effect brought to Virgil's mind the clouded nature of their case. Obscured by secret codes, shredded paper, a dead spy and a one-eyed man who only became more mysterious the longer they knew him.

The bonito arrived, flayed and grilled expertly with drizzled olive oil, two lemon halves and a sprinkling of diced basil leaf. It was a simple dish, absolutely fresh, and piping hot; the perfect contrast with the morning. This was what life should be — especially on this island. The murder of Reginald Wellesley. The smuggling of Kalashnikov rifles and RPGs. The disappearances of Zoe Kordatos and the *Πολύφημος*.

These things happen, Virgil thought to himself as he ate the bonito and looked at the harbour, *but they should not happen* here!

When they had finished the fish and ouzo, mostly in silence, they looked at each other and knew they were going to have to bite the bullet and discuss the case before heading back to the station to see if the tunes of the arrested men had changed. Before either could break the delightful silence of lunch, Kyriakos arrived, a bit out of breath.

"*Ar-khe-gos*!" the winded man blurted out, coming to a stop from his jog from the plaza. "I... have... news!" he gasped in between gathering gulps of air.

"Calm down, Kyriakos!" Costas said with a concerned tone, offering a chair. Kyriakos sat down and drank some of the sparkling water that Costas offered him from his untouched water glass.

"*Ar-khe-gos*, the woman Kordatos, we cannot find her. No one knows anything about where she is,"

Kyriakos was finally able to say. He drank a little more water, then continued, "*Monsieur* Deflers picked up Circe before Demetrios could make an arrest, *Ar-khegos.*"

"Where did they go?" Virgil interjected.

"Towards Project Odysseus, as best we could find," Kyriakos answered.

"What?" Costas asked. "Why do they go there? Mr Colvin" — Costas turned to Virgil — "what do you make of this?"

"I think we should go to Project Odysseus, now," Virgil said with obvious urgency.

"Why? Why not continue to talk to Nikos and Nobody?" Costas said with a twinkle of amusement in his eye.

"Because we need to prevent a murder!" Virgil said in deadly seriousness.

"I do not understand." Costas shrugged, but agreed to go to the isthmus immediately. "Kyriakos, get back to the station, make sure the fisherman and Nikos do not go anywhere, yes?

Kyriakos assented and sprinted off towards Enmeou Street and the police station.

Virgil tossed a wad of Euros on the table and then jogged with Costas to the south end of the plaza where he had parked earlier that morning.

As they climbed into the car, Costas asked, "Mr Colvin, who is killing who?"

“Jesus, Costas!” Virgil said with impatience while starting the car, slipping it into gear and pulling around the plaza and onto the main road around the harbour to the isthmus. “How can you not know?”

CHAPTER EIGHTEEN
AGROS LAERTOU

As they drove towards the isthmus, Costas and Virgil discussed the status of the case. Or, more accurately, Virgil told Costas the basic facts of the case as he now understood them.

"Look, Costas, this homicide, like all of them, begins with the victim — for us, it's Reginald Wellesley. We know he was British Intelligence, no doubt sent here to discover or prevent illicit shipments of arms to the forces of the coup against the Turkish dictator, Onur Gündüz. British Intelligence obviously gave him information on likely smuggling stash points on the island as well as likely suspects to watch. First, there is Nikos Kordatos, the leader of the communists on the island, who might be hopeful that overthrowing Gündüz could advance a bizarre dream that in the aftermath the Turkish military would tolerate a powerful Turkish communist party. Ultimately, it doesn't make sense, but as the leader of the communist party in Ithaca, since when does making sense matter? Then there is François Deflers." Virgil rounded the inner loop of Vathy harbour heading along the western edge before turning left to pass Dexia Bay. "Reggie looks at him because his associates are Eastern European and Russian arms dealers and black-market oligarchs, but François wants to build a tourist resort on the island. That resort is going to be a much tougher sell if Greece, and the island of Ithaca itself, gets caught up in this ill-fated political intrigue. Obviously, Reggie quickly concludes that Nikos is the mark that matters. Being something of a Casanova, he decides to romance the stone. He sleeps with Zoe Kordatos to gather information, and keep tabs on, Nikos. Reggie does this to save himself time — why does he have to follow Nikos around all the time if Zoe is doing that for him when they aren't together? Also, he hopes that the affair might cause Nikos to respond erratically — to make a mistake. It's a risky approach. Obviously, it helps that Zoe Kordatos is a dish; that must have made it easier to downplay the risks. If it didn't get him killed, it probably would have resulted in some sort of ruckus eventually. I suspect that, seeing Nikos Kordatos, Reggie believed he could never be taken unawares by a man so easily cuckholded."

"I follow you so far," Costas said, though he did not pick up on all the linguistic oddities Virgil had employed. "Please, is there more? What about Circe?"

"The gun running is clearly being done by the Cyclopes. Our island, Thiakí, is just a way station through the Balkans and around the Peloponnese, probably to get the weapons to Rhodes and Izmir."

Costas smiled to himself — it was the first time Virgil Colvin used the native word for the island. Unaware, Colvin continued, "The Turkish navy blocks all the shorter routes through the Black Sea and no one would suspect this island of anything in a million years, Costas. It is out of the way, but close enough to the exit points for the weapons somewhere up on the Dalmatian coast. The idea of smuggling on a fishing boat is genius. They are all over the waters in this area. They all look alike and are totally non-descript. Only the earthquake and the murder put us onto any of it. Had neither of those events occurred, would we have ever been the wiser?"

"Well, Mr Colvin, my men may not be Chicago police—" Costas began to defend his police force, his family.

"It isn't that, Costas. We simply had no reason to think anything was happening. Without Reggie's body in the street, they would have carried on just as they had been."

"Had been?"

"Yes, Costas, they must have been doing this for a while now — there is no way the coup wasn't supplied for months before getting under way in multiple cities simultaneously. Now, who is the 'they'? Nikos and Circe are the most obviously involved of the island's citizens in aiding and abetting this smuggling with the Cyclopes, though for wildly different motives. However, if one of them killed Reggie, then they all killed Reggie. Like the *Murder on the Orient Express* — ever read it?" Costas shook his head. "Well, so far as I am concerned, they are one suspect — though they all have different reasons for being involved to begin with. Regardless of those different motives to smuggle arms, the threat Reggie posed to all of them was the same. The only real issue with the three of them is that Reggie was watching all of them in some way. He must have known about all of them, even the Cyclopes. Getting the drop on a spy is like sneaking up on an Indian, Costas."

"What does this mean?"

"Oh, it's just an old expression where I come from — no one sneaks up on an Indian, Costas, especially if he's already looking at you!"

"I see. What about Zoe?" Costas asked as they made their way into the hills towards Mt Aetos before the descent into the isthmus.

"Zoe is a problem, Costas. She may have murdered Reggie to protect Nikos, but I seriously doubt that for a couple of reasons. Her disappearance was either intentional or she may be the victim of foul play. I suspect the former, but I suppose it is possible that she ran afoul of someone."

"Intentional?" Costas queried.

"Zoe knows more than she lets on, Costas; you know this." Costas nodded in agreement. "She is not the mild-mannered receptionist. The real question is whether she's just another pawn on the board, or a more important piece — or the most important. I don't know yet. Circe's suggestion that we talk to Zoe and then her amusement at my question of 'why not Nikos?' suggests to me that she's more central to what is going on. But Circe may have just been referencing the affair with Reggie. Perhaps it was something else entirely, but I doubt it, and I also have no idea what it might be if it was."

"So, Nikos and 'Nobody' are arrested at my station" — Costas took over the conversation for a moment — "so what are François and Circe up to? Do they move guns at the *Agros*? Do they smuggle antiquities? Where does Mr Wellesley fit in with those two and what they are doing? Or was he never involved or aware of them or their activities at all?"

"Reggie was aware of their activities, Costas, but that isn't the point of our getting to the *Agros* as quickly as we can," Virgil said as his knuckles turned white gripping the wheel of the G-6 through the descent into the isthmus — shuttered *Chani* was coming up fast on the right.

"Well, what *is* the point?" Costas asked, genuinely curious and a bit confused.

"Because, Costas, if we don't get there in time, François Deflers is a dead man."

***

They pulled up next to Francois Deflers' black Citroën Elysée, parked the G-6, and then exited quickly into the construction camp surrounding the *Agros Laertou*. The local Ithacans had long regarded this spearhead of flat land on the otherwise rocky and craggy isthmus as the mythical fields of the father of Odysseus. The curiously retired King Laertes had arrived in Ithaca and greater Kefalonia in the generation before the events of the *Iliad* and the *Odyssey*, conquering the local potentates and then transferring the kingdom to his son at some point before Agamemnon and Menelaus came to call the new father to Troy. More peculiarly, during the supposed two-decade absence of his son, the retired king remained retired on his farm. He also remained retired as dozens, eventually over a hundred, suitors besieged the palace of his absent son and very present daughter-in-law. Eventually, Odysseus called upon his retired father for aid — at the very end, as he feared the angry relatives of the suitors that he slew. Then, and only then, Laertes rose from his retirement. So ready to do grim battle to the death alongside his son, grandson and their servants and loyal slaves was he that Laertes flung his bronze tipped spear into the neck of the angriest and most aggrieved of the suitors' fathers. Were it not for the intervention of the Goddess Athena, Homer tells us, that act surely would have led to an epic bloodbath in the fields of Laertes. Ithaca might have emerged rudderless, ripe for the first ambitious warlord who caught word of the elimination of so many of the island's patriarchs. Such a man, very much like Laertes two generations earlier, would have come to stake his own claim to rule. The flat plain on the isthmus was an odd geographical feature attributed to one of the *Odyssey*'s oddest characters.

Now it was the home of the mobile trailer HQ for Project Odysseus and surveyor's flags all over the plain and the hills running beneath the road to Anogi. The stone walls, many running in parallel lines, seemingly signs of ancient terracing for an ancient farm, were still very present at the site. A joint team of archaeologists from the British School at Athens and the University of Cincinnati had been slated to arrive in September to begin working. They would excavate, save and plot all finds, photograph the site as they painstakingly removed one layer after another of earth and exhaust all the arts and techniques of stratigraphy on the dime of Project Odysseus.

Whether that was still going to happen with the earthquake, the coup, the murder, the guns etc. was anyone's guess. While a bit of money, had been invested in permitting and land purchases — millions of Euros — the syndicate had not sunk so much into it yet that they wouldn't still pull the plug if they got too nervous. François, of course, stood to be blamed for that failure, whether that made sense or not. This certainly contributed to his general impatience to keep the project going without interruption.

Costas and Virgil immediately suspected something wasn't right when they got out of the car. The door of the trailer was not fully closed, instead it creaked back and forth in the breeze, picking up on the Isthmus. Virgil Colvin looked into the sky. The sun had moved past its zenith and was moving slowly down towards Kefalonia, it was early afternoon. Clouds were blowing in from the northeast, they looked heavy and dark, and they were moving quickly. The few trees in the *Agros* rustled quietly in the background. Colvin felt a slight shivering tingle go up his back. He was suddenly aware of being unarmed.

"Shall we?" Virgil said to Costas, moving tentatively towards the door of the trailer as it moved and creaked a bit more dramatically while a gust blew through before subsiding just as quickly.

"Yes, Mr Colvin, I go first." Costas took the lead and opened the door before freezing in the entrance.

"Costas, I can't get by you," Virgil said, stuck on the stairs leading up to the trailer's door.

"Mr Colvin..." Costas muttered, turning around with a horrified and questioning look in his eyes.

"What Costas, let me by you." Costas pinned himself on the right of the doorjamb so that Virgil could squeeze by and enter the trailer.

As he entered, even before his eyes could tell him the story, the smell of blood — warm, wet and human — blasted his olfactory senses. As a homicide detective, Virgil Colvin had seen many corpses in various states of exsanguination, some fresh and recent, others long dead, bloated and empty. He stepped gingerly into the trailer, careful to avoid the visible smudges of blood and larger puddles. François Deflers had died within the hour. The blood that splattered from the repeated stabbing with the *xiphos* — now sticking out of his back as his body slumped over his desk — had sprayed all over the floor and trailer ceiling behind his seat. He silently motioned to Costas for latex gloves before touching anything, expertly putting them on while looking incredibly closely at the Frenchman's wounds. That smell. You never forget it. Virgil felt the dead man's neck, not for a pulse, but simply to see how warm he was. Still felt alive, though very clearly not. *It wouldn't last much longer,* Virgil thought to himself. There was a bottle of French claret on the table, opened. Costas came into the trailer a few steps as Virgil gingerly examined the back of the Frenchman.

"Shall we?" Virgil asked Costas, motioning to the wine.

Costas looked disgusted; he was speechless.

Without apologising, Virgil resumed his examination. The bronze *xiphos* had been pushed through the body during the *coup de grâce*, but it seemed as if there were at least five or six other thrusting wounds as well as a deep gash on the left shoulder that had sprayed blood all over the wall to the left of where Deflers was seated, no doubt caused by the removal of the blade. This had almost certainly been the first blow. François would have been so stunned and wounded that the thrusts after this opening thrashing attack would have simply been so much overkill. The murderer must have been quite upset.

"Well, Costas," Virgil said after his examination, cursory though it was, ended, "this is my first bronze age murder scene. In terms of bloody messes, it's not bad."

Costas looked horrified, and Virgil suddenly remembered where he was and whom he was talking to.

"I'm sorry, Costas, I forgot I'm not a rookie working through South-side carnage any more. This looks like your typical intimate stabbing crime. When people who know each other murder one another, they often tend to overdo it, especially when they murder with knives and guns. Bronze Age swords are apparently in the same boat."

"Do we know anything more?" Costas mumbled.

"Circe did this, we need to find her. Let's lock this place up, we can fetch him" — pointing to François — "later. I'm sure he won't mind some time away from his two favourite detectives, right?"

Costas looked horrified again.

"OK, OK, I'll stop, I swear!" Virgil fished around in François' pockets as he suppressed a laugh. Finding the dead man's keys, they backed out of the trailer, trying not to step on or disturb anything any more than they already had. Once they locked the door. They noticed how much darker it was outside. The sky now seemed dominated by the incoming clouds. A low rumbling thunder was permeating the background every thirty or forty seconds. They moved around the trailer to examine the ground of the *Agros* and see if there was any sign of Circe.

As they entered the ancient terraces, they both stopped dead in their strides. To the left, at the edge of the field, overlooking the steep and rocky descent into the Gulf of Molos stood Circe, her back to the detectives. Her head was angled up to the sky. Costas and Virgil approached very slowly, unsure of what her state of mind was, or what was in her right hand which they could not see. It was possible she was still armed and ready to dispatch more people to the realm of Hades and Persephone.

"That's far enough, policemen!" Circe thundered, stopping them both cold, again.

She turned slowly in a clockwise direction. As she faced them, her countenance was terrible and ghastly. Her clothes and face were covered in blood. Had they not already seen François Deflers, they would have assumed she was the victim. Instead, they knew that the blood was that of the skewered Frenchman. In her right hand was a small piece of paper, or something with a bit more substance, but it was hard to tell. It was slightly smeared with François' blood, whatever it was. Her eyes were wild-looking, offset by the crimson mask on her face. Those windows to her soul looked back and forth between Costas and Virgil who stood as statues that had looked into the eyes of Medusa. With the heavens in disorder behind and above her, she certainly appeared to hold some sort of mystical power over the elements. A sorceress worthy of her namesake.

"Circe," Costas called out gently, "what happened? What have you done?"

"He had to die, Costas, and no one else would do it," Circe said with full authority suffusing her voice as it flowed electrically through the charged air of the isthmus.

"But why?" Costas asked.

"He was going to stop the weapons, Costas! Use his connections to stop them being sold through us! The forces of freedom and God are fighting, Costas! They need our help and that man was going to stop us from delivering it! He had to die. I would kill him again if I could."

"What is in your hand?" Virgil asked.

"This?" She held up the fragment; it appeared thicker and more solid than paper now, but what was it? Could it be a fragment of metal or a piece of porcelain or pottery? "This," Circe intoned, "is the other reason he had to die. I would have killed him for this whether he was trying to stop the guns or not."

"What is it, Circe?" Costas reiterated the question.

"It is Thiakí! This island is remote. It is isolated. It is special. It is mythical. It is this!" she said, holding the object up to her wild eyes. For a moment, she was lost in examining the object in her blood-soaked fingers before her eyes refocused on the two men beyond the treasure in her grasp. "His Project Odysseus," Circe spat, "would have destroyed this spot and this island. He did not even care that this object meant that this spot needed to be preserved and never developed. He said that he already got all the permits and paid everyone. After the archaeologists arrived and did their work, he said, this whole area would be flattened, destroyed and never the magical resting place of the myths that it is and ever should be. Then he told me to get the hell out of his office and worry about getting myself arrested by the two of you for the guns." She stopped to look to the sky, her wild eyes scanning the clouds.

"What happened after that?" Costas prompted her.

"He does not know that I had the *xiphos* under my skirts, I always hide weapons when I wear skirts! Stupid, arrogant man! I did what had to be done, for God, for Greece and for Thiakí!"

"Why are you still here, Circe?" Virgil asked.

She threw the object to Virgil with a quick flip of her wrist. It spun through the air in a slightly curving line and Virgil had to move down and to the left to avoid letting the fragment hit the rocky ground, while still attempting to catch it gingerly. He managed it. Barely. He felt the object with his fingers and he finally knew what it was. Pottery. It was about three or four inches of curved surface, perhaps from a bowl, maybe an amphora? Faint traces of ancient colouring were visible, but the notable thing about this fragment was the etching into the clay of strange, but deliberate, symbols.

They looked vaguely familiar. François' blood was smeared on both sides of the sherd.

After showing it to Costas, Virgil looked back to Circe. "Where did you find this?"

She waved her arm over the entirety of the *Agros*, but then she spoke, "François allowed me to dig a narrow trench behind the trees over there." She pointed to some fig trees off to the right, and as she did so a bright streak of lightning split the darkened horizon behind her, the thunderous report following a couple of seconds later. The wind, cold now, blew swiftly across the isthmus. There was something else in the air, Virgil thought. Something rotten and foul.

"I went down two meters and found this sherd. So much for the 'Thiakí question'! You know what it is. It is Thiakí!"

As she concluded, the simultaneous roar of thunder and the rumble of the earth drowned her out. This quake was far more powerful than anything Virgil experienced over the previous day. The ground seemed to be the sea and it was impossible to stand. Both Costas and Virgil fell to the ground and hugged it, hoping it would stop behaving as a rippling liquid. The rotten smell, the loss of stability familiar to those who walk upon the earth and take its immobility as a given, and the strange all-encompassing rumbling noise went on, and on, and on. He could hear the earth breaking apart and rocks cascading into the Gulf below. Virgil Colvin shut his eyes and thought about dying here in Ithaca, on a cliffside at the *Agros Laertou*. There was something terribly tragic and pointless about the idea, but also something terribly romantic about it. The most terrible thing that kept recurring, as the earth rattled and moved, was losing Janet for good. She existed so long as he was still alive to remember and cherish their time together. The moment he ceased to exist, so would those memories of who they were and how they loved one another. He cried, waiting for the shaking to stop. It seemed like an hour when he felt the tapping on his shoulder; it was seemingly another minute or so until he heard Costas whispering, "Mr Colvin! Mr Colvin! Are you all right?"

Virgil opened his eyes, his vision blurred from his sobbing and blubbering. *He must appear quite the enormous coward to his friend*, he thought. Before he could sit up, he needed to unclench the earth. During the quake, he had spread his arms out as wide as he could and dug his fingers into the soil. He must have been hoping subconsciously to stop the earth from moving, or it was simply a desperate ploy to avoid being tossed into the sea. It took a few seconds of conscious effort to unclench his buried fists and then he stood. His legs were like jelly at first, like he had just stepped off a sailboat after a particularly jostled voyage. His Cubs hat was no longer on his head. He looked around for it, but it had vanished. His friend appeared entirely unshaken by the tremor. Costas, instead, was only concerned for Virgil, who must have appeared a total shambles. Wiping his eyes and thanking Costas, Virgil saw that the *Agros Laertou* had cleaved in several spots during the shaking, near the edge of the descent to the Gulf of Molos. Circe was nowhere to be seen.

"Where is Circe?" Virgil asked, as the earth shook again for a moment, but far less severely than before.

"No idea, Mr Colvin," Costas shrugged.

They walked to the edge of the *Agros* and peered down the rocky descent into the sea. There was no sign of Circe in the rocks below. She was gone.

"What the fuck? How long did that quake last, Costas?"

"Oh, about a minute, maybe more, Mr Colvin, quite large." Costas exhaled.

They looked back at the cleavages in the earth. The natural trench that opened up nearest to where Circe had stood was about five or six feet deep and ran all the way to her narrow exploratory trench and beyond. Had they not seen her trench before the earthquake, they would not have been able to spot it now. It was clear that the trench had not swallowed Circe. It was also clear that it had exposed more pottery sherds, some of which were plainly visible. Colvin picked up one that seemed relatively exposed and stared at it for a while. It was a rather large triangular sherd that had the same signs of previous colouring, perhaps a design or figures on the body — were they people? He couldn't make it out very well. More interesting were the etchings on the curved end — again vaguely familiar looking symbols, etched into the clay. The previous sherd was still on the ground where Virgil had hugged the earth. He walked over with the new sherd and picked up the one smeared with Francois' blood. The etchings looked similar, but they were different, no repeats.

"Do you recognise these symbols, Costas?" The chief shook his head quickly after looking briefly.

"Mr Colvin, we need to get back to Vathy, the city has had a disaster," Costas demanded, bringing Virgil back to the ongoing emergency.

They went back to the G-6. Virgil found a plastic bag in the back and a roll of paper towels. He wrapped the sherds in paper towel as gently as he could, creating two bulky white piles. He then gently placed them in the bag and sealed it. He brought the bag to the front seat and handed it to Costas. "Hold this, please." Costas held the bag on his lap and Virgil shifted the G-6 into reverse to regain the road back to Vathy.

"We need to stop at my villa, Costas, there is a book I need to get," Virgil said as they slowly made their way south back towards Mt Aetos and Vathy.

"Mr Colvin, we really need to get into the town and offer assistance — many may be injured!" Costas was, of course, correct.

"I understand, Costas, but this is related to the case," Virgil pleaded.

"How?" Costas asked, keeping his emotions in check.

"I don't know, but if you don't want to go, that's fine, I can drop you off and catch up," Virgil said adamantly.

"If it is important, we can stop, but no longer than a minute or two, yes?"

"Yes." Virgil promised.

They drove until the isthmus began to move into the hills again and then Virgil stopped and turned off the vehicle. The road was entirely blocked to cars by boulders, rocks, dirt and rubble. It was blocked as far as they could see. Even if the blockage let up a few hundred yards ahead, there was no way to drive there. They would have to proceed on foot. It was a little over three miles to downtown Vathy from where Virgil parked the car off the west end of the horseshoe road around the Bay of Molos. Under normal circumstances, the walk should have taken a little over an hour due to the uphill climbs. The uneven walking they now had to do over the dangerously unsettled debris, stretched the time to more than two and a half hours just to get back to the descent into the city along the western road abutting Vathy Harbour.

Virgil now carried the bag of pottery sherds, doing his best to avoid making any contact between it and anything, including himself. He and Costas did not talk much during the hike due to the desire of both of them to be careful. Costas was also motivated by an intense desire to get to his friends, his family, his people, as quickly as he could. He took point as soon as they set out and he never relinquished it — generally staying five to ten yards ahead the entire time. They were winded, but not exhausted when they reached the western heights above Vathy. The road was largely blocked the entire way into the town. Even from this distance, smoke was clearly rising from some of the buildings, and the miniature forms of cars and people were moving about the streets with no discernible order or plan. It was eerily silent as they caught their breath, watching from above. Only the thundering of the clouds broke the silence. Virgil felt a large glob of water land on his bald head, then another on his arm. In another minute, he was entirely drenched.

Costas raised his arms to the heavens and said loudly, "*Thav-ma*!" He then turned to Virgil and said simply, "No fires!"

Indeed, it was hard to imagine any fire managing to survive the deluge that now drenched the earthquake-stricken people of Vathy. The rain, however, did not make the descent through the rubble along the boulder-strewn road any easier. Their previously 'impressive' pace literally bogged down to a crawl as the dirt turned to mud. Footing was their constant worry. It took another hour to get to the hillside where Virgil left his villa that morning. The wall that made up the right side of the villa — the kitchen wall and the right wall of his bedroom — had fallen away from the villa about three feet from the ground. The roof had caved into the villa itself, providing imperfect protection to part of the living room. The kitchen, part of his bedroom, and part of the living room were entirely exposed to the rain. Some large boulders from the hillside had missed the villa and stopped in the driveway where he normally parked.

"Insurance," he kept muttering to himself.

It was still possible to get into the villa through the door — he only needed to get to the books, which hopefully were not all exposed to the water. The books were largely protected from direct rainfall, but the large bookcase had collapsed forward during the quake and made the left side of a Greek letter Λ with the fallen roof as the right side — of course spilling most of the books upon the floor. There was no way he was going to be able to find the book he needed in a minute or two. It was clear that Costas wanted to leave. It was clear that the city needed help. He placed the bag of sherds just inside the door. *They should be OK here*, he thought. Unless there were another earthquake.

They descended into the town to do what they could to help the wounded and those trying to find loved ones who were missing or trapped beneath the rubble of collapsed homes and buildings. Transporting people to the hospital on makeshift stretchers — usually just boards — became their main task. The Mentor Hotel, just off Drakoulis Street on the east end of the harbour, had collapsed. Ithacans were working through the rubble to find trapped survivors when Virgil and Costas arrived. They immediately got to work heaving concrete out of the rubble pile. It was hard work, especially in the driving rain, but every moment counted. After about thirty minutes of clearing the pile, they heard moaning.

"Careful!" Virgil shouted as overeager rescuers abandoned their previously careful and even clearing of rubble. Only clearing in one specific spot risked having the surrounding rubble collapse onto rescuers and trapped alike. Order was soon restored as Costas translated Virgil's commands to the others. Within fifteen minutes, four wounded tourists and two of the hotel's staff were safely extricated from the collapsed hotel. All were carried to the hospital on makeshift 'stretchers' by twelve of the rescuers while those who remained on the pile, Virgil and Costas among them, made sure there were no others trapped beneath what was left.

A woman ran up to the soaked men as they were finishing, shouting in Greek. Costas ran to her and talked to her for a few moments before turning to Virgil. "She says her grandfather has had a heart attack, her home is up the hill behind Circe's."

"Well, let's go get him to the hospital!" Virgil got a couple of the men to pick up a wide wooden plank from the rubble, and the four of them followed the woman up the road into the hills on the east-side of the harbour. When they arrived, they found a largely collapsed house. Carefully, the woman led them into the home, and into a back room where other relatives were trying to provide aide to an elderly man laying upon a bed. Costas and one of the men hefted the man gingerly onto the board. Virgil got one of the man's relatives to strip the bed of a sheet that he and the other man could hold over the old man to shelter him from the rain. The trek back to the hospital took almost half an hour as they tried to get there without straining the man as much as possible. When the orderlies got the man from the plank, triaging him immediately to doctors, the woman kissed all the men for their efforts.

Before Virgil and Costas could get their bearings for where they might go next, one of the nurses ran up to Costas and urgently related something important. After a short back and forth, Costas turned to Virgil. "She says they need bandages and dressings — they are out and have already repurposed their spare sheets." He looked quite perplexed.

"What's the problem, Costas? Let's go!"

"If the hospital has none, Mr Colvin, where will we get more?"

"Where there are clothes or lots of sheets?"

"Of course, but why…" Then it dawned on Costas. He motioned to the two men who just assisted with the old man. "*Pah-may*!"[44]

They made their way back across the town to the dry cleaners. The building seemed undamaged by the quake, but there didn't seem to be anyone inside, and the door was locked. Virgil kicked the wooden door in

---

[44] πάμε! — let's go!

— the second time that day. The machines were askew and akimbo, making for a peculiar labyrinth inside. Supplies and folded orders were scattered upon the damp floor, wetted by several leaks in the ceiling. The men searched for dry bed sheets, towels, and other linens that could double as dressings and bandages for wounds. They piled the haul into the bags the dry cleaners used to segregate the cleaned from the uncleaned before setting off under the vital burden. When they arrived back at the hospital with eight bags of dressing and bandage substitutes, that were greeted by several very happy nurses who distributed more kisses to their deliverers.

“Let’s get back to it, boys!” Virgil Colvin declared as he turned and ran out of the hospital, his neighbours and friends in tow. And so it was, for what remained of the day. Just after sunset, Virgil and Costas managed to return to the police station, the left side of which had collapsed in the earthquake. No one, fortunately, was hurt. Alexis and Ariadne had hunkered down with Nikos Kordatos in his holding room, all of them against the far wall underneath the table, which they had pushed into the corner. Demetrios, Alexandros and Kyriakos were all in the town helping to find people and transport the severely wounded to the hospital. The fisherman was gone.

“Costas,” Virgil said as they sat down at one of the desks in the main station room in the darkness of sunset — power was out everywhere in Vathy. They were silent for a few moments. Virgil could see Costas' anguish and exhaustion, but he also knew there was a loose end to tie up. The chaos of the earthquake already freed one guilty man. "Costas, I need to run an errand. It won't take long. Do you need me to do anything or bring anyone, or anything, back with me?"

Costas, completely soaked through and staring towards the ground, spoke lowly and from faraway, "When I married Eleni, I thought it was the beginning of the greatest happiness I would ever know in my homeland." He paused, looking to Virgil who sat down across from his friend before looking back into the abyss. "We had three marvellous days before she told me." He sat quietly for a long, pregnant moment. "She expected me to get her out of Thiakí, out of Greece if possible" — he trailed off for a bit before becoming audible again — "it was her life's ambition to pursue a career in a big city and she assumed my devotion would follow her ambition to the ends of the earth." He sat quietly for a minute or two before resuming, "We argued the old argument of the rural Greeks. She wanted the big city, the bigger world; your world, Mr Colvin. But this island, Thiakí, this is me. I cannot leave it, even in death. I assumed she knew that. I am so obvious and open. No one who knows Costas can pretend he can ever live any other place than Thiakí. She assumed I could not live without her. Until this day, I have tormented myself about what happened all those years ago, Mr Colvin." He looked up at Virgil. "Should have

I gone away with her? Was I correct to stay here? Here, alone? These questions. Every day. For twenty years!"

"Costas," Virgil muttered, "I don't know what to tell you. I'm sorry."

"No, Mr Colvin, don't be sorry," Costas said, exhausted. "This day has ended my doubts. This terrible, disastrous, day. This is my home. This place is where I belong. The woman for me — this needs to be her place, too. Eleni was the most wonderful girl I have ever known, but without Thiakí I would have been adrift in life — lost at sea like Odysseus. Here I know who I am. I know what I am. I know how I belong. This place is me, and I am Thiakí, Mr Colvin."

Realising that he had never felt so deeply for a place during his life in Chicago, Virgil Colvin was at a loss for words. But he understood, on some level, Costas' attachment. This island was magnetic. Not everyone felt the attraction. Not everyone always felt it. When you did, there was no keeping yourself away from Thiakí. Spiritually, emotionally, psychically, physically — it was all-consuming. Costas Pantakalas would never be able to leave this place permanently. Virgil Colvin was wondering if he could ever leave.

The chief lifted his weary head. "Mr Colvin, what errand do you need to perform?"

"Just something to figure out who killed Reggie," Virgil answered.

"You have done more than ten men this day," Costas said slowly and methodically, "this city will never forget it while I still breathe. I do not know how you're still able to think about the murder case. Or anything. Go! The gods be with you!"

Virgil shook his friend's hand in silence with a slight nod of the head. He stepped back onto Enmeou Street, as the patter of the rain transitioned to a constant drizzle. It was completely dark — the clouds blocked the moon and the stars from any sort of illumination. Only the hospital, to the right, had any light due to its emergency generator. There were a few lanterns and candles moving about in the streets of the town beneath him, floating as if by magic. The periodic shouts of voices, from all directions and all distances, along with the disembodied floating lights, created a haunted effect as he made his way carefully back into the western hills, towards his villa.

***

His exhaustion hit him as soon as he was inside his front door. He wanted to collapse into bed, but he remembered that the bed had been exposed to the rain for the last several hours. Those hours of chaos, mayhem and sustained effort to help his neighbours. It was all a weary blur now. Had he really done anything special? Wouldn't anyone have done the same for their neighbours? Their town? Their home? *Their home*. The thought was like a bolt of lightning. Thiakí was *his* home, now. These were *his* friends; *his* neighbours; *his* family. They had welcomed him at the lowest moment of his life and had gladly tolerated his six-month bender. Mostly tolerated. He felt good, truly good, for the first time in many months. Not sad. Not melancholy. Not self-pitying. Just purposeful and good.

He looked down at the plastic bag with the wrapped pottery sherds. It took a few minutes to locate the book he had thought of earlier at the *Agros Laertou*; John Chadwick's *The Decipherment of Linear B*. Moving back to the doorway, where it was dry and he could use the flashlight from his cell phone, Colvin unwrapped the sherds of pottery. He then opened the book to the end of the preface, where the chart of eighty-seven Linear B symbols and their syllabic values was conveniently located. It took several minutes to scribble out the meanings from the sherds with a pen in the back of the book. It took a while, but he never tried to read Linear B before and he was bone-tired. When he was done, he rewrapped the sherds and put them back in the bag as gently as he could. Then he stood and tossed the book back into the pile on the living room floor, stretching his torso and arms.

"Son of a bitch," Virgil said to the empty and dilapidated villa, reflecting on what he had just discovered. According to the spot translation, the sherd that Circe tossed to Virgil said, '*ra — er — te*,' while the one from the trench opened by the earthquake read, '*pa — ne — o — p*'. It would seem like baby talk to anyone who came upon it. But Linear B was an early

Greek shorthand. Ventris and Chadwick claimed that the syllabic suggestion of R was interchangeable with L. Circe's sherd could be read, '*la — er — te*' — Laertes. Along with the far more obvious evidence of Penelope — *'pa — ne — o — p'* — the sherds stood to strongly bolster modern Ithaca's claim to being the ancient Ithaca of Odysseus.

Virgil Colvin was wide awake, again. And Virgil Colvin was angry. His day wasn't done yet. Thiakí *was* ancient Ithaca. This evidence came as close as anything in almost three millennia to proving it. Someone had tried to bury it. Someone had tried to deny *his* friends; *his* neighbours; *his* family from basking in the glory of their rightful heritage. They had killed for it. Virgil Colvin was going to make them pay.

He exited the villa with the bag of mythical evidence in his hand. Since arriving in the villa, a chill had entered the night air, creating a dense fog that added to the low visibility of the night's darkness. The atmospheric ouzo effect stood in stark and diametrical contrast to the clarity and certainty that Virgil Colvin had about the case, about his island, about himself. No one would take that from him, not again. After a brief pause to prepare for what was ahead, Virgil Colvin marched down, into the fuzzy darkness.

CHAPTER NINETEEN
RETURN TO HOTEL FAMILIA

While the Hotel Familia appeared to be constructed of stone and brick — perhaps the worst material to use to withstand frequent and severe earthquakes — it was constructed to only superficially appear so sturdy. Its underlying structure was actually wooden, and like all good construction in fault zones, it was not anchored to the bedrock. Wood had much more flexibility and give during earthquakes and could sway with the rocky earth beneath. Not being anchored into the bedrock allowed structures above to move without breaking at the foundation. In contrast, the stone and concrete structures in the town suffered the most catastrophic damage due to their rigid, unbending construction. That they had ever been built after the massive quake in 1953 would be the subject of much consternation in the coming months, and then they would almost certainly be rebuilt just as before.

Given the severity of the quake, the two-storey hotel was in good shape. The superficial façade had cracked and fallen away in places, but the basic structure was intact. Nothing had collapsed. Low light emanated from the front door whose glass panelling now lay in pieces on the ground. Virgil opened the door and entered the lobby, glad to be out of the rain again. He still had his bag of dry and safe Mycenaean pottery sherds in his hands, which were shaking a bit with cold. The lobby had several oil and gas lanterns posted around and it took a few moments to adjust to the 'intense' illumination after being in near total darkness for so long.

Katerina came up to the drenched detective, quite alarmed at his appearance. "Mr Colvin! You are soaked through! Please, let me get you a towel!" She ran off to the room behind her bar and came back in a few moments with several big fluffy white towels that Virgil used to try to soak up some of the water from his torn Khakis and shirt. He put one of the towels on a bar stool and sat down.

"Any chance you have some bourbon here, Katerina?" he asked. He noticed for the first time that his teeth were clattering together from the chill in his body.

"Of course, Mr Colvin, ah, I mean Virgil, sorry!" She poured him a double.

"It's fine, don't worry." He downed the bourbon in one gulp. Katerina poured him another without waiting for him to ask.

"Have you been out in this all day?" she asked.

"Sadly, yes. Been quite a day! How have you been holding up?" He looked around the lobby for the first time since coming in. There were some people lying down on the floor against the wall. "Who are they?"

"Their hotels and rentals were damaged or destroyed. I don't have any more rooms, but I could not send them away. I give them blankets and pillows. They make the best of the floor. The hotel has no water or power, but it is still here!" Her infectious smile warmed the cold detective as he drank a third of the second pour.

"Thank god for that!" Virgil drank some more. The chill was subsiding. He looked back at the people against the wall. He noticed Blake and Ellen Sheridan, asleep against the wall.

What a honeymoon! he thought.

Ellen Sheridan's face was streaked in bizarre orange, and pink-skin-coloured lines. *So much for spray tans!* Virgil chuckled as he turned back to Katerina, who was still looking at him with tender concern in her eyes.

"Virgil, all of my guests are accounted for, except François. Have you seen him anywhere?"

Dreading to have to tell her, Virgil looked down into the rich amber liquid in his glass. He paused for a moment.

"Katerina, when the earthquake hit, Costas and I were at Project Odysseus."

"Oh, so he is fine!"

"No, Katerina." He drank a bit more bourbon. "François is dead. Murdered before we got there. Not sure when anyone is going to be able to make it back out there to retrieve him. I'm sorry, Katerina," Virgil concluded. *Always do it quick,* he reminded himself. It never got any easier. The quicker you did it, the faster it was over.

"What? My god, Virgil! That is… terrible! What is happening to our island?" She went silent in thought. She poured herself a shot of whiskey and downed it before pouring another. She didn't cry. *Tough broad,* thought Virgil.

"It has been a bizarre couple of days, Katerina," Virgil said before finishing his drink. Katerina moved to pour a third and would have done so, but Virgil's hand covered the glass. "I'm still working, Katerina."

"What? On what?" She downed her second shot and poured a third.

"Reginald Wellesley." He opened his plastic bag and unwrapped the sherds of pottery and laid them gently upon the bar. "Katerina, have you seen anything like these recently?"

She leaned over. She was about to grab one of the sherds before stopping herself. "May I touch these?"

Before he could answer, a woman's voice tersely interrupted them, "Excuse me? When will cellular service be restored?"

Ellen Sheridan was even more a sight up close — Virgil had not seen the black mascara streaks when he examined her earlier.

"Oh, I don't know, miss," Katerina said with beguiling charm, "I imagine it will be quite a while. Was there something I could help you with?"

"How are we ever supposed to get out of here?" Ellen said, gripping her phone like a vice at her side.

Virgil looked to Katerina. He could tell her illimitable hospitality was running out. Her smile was subtly collapsing. Ellen Sheridan may have been the last straw for this day. Virgil was surprised that he wasn't the angry and pitiless cynic of the day before. Instead, he saw a friend, Katerina, who needed a boost; and a frightened tourist on the verge of breaking down.

"Ellen," Virgil soothed, "the navies of the Mediterranean are on their way here now and will evacuate everyone who wants to leave in the next twenty-four hours or so. You just need to hang in there until then. Is there anything we can get you, right now?" Katerina regained her usual hospitable and generous smile as Virgil spoke.

Ellen Sheridan looked mildly assuaged by Colvin's suppositions before shaking her head and walking back to her sleeping husband, clutching her phone in both hands. *What would she do when it died?* he wondered.

"She's… pleasant?" Katerina whispered.

"*Ha!* The worst thing I've heard you say of anyone, Katerina!" They giggled briefly, before Virgil redirected them to their previous conversation. "Anyway, yes, you can touch these, very gently. Katerina, they may be three thousand years old, at least." He looked around to make sure no one else was nearby. Any museum curator would be appalled. Good thing there wasn't one around!

She picked the pieces up with both hands, one at a time. Her delightfully tiny fingers made the sherds appear much larger than they were. She noticed the dried blood smeared on the smaller sherd that Circe tossed at Virgil. She looked at Virgil. He nodded. She put them back on the bar and wiped her hands. She downed her third shot and poured another.

"Katerina," Virgil whispered, "have you seen anything like these recently?"

"Yes."

"When? Where? Who showed it to you? It had etchings like these?" Virgil was struggling to contain his excitement.

"Yes, I have seen one piece of pottery like this recently, it had three or four etchings. One was just like this one." She pointed to the third symbol on the Penelope sherd, the larger of the two. The symbol stood for the syllable '*o*'.

"Do you remember where it was among the symbols? First? Last?"

"It was first," Katerina sipped a little of the fourth shot.

"Who? Where? When? Katerina?" Virgil's excitement was boiling over.

"The dead man, Wellesley. He had a small pottery fragment like this too. He came back from a long day, more than a week ago. He had a drink. He showed it to me and asked if I knew what the etchings meant. I said 'no'. He ordered another drink and went to his room. He left the next morning for another long day. He didn't say it was important or anything and I didn't see him with it again. What does it mean, Virgil?" She looked curious and suddenly worried.

"Why didn't you mention this earlier, Katerina?" Virgil asked cautiously.

"I'm sorry, Virgil, I forgot. So much was happening! People are always showing me things they find on the island, I don't really pay too much attention. Don't tell anyone!" She begged, with genuine sweetness.

"OK, Katerina, well, these little pieces of pottery mean that I need you to do me two favours. First, I need you to go to Costas. He should still be at the police station. Tell him to get here as quickly as he can."

"*Ve-vay-os*! What is the second thing?"

"What room is Sir Nigel Blasingame staying in?"

***

Virgil knocked firmly on room #2. The low glow of lantern light flickered around the edges of the door. There was no sound or response from behind the door. He knocked again. Still, nothing.

"Nigel? It's me, Virgil Colvin. I'm just checking in. Is everything OK?" he said in his most empathetic and concerned tone.

Silence for another few moments, and then the noise of weight shifting in a chair. "That's very nice of you, Detective," Sir Nigel said, somewhat weakly, "but I'm not feeling too well. I hope you'll forgive me for the anti-social reception!"

"No worries, Nigel," Virgil lied, "it's just, we found some pottery sherds at *Agros Laertou* today, I was hoping you could look at them? But I suppose it can wait. I hope you feel better tomorrow." Virgil began to walk away very deliberately, much slower than he normally walked. Behind him, he heard the sound of a door opening.

"Detective!" Blasingame called after him.

Virgil turned. Sir Nigel was barefoot, in lounging pants and a linen shirt. He sort of looked like a 19 century British gentleman at home — or at least how they always looked in those BBC programs Janet insisted they watch together on the weekends. Some of them were pretty good. When they weren't, he always tried to convince her to get to know him a little better — in the biblical sense. That sometimes worked, but sometimes, after they were done, she made them finish the program anyway. Sir Nigel looked rather pallid and sweaty — *ironic*, Virgil thought, *after his performance during the Arethusa hike*. His eyes bulged widely. They were not quite as wild as Circe's earlier in the day, but close.

Making sure to remain totally in control of the effect his thoughts and emotions had on his face, expressions and tone, Virgil politely responded, "Yes, Nigel?"

"We can look at them tonight, Detective. The flesh may not be up to it, but the spirit is willing!" He smiled invitingly as he motioned for Colvin to come into his room.

When Virgil entered, he was blasted in the face by an incredible cloud of stale cigarette smoke. The bed was straight ahead, the desk was against the wall opposite the foot. There was a wardrobe to the left as he entered. On the opposite side of the bed, nearest the window to the outside, there were two chairs with a small table in between them. The bathroom door was on the opposite side of the bed, perpendicular to the front door and the parallel window. The bathroom looked directly upon the chairs, table, and left side of the bed. Virgil noticed the large stone ashtray on the small table, full to the brim with ash and butts. The pack of Chesterfields lay open next to the ashtray. There was a lit cigarette leaning into the pile of ash, the trail of smoke thinly drifting vertically into the air, dissipating broadly and slowly as the wind from the outside darkness caught it through the open window, making it dance as it melted away into the air. The oil lantern on the desk provided a dim light around the room.

Aside from the thick atmosphere of smoke, there was nothing amiss about the room. Having surveyed the room and its layout, Virgil quickly plotted how he was going to get to the bathroom. If it was anything like the facility in Reggie's room, it would be all high-end finishes and a dark cold stone floor.

He pretended not to hear Sir Nigel locking the door behind him. "Nigel, I have two pottery sherds here with interesting etchings on them. I don't know for sure," he dissembled, "but I was thinking they might be Linear B?"

As he spoke, he unwrapped the sherds and placed them on the bed while he made sure to angle his own body at the foot of the bed. Once the sherds were displayed, he reached for the lantern and handed it to Blasingame, so that he could examine the sherds under the light.

"Yes, Detective," Sir Nigel said with the '*la — er — te*' sherd in his left hand while the lantern was held up in his right, "these etchings do look like Linear B." He was silent while he thoroughly examined the sherds. Either he didn't notice François Deflers' blood, or he didn't care enough to ask about it.

Virgil now drifted into the far side of the room. He noticed that Sir Nigel's very own copy of his own book, *Getting Odysseus Home*, was open on the left-hand side of the bed. There was also a copy of Emily Wilson's translation of *The Odyssey* on the chair that the lit end of the cigarette was pointed at. Virgil picked it up to look it over, flipping through the pages. He noticed the heavy annotations in the margins. He had seen these cramped notations before. He closed the book and looked over across the bed at Sir Nigel Blasingame. Sir Nigel Blasingame was looking directly at Virgil Colvin. His face was hard and drawn. The shadows from the lantern made the man's tremendous bulk loom quite large on the wall and ceiling behind him, while his countenance, lit from below, was ghastly looking. Hitchcock would have loved it.

"He brought it over," Sir Nigel broke the silence, placing the lantern on the desk, but then drifted back to the bed across from Virgil, looking over the sherds, "along with one of these." He picked up the large '*pa — ne — o — p*' sherd and broke it in half between his fingers. "They break so easily, these all-important sherds." He laughed. "One minute they are the greatest archaeological finds of the century, the next moment they are at the bottom of Vathy Harbour, never to be seen or found ever again."

"What did the sherd he brought say?" Virgil calculated his chances of getting by the enormous historian if he leaped across the bed. He decided to begin edging very slowly towards the bathroom door.

"'*O — di — se — u*,' of course! He and that blasted bitch, Circe, went digging at the *Agros* and found sherds early last week. Reginald was a classics and archaeology student, he received high honours at Oxford under the classicist Hugh Smithson. Hugh, of course, was the one who helped me with my book. So, Reginald was familiar with my work, obviously. When he started poking around the sites — breaking into the trench at the *Agios Athanasios* for instance — he got in touch with Hugh, wanted him to come down here. Hugh couldn't, but suggested me, knowing I was in Paliki on business. Reginald sent me a message about finding something, offered to pay for room and board if I popped over. I came over that day, and here I still am, trapped on this dingy little rock! He waltzes in here, no bragging, no sense of triumph, no awareness that he is going to crush twenty years of painstaking work against the odds, against the scholarly community, against the archaeologists and lays that damned sherd on the table there and tells me what is says and what it means."

Virgil continued to slide slowly to the bathroom door. "But Linear B sherds that say Laertes, Penelope and Odysseus are still not definitive proof that this was ancient Ithaca, right?" He tried to sound as understanding and sympathetic as he could. "It could just be a bowl that happened to end up here, right?"

"Of course!" He thundered. "Of course they are just sherds from some bowl that just happened to end up here, Detective! I told you already, this *is* Doulichion! There is no 'Ithaca question' — Paliki *is* Ithaca! But we both know the damned archaeologists will never go to Paliki, or even dream of it, if these sherds are ever known. The moment those lazy bastards 'oooh' and 'ahhh' over these sherds, it will be just like those fucking bronze pots at Loizos! It will take a half century or more before anyone bothers to point out the obvious and look at the problem anew. I do not want to be long dead, Detective, to bask in my rightful due as the true discoverer of Odysseus' home. Even Schliemann will sink into second place in comparison to such an astounding discovery. Stop moving to the bathroom door!"

Virgil ceased moving, but he didn't stop doing the calculations — he could make it to the door and open it, the question was whether he could close it in time to lock it or withstand what was going to be Sir Nigel's mountainous bulk smashing into it? "So, you killed him on the spur of the moment?" he asked, not dealing with the admonition. "You had no idea why he was here?"

Ignoring the latter question, Sir Nigel answered, "I did the math, Detective, I calculated how long it would take before the archaeologists stopped being blinded by that blasted sherd. If I thought he would let me destroy it, I wouldn't have killed him — but he was the sort of man you would never be able to convince of something like that. Instead, I played the happy loser. I offered him a glass of wine, to celebrate his find. He went to the bathroom and I crushed up six of my Xanax tablets and poured them into his glass. I've had trouble unwinding the last five or six years, so they are always with me. You shouldn't drink if you're taking them, but a little wine now and then won't kill you. He drank it down. Why wouldn't he?" Sir Nigel started laughing as he began moving slowly around the corner of the bed.

"What's so funny?" Virgil asked, moving by centimetres towards the bathroom door.

"Oh, Reginald" — Sir Nigel stopped laughing, catching his breath — "after he drank the wine and sat down to enjoy a cigarette with me, he told me he was going to let me take the credit! He wouldn't tell me why, but he said he could not be associated with the discovery, but he was happy to let me get all the glory! Can you believe it? He destroys my life's work and he tosses me a worthless chicken bone as a consolation prize!" He laughed again, still moving down the end of the bed.

"Then what happened?" Virgil was mentally preparing for the quick burst of activity he was going to have to make at any moment. Sir Nigel was more than ten years older than him, and in his 60s, but he was taller, weighed more and much of the extra bulk was muscle. Virgil might be able to fight and grapple his way out of this, but that hadn't worked for the much younger spy. Plus, Virgil was exhausted from the day's exertions, adrenaline boost or not. Better to buy time and hope Costas arrived before he would have to get into a good old-fashioned knockdown, drag out, eye gouging, teeth gnashing, groin hitting, hand-to-hand fight to the death. *Costas had to be on his way, right?* Before he could ponder all the ways in which Katerina might not have found Costas, or that Costas might have refused to come to the hotel, Sir Nigel answered his question.

"Well, he stood up to shake my hand and leave, the good, disinterested, scholarly Samaritan! He could not keep his balance. He immediately understood that I had done something to the wine, but he just looked stupidly confused as he stumbled back into the bathroom. Not terribly unlike you are trying to do right now, Detective" — Sir Nigel was nearly clear of the bed, which would allow him a clear run at Virgil — "and he fell backwards as I got closer to him. He hit the back of his head, hard, on the bathroom tile. The blood was already pooling when I came to him. I couldn't tell if he was simply stunned or dead, but I lifted his head and gave him a couple more capital hits to the stone to be sure. Katerina and Deflers retired for the night quite a bit before, I sometimes hear that ghastly Frenchman whistling by here on his way back to his room afterwards. Insipid man!" Sir Nigel got lost in his contemptuous digression.

"How was the body still warm?" Virgil asked, playing for time.

Snapped out of his reverie, Sir Nigel smiled. "Oh, that! A hot shower, Detective. About an hour or so, just to muddy the time of death. All those detective shows, you understand? I assumed it couldn't hurt my case while I thought about how to get rid of him. After an hour, I dried him off and redressed him, wrapped him in a bedsheet and carried him to the statue of Odysseus." Here, Sir Nigel stopped to cackle. "It was such an inspired spot to put him, don't you think? I tossed the sherd into the drink and came back here. Then the earthquake, and I have been trapped here. I've had a devil of a time keeping Katerina and her people out of here. And now these damned sherds! And *you*!"

It was now or never. Virgil bolted for the bathroom door, which opened easily and almost closed it before

Sir Nigel, a kinetic battering ram of energy, smashed into it. It was like being hit by a car, Virgil thought, and he struggled to absorb the blow and move the door back to closed. Sir Nigel grunted and huffed as he tried to wedge his body further into the gap between the door and the jamb. Having survived the initial blow — had he had an extra five steps, there would have been no stopping Sir Nigel when he collided into the door — Virgil now had the advantage of pressing his weight into the door, pinning the historian in a painful vice. Sir Nigel tried to reach around the door to grab Virgil and pull him away. Seizing the opportunity, Virgil grabbed the searching hand in the darkness and bit down on the index finger — hard. He drew blood and Sir Nigel howled before falling back from the jamb. As soon as he moved away, Virgil pressed his advantage, hit Sir Nigel's foot between the jamb and the door with all the pressure he could muster. Again, Sir Nigel cried out and pried his foot away. The door slammed shut, Virgil locked the handle. He then wedged his body against the door, pinning his feet against the wall of the shower stall. He was not fully extended, so he would be able to push with his legs against the wall. That should keep Sir Nigel at bay unless he broke through the door itself, Virgil thought as he tried to catch his breath. It was completely black inside the closed bathroom. It felt damp. It smelled like blood.

Almost as if doing the same math, Sir Nigel began beating and punching the door with his shoulders and enormous fists. He had devolved into a lower form of primate, oblivious to the pain of repetitive blows to his own fists and shoulders. Virgil tried to breathe regularly, absorbing each additional hit upon the door, trying to time his own pushback from the wall. It was the second time in one day that he contemplated his own death. While he was preoccupied with the tragic-romantic possibilities and sheer terror of death by earthquake on the isthmus, this death was pure comedy. Aristophanes could not have written a more humorous demise. *Murdered by the crazed historian!* Virgil tried to think about how many times he felt like he was going to die when he worked homicide in Chicago. He had only fired his service revolver three times in nearly thirty years on the job. He had been shot at six times. His car had taken a bullet once. Virgil had never been hit himself. He had always been careful and responsible and aware. He wanted to come home to Janet. The last thing he wanted was for her to have to recuse herself one day from her operating room because her husband was there with a GSW. Yet here he was, in the pitch-black darkness on the floor of a bathroom while a murderous academic tried to get close enough to murder him with his bare hands. Virgil Colvin didn't want to try to calculate the odds, but they had to be hilariously astounding!

"It's over, Nigel!" he shouted. "There is no way you're getting out of this! Also, you know your theory is wrong! This *is* Thiakí!"

"We will" — he rammed the door with his left shoulder — "see about that!" Again, his left shoulder.

Using his left shoulder kept Sir Nigel Blasingame's back to his room's door, so he did not notice the gentle reversing of the lock and the door's silent opening and nearly as quiet closing. Costas Pantakalas could not believe the scene. The enormous British historian was ramming his left shoulder into the bathroom door over, and over, and over again, while threatening to kill Virgil on the other side of his only protection.

Virgil's muffled voice was occasionally clear, telling Sir Nigel that it was over, that killing him was not going to stop Costas from catching him or the archaeologists from proving that Thiakí was also ancient Thiakí. This last communication seemed to redouble Sir Nigel's effort with what must have been a heavily bruised left shoulder. Costas got down low to the ground and slowly crept around the bed, being careful to stay out of Sir Nigel's peripheral vision. While he struggled to remain absolutely silent, he was sure that Sir Nigel wasn't able to hear much besides his own struggle to break through the door.

Suddenly, Sir Nigel turned to the table — Costas went flat behind the bed just quickly enough not to be seen — and picked up the heavy thick stone ashtray, emptying it on the floor. Then, turning back to the door, with both hands on the ashtray and heaving it over his head he brought it down with tremendous smashing force. The previous small dents that his shoulders and fists had made became a large gaping hole. Sir Nigel now redoubled his brutish efforts with the effective tool he had improvised, hefting the stone hammer back and forth, busting more and more of the upper half of the door with each succeeding blow. With his back now to Costas again and his attention completely lost with his murderous task, the Vathy Police Chief could resume creeping up behind the enormous man. Costas gripped Reginald Wellesley's Sig Sauer firmly in his right hand, plotting the angle he was going to need to take. Given the enormity of the historian, his only hope was to land a blow on the side of his head, clean, without hitting an arm or his neck by mistake. He was so tall, however, that Costas was going to have to stretch a bit to make contact around the right temple of the savagely enraged man. He had never pistol-whipped anyone before. Costas, now clear of the bed, waited for the timing by watching two more smashing blows against what remained of the door's upper half. Then he leapt, quite literally, into action. With a couple of steps, he was in the air ready to land the blow. The timing was perfect. As Costas leapt, Sir Nigel came down against the door with the ashtray. Before he could rear back for the final blow to get into the bathroom, everything suddenly went entirely dark.

Sir Nigel crumpled to the bed and then the floor quickly, the ashtray fell to the floor outside the bathroom door. He was totally out.

"Mr Colvin?" Costas called out while he collected the lantern from the desk.

"Costas! Is that you? Thank God!" Virgil sprawled out onto the floor to stretch his legs. Releasing them from their pinioned position of constant strain and tension was incredibly painful. The adrenaline pumps also shut down immediately upon the removal of the deadly danger of Sir Nigel Blasingame. He just needed a moment to calm down and relax. The stone floor of the bathroom was incredibly cold. It felt lovely.

Costas handcuffed the limp wrists of Blasingame behind his back. Then he reached through the door to unlock the handle. He grabbed the lantern and opened the bathroom door. Virgil Colvin was splayed out on the stone tile, a large pool of blood beneath him.

"My god, Mr Colvin! What has happened to you? Are you badly hurt, my friend?"

Virgil looked up at the glare of the lantern and then propped himself up on his elbow to look at the floor. The dark stain of Reginald Wellesley's blood. There was a pile of blood-stained towels and a bed sheet in the far corner of the bathroom.

"It's not mine, Costas, it's Reggie's." Virgil groaned as he got back to his feet on his unsteady legs.

"So this was your errand?" Costas asked, looking his friend in the eye.

"What took you so long?" Virgil replied, smiling.

"Come, we get Sir Nigel to the station. You can tell me the epic tale of how you solved this case, Mr

Colvin." Costas offered him unobstructed egress from the bathroom.

"Please, Costas," Virgil said as he knelt down beside the groaning body of the gigantic and groggy knight of the realm, "will you call me Virgil, already?"

"Yes, Mr Colvin."

CHAPTER TWENTY
LAZARETTO

One week later.

Costas Pantakalas and Virgil Colvin waited in the dark. One of the American patrol boats had quickly and discreetly dropped them at Lazaretto Island in the middle of Vathy Harbour on its way out to Sami in Kefalonia. The small mass of land was home to a dozen tall trees and a low stone wall looping around the island that Virgil and Costas were currently hiding behind while sitting on the ground, waiting. It was also home to a very small Orthodox shrine dedicated to *Agios Sotiros* — the Saviour. The Venetians used the island for worship and to tax merchant vessels on their way to Vathy. It had also served as a quarantine site for the ill or plague-exposed. The island was now a stopover for prayer, weddings, pictures and an annual *paneyeri* in August that Virgil looked forward to attending. It would probably be a couple of years before it was back to normal, if there ever was such a thing as normal again in Vathy.

Since they arrived at the police station on a similarly dark evening a week earlier, small earthquakes continued to rock the islands. High 3s, low 4s. None was the 8.0 of the massive quake, that struck somewhere on the sea floor between Zakynthos and Kefalonia on the afternoon that Circe killed François Deflers. The humanitarian disaster on the Ionian islands brought some of the media covering the coup in Turkey across the Aegean and the Peloponnese to get stock footage of buildings reduced to rubble and tourists crowded onto the beaches and remaining docks, waiting for boats, helicopters and ferries to rescue them. Ellen Sheridan's face had gone viral around the world. Tearful frown, the coloured streaks and the dead phone clutched in hand represented the plight of the modern tourist in a disaster. For some commentators, it was the quintessential portrait of the ugly American abroad. For others, in turn, it became an example of modern media misogyny.

The rockfall caused by the calamitous shaking greatly impeded movement within the islands themselves. It was easy to get to the bay of Frikes, for instance, to transport Panagis Metaxas, wounded by a collapsing building, to Patras on the mainland. It was, however, quite difficult to check on the people of Exogi and Anogi in their mountain enclaves. Greek fisherman and yacht owners sprang into action, creating an impromptu ferry service that operated around the clock. The 'Ionian Navy', as it was dubbed by the international press, greatly alleviated the pressure on relief services to transport food and water to the islands for those who could not, or would not, leave. The US 6th Fleet, steaming towards the crisis in Turkey from its base in Italy, detached cruisers and patrol vessels to ferry supplies and emergency personnel between the mainland and the islands. The thirty-mile stretch between the islands and the main ports on the Greek coast was constantly full of traffic. The rest of the fleet made for the Aegean to keep the peace between Greek and Turkish vessels, in the 'other' Ionian Sea, ironically enough.

Virgil and Costas spent most of their time over the previous week performing Herculean labours around the island — working in the hospital, shovelling and clearing roads, piling up rubble in the plaza, and a thousand miscellaneous tasks that needed doing in the stricken capital. During the crisis, Virgil met a great many of his neighbours for the first time — trying to keep all the other Costas' straight, along with the multiple Yiannis', Spyros', Zoe's and Eleni's. He also did his best to employ their language during his sudden immersion in constant work and conversation more than thirteen hours every day. He found he knew more of the language already than he imagined possible. Picking individual words out of the cacophony was difficult during the first few days, but it was getting noticeably easier. He was certain his pronunciation and grammar were atrocious, but everyone seemed patient and happy to help. *Why had he waited so long?* He wondered.

The world's archaeologists got word of the discovery of Linear B pottery sherds at the *Agros*

Laertou, despite the overwhelming focus on the earthquake and the disaster that befell the islands as a result. That they were discovered by a beautiful, mysterious and crazed taverna operator and a philandering British spy, who died for his troubles, added to the allure. Sales of *The Odyssey* went through the roof around the world, easily outpacing the most recent biography of Onur Gündüz. Undoubtedly, it would end up on every American teenager's summer reading list. Lengthy scholarly posts had already appeared on the faculty pages in archaeology departments at the universities of Chicago and Cincinnati, Leiden University and the University of Tübingen, speculating on what the sherds meant exactly. One question that had already emerged was: "Why Penelope and Laertes, rather than Odysseus and Telemachos?" While there was no hope of getting to Ithaca for excavations anytime soon, they were already booking flights and lining up funding for four separate expeditions to Ithaca. The island, once the disaster was surmounted, would be overrun by international archaeological authorities, antiquities experts in Athens and graduate students hoping to turn the experience into successful articles, master's theses and doctoral dissertations. In that regard, Sir Nigel Blasingame was prophetic. There were no archaeological teams preparing to visit the Paliki peninsula in neighbouring Kefalonia.

The sudden and stunning crime spree on the island had finally come to an end. No one had seen, or really even looked for, the Cyclopes 'Nobody' who had vanished from the Vathy Police Station. Most everyone assumed that such a noticeable man would turn up at some point, somewhere. They were stranded on an island after all. Word that the *Πολύφημος* vanished only an hour or so before the big quake did not circulate widely.

Circe was not found, or recovered. Rumours already ran wild throughout the island as to her whereabouts. Some speculated that she had simply cascaded into the sea below the *Agros Laertou* and would float onto a beach somewhere at some point — or already had, waiting to be found. Others imagined that she had run off into the hills of Mt Neriton to live the life of a wild bandit, befitting her traditional 19 century Greek dress — usually the dress of a 19 century Greek man, except for the skirts she wore the day she murdered Deflers. The more superstitious of the gossiping islanders imagined that she was spirited away to Olympus and that she was *actually* the witch of ancient myth and legend. They whispered knowingly that she had been sent to save the island from the evil forces of modernity represented, ironically, by Project Odysseus.

The financiers of that development placed all their plans on hold and donated their helicopter fleet to bringing in specialists and emergency supplies, as well as flying out critical patients to larger hospitals in mainland Greece. Quietly, they also landed at the isthmus to remove the body of François Deflers, as well as all the paperwork and documentation from their trailer. Aside from the spattered blood, long since dried on the floor, desk, walls and ceiling, there was little left indicating any sort of project at all. The black Citroën Elysée mournfully sat on the isthmus, awaiting an impatient master who would never command it again.

Nikos Kordatos, the head of the Ithaca KKE, was released the morning following his arrest under orders not to leave the island pending the resumption of normal legal proceedings. He promptly disappeared. He offered no aid or comfort to the people of his city whom he was allegedly supposed to champion. Zoe Kordatos did not reappear either. The gossip among the Ithacans was that he had killed her and then himself, or the other way around, or, less dramatically, that they were hiding somewhere — perhaps with 'Nobody'.

The coup in Turkey was on its final legs, after being brutally crushed in Ankara and Istanbul, but managing to hold a footing in the city of Izmir. Once ancient Smyrna, Izmir was one of the claimants to be the birthplace of Homer, on the Ionian coast of Asia Minor. Modern Turkey's liberals, communists and forces of western secularism fought their rear-guard action of mutual convenience, with no particularly unified or coherent message beyond disdain for the increasingly dictatorial strongman who now surrounded the city by land and sea. Sadly, the people of the countryside remained largely unmoved when they weren't actually rallying to Gündüz's support. The international community called for a peaceful settlement and an amnesty. Onur Gündüz told the world to fuck off in a very Turkish and mostly diplomatic manner. Some of the people in Vathy speculated that the Kordatos couple and the Cyclopes were in Izmir now, heroically awaiting their doom. Some said Circe was there, too.

Sir Nigel Blasingame, the evening after his arrest, gave a full statement to Costas Pantakalas. Ariadne Konstantinos typed it up on an old, but still quite functional, typewriter. Blasingame signed the confession. Costas still couldn't believe it. The British consul arrived two days later and couldn't believe it either. She immediately contested the statement on Blasingame's behalf. The consul also successfully pushed her advantage in the chaos to remove the body of Reginald Wellesley from the island. She claimed it was for his family back in England, and to free up space and resources in the Vathy Hospital. Costas and Virgil suspected the predictable coverup of an international embarrassment. Costas had so far successfully argued to keep Sir Nigel detained in Ithaca based on the signed confession. However, with the victim gone, and the application of diplomatic pressure beginning even in the midst of a catastrophe, circumstances did not bode well for justice being done in Greece — maybe not even in England.

Virgil's villa was uninhabitable — it was unclear when he would be able to get back in. His insurer agreed they were on the hook for the damages, but were blunt about when they would be able to get him a check: "No idea." He wanted to smash the satellite phone when he got that answer, but fortunately remembered that the American naval officer who loaned it to him would probably be displeased. The bigger challenge was going to be contracting with someone to do the major repairs out here in the middle of nowhere. It was likely that he would not be able to move back in for many months. He tied down a series of tarps around the collapsed walls and caved in roof to halt further damage through exposure to the elements. He moved the books to the space where the bed once stood — it was soaked through and went to the town's overwhelmed and improvised trash heap — and covered them with another tarp. Most of them were relatively undamaged. Several were totally soaked through, including his copy of *Getting Odysseus Home*.

I guess I won't be getting it autographed, now, Virgil thought to himself and laughed.

The picture of Janet fell with the bedroom wall and was ruined in the rain. He would get another, but the experience on the isthmus reminded him that his memories were a port of comfort and safety rather than sad and morose. It had been an epiphany.

He went to Katerina first to find a place to stay, but her available rooms were already double occupied in addition to her lobby floors. She, of course, had two empty rooms, but Costas ordered them sealed until the investigation could be completed in the wake of the disaster. She smiled delightfully at Virgil, as ever, but she had to turn him away. Invites from all over Vathy and the surrounding areas poured in. Virgil Colvin's neighbours rallied to the '*a-mer-ee-ka-nos ear-o-as*' and he was now part of the city and the lore of the island.[45] But Costas Pantakalas pre-empted everyone else by simply declaring, "You stay with me, Virgil!" It was the first time Costas had called him by his first name.

Living on the Pantakalas farm south of Vathy — Spyridon and Giorgios were, indeed, Costas' neighbours — had been an experience. Costas was a bachelor, but his family was constantly cycling through the place. After nearly a week there, Virgil wasn't sure he had seen anyone twice, yet. Brothers, sisters, some aunts and uncles and a torrent of cousins — and they all had spouses and children. They had arrived to help Costas repair the damages to his home, while Costas and Virgil, the rest of the family, and all the other neighbours in the hills south of the city took their turns to pay visits of consolation, commiseration and repair.

The farm was functional in terms of providing much of the food that Costas consumed. Figs, olives and pears grew on the grounds and Costas got milk and

---

[45] Ο αμερικανός ήρωας — the American hero

cheese from the goats that roamed his walled plot. Everyone who arrived brought him food and ate freely of his table. Even the farmer who made the island's best goat cheese visited. Virgil found him quite a charming old man. His cheese continued to be otherworldly. During the nights, after the long days of triage on the bleeding town in the plain below his farm, local men would come to Costas, many of them related to him somehow, and all would drink ouzo and *retsina*. They talked about the previous earthquakes, the crimes, the disaster unfolding in the other islands — particularly on Kefalonia at Sami and Argostoli — and the mundane aspects of days that still managed to look disturbingly and reassuringly normal. When the large power generators were shipped into Vathy and Frikes, limited power and water came back to the island for portions of the day and night. When the curfew hit the island at night and power went off everywhere except the hospital, the stars reclaimed their pre-eminence while the gift of Prometheus illuminated and warmed those with enough debris or fuel to burn. The children came to hear the men, taking turns, tell the old stories about how the constellations came to be. Virgil was as entranced by the tales, and their telling, as the kids were. Even the *retsina* started to taste somewhat decent. There was magic in the air. *Curious how disaster often leads to these transcendently happy and sublime moments,* he thought.

Then there was Eurydice Pantakalas. Costas' beautiful cousin had been in the midst of the relief efforts almost from the beginning, working alongside the rest of the community, hour after hour. She helped Virgil with his grammar and vocabulary during the days working with his new friends, while at night, back on the Pantakalas farm, she worked with him more formally in between listening to the stories under the stars. One night, she arrived late with a surprise — a new amphora. It was decorated with a painted scene of Orpheus' fateful decision to look back at her namesake, condemning his beloved wife to the underworld. *It must have been from Eurydice's own collection*, Virgil surmised. She wanted him to have genuine Thiakían pottery for his villa, when it was one day reconstructed. While they were not 'dating' in any formal sense, Virgil realised he had spent nearly a week in her company without interruption. He realised that he liked her quite a lot — and he knew she liked him. She was vibrant, lovely, industrious and full of decency and common sense. She was different in many ways from Janet, but they shared many fundamental qualities that Virgil Colvin loved and admired. Whatever happened moving forward, he knew that he no longer felt guilty about pursuing his own happiness in this place — *his* place.

Those same bright and lovely stars were shining down on them now as they sat against the wall on Lazaretto. Costas and Virgil chewed on some jerky, distributed from relief shipments that flooded the island.

Jerky and cigarettes became the medium of exchange throughout the island. It was unclear why the world's jerky and cigarette supplies were directed to the islands off the western coast of Greece, but no one was really complaining — just haggling, chewing and puffing. Lots of chewing. They listened to the water around the island. This was their second night of waiting. The previous day, Kyriakos, now sporting nearly a full beard — in fact, nearly full beards were on display almost everywhere — brought in a new prisoner. The mate from the *Πολύφημος* readily gave his name when he turned himself in to Kyriakos: Constantine Gregorios. The name was meaningless to Costas as he wasn't from Ithaca. Aside from giving himself up — for food and rest as it became quite obvious soon enough — he really offered no other information. He would not say what happened to the Cylcopes or the *Πολύφημος*. All he would say in between demands for food and water was that his boss would fetch him soon and that he was '*kon-da*' — near. Aside from these teases, the man was an annoying nuisance.

Now here they were, the holy little island in the harbour — once a refuge of lepers — sitting in the dark and gnawing on dried, salted beef.

"Virgil," Costas said quietly, "are you sure this is the right spot?"

"No," Virgil whispered back, swallowing some jerky before talking again, "we've had this conversation already; it's just a hunch and more likely than your farm, OK?"

"But this 'hunch'," Costas tried to contain his whispered demand, "explain it again."

"Why?" Virgil asked. "Next, you'll want me to tell the story of solving Reggie's murder again."

"Virgil," Costas chewed, "you must know by now that we Greeks, and we Thiakíans especially, never tire of hearing the same stories, told the same ways and different ways, over and over and over. Please, proceed!"

Virgil laughed quietly as he prepared his thoughts to tell the stories again. He realised Costas was just trying to pass the time and stay awake and alert. It was not that dissimilar from the pointless and meandering conversations that got him through all-day and all-night stakeouts in Chicago. The air, the sky and the company were better here, though lately the food was better in Chicago.

"Well," he began, "we never figured out where the weapons were stored, transferred or dropped off. We guessed there had to be some sort of intermediate stage associated with the island because why else would our old Cyclopes friend be here? He would just go on by to the Aegean and skip Ithaca altogether. But he didn't. He was just lingering around here. The earthquakes and the murders and his own arrest fouled up the whole plan. His escape, the disappearance of the *Πολύφημος* and the disappearance of Nikos and Zoe Kordatos suggested they all left. *Or*, they still need to fetch a stash. They know the weapons taken from the *Πολύφημος* are gone, but yet they are still around if we are to believe the mate, Constantine. Keep in mind, Costas, he's the weakest part of this whole hunch. The man is useless and almost certainly a liar. But if we believe him this once, then it is a question as to where they would have tried to stash things easily accessible, while being someplace we hadn't already looked or where we weren't already looking. It occurred to me that it was odd that a patriotic Greek mystic like Circe was working with a couple of godless commies like Nikos and Zoe. The Cyclopes, too, had an enormous golden Orthodox crucifix around his neck." He paused to listen to the water. Nothing. Silence.

He took a sip of water before continuing, "So, anyway, it occurred to me that two of the islands off the coast had little chapels or shrines on them and that ships were often stopping at and going by those islands. So it wouldn't seem suspicious for people to be going to or from either of those islands, day or night. One is this island, with its ruined and rebuilt stonework, chapel and trees. The other is Deskalio in the Channel, which also has a shrine. That seems the less likely given how small, unapproachable and exposed it is. So here we are, armed and fed, waiting to see if the rats fall into the trap." He hefted his Colt .45 automatic pistol, on loan from one of the captains of the 6th Fleet. Against regulations, of course, but the captain was from Aurora. Not exactly

Chicago, but close enough for them both. It felt pretty nice. It felt like safety.

On a few nights that week, he woke up in a cold sweat, imagining that Blasingame was wailing away on the door directly above his head, while he sat there waiting for Costas. What wouldn't he have given for this Colt at that moment?

"Or if the cats are at the wrong hole!" Costas laughed, holding onto Reginald Wellesley's Sig Sauer P226.

"Well, yes, but I think not. I think the mystics and the atheists who teamed up here would both be drawn to these islands for practical reasons and far different ideological reasons." Virgil bit off a piece of jerky, chewed and listened to the water. It was a quarter to one a.m. "Practical," he continued, "because of ease of access. The Cyclopes and Circe saw their mission as godly — so where better to sanctify their weapons? Zoe and Nikos would simply be amused by their own sacrilege."

"Now the murder case!" Costas said after a few moments of silence.

"Yes, yes" — Virgil chewed and swallowed his jerky, took another drink of water — "well, Reggie was a spy, we start there. He seemed intelligent, and well-briefed on the gun-running and the forces surrounding Project Odysseus. He already had the main players under his eye. Zoe Kordatos because he was sleeping with her; Nikos Kordatos through his wife; Circe through their mutual interest in the island's antiquities; and François through Circe on one side, and Katerina and their mutual hotel on the other. The Cyclopes too, he surveilled actively around the island under the semi-guise of touristic sightseeing at places giving him clear observation points of the bays and harbours around the island. All the major suspects in the case, in short, were on his radar in very obvious ways. Which means that if one of them killed him, they caught him entirely off his guard. Even Zoe Kordatos, in their moments of intimacy, wouldn't have had him at such a disadvantage. He wasn't here for leisure, he was working. Everything in his room pointed to a serious man capable of doing multiple things at once, rather than an incompetent scatterbrain. If that was true, then there was a serious possibility that we had to consider, that his murder came about through the agency of a different suspect with a different motive. But the most damning piece of evidence for it not being the gun-running conspirators, or François, was the very public dumping of the body at the Odysseus statue. Nothing can have been more damaging to all of their interests than having a dead spy — and they all would have known he was a spy by the time they murdered him — turn up in the middle of town to get even an incompetent police force" — he paused to look at Costas — "which this island most certainly *does not* have, to get even such a force to start looking around and poking into things."

"Very good, continue." Costas chomped some more jerky and stared into the sky.

"That was the other thing that did not make any sense. Not only would they not drop a dead spy out in the open, but they would have taken the trouble to clear his room of evidence related to them. Instead, we found all manner of incriminating things in his room leading us straight to the lot of them. So, either they had been unable to tidy up in haste and with the earthquake, or whoever killed Reggie had no idea he was a spy and had no reason to clear Reggie's room of evidence."

"Now, Sir Nigel, what about him?" Costas continued to stare at the stars.

"Well, I left the Hotel Familia convinced it might be some unknown person, given the oddities surrounding the context of where we found Reggie and the condition of his room. But as to who that might have been or why, I hadn't the foggiest. Then we began to talk to all the more obvious suspects and some of them behaved very bizarrely — as we might expect since they *were* all involved in their own petty conspiracies. However, their guilt clouded the issue. And they almost all had a compelling motive to kill Reggie. But when you were praying to the Panagia and I was overlooking the Gulf, my conversation with Sir Nigel started the seeds of a suspicion for me. I couldn't really figure out why he was here — that and his staying at Reggie's hotel gave me a mild inkling. His myopic obsession with his theory about the island, and how much he lost himself in it, became very obvious there on the bluff. You read his book, Costas, it oozes out of every page and culminates with that absurdly melodramatic conclusion about the importance of finding Odysseus' Ithaca for world peace. When I first met him in the Plaza, I simply thought he was a harmless aristocratic antiquarian. But on Neriton, and then again at the School of Homer, his reactions and petty manias, like the fanatic, bled through. At Frikes, I started to turn over the possibility in my head quite seriously and things began to make sense. He had the opportunity, he was in the same hotel; he had the capability, he is enormous and powerful despite his age; he would have the element of surprise, there is no obvious reason why Reggie would need to believe he was in danger from Sir Nigel. The only problem was motive — what could push Sir Nigel over the edge? The only thing that would obviously do that was threatening his baby; his theory; his whole monomaniacal universe. But the only thing that could do that would be some new piece of evidence or find. We found nothing in Reggie's room, bags or pockets. Then there was Sir Nigel's reaction to the damaged trench. It certainly indicated a hypersensitivity to something — even you were not so alarmed to the damage, Costas, and you're the cop and it's your island!"

"*Our* island, Virgil," the chief corrected.

"Yes, *our* island."

"Good, now Circe!" Costas had some water and they both listened before Virgil continued the tale.

"Well, François never fit into the gun-running conspiracy. One sure way to ruin the whole project here would be to have the island embroiled in an international incident. On top of that, all the property of the financiers he represented here would be in jeopardy of being seized and held, or lost altogether. Governments don't normally take well to foreign syndicates buying land and then running guns and weapons through their territory. So, while Cyclopes, Circe, Nikos and Zoe Kordatos were all clearly involved in the gun-running operation, it wasn't clear what, if any, involvement François had with all of it. That changed when you read the report about his syndicate and when we saw him arguing with Circe. It suddenly occurred to me that François must have connected his backers to whoever was doing the buying of the weapons and that he thought they would never end up anywhere near the island or Project Odysseus. His presence here, representing gun dealers and black marketeers in eastern Europe and Russia, and the presence here of smuggled arms is all too much of a coincidence to not be connected. The argument with Circe clinched it. They had no other reason to be together, let alone arguing with one another. François wanted the weapons gone — and I'm sure his dangerous friends did as well. God only knows what sorts of blunt and jerkoff threats he made to her before we arrived.

When Kyriakos told us that François scooped her up to head off to the isthmus, I figured one or the other of them was going to bite it — and when I had a moment to think about who would win that encounter, it wasn't even a question. François was a dead man. Of course, when we got there and Circe gave me the pottery sherd with the Linear B etchings, and then we found the other after the quake, it became clear that Reggie must have been involved. She told us all the places Reggie wanted to go and visit, except the *Agros Laertou*. It was totally absent. It was on his way from Alalkomenai, but he went right by it to get to the School of Homer? He's a scholar of classics and archaeology and misses such a place? No. She held it back. She and Reggie dug there clandestinely, surely out of his innate interest and to develop her as a source for intelligence. Her digging there, and her finding something — a big something — was her only rationale for misleading us and making sure we did not stop there. If we had, we would have seen the trench fairly quickly upon walking the grounds."

"And, so, the etchings?" Costas sounded content.

"Well, they were etchings in the pottery of Linear B, the written Greek shorthand of the Mycenaean palaces on the mainland. Their presence here, particularly at a place associated in local island lore with Laertes, meant that there were Mycenaean settlements here at the right time to place Laertes, Odysseus, Penelope, Telemachos, all of them, here in Thiakí. At the very least, they would constitute the most solid evidence of contemporary writing and commemoration of the important figures of Homer's poem on this conveniently named island. Such a piece of evidence would threaten to destroy the entire edifice that Sir Nigel had so cleverly fashioned in his enormous book and the many years of obscurity and persistence that he put into pursuing proof ever since. If anything could make him totally lose it, I realised when I held the sherds, it would be one of these. Translating them merely confirmed how dangerous they would be to him — but honestly, any Linear B sherds here would have focused all Ionian archaeology dollars on this island for the foreseeable future. Sir Nigel would have died without ever seeing the archaeologists confirm — and confirm it they had to — his theory, his life, his glory. When they eventually did confirm it — and confirm it they would — he would be long dead and not able to enjoy the glory of Heinrich Schliemann, Sir Arthur Evans, and Carl Blegen, the giants of Bronze Age archaeology and discovery. Once I had the pottery sherds, I had the motive. The oddities of Reggie's room, the dumping ground of the body, the means, the opportunity and the motive — they all pointed to Sir Nigel. And indeed, when I arrived with more sherds, the same switch flipped that had led to Reggie's unsuspecting death. Fortunately, I was semi-ready for it, or he likely would have broken my head as well. And that's it, Costas! Finished! Done! End! *Ef-ha-ris-to*! *Par-a-ka-lo*!"[46]

They chuckled quietly for a moment. Then, both stopped suddenly. They listened very intently. It was not a motor. It was not voices. It was the quiet noise of water being moved systematically, like when a swimmer's arm goes over their head to cut and push them forward. This was not a swimmer. They could not look over the wall, but it sounded like paddles as the noises got closer and more distinct. Still, no voices carried over the water.

"Are you ready for the final surprise, Costas," Virgil whispered so that he was barely audible — yet it still sounded too loud.

Costas looked at him, clearly puzzled. He grimaced and shrugged, indicating he had no clue what Virgil was talking about. Virgil pointed to his ears and eyes and then straight ahead, where the black silhouette of a pontoon boat pulled alongside the opposite end of the tiny island. Now they heard the authoritative commands of the person in charge as they saw the slim and tall speaker, decked out entirely in back, jump to the shore. The smaller figure aboard the vessel tossed a rope to the first person, who then tied the boat to the boat hook on the wall that ran around the island. The smallish figure then jumped to the shore as well. Zoe Kordatos threw a shovel near one of the trees and issued a command.

---

[46] Ευχαριστώ! Παρακαλώ! — Thank you! You're welcome!

Nikos slowly picked up the tool and began digging close to where the shovel landed.

Virgil looked over at Costas who was just shaking his head and smiling. "I told you *she* had them!" Virgil whispered.

"Shall we?" Costas asked as lowly as he could.

Virgil looked at the guns in their hands and nodded. They stood up and walked into the light of the moon and the stars.

EPILOGUE
ANCIENT ITHACA, CIRCA 1165 BCE

Helios' chariot was diving quickly into the garden of the Hesperides as Eukalos made his way up onto the slopes of Mt Neriton, towards the sanctuary of Athena. The bleeding of the gash on half left calf had ceased an hour or so ago. It was the most severe of the several wounds he carried with him from the field that day. The two best men he knew, his surrogate fathers in many ways, Okuwanos and Ekhemedes had fallen before his eyes that afternoon. Surrounded by the savage invaders, they were cut to pieces. They died for the island that was their birth-right. They died to give the orphaned interloper a chance to escape and live another day. Eukalos tried not to think about it, but the image of his dearest friends being killed before him kept appearing, and reappearing and reappearing.

How had he escaped? Why had he escaped? These questions kept coming back. Over and over again. The 'how' was fairly easy — he ran. When he and Ekhemedes gathered the herders of the isthmus and Aetos together, they held the invaders on the steep shore for several moments that seemed like no time at all before retreating up the mounting and using the walls for protection. Ekhemedes fought like the grand heroes at Troy, boundless energy and ferociousness. Eukalos mainly just kept him from being hit in his exposed sides by deflected incoming blows and missiles — occasionally absorbing their final bits of energy into several of his own wounds, including the gash on his calf. Eventually, Ithacans from the North, under the king and Okuwanos, emerged to attack the barbarians from behind. For a while, it seemed like the tide had turned, the island would be saved! But they kept coming, wave after wave, ship after ship. Eventually, as the barbarians closed in and nearly surrounded their position, Ekhemedes turned to Eukalos and said, "Run up the mountain and work your way around and back to the isthmus. Your wife is with Athena! Go to her! Now!"

The roar of Ekhemedes was enough to make Achilles quake. Eukalos ran up the mountain. After what seemed like a safe distance, he turned around in time to see Okuwanos and Ekhemedes fighting side by side. There was no sign of King Telemachos any more in the melee below. Okuwanos was hit first, in the right flank with a bronze spear. The polished brown metal turned almost black as the warm blood of his friend gushed out upon it. He kept fighting, but he was crippled in terms of mobility and after about a minute he fell to his knees. Another spear thrust pierced his neck and he collapsed upon the ground. It was awful, but Eukalos could not bring himself to look away. Once Okuwanos had fallen, Ekhemedes was surrounded. He fought through several spear thrusts until he toppled over like a great statue pulled down by the gods themselves. The barbarian horde surrounded him and stabbed repeatedly as if to make sure their stalwart enemy were truly dead. Or maybe it was to make sure all of them could later claim the honour of having killed the ferocious beast of eagle mountain? Eukalos could not watch any longer and looked away from the demise of the men he loved like the father he did not remember having.

Suddenly, Eukalos realised he was still quite visible to the invaders and overwhelming panic overcame him. He finally obeyed Ekhemedes and took to flight up the mountain, past the deserted shrine to Zeus, and then spent the rest of the day working his way through the steep cliffs and rocks back to the isthmus. He had had to wait for the flat spaces to clear of invaders before bolting across the isthmus, past the fields of Ekhemedes and the shattered remains of Okuwanos and Idomeneia's masterpiece, and finally following the path that Amphidora pursued all those hours earlier. Towards the sanctuary of Athena he ran and stumbled, picking up additional minor cuts and wounds along the way. A scraped knee here. A tweaked ankle there. He only realised how exhausted he was when he finally saw the sanctuary after what seemed like a day of climbing.

He heard it before he could distinguish the wooden building from the surrounding mountainside. The wailing. The lamentation. Women and children. It was a woeful and terrible noise. It only got louder and more ominous as Eukalos neared the temple. Several men with bronze swords stood guard and ran at Eukalos when he appeared on the plain where the temple looked out over the gulf below. They realised that he was not one of the barbarians as they neared him and allowed him to pass into the temple. As Eukalos entered the sanctuary, the noise overwhelmed his senses. Two bronze tripods, burning oil, provided a cloudy illumination of the interior that stung the eyes at first. Then the mass of sobbing children and moaning women came into focus. He scanned the faces, looking for a familiar one. He did not see Idomeneia or Philona. He did not see old Queen Penelope or Nausicaa, the wife of Telemachos. He did not see Amphidora! He shuddered as he thought of the fate that may have befallen them all in the city of Ithaca once the barbarian invaders arrived. They must have sacked the town by now. Suddenly, a hand grabbed his left arm from behind. He whirled around into the arms of Amphidora, who embraced the ghost of the man she loved. But Eukalos was real — weary and barely able to stand, but real.

"What happened?" Amphidora looked up into his eyes, tears streaming down her face.

"The island is overrun," was all Eukalos could say before he lost his train of thought; before he lost his voice. He couldn't say anything else as he stared into Amphidora's eyes. He realised that he, too, was crying.

“What about Ekhemedes and Philona?” Amphidora pleaded.

“I thought Philona would be here with you,” Eukalos said, looking at the crowd to scan for the widow’s face, but more to avoid Amphidora’s searching gaze.

“And Ekhemedes? You must tell me what happened! You are all I have now!” Amphidora’s voice was solid as stone as she commanded Eukalos. These were not questions.

Eukalos looked down into the eyes of the woman he loved, opened his mouth to comply, but nothing happened. She knew. His eyes told the story. They embraced for a few moments.

“Will you come to the cliffs with me?” Eukalos asked her.

“Of course, I will.” Amphidora walked beside him as they exited Athena’s sanctuary and made their way to the overlook above the steep decline to the sea below. The panorama, now illuminated by the last fading embers of dusk and the rising spectacular glory of Artemis, allowed them to see the sea, the isthmus, and the fires of the invaders’ camps strewn about the landscape across the chasm. They stood there staring at the small flickering orange lights in silence, each one representing the demise of a loved one sent to Hades and Persephone. After a long while, Eukalos spoke, still looking across the water at the fires.

"My life is a confusing story. The gods play with me; my fate; my happiness. I lost my family in Poseidon's realm as a boy. For some reason, I was saved upon the shore of this island and taken in by Mentor, Okuwanos and everyone else in the city. I eventually came to feel a part of this place. Like a son of this island — as much as Okuwanos was. I fell in love with a daughter of this soil. I planned to make a family here with her. Men from the sea arrived to take it all away. I marched with Ekhemedes to defend this land. It never felt more like my home than when we went into battle. And then I saw my brothers, my friends, my family cut down and slain. I never felt more homeless and desolated." He turned to Amphidora. "I still have you, but what have we to look forward to in the morning? These men will follow us up here, and then…" He looked away, the tears streaming from his eyes.

"This is your home, still, Eukalos — *our* home! We will not stay here till morning!" She grabbed his arms and shook him. "The priestesses told us all of sanctuary further up on Neriton's slopes where food is stored, water is unending and where we might hide from these men for a long while. The king prepared it for a day like this. They said the approaches are narrow and easy to defend with only a few men and a number of stout women who could hurl stones upon the heads of those making the climb. We are all going to make the march before Helios returns — one of the priestesses will guide us. We are going to live, Eukalos. We are going to live together!"

"Maybe you will all be better off without me, Amphidora — the gods seem to have their eyes on me, and they seem to desire that I suffer. I am better off rallying whatever men are left to draw these barbarians away from your sanctuary," Eukalos resignedly replied.

"You will not abandon me again, Eukalos!" Amphidora ordered.

"But my love—"

"No! You will live with me on the slopes of Neriton for as long as the gods desire us to be alive together, or I will rally the men with you and share your suffering. This is our home, Eukalos. You are my home. Whatever happens to you, happens to me! Do you understand?" her voice was unbreakable and her countenance, so young and lovely, was on fire with implacable steadfastness.

Unable to contest her will at full strength, Eukalos was not going to try in his weakened and spent condition. Instead, he kissed her cheek, and drew back to look at her animated and resolute face. "I march with you up the mountain, my love. Lead, and I shall follow. Wherever you are, I will be, too. Whatever place you call home, I call home as well!" His dismay, self-doubt and self-pity evaporated staring into the adamantine eyes of the woman before him. He did truly feel that he belonged here, at this moment, at this place, on this island, with this tower of strength. Athena herself would be hard-pressed to match the resolve of this woman, Eukalos seriously believed — as firmly as he believed anything in his life.

They kissed as Artemis showered her rays upon them. One hoped that they might find more moments of happiness like this tomorrow, the other knew that things would never be this easy again for a long while, if ever. They both never loved each other more than at that moment, locked in passionate and exhausted embrace while the fires of the invaders from the sea flickered and swayed below them.

THE END

NOTE ON SOURCES
ITHACA LOST?

Robert Bittlestone was the inspiration for Sir Nigel Blasingame. I hope he takes as a consolation, should he ever read this novel, that final confirmation for modern Ithaca as ancient Ithaca was only attained through the agency of fictional archaeology with the assist of a massive seismic disaster. Who knows, such an earthquake may be the mechanism of confirming *his* theory one day. The ironies of myth and history never cease to surprise and amaze.

When I first visited modern Thiakí in July 2018, the magic of the Ionian islands impressed itself upon me instantly. Just giddily thinking that Odysseus stomped through the hills I was stomping through was enough to create a perpetual sense of living within a myth. Only after arriving in the Ionian islands, did I begin to hear about the question surrounding the identity of ancient Ithaca being in some doubt. Ironically enough, we heard about this in Kefalonia — the prime candidate for several of the leading alternative theories for the location of the ancient home of Odysseus. But I did not investigate the issue in any serious way until the

COVID-19 pandemic provided me with a tremendous amount of free time unexpectedly to do some reading. The competing theories of J V Luce, Robert Bittlestone, and Cees H Goekoop are all compelling in their own ways and are all ably argued in various respects. Whether the debate ultimately matters to anyone outside the classicist and archaeological community is dubious, but it certainly matters to the people who call the Ionian islands home and rely on annual tourist dollars for their livelihoods. Were modern Ithaca officially declared to not be the home of Odysseus, it seems difficult to imagine that anything but a fraction of the annual tourist visitors (on any given day in a six-week stretch of July and August, there are about 10,000 tourists on an island home to only about 3,000 permanent residents) would make the somewhat difficult journey to the island any more.

The notion of setting a murder-mystery on the island came to me in embryo when I saw the story of the beating death of British tourist Iain Armstrong by local supermarket operator Kostas Skarmeas in November 2019. Armstrong, staying at the real Hotel Familia, was stepping out with Skarmeas' wife — it was a tale as old as time in many ways, on an island wrapped in one of the oldest tales of western literature. It suddenly occurred to me that a murder on the island could be fascinating, especially if the island were truly cut off from the rest of the world somehow.

The rest of the plot filled out easily enough when I began to seriously consider writing such a novel myself during the pandemic. A resort project, 'Ithaca Odyssey', provided the basis of the François Deflers character and his Eastern European syndicate — where there is an illicit arms trade to this day. Whether a large resort project ever gets built on the island post-pandemic is still up in the air, but such a development will undoubtedly change the character of the place in some important ways. Continuing problems in Turkey as well as the mutual enmity with Greece going back centuries made the ominous coup against the more-ominous strongman Onur Gündüz an obvious and plausible cause for the overarching conspiracy surrounding the murder victim, Reginald Wellesley, and the other suspects in the case.

The communist party's Ithaca office, when I first saw it after the tiring and harrowing hike to Arethusa's Fountain, drew my immediate laughter. "Dump" doesn't really do it justice, though it did seem appropriate given the ideas and party it represented on the island. As I got serious about writing a novel and filling it out with characters, I knew that the KKE would have to play an important and comical role. Hence, Nikos and Zoe Kordatos.

Sadly, while there are many fine tavernas and restaurants in Ithaca, Circe's Well is not among them. All the other places described in the novel are real places and were open for business as of July 2021, when

I visited the island a second breath-taking time. Sadly, I cannot comment on their survival past that date. If you ever have a chance to visit any of them, you will not be disappointed!

Finally, the places of myth and history around the island are represented here in one form or another. They are all quite spectacular and worthy of visitation. My then-wife and I did not actually manage to visit all of the sites described here in the novel, but the wonderful age of the internet, and the ongoing phenomenon of travel writing, allowed me to fill in a few gaps in my own knowledge and experience. During my second voyage in 2021, this time alone, I managed to visit many more sites on the island to confirm various small details for myself.

I cannot end this coda to this creative endeavour without tipping my cap to the forces and people who allowed me to produce it and make it better. First, with discomfort and great guilt, I need to acknowledge my debt to the COVID-19 pandemic. While an awful pathogen that has wreaked havoc upon the world, people's lives and livelihoods, I do not think I would have had the time to devote to this project in many years without the sudden halt to normal human life in the United States in the spring and summer months of 2020. I began learning modern Greek and writing this novel —and reading voluminously on Mycenaean Greece and modern archaeology, much to the detriment of my other research and writing projects. But it was fun and helped distract me from the troubles of the pandemic. Deena Metaxas and Katerina Kontogeorgaki of the Annunciation Greek Language & Culture School deserve public acknowledgement here for helping me to turn a pipe-dream goal of learning Greek into something far more real. I believe (and hope!) that it greatly helped to add depth to my Greek characters.

Second, I can guiltlessly and joyously thank my friends and family for their support. I begin with my parents, who always encouraged me to write and create from an early age. While I have only dabbled in creative writing since I was a teenager, it is all I did for a significant chunk of my early childhood. Author and illustrator of fantastic tales! Lost tales now. My sister, colleagues and friends have all been supportive during the many months I was working on the novel — everyone of course wanting to eventually read it. Fortunately, unlike my PhD dissertation, no one seemed to be poking me about its eventual completion — in fact, I seemed to be the one bringing it up most of the time! Special thanks to Ramin Oskoui and Paul Aranson for being good friends throughout this process and always supportive of me in all of the travails of the *annus horribilus* known as 2020. I must also thank Mirabai Simon, for her encouragement and support throughout the drafting and completion of the novel. When I was ready to blow it off, she sent me back to work. Ευχαριστώ πολή!

My second draft readers deserve special mention for their time, patience and good humour — being given a reading assignment over Thanksgiving and Christmas season is a burden they all bore with good humour. My sister, Nicole Fronczek; and my colleagues, current and past, Kim F Beaton and Johanna Hume. To you all, my never-ending thanks! Your feedback was valuable and made the novel better.

Lastly, I must single out my fellow historian and greatest of friends — Dan Roberts. I could not have done this without him — so if you don't like the novel, it's his fault! At every stage from conception, outlining, drafting and editing, he was brutally critical and insightful about the story, the characters and my own rationale for writing a murder-mystery set in such a specific place. He helped to make sure that the island of Ithaca itself — its sights, its people, its food and drink and its myths — remained the centre of the story. When I got lost on some other minutiae, he always brought me back to what mattered. I once performed a vaguely similar service for his admirable biographical work — *The American: The Life, Times and War of Basil Antonelli* — so I am glad that he was able to more than even the score on this project. I know it was keeping him up at night! Thanks, Dan. I love you, buddy!

Bibliography

Aesop. *The Complete Fables*. Translated by Olivia and Robert Temple. London: Penguin, 1998.

Archibald, Zosia, Catherine Morgan, Irene S Lemos, Robert Pitt, Rebecca Sweetman, Daniel Stewart, John Bennet, Maria Stamatopoulou and Archie Dunn. "Archaeology in Greece 2011 – 2012." *Archaeological Reports*, no. 58 (2011): 1 – 121. Accessed 3 July 2020. www.jstor.org/stable/23621598

BBC. "Ithaca: Family's 'total devastation' at Greek island death." *BBC News*. 25 November 2019. Accessed 10 August 2020. https://www.bbc.com/news/uk-england-norfolk-50550165

Benton, Sylvia. "Excavations in Ithaca, III." *The Annual of the British School at Athens* 35 (1934): 45 – 73. Accessed 25 June 2020. www.jstor.org/stable/30104419

________. "Second Thoughts on 'Mycenaean' Pottery in Ithaca." *The Annual of the British School at Athens* 44 (1949): 307 – 12. Accessed 25 June 2020. www.jstor.org/stable/30096735

Bittlestone, Robert, with James Diggle and John Underhill. *Odysseus Unbound: The Search for Homer's Ithaca*. New York: Cambridge University Press, 2005.

Chadwick, John. *The Decipherment of Linear B*. 2nd ed. Cambridge: Cambridge University Press, 1967.

________. *The Mycenaean World*. Cambridge: Cambridge University Press, 1976.

Cline, Eric H. *1177 BC: The Year Civilization Collapsed*. Princeton: Princeton University Press, 2014.

________. *Three Stones Make a Wall: The Story of Archaeology*. Princeton: Princeton University Press, 2017.

Coulson, William D E. "The 'Protogeometric' from Polis Reconsidered." *The Annual of the British School at Athens* 86 (1991): 43 – 64. Accessed 25 June 2020. www.jstor.org/stable/30102871

Dickinson, Oliver. *The Aegean Bronze Age*. Cambridge: Cambridge University Press, 1994.

Finley, M I. *The World of Odysseus*. New York: New York Review of Books, 1982.

Freely, John. The Ionian Islands: Corfu, Cephalonia, Ithaka and Beyond. London: I B Tauris, 2008.

Fry, Stephen. *Mythos: The Greek Myths Reimagined*. Read by Stephen Fry. New York: Hatchett Audio, 2019.

________. *Heroes: The Greek Myths Reimagined.* Read by Stephen Fry. New York: Hatchett Audio, 2020.

Gallant, Thomas W Modern Greece: From the War of Independence to the Present. 2nd ed. London: Bloomsbury, 2016.

Gell, William. *The Geography and Antiquities of Ithaca.* United Kingdom: Wright, 1807.

Goekoop, Cees H. *Where on Earth is Ithaca? A Quest for the Homeland of Odysseus.* Delft, the Netherlands: Eburon, 2010.

Grant, Michael. *A Guide to the Ancient World: A Dictionary of Classical Place Names.* New York: Barnes and Noble, 1986.

GTP editing team. "'Ithaca Odyssey' to Move Ahead as Fast Track Tourism Venture." *GTP Headlines.* 19 August 2019. Accessed August 10, 2020. https://news.gtp.gr/2019/08/19/ithaca-odyssey-move-ahead-fast-track-tourism-venture/

Hague, Rebecca H. "Ancient Greek Wedding Songs: The Tradition of Praise." *Journal of Folklore Research* 20, no. 2/3 (1983): 131 – 43. Accessed 29 June 2020. www.jstor.org/stable/3814526

Haller, Benjamin. "Ithaca (Ἰθάκη)." In *The Homer Encyclopedia*, edited by Margalit Finkelberg. Wiley,

2011.
https://search.credoreference.com/content/entry/wileyhom/ithaca_%E1%BC%B0thaki/0

Hamilton, Edith. *Mythology: Timeless Tales of Gods and Heroes*. New York: Grand Central Publishing, 1942.

Haywood, Christina. *Classics Ireland* 14 (2007): 89 – 91. Accessed 28 June 2020. www.jstor.org/stable/25528473

Heurtley, W A. "Excavations in Ithaca, II." *The Annual of the British School at Athens* 35 (1934): 1 – 44. Accessed 25 June 2020. www.jstor.org/stable/30104418

________. "Excavations in Ithaca, 1930 – 35." *The Annual of the British School at Athens* 40 (1939): 1 – 13. Accessed 25 June 2020. www.jstor.org/stable/30096706

Heurtley, W A, and Martin Robertson. "Excavations in Ithaca, V: The Geometric and Later Finds from Aetos." *The Annual of the British School at Athens* 43 (1948): 1 – 124. Accessed 25 June 2020. www.jstor.org/stable/30104427

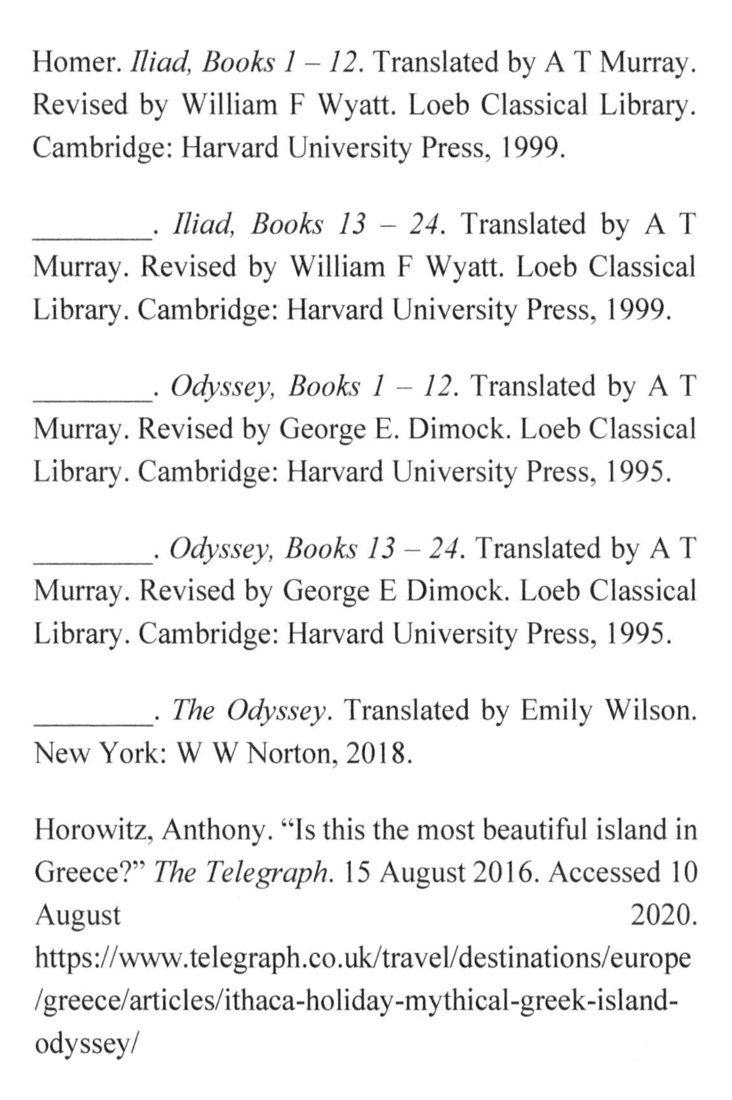

Homer. *Iliad, Books 1 – 12*. Translated by A T Murray. Revised by William F Wyatt. Loeb Classical Library. Cambridge: Harvard University Press, 1999.

________. *Iliad, Books 13 – 24*. Translated by A T Murray. Revised by William F Wyatt. Loeb Classical Library. Cambridge: Harvard University Press, 1999.

________. *Odyssey, Books 1 – 12*. Translated by A T Murray. Revised by George E. Dimock. Loeb Classical Library. Cambridge: Harvard University Press, 1995.

________. *Odyssey, Books 13 – 24*. Translated by A T Murray. Revised by George E Dimock. Loeb Classical Library. Cambridge: Harvard University Press, 1995.

________. *The Odyssey*. Translated by Emily Wilson. New York: W W Norton, 2018.

Horowitz, Anthony. "Is this the most beautiful island in Greece?" *The Telegraph*. 15 August 2016. Accessed 10 August 2020. https://www.telegraph.co.uk/travel/destinations/europe/greece/articles/ithaca-holiday-mythical-greek-island-odyssey/

Iyer, Pico. "A Journey into Greece's Land of a Thousand Stories: One writer chronicles his voyage to the island of Ithaca, where Odysseus was once reputedly king." *The New York Times Magazine*. 13 May 2019.

Accessed 10 August 2020. https://www.nytimes.com/2019/05/13/t-magazine/greece-ithaca-visit.html

Livitsanis, Gerasimos. "The archaeological work of the 35th Ephorate for Prehistoric and Classical Antiquities at Ithaca: A brief presentation." *Pharos* 19 (2013): 95 – 126.

________. "Ithacans Bearing Pots: Pottery and Social Dynamics in Late Archaic and Classical Polis Valley, Ithaca Island." Master's Thesis (Archaeology), University of Leiden, 2014.

Lord Rennell of Rodd. "The Ithaca of the Odyssey." *The Annual of the British School at Athens* 33 (1932): 1 – 21. Accessed 25 June 2020. www.jstor.org/stable/30096944

Luce, J V Celebrating Homer's Landscapes: Troy and Ithaca Revisited. New Haven: Yale University Press, 1998.

Martin, Thomas R. *Ancient Greece: From Prehistoric to Hellenistic Times*. 2nd ed. New Haven: Yale University Press, 2013.

Morgan, Catherine. "From Odysseus to Augustus. Ithaka from the Early Iron Age to Roman times." *Pallas*, no. 73 (2007): 71 – XIV. Accessed July 3, 2020. www.jstor.org/stable/43684954.

________. "Figurative Iconography from Corinth, Ithaka and Pithekoussai: Aetos 600 Reconsidered." *The Annual of the British School at Athens* 96 (2001): 195 – 227. Accessed 3 July 2020. www.jstor.org/stable/30073277

Mylonopoulos, Joannis. "Terracotta Figurines from Ithaca. Local Production and Imported Ware." *Bulletin de Corresondance Hellénique Supplément* 1 (2016): 239 – 251.

Neos Kosmos. "British tourist murdered by lover's jealous husband on Greek island of Ithaca." *Neos Kosmos*. 21 November 2019. Accessed 10 August 2020. https://neoskosmos.com/en/151885/british-tourist-murdered-by-lovers-jealous-husband-on-greek-island-of-ithaca/

Noack, Rick. "For Europe's criminals and terrorists, buying a gun is getting easier." *The Washington Post*. 18 April 2018. Accessed 10 August 2020. https://www.washingtonpost.com/news/worldviews/wp/2018/04/18/for-europes-criminals-and-terrorists-buying-a-gun-is-getting-easier/

Norwich, John Julius. *A History of Venice*. New York: Vintage, 1982.

Severin, Tim. *The Ulysses Voyage*. London: Lume Books, 2018.

Strauss, Barry. *The Trojan War: A New History*. New York: Simon and Schuster, 2006.

Tick, Edward. “Ithaca; Odysseus’ Isle.” *The New York Times*. 4 August 1985. Accessed August 10, 2020. https://www.nytimes.com/1985/08/04/travel/ithaca-odysseus-isle.html

Traill, David A. *Schliemann of Troy: Treasure and Deceit*. New York: St. Martin’s Griffin, 1995.

Ventris, Michael, and John Chadwick. Documents in Mycenaean Greek: Three Hundred Selected Tablets from Knossos, Pylos and Mycenae with Commentary and Vocabulary. 2nd ed. Cambridge: Cambridge University Press, 1973.

Waterhouse, Helen. “Excavations at Stavros, Ithaca, in 1937.” *The Annual of the British School at Athens* 47 (1952): 227 – 42. Accessed 25 June 2020. www.jstor.org/stable/30096895

________. “From Ithaca to the Odyssey.” *The Annual of the British School at Athens* 91 (1996): 301 – 17. Accessed 25 June 2020. www.jstor.org/stable/30102552

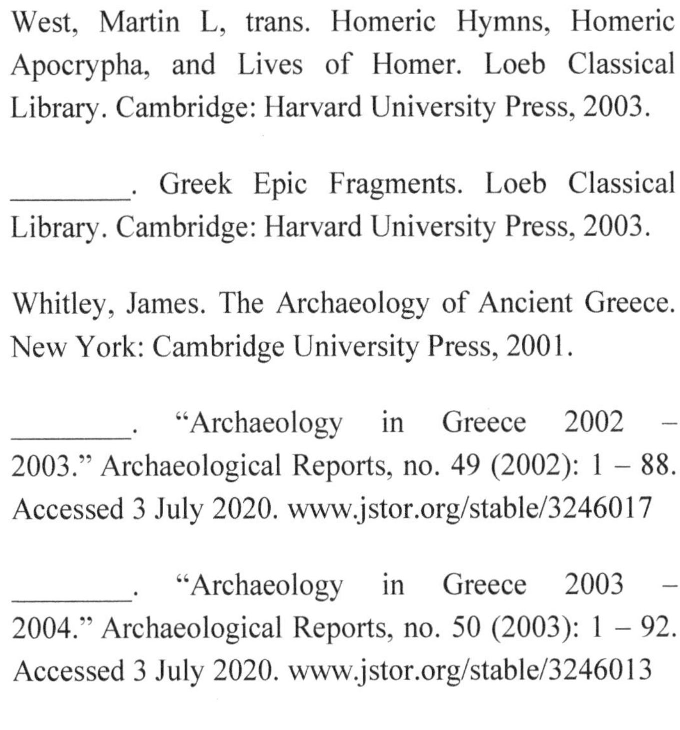

West, Martin L, trans. Homeric Hymns, Homeric Apocrypha, and Lives of Homer. Loeb Classical Library. Cambridge: Harvard University Press, 2003.

________. Greek Epic Fragments. Loeb Classical Library. Cambridge: Harvard University Press, 2003.

Whitley, James. The Archaeology of Ancient Greece. New York: Cambridge University Press, 2001.

________. "Archaeology in Greece 2002 – 2003." Archaeological Reports, no. 49 (2002): 1 – 88. Accessed 3 July 2020. www.jstor.org/stable/3246017

________. "Archaeology in Greece 2003 – 2004." Archaeological Reports, no. 50 (2003): 1 – 92. Accessed 3 July 2020. www.jstor.org/stable/3246013

Whitley, James, Sophia Germanidou, Dusanka Urem-Kotsou, Anastasia Dimoula, Irene Nikolakopoulou, Artemis Karnava, and Don Evely. "Archaeology in Greece 2006 – 2007." Archaeological Reports, no. 53 (2006): 1 – 121. Accessed 3 July 2020. www.jstor.org/stable/25066685

Zimmerman, J E. Dictionary of Classical Mythology. New York: Bantam Books, 1964.

Printed in the USA
CPSIA information can be obtained
at www.ICGtesting.com
JSHW022339180923
48470JS00001B/8